SWORDS
OF THE
DOUBLE SUN

Book 4 of the Maalstrom Series
Glenn Lazar Roberts

2026, TWB Press
https://www.twbpress.com

Edited by Terry Wright

Cover Art by Terry Wright

ISBN: 978-1-967888-14-6

"He looked from the planks to heaven,"
Said the man called 'Youth':
"Immortal... one thousand years before now...
Passing into the point of the cone
You begin by making the replica."
But the old man did not know how he felt
Nor could remember what prompted the utterance.
"What I know, I have known,
How can the knowing cease knowing?
Matter is the lightest of all things,
Light also proceeds from the Eye;
The globe over my head
Glassy, the glaring surface –
There are many reflections
One sees them turning and moving
With heads now down, now up."

Of Ezra Pound, Canto XXIX

Glenn Lazar Roberts

CHAPTER 1

From the darkness they came, the hissing of reven-na in rough folds of night, cries of men waving swords amid squeals of the stricken, surprised in crude camp tents as black ghosts enveloped them, sealing their fates like bad luck.

"Flores!" A frantic voice pealed as a veiled figure was strong-armed by several ghosts from beneath the folds of one trampled tent. She of the yellow-auburn hair, amber-green eyes, and indigo lashes, haughty as a child, the passionate lover now dragged like carrion by a phalanx of ghosts.

Flores tossed aside the remains of their tent and lurched to intervene, flexing newly strengthened massive arms. The Lord of the Turlicum clan of the imperial city of Ven let loose with a heavy axe, severing a bandoleer-crisscrossed specter from its limb that bore an iron sword—iron for evil deeds at night as irsrem tear-glass would sparkle with moonlight. The slaver's impetus sent his limb topsy-turvy, clutching the sword like a snake, its fangs still buried though headless, the specter's blood spraying darker layers over the splotched night.

"Crestal," Flores bellowed, lyart-loud.

Before Flores could intervene, more floating specters closed, more shadows emerging from the forest while two score of Ven soldiery spilled from other tents. Dense branches of thick forest whipped as the amphibious reven-na that the intruders rode materialized in numbers from the surrounding midnight forest, rushing to engage.

Flores swung the axe blindly—a guttural whimper answered, the Turlicum's axe removing the attacker's head to bounce off its fellows, bringing several of the assailants' reven-na mounts to a shocked halt near the guttered ash heap in the center of the Vens' campsite, the embers no longer alerting to intruders.

The angry Vens poured from their tents, iron and irsrem throwing a cloud of invisible ozone among the combatants, emitted where tear-glass met iron, the sparks threatening to ignite tinder beneath their feet. Between the surrounding leafy boughs, a ghastly green blanketed patches of ground as the hurtling moon Tumsenet cast its unsympathetic gaze on this secret arena of the medieval planet called Maalstrom.

Tumsenet's velvet coat grew greener, as if the god in its fulsome moon sought to punish the source of the night's disturbance. Another score of intruders took form, intermingling with outraged Vens still half-asleep, more ruffians inrushing from the depths of Tartarus. Most were bare-chested slavers with crossed leather straps, some sporting bandoleers filled with glass or iron darts, while others brandished rawhide whips of lyart hide. All wielded stubby iron swords so the light of the just gods would not discover them.

As tan rays of the moon-god Talen poured suddenly forth, the fresh wave of slavers atop their reven-na mounts paused and glanced skyward like vermin exposed in sudden illumination, the green blanket now spotted with brown rippling from the figures knotted in combat like fish flopping out of water. Then they too hurried to slaughter the Vens.

Across the clearing between still-standing tents, grim-faced slavers hauled Crestal, the gila from the ancient land of Mok-sa, who knew better than any the fate of disobedience to the masters of the Eunuch Guild, those discreet marketers of sex to the insect cities of Vensor-sa which were strewn wide across the world's surface. The slavers halted at the far edge before a single mounted figure, as presenting a prize to an admired superior.

Flores caught a single glance of a man with prismed

face and arrogant turn of lip, clothed in the black robe with the red thread, the one *not* blind, the one *not* cut, but sitting atop a reven, the amphibious beast's sinuous neck squirming against the steely reins of its owners. The beast yawned its purple-tongued mouth, its sabered canines white and glowing even in shadow, its gills working spasmodically. Foot-shod slavers thrust Crestal onto the saddle behind the Chief of Ven's Eunuch Guild.

"Soorkrul," Flores shouted. And flung a knife from his boot across the interval, missing the Eunuch Chief by inches. The Eunuch lord responded with another smirk of triumph and whipped his reven into the undergrowth to vanish, Crestal tied to his saddle behind him.

Flores found himself pressed back by a wall of iron and razored irsrem-glass, the rapiers and swords of the slavers forming a net that steadily shrank, forcing him to retreat. At length he felt a boulder contact his back and Flores knew he was safe for the moment from that direction. Around him yet another human wave was illuminated by the green and tan lights of the swift moons Tumsenet and Talen, as the wave flooded from some netherworld to murder the Guild's foes.

Vens fell by ones, then twos, then multiples. Several strove to protect their feudal lord, Flores of the Turlicum. Before they could reach Flores' side, they too were cut down. The light of dawn gradually cast the yellow glory of twin barbelled suns over the clearing, hardly a spot of earth visible that was not covered by red gore and the sliced flesh of an abattoir.

A thought that the slavers must be imbrued with some drugged-up madness to ignore such bloody death flashed across Flores' mind. He swung his axe with greater ferocity. With no time to think, much less respond to the theft of his mate, Flores delivered himself to the automaton of the born killer, the ozone-laden red lust of the god Atasan, Ruler of the Abyss, erupting into the prison of time and space where mortals live and die.

For himself, Flores cared not a whit. For his enemies, not a whit inverted. The skull that he split with his heavy axe, named Nebelroc, the heart that he punctured with the glass dagger which he wielded in his versatile left hand, the limbs he severed and sent flying into the ranks of the impervious enemy with the long practice of a Simet lord of the city of Ven, were no more than the calculated berserk that Simet warriors are trained to from birth. Insect soldiers in an insect world.

The bodies stacked in front of Flores like cordwood. Still the slavers came.

Dawn finally broke. Vensor and His twin Vensed glared down upon the scene with aloof indifference, not even the heroic struggle of one against many sufficing to stir the gods to help a loyal subject.

And still the slavers came. Thrusting and slashing, the red haze of Atasan seemed to accentuate, to penetrate deeper into Flores' brain as he parried and jabbed, only a tough redentine fiber jacket turning aside the occasional weapon that found gaps in his own net of weaponry, from the many darts flung at his body.

His arm grew tired with the hours. Even he, despite the years of punishing exercise in the martial yards of his Turlicum clan in the City of Ven, Emperor of the Three Valleys and beyond. Yet another slaver threw himself at Flores as if impelled by invisible forces, as if Soorkrul the Eunuch Lord's wrists still wore his talismans. Flores raked his attacker's neck with a backward slice of his dagger and the man's head rolled off, striking the ground before the gore-gushing corpse could follow.

Flores grunted. Dagger and axe at the ready, he peered through a mist of blood and sweat and stench of ozone and a flop of blood-encrusted hair from his own forehead, weaving evilly, awaiting the next red kiss.

He was alone.

All were dead.

"Hoom," he muttered.

No more slavers. No more Ven soldiery either. Only the lazy flapping of the Sun-God's malkops gathering overhead to collect the bodies of the dead, forever obedient to their eternal duty.

He let his gaze wander over the corpses scattered about his feet and across the wide clearing. The moons had paled and raced away, his expedition's reven-na had bolted, and his clan slaughtered. Crestal and Soorkrul had long vanished in the thick night, hours hence.

"So, the pits beneath Ven's Hall of Vim were not enough to hold you, chief of whores. I wonder if any pit could." Flores fingered his axe. "Next time we meet...I shall opt for a different solution than a prison cell. Some traitor apparently let you out." Flores sighted Crestal's veil on the ground. "And we shall meet again. Yes, by Vensor, we shall meet."

A moan rose, like the crying of a child. Flores scanned the landscape for signs of life amid the stark remnants of dead, saw no movement. He climbed the stack of corpses piled around his legs and stepped with care to avoid tangling his feet in mud-pools of blood.

Behind a tree, a leg stirred.

Moving carefully but swiftly, Flores approached—both eyes peered intently into the surrounding brush along the tree line, wary of eunuchs' tricks.

"Flores..." the figure moaned.

He stepped closer.

Prone on the forest floor lay his former chieftain, most loyal through the years. An arm and a leg had been hacked off and the other arm fractured.

Flores kneeled. "Isav. After all our time together in foreign climes. Now this..."

"I cannot see, Flores. Is it as it feels?"

"No lies between us, old friend. It is worse." Flores leaned and gently lifted Isav's head off the bed of leaves so he could take breath.

Isav sighed. "To the Eye of Vensor I go first, Flores, sword in hand. I will await you there."

"If Vensor permits me the boon."

"The greatest warrior Ven has ever seen? Vensor will seat you at the head of the warriors' hall."

"I will not take what belongs to *you*," Flores chuckled.

Isav grinned grimly as his blood flowed steadily into the earth.

"Will you...will you return now to Ven?"

Flores looked up, again scanned the forest. "The chief of Ven's House of Prostitution, that leader of the eunuch whores of the city, has stolen Crestal from under my very nose. I will find Crestal and even the score."

A genuine smile crossed Isav's cold, pallid face. "Another quest? Roaming the world in pursuit of...another gila? Was it not enough...that Ven's Assembly...expelled you for your sacrilege? That only part of your own clan...still supports you?"

Rough scorn rumbled deep in Flores' chest. "What I have seen, Isav, I cannot unsee. I have witnessed more miracles than Ven and its Assembly could dream of. To gain knowledge, one must sacrifice rather than prosper."

Horrid coughing shook Isav. He breathed deeply. "So, you will go on, my king?"

"Ex-king. And yes, Crestal was leading me to the land of her birth, the land of Mok-sa. We were taking a detour around the Guild's cult city of Klopus. But now, having traveled across half of Maalstrom, it seems I must visit Klopus first to regain what is mine."

Isav did not hear.

Flores looked down. Isav's eyes were closed and breath no longer came. The Turlicum chief, half-reverted to a primitive chief of the wilds, stood straight. Brandishing axe and gore-dripping dagger, he turned his grimy face to the sky and let loose a howl like a predator ros seeking prey, the sound sending the malkops rippling away in panic, only soon to return.

Satisfied that they would do their sacred duty, Flores began to walk.

Behind him, spiders as large as one's hand crawled from the forest to consume the dead but retreated as Atasan's messengers, the winged malkops of the air, descended *en masse* from a cloudless sky.

One glance back at the field of slaughter and Flores once more glimpsed the denizens of Heavenhell in their grim duty, paragons of beauty, blond strands flowing over fulsome human-like breasts as well as massive spinal muscles for their partly feathered wings, no word spoken by the mute vultures as they lifted the dead warriors in their deceptively weak but immensely strong arms and flew with a rush toward the southern ocean in their long flight to the Island of the Eye of Vensor and its pyramid of glass.

Flores shuddered. "One visit to that charnel island is enough for me." He watched as two malkops dragged Isav from his bower and flew skyward, followed by two more who collected his disarticulated arm and leg. Soon nothing remained on the entire clearing of slaughter but reddish-purple pools, even that sinking quickly into the earth.

No more bodies. No more spiders. Nothing more to see.

He shrugged. "A long walk lies ahead just to locate one of my lost reven-na." A thought occurred. Returning to his flattened tent, he pulled from beneath a canvas-fold a wrapped fish. Extracting iron and flint from a pocket, he soon lit a fire and let the fish roast.

Striding into the forest, he let the aroma waft and before long heard the soft padding of several reven-na in the forest's dark recesses. A sinuous neck cautiously emerged from between two sercotrope stands and two watery eyes gazed in his direction.

"Come out, my friend. I have need of another Tha, my former mount. Are you strong enough to carry me?"

The amphibious beast approached. Slowly at first, then quickly as it recognized one of its life-long keepers, the two-legged creatures who kept it clean and fed.

Nearing Flores, the chieftain took its limp reins, stroked its long grey neck and spat on its gills. Although this reven belonged to one of his attackers and was not one that his clansmen had brought from Ven, it nudged him with affection. Flores stepped back. The affection of reven-na could lead to a friendly nip with two-inch fangs—less than helpful.

One more digression to collect what weapons he may need and which the now vanished bodies had left in the clearing, and Flores mounted his new charge and urged the animal forward, away from the hazards of the forest, and he hoped in the direction of the mysterious place called Klopus, which only his beloved Crestal, of all the people of his home city of Ven, had ever visited—except, of course, Soorkrul himself, Chief of Ven's Eunuch Guild, whose cult was headquartered in that distant place.

But how to find Klopus? His only guide, Crestal, was gone.

Impatient, Flores spurred the animal to a trot. A trot rather than a hop, which latter was just as natural to the water-borne beast, but a hop would be even more inconvenient for a man burdened with a menagerie of weapons than a nip with fangs.

CHAPTER 2

Flores rode under a clean, clear sky on a gorgeous cool day. The weather was growing cooler as the barbelled suns slowly joined until they would eventually merge into a single glowing ball, halving the energy that met Maalstrom below. Curious, he thought, how the Divine Twin, Vensor and Vensed, had from time immemorial been worshiped by His offspring as a single god, the Sun-God Vensor. But Vensor ruled jointly with Atasan, enemy of life itself. They may as well be a triune god.

The Turlicum's face grew dark. Myths all. He had learned to his shock and chagrin the previous year the truth of things in his invasion of Vensor's distant Island when he discovered the charnel caves, and the colossal Black Pillar with its sculptures of iron-hard tachylite, and had to slaughter his way through Atasan's city in the clouds to rescue Amina, cornering at last Atasan Himself, the Adversary of Men, in the very Eye of God...only to relent and allow Atasan to live. Assuming that he had ever truly held the god's life in his hands. Perhaps even that was illusion. Who was he, Flores, a mere mortal, to think to overthrow the eternal Plan of God?

Then he had discovered that the object of his quest, the gila-woman Amina, was not in Atasan's city. That she had never been on the Island of Vensor at all but had all along been in his home city of Ven, inside Ven's forbidden Temple, giving birth to a new generation of Vensor-sa as Ven's sole Queen, without Flores ever knowing, and without Amina ever informing him, though he had been her devoted paramour.

Think carefully before one begins a crusade, Flores thought, swallowing a tinge of bitterness. One may well be hurrying only to an ignorant, violent end, sacrificing oneself merely for the joy of action.

Yet for action he lived. And for action would he die. Vensor still rules in Heaven. And winged Atasan still rules in his glass pyramid Heavenhell. And a new Vensa—his former lover Amina—having adopted the name of the former queen of Ven from political necessity, even now gives Her instructions to Her followers at Her periodic Calling for Sons, accompanied by the hissing of steam from Her giant golden statue. It was just as well that Amina had forgotten Flores, else, for some imagined slight, She could command the city to tear him to pieces. And they would obey, even to their very own king.

As it was, only the Assembly had banished him, for trafficking with one of the forbidden sex, the gila Crestal, a woman like Amina Herself, leaving him with little other purpose than to accompany his new homesick mate as she sought to return to the land of her birth. Crestal needed Flores more than ever—for the protection of his warrior's arm and of what remained of his clan. Just as he needed her, though precisely why he was not quite sure.

And he had failed her. Or, rather, by failing to execute Soorkrul when he had had the chance. It was being tricked by Soorkrul yet again, at least as much as for Soorkrul's theft of Crestal, that made Flores' face burn the most. And not even by a man, but by a half-man!

Flores' hand wandered to Nebelroc and fingered the edge of his axe. Next time...no more talk.

Searching for signs of Soorkrul's party, Flores prodded his reven, and to Flores' surprise, the animal seemed to follow a known path. It followed the banks of the river Hedronmas upstream, in a northeast direction, where, Crestal had told him, the river's headwaters emerged from a series of high crags. There, somewhere among the high valleys, lay the fabled land of the Mok-sa. If he was careful, even if he was incapable of perfect subtlety, just, perhaps, Flores could evade discovery by the slavers of Klopus long enough to scout the terrain.

That may not be easy. Above him, as he trotted across open yellow-tan expanses of grass while avoiding thick groves along the river's marshy banks, the usual flock of malkops circled, almost as if they knew that wherever Flores ventured, bodies fell. He could not quite come to call the malkops 'selks', as foreign cities did. Not after his ghastly discoveries across the ocean on Vensor's 'holy' isle, discoveries that in his view undermined the global religion that was entrenched in every city on Maalstrom, but which he could never explain to the uninformed, credulous, and simple-minded Vensor-sa that inhabited most of Maalstrom. Isolation is the life of all heretics, Flores reminded himself. It is the high price demanded by knowledge, by Marco Polos of the mind.

But exposure was something to be avoided. How could he shake the denizens of the sky? They hovered, always visible out of the corner of one's eye, like vultures eager for the feast, always ready to fasten their forms on the unlucky, but remaining always just out of reach, their bare breasts— organs common among the beasts of Talen but entirely absent among Vensor-sa—tempting those men who allowed Atasan's passions to creep into their souls. Flores knew even what lay beneath their dirty brown rope-tied loin cloths: the other feminine charm, evident among beasts, but entirely absent among the rational male-only societies of Maalstrom, who, to a city, had banned all women, returning women upon discovery to their respective temples to suffer whatever fate each city's temple decreed.

Flores knew who would arrange their punishment. And what the punishment was. And what lay beneath the loincloth. As he, and he alone among men in recent Vensor memory, had lain with two gilas—not only with Amina, but with the fugitive Crestal.

A drone in an insect world.

And a double indulgence in the crime of feminality, making of Flores a universal criminal and heretic, twice over.

Prodding his reven into a dense thicket of foliage, he hoped to escape the ever-watchful eyes of the denizens of heaven. To his surprise, this seemed to work. Peering from between branches, his searching gaze sighted no malkops, for the first in hours.

He ventured out.

Malkops returned immediately to sight.

He humphed. No matter. They were no threat, only a pest. All men everywhere lived under their eternal gaze. Even heretics.

A smudge seemed to nick the horizon. Far across the open plain strewn with yellow altheas and rippling fields of tan grass, a denser strand of tan moved.

Flores watched, thought, remaining immobile for a full minute with puzzlement on his face.

The strand grew thicker, turned into a smear. The smear became a belt.

A memory clicked and Flores yanked the reins of his mount and spurred it hastily back towards the brush that lined the Hedronmas. He barely had time to gain the shelter of the first tree when the tan belt erupted in full view. A horde of bizarre animals dashed almost upon him, each biped displaying a large bird-like beak flanked by enormous tufts of thick whiskers that shook with each step of hugely muscled legs on splayed toes, each ending in a hook the size of a man's arm. Vestigial wings flapped. One would not want to be caught helpless on the plains when such a horde came barreling down in its endless thousands like an avalanche.

"Nearly another bad day," Flores muttered. "The rumna are restless."

The horde raced past in a flood, then in minutes their

numbers lessened and soon only stragglers remained, including a few which had been injured by the frantic pace of the rest. They limped after with broken toes and frightened expressions—assuming one could distinguish fright from their usual constant head-spinning in reaction to real or perceived threats, rum-na always stampeding at the least perceived danger.

"My stomach rumbles." Flores addressed his mount, lacking any Vensor to speak with. "Let's see if they can run on one leg as well as two."

Spurring out of the thick brush, Flores drove his reven across the yellow plain until he came up beside an older rum, one that had broken an ankle and limped. The creature saw him coming long before Flores could get near and immediately sprang forward in an attempt to gain the security of the flock. But the flock had gone.

Flores caught up to the injured animal, and taking a chance since his throwing skills were not what he desired, as proven by his error when he had flung the dagger at Soorkrul, he flung his heavy axe.

"Damned of Vensor," he swore as the axe missed and the animal lurched away. A second slow rum jerked unexpectedly sideways and collided with Flores' prey. The creature stumbled—Flores closed for the kill.

A single dagger thrust to the heart and the rum closed its two large eyes and died, its blood spilling across its legs, which continued to pump and its hooked claws to swipe the air in futile gestures. Finally, it ceased moving.

"I hope it smells better after it's cooked," Flores said.

Tying his beast's reins to a clump of redentine so the reven could browse, Flores recovered his axe and set about slicing off a thick steak from the rum's thigh and lit a fire. There would be no more malkops than those already fluttering overhead. They had no interest in dead animals too heavy for them to carry, preferring human corpses.

"Not bad eating," he mumbled after satiating his

hunger. Wrapping several more broiled steaks in the animal's hide, he stored them for future needs, and mounting the reven, let the animal resume following the spoor of Soorkrul's band—or what he hoped was its spoor—Flores not possessing the tracking abilities of his former companion, Macius.

Who knew where the greatest thief had gone after Flores reclaimed his throne in Ven? Having learned that the person to whom Flores had handed the irsrem bracelets was not Macius, but that the thief had been on the docks the whole time that Flores had fought Soorkrul in the throne room of Ven, Macius had chosen to go his own way. That way was not with Flores in his new quest to accompany Crestal to the land of the legendary Mok-sa. He had gone without even a companionable goodbye.

Covering half the distance to the protecting tree line, Flores paused. He felt someone was watching him. Deciding not to give indication that he was aware or merely suspected, he continued until he regained the brush where he proceeded to pick his way forward again, following the Hedronmas upriver. Whoever it is, let him follow if he can.

More miles fell beneath the soft pads of his reven. A break intervened to snag fish for the animal, not difficult given that a threaded net was standard equipage for all Simet warriors who rode amphibious reven-na for the purpose of feeding them. Which meant all Simet warriors. When there was no time for netting fish, redentine grass sufficed, though the grass alone was a poor diet for them.

Despite the feeling that someone continued to stare, Flores found himself threading a deep forest, whorls of huge trees spinning into the firmament to leave him puzzled as to which way was which, though the reven still seemed to know which way to go. An autumn breeze shook the forest and to Flores' joy and amazement, clouds of silver and red three-pronged leaves descended in spirals and flutters so that he could not tell whether they were leaves or scarlet fragments of the sun, Vensor Himself, that spun about his head.

With a start, Flores felt unsuspected emotions surface unbidden. What was this alien sensation that seemed to grab his soul and squeeze him like a seed-pip? His rational mind, that structure that he so carefully constructed about himself like a cage, bent and stretched as he felt... What... Despair? Disappointment? Rage?

"What kind of world is this?" his mouth spat out, his reven stilled, its neck twisting so its two eyes might stare directly into the two eyes of its owner, whose emotion had spread to the beast. "Why is it so full of wonders, yet has oceans of blood? Atasan rapes our queens. Instead of halting this, Vensor abducts the dead and gives them to the Adversary of Men—to Atasan himself! Yet all remains in balance. I looked from the planks to heaven. I thus thought to storm the ramparts of Heavenhell and challenge God in his lair, but all I achieved was an ocean of blood. And nothing changed. Yes, Isav my friend, I know what I have known. I cannot unknow it. The gods are indeed great. But can Man be greater? Can I be greater? Is that not my right as mind and flesh of this world? Clearly the Eye lies within a cone, and as I witnessed, it is sometimes up and sometimes down. What does fate and the god Gethos have yet in store for me? Is it not my right to defy the gods, since their crimes are even greater than those committed by Vensor-sa?"

The leaves poured their generous treasure over Flores' head, gracing him with layers of gold on his black curly-haired skull and shoulders and the head and rump of his mount.

They stepped forward to resume the quest—Flores jerked the reins in surprise.

CHAPTER 3

"Aghh!"

The sound sprang from Soorkrul as he squatted on the bulky throne of glass in the Assembly Hall of the City of Ven. Blinded by the sprinkle of salt tossed in his eyes, his spell—the spell cast by means of the half-dozen irsrem bracelets that adorned his wrists—was broken, and Flores, at last freed from the phantasm that Soorkrul had implanted in his mind, stood erect, the evil dream vanished.

Hurrying up the steps to the throne, Flores grabbed the Eunuch Lord by his throat and dragged him down. As Soorkrul's fearful slavers watched, the Lord of the Turlicum ripped both of Soorkrul's wrists free of the devices and handed them to Macius, who stood behind the Eunuch Lord still holding the purse of salt, having freed Flores and Ven from the Eunuch Lord's power. As Flores delivered the half-dozen devices to Macius for safekeeping, the latter watched Flores without expression.

"Hold these, my friend." Flores made the sign of Vensor on his chest. "I trust no one else that dwells beneath the eternal spheres with these talismans. Take them yourself to my clan estate and see personally that they are placed in my most guarded safe, which my manservants will show you."

Without a word and only a quick nod, as was the wont of Macius, the thief of Vaw hurried out of the Hall and away in the direction of the Turlicum estate as Flores summoned his captains to hurriedly restore his rule over the stricken city.

Once striding out of Flores' sight, Macius paused. Noting that Flores had assigned no one to follow and watch him, the thief stood silently for a moment between alleyway entrances as if inwardly debating a matter of import, his amphibian features as inscrutable as ever, his eyes rolling across the wide plain of his face like castanets. At long last, he made his decision and darted into an alley and less than a minute later arrived on the docks of the City of Ven, where boats and pirogues already jockeyed for room, their owners eager to recommence their long-interrupted water trade.

Singling out an abandoned pirogue, Macius prepared to enter it when, to his surprise, Flores suddenly appeared and hurried to meet him, the Turlicum's face showing some confusion at having found his friend at some other activity than safeguarding the crystal talismans in Flores' walled estate.

"Are the bracelets now well-guarded in my safe, my friend? Whom did you assign to watch over them?"

Macius gazed back at Flores blankly. "Safe? What safe? Watch over which devices?"

"Why, Macius! I mean the clutch of bracelets, of course, which I gave you not ten minutes ago after you threw salt on Soorkrul in the Assembly Hall and saved the city of Ven from the delusions of the mad chief of the eunuchs. Are you ill that you are so confused?"

The dark man moved his arms in characteristic fashion parallel with the horizon. "Flores, my friend. I have been on the docks seeing that the ships are well tended in case we had to make a quick getaway. I have not been in the Assembly Hall since we arrived."

No man showed disappointment and shock more than Flores did in that moment, upon realizing that after all his efforts and sacrifices and his quest that had led to the slaughter of so many thousands of lives, the one positive result that he had seemingly accomplished had slipped from his grasp due to a moment's oversight.

"Yezd," Flores muttered. He collapsed onto a concrete bench. "This mysterious man has foiled me yet again. Only he possessed the seventh and last bracelet, which he must have used to emulate your appearance. Now Yezd has them all. And I—and my city of Ven, the fairest and first of the cities of civilization on the surface of Vensor's world—have lost the lot!"

Macius said nothing but stood and hopped from one leg to the other.

"You dance even in despair, Macius. I know that much at least about you by now."

The thief cocked his head sideways. "You had best see to Crestal, Flores. There are still those who view her with unreasoning suspicions."

"Not to mention her need to renew the sting of the hornet," Flores said. "To avert the..."

No need to repeat the eeriest secret of Maalstrom: the concept of pregnancy, an alien condition to the inhabitants of the overweening masculine cities of Vensor.

"There may be only one queen in Ven, Flores. As in every city that sprinkles this world. Only one queen to a city. If Amina learns that another gila resides in Ven..."

Flores omitted asking why Macius—or 'Surge', one of who knew how many aliases the thief possessed—had said 'this world' as if there may be more worlds than this one.

"My subjects shall accept Crestal as my own queen, or they will pay the consequence," Flores said sharply, steel flashing in his grey eyes. "I will not allow even my own clan to come between Crestal and me again."

Macius' eyes betrayed the slightest glimmer of... skepticism? Humor? The thief of Vaw turned his glance away.

A motley collection of chieftains of the various clans of Ven approached, sullen faces and insistent voices demanding the attention of their returned king.

"I must tend to affairs of state, Macius. First on the

agenda is to safeguard Crestal. Second is to ensure that the city of Ven is safe from invasion. Third..." Flores gazed skyward where he eyed the growing flocks of malkops as they glided lower, seeking to execute their immemorial task. "Third, we must desert the streets so that the malkops may retrieve the corpses and transport them to the Eye of Vensor."

Was that more glints of humor in Macius' eyes?

"I know, Macius. I know the truth of it. All is illusion, as I learned on the Isle and in the Eye. Even perhaps for you and me."

Macius averted his gaze.

With that, Flores hurried off surrounded by an ever-growing collection of clan heads who had survived Soorkrul's holocaust with their skin intact, while Macius stood and watched, once more silent, once more still.

When Flores had disappeared toward the Hall, Macius still stood. Dare he move? Might the favors of the god Gethos, the blue god of luck, have finally shined down upon him with full gaze, more fully even than Vensor Himself?

Before ought could intervene at his moment of triumph, Macius turned toward the water. Pulling on a rope that tied the abandoned canoe, Macius climbed carefully but quickly within, pushed out from the dock, and taking up the one half-intact paddle, pushed to the center of the river Suma. Bending low to disguise his silhouette in the growing evening, he paddled slowly but deliberately upstream in the direction of the city of Sish and the slave-worked Mines of Maanus.

The duskline overtook him with the speed of a flitting bird, signaling the end of another short sixteen-hour Maalstrom day. Under cover of the rapidly deepening night, the cool air of late autumn stirring whirls of mist about him, the thief—the most famous thief of all the southern seas—paddled quietly against the slow current. He must put as much distance as possible between his little canoe and the City of Ven before suspicions were raised.

"Yezd," he whispered as if casting a spell upon the rippling blue-grey surface. "Yezd, indeed." If any had been present to see, he would have witnessed the greatest of shocks—the famous thief's lips stretching into a smile. The first, and perhaps last occasion, that such a unique event would grace Vensor's Creation. By Vensor and the heavens, Macius was indeed capable of a smile.

Almost unconsciously, he fingered the bracelets, three fitting snugly about each wrist. Six in total. Their powers had come to him at last. How much time had passed since he had first learned of them? How much time since he had attached them to the ankle of a captive malkop in Yezd's remote castle, then with a heavy axe severed the chain that let the creature fly into the night with all seven of Yezd's crystal devices on its ankle, removing them, seemingly forever, from the grasp of the enraged red-robed scribe?

Only for Macius himself to witness Flores discover one of the talismans on the Isle of the Sun-God, frustrating Macius yet again; then to learn that the clumsy noble, Sendas, had been sprinkling the remaining bracelets about the city of Ven like God's tears while Macius wasted his time far away. Correction: God's tear-*glass*, called irsrem. Harder than iron once 'essence', that substance of mysterious origin brought to Ven by the eunuchs' monopoly, was annealed with the corta produced by condemned slaves in Ven's imperial Mines of Maanus.

Best to focus. After all his exploits, after all his efforts, it would not do to lose his blue luck once more just as he was on the verge of finally completing the greatest exploit, of which no other thief in all the watery seas could boast.

For the remainder of the night, Macius paddled, his indefatigable muscles infused with the energy of the noble suns, never tiring. When he approached the port of the city of Sish, caution took him and he directed his little pirogue to the far side where he found shelter in an overhang before the suns spread their glory over the misty deep. To his happiness, he found the wrecked remains of another small boat similarly ditched and was able to locate a pair of ruddy and worn paddles left to rot by their previous owner, his bones perhaps resting on the bottom of the river since the war of Nesos of Neset had overwhelmed the Three Valleys in the previous year.

Here, in the shadows of a clayey escarp well hidden from prying eyes, Macius finally attempted to learn how to use the trinkets of Vensor as he had witnessed Flores use them, peering into the water for verification.

Before he was aware, the day had passed, not one moment having registered with him, wholly absorbed as he was with the image-altering miracle of the talismans. Breathing deeply, he at last woke from his hypnotic reverie, and as the suns plummeted behind the escarpment, the pirogue slipped quietly into the stream, again venturing upriver. But it was a pirogue no longer, to observers become nothing more than a crease among the ripples of water interspersed by regular hollows as of invisible paddles dipping.

Sish no longer posing a threat of discovery, Macius paddled past the torch-lit docks where even the advent of night did not pause the traffic of boats as merchants plied their trade by night as well as day.

Once he was well beyond the city and its lights, the river Suma commenced to narrow and Macius was compelled finally to leave the river as he arrived at the portage. The peaks of the Amanus-nama mountains towering on his right, he lifted the small boat—after once more assuring himself that his new image-altering skill was working as he had hoped. A steady stream of boats, and even sizable ships, were hauled by their owners up the portage, the night relieved by a succession of guttering torches and in more peaceful times monitored by garrison guards of Ven. The chaos caused by Soorkrul in Ven had, for the moment at least, removed the gendarmes.

Even so, as voices approached, swearing at the weight of their own boat despite having placed it on rollers, Macius froze. Would his new skill be sufficient to avoid detection? As the others staggered past, almost close enough to brush his sleeve, without detecting him, the thief sighed in relief. The devices work! For him, as well as they had for Flores.

By dawn, Macius was again in the Suma, paddling still upstream, moving steadily toward his goal.

CHAPTER 4

Flores' attempt to avoid the impact came too late.

A net of dense fibers rose from the floor of the forest path with the suddenness of a blink. Leaves circled Flores and his mount in a whirlwind, thrown up by the net which encompassed them left and right, and thicker strands pulled by unseen hands, wrapped both in what amounted to a gargantuan cocoon.

Flores had only time to lift one arm—he fell from the reven. The act of falling tangled him in greater stretches of fiber, and the reven, panicked by the attack, also stumbled. As Flores watched from his position stretched out on the ground, the animal managed to stand. Rearing up, it snapped half the strands, and with a hop, it snapped the remaining half, and quickly vanished among the trees.

Slowly, Flores stood. He noticed that several of his strands were dissevered by that simple act and he began to think that without much effort he could snap the rest that entangled him and free himself as his reven had done. But not yet. He wanted to see just who had implemented this undignified assault. Beneath the concealing strands, one hand fingered his axe; the other his rapier.

From between the boles of forest trees, several figures cautiously emerged.

Yes, these were the eyes Flores had sensed staring upon him for some time.

To his surprise, the eyes were not those of Vensor-sa, at least as Flores knew them, the people birthed by Vensor queens in their numerous cities strewn across the face of the world. Each figure had two eyes, like any Vensor. He noted next each had a single body much like Flores' own, if rather thinner. The similarity stopped there.

To Flores' shock, he realized that his captors had no arms. How then did they manage to manipulate the ropes that controlled the trap of nets upon the floor of the forest? Or make the nets?

As they stepped clear of the protecting forest, their bodies became distinct. Yes, Flores noted, they did have arms. But his shock was not done yet. Their arms appeared to be the wings of birds, though much shortened as if the pedestrian nature of the creatures had rendered wings more burdensome than helpful. And each shortened wing did end in hands, though these hands seemed weak but sharp, their five fingers ending in dangerous-looking claws. How could the limbs of these animals—and, Flores thought, how could these be anything but intelligent animals—manufacture anything?

Their legs were also odd. Flores noted—still peering through the cocoon of off-white fibers that crowned his head—that their legs appeared to be exceedingly strong, more massive than Flores', indeed more massive than the legs of any Vensor Flores had ever known. And in the place of feet, he noted immense splayed toes, such as might negotiate any terrain, however rough. Those legs and those sturdy feet with their toes ending in more sharp claws, Flores at once concluded, could only be built for running.

His eyes settled on the creatures' faces. Here Flores received yet another surprise. They had no jaw, but rather only an extended bird's upper beak, and on either side of their two eyes outthrust shocks of rough whiskers that bounced with each step they took, more straw-colored 'hair' upending almost vertically on their heads.

Never before had Flores heard of these peculiar creatures, he who had traveled over much of Maalstrom.

Before Flores could speculate further on the nature of his captors, they approached nearer. Not by slow steps, but by impatient little rushes, hurrying up to his side where each stared briefly full-on Flores' face, then rushing back where each had come, the creatures taking turns with approaching then quickly retreating.

The largest of the creatures finally came quite close to Flores, its eyes staring full into Flores' own.

"Have you seen enough of our power, O disgusting one?"

The latest surprise, as Flores realized that these creatures could speak the universal language of Vensor-sa, quickly passed, though he could not quite see how they could speak since at least one-half of their jaw was bird-beak. But it spoke well enough for Flores to make out his own familiar language, interspersed with titillations and whistles.

"I don't know what kind of Vensor-sa you may be," Flores said through the intervening captive strands of fiber, "but on what grounds do you consider me disgusting?"

"Hoo-hoo," several pealed at once, turning their beaks to each other, then back to Flores. "Why, just look at you. Two arms, two legs, booted feet, head full of limp disgusting hair, even your chin. What other word could possibly fit you than 'disgusting'?"

Flores decided that these flitting creatures must not be quite right in the head. He began evaluating the strength of the fibers again, but held off from testing it, as the creatures proceeded to unwrap most of the cocoon from about his head.

"You will have to come with us, you absurd-looking targan," the largest said, labeling him a pet common to Maalstrom. They soon had unwrapped all the untorn stretches of fiber but that which surrounded Flores' waist, apparently wary of his reach and desiring to keep his arms pinioned. "And we know the purpose of these hard objects about your person. We won't be tricked again."

With that, quick hands, feeble though they appeared to Flores, robbed him of his axes and rapier. These beak people, as Flores decided to regard them, seemed unaware of how to use his warrior's tools, handling them as if they were mere sticks of wood. So, others had fallen into their trap before him, Flores speculated, very likely Soorkrul and his party, confirming from that small statement that he, Flores, remained on the track of his nemesis.

The large one resumed, "And don't imagine you can escape us. These fibers are so tough that even the huge lumbering lyarts of the plains cannot break them."

Flores thought better than to retort that his reven alone had shredded half the net. Best to see just what these creatures had in mind for him before attempting to even scores.

Well that he did so, he postscripted. For out of the forest a veritable sea of such creatures now appeared, numbering at least a hundred, and crowding around their newest prize, the crowd dragged and pushed him forward onto a wide forest path. If he had thought an opportunity to resist may soon appear, he was soon disappointed since the motley band did not cease its progress until the suns had almost set.

At last, they emerged free of the forest and Flores found himself in a wide broad valley with gently rising bluffs on each side, knee-high amethyst and oceans of grass mixed with eternal yellow altheas spreading the length of the valley. A fine water mist began to settle over them as the effects of the coming winter made its first droplets felt.

More surprises came. No village could he see. Just as no fires, no structures of any sort, or even walls or fences. Just wide-open spaces beneath the wide expanse of sky, patches of stars and the ecliptic of Teknos peeking through darkening gaps in the high-floating clouds as another fleeting day of sixteen hours sped by on the planet Maalstrom.

Yet more hundreds of the creatures appeared around him, now numbering at least a thousand, arriving from all directions to see the accomplishment of their leader. As the largest also spoke the loudest, Flores concluded that he must be their leader and he noted that all let their eyes follow this one's every movement and attended to his every utterance. No democratic principles prevailed here as did in his home city of Ven, Flores concluded.

With all the attention that this vast and growing assemblage put upon him, Flores began to wonder just what they may have in mind, just as he began to wonder by what means he might make his escape, given that their numbers kept accumulating.

So far, at least, none had harmed or abused him. They seemed quite free of any anger or malice. But for their numbers, Flores began to think that they must have something else in mind. But what? What malicious purpose could these creatures have in mind for their 'disgusting' captive, with their constant fluttering and flitting about?

Their leader stepped closer again. He seemed more bent on preening himself and showing off his captive by dragging Flores around by means of the remaining strands of net than in anything else.

Fed up with this undignified treatment, Flores dug in his heels, bringing the dragging to a halt.

The leader paused mid-step, as if debating whether to flee or hold its ground.

"Kind sir, do you have a name?" Flores asked.

It paused, seemingly not annoyed in the least by Flores' interruption of his itinerary, only showing more apprehension. "Name? How do you mean?"

"As in yours. Everyone has a name. What is your name?"

Comprehending, the leader nodded his head with pride, his top-shock rippling. "Of course I have a name. Not to have a name would be crazy."

"And it is..?"

"Why, everyone knows it. Only a disgusting thing like yourself could possibly not know what even the stars and the grass know."

"Well, I do not."

His chest swelled. "It is Swift of Foot." No man ever spoke words with greater pride and emphasis than did this bird-beaked creature bolstered by a vast throng of his own.

Flores nodded. "That is a good name. And what of your people? Do they have a name, too?"

Swift of Foot stared at Flores like he had gone mad. "What did I just tell you, disgusting one! The name is Swift of Foot."

"But," Flores inquired, "that is your name. What do you call your people?"

"How many times must I tell you, you perverse deviant. We are Swift of Foot!"

"Your people are Swift of Foot. And your name also is Swift of Foot?"

"Of course, you great moronic fool! But how could anyone expect a perversion from the herd to understand what Swift of Foot may say? Just look at yourself." The leader pointed at Flores and immediately the entire crowd tittered with high-pitched laughter, all pointing at Flores with guffaws and hilarity.

Without thinking, Flores glanced down at his body. Nothing unusual about him. So why did his captors find him so amusing and disgusting?

Out of patience, Flores took a firm step.

At this unexpected movement, the crowd jerked back in fright and every eye grew large.

As in a flash, it came to Flores what had been percolating in his mind since the creatures had first appeared. They all looked familiar. Too familiar. Half-Vensor they seemed—but only half. There was another half, or at least some significant portion, that was decidedly not of the ancestry of Vensor-sa, but of something else, something profoundly different, something he had seen recently, but which had somehow, in some inglorious—even shameful—

way must have merged with Vensor's own children who lived in civilized cities across the face of Maalstrom, his Vensor-sa.

Flores decided to test his hypothesis.

"So, you are all Swift of Foot. And not just you yourself."

"Yes. All of us. What an absurd notion that anyone that is Swift might exist in and of himself. That is what makes you a deviant. And deviant is what makes you disgusting. And disgusting is what makes you laughable. We have a name from our ancient lore for creatures that imagine themselves to be single like you."

"And that word might be..."

The Swift leader turned and for a moment discoursed in quieter tones with several others before he finally returned his attention to Flores.

"Freak."

Flores smiled. "I prefer a word even older. One that matches my nature more exactly: a walker. One who walks."

Swift of Foot stepped back, his whiskers shaking. He again consulted the others, including several who seemed older than the rest, even aged ones. Back to Flores. "We have heard of that word also. You must be ashamed, disgusting one. No creature can imagine walking its way alone through life without a speedy herd to protect and comfort him. That is not just unthinkable, but the ultimate crime, a crime against nature. One must run. One must run with the herd, for that is the purpose of all living things. He who cannot run, is a deviant freak and violates the sacred rule of the Running God."

With that, Swift of Foot gazed skyward where the last slice of suns was even now vanishing below the horizon. "The prize goes to the swiftest. Heaven awaits only those who win the race. And looking at you, O perverse one, you 'walker': you are marked for death by our God who runs across the sky. Such is the fate of the slow and of, as you say, a person that *walks*."

"No, Swift of Foot. You are wrong. I am not just a walker, but a predator."

The little wings with their feeble hands flipped upward to cover Swift's ears, and a hundred other Swifters followed, not waiting for instructions from their leader, but all responding at once upon hearing the ultimate heresy.

"We will not listen to such blasphemy! You must not say such things. You will be banned from running with the herd. No Swift of Foot will speak with you again, you will not mate, you will no longer be swift in the running, you will have no protection from the hunts of the ros. That is what our God decrees for slow-footed ones that eat meat!"

That was the confirmation Flores needed. "Know this, O Swift of Foot, that I am not only a heretic and a deviant, but that I prey on rum-na. I hunt them down and eat them!" Grasping the fibers with his hands, he exerted his full strength and in less than a second the net ripped apart. With a growl, he stepped forward, arms upraised.

Screeches sounded and the entire crowd, Swift of Foot as well as the Swift of Feet, belted away in panic, flowers and tufts of dirt filling the air as they scampered *en masse* to put as much distance as possible between themselves and their erstwhile captive.

As the dust settled, Flores shook his head. "What strange force has joined my own kind, we Vensor-sa, with the rum-na of the plains?" Flores continued to stare as the vast concourse of Swifters ran like the fastest of athletes—faster—to the far horizon, leaving the wide valley empty, the herd, doubtless, not stopping until distracted by some new field of succulent grass.

CHAPTER 5

D ust still in the air about Flores, far away under the Maalstrom sky and the Maalstrom moons, in the ancient city of Vaw, or more precisely beneath it, a squat monstrosity opened one eye in the blackest of Stygian underworlds submerged in a pool of water that contained a backwash from the sea.

A second eye opened. As blind as any sightless dweller in cave brine, the two eyes blinked. A fleshy landscape twitched, sensing as if by insensate perceptions, on a wide bullet head and the ichthyous brain within commenced to stir. It took stock of its shattered body, and without purpose or intent, dispatched a rare signal to nerves and fibers and striatonated muscles and cartilage to resume a growth once thought forever outgrown as a man outgrows the ability to regrow a limb.

But as even a man may grow new teeth once his infant teeth are gone, this man sensed rather than felt the initiation of a new stimulus of growth where arms and legs had once lived. More than arms and legs. On his bullet head, flanks that substituted for his lack of a measurable neck, slits appeared. One upon another they took shape in tandem with pink feathers along their outer edges. Bubbles escaped the slits. More bubbles, until finally—and who could calculate the passage of time for such a biological process to complete?—they became functioning gills, if not as serviceable as true fish, at least sufficing to keep the head and the brain within alive in the absence of temporarily non-functional oxygen-breathing lungs.

The weeks elapsed and one day... Or perhaps it was a

dawn? Or an evening? Or blue-bathed night? New signals filtered down the spine to its new arms and legs that they should move. And the eyes blinked in blackness, and the arms marched to prehensile hands and to feet that merged into flaps instead of toes, and the brain directed the body to rise up, and with a jerk to lift itself out of the inky darkness which even its blubbery soul found confining.

The surface of the black pool broke into ripples as from a tossed pebble and the bullet head lifted clear of the ink and laid its flat gaze upon two parallel walkways that oppositely bordered the watery depths beneath a wall of raw stone at right angles to another wall composed entirely of translucent irsrem. A staid figure stood upon one of the walkways, arms calmly by its side.

The bullet eyes in the bullet head focused on the figure. A gurgle sounded.

"Do not attempt to speak so soon, Initiate. You have been underwater for the better part of a year. I have been waiting for you since I saw the first bubble escape this dark pit. I knew that if I was but patient, your spawning from the loins of the Golden Cyclops would come to your rescue, even though your mother Morla tore you limb from limb."

Fish floated as freely in the water, at home as any denizen of the seas.

The figure continued, "O Third Initiate of the Cult of the living Kot, slave of the Golden Cyclops and the Eternal Whirling Sceptre...the obsidian throne and your piebald raiment await! The city of Vaw has need of your strength and a new living Kot. One who values statecraft more than bundles of sticks."

The bullet head split in an obscene grin, wine-dark water streaming down its pink cheeks.

"Mens," he gurgled. "I have need of my vizier. Let us talk."

* * *

Crestal's mien collapsed. "Why, Soorkrul? Is it not enough that you have taken me again and that your slavers are ending my lord's life even as we stand here?"

The prismed landscape of pale flesh glinted with dawnlight as the twin suns Vensor and Vensed rose above the horizon, their quickly contracting barbell signaling the coming of cooler weather. Soorkrul motioned with a wave of his hand to the two remaining slavers that still accompanied him.

"Is it not enough? The devil slaughtered my followers as easily as we slaughter lyarts and reven-na for our evening meal. It was only by the fortune of a cached tunic squeezed in the interstices of the dungeon of Vim, which I in my caution placed there for just such an eventuality as happened, that I managed to escape from the Turlicum's clutches." His brown eyes flashed—Crestal noted once more that, despite all his representations, the Eunuch Lord was not blind like the others who had been selected by the Order for the highest duty of seeking the Thirteenth Revelation. "That, and the ministrations of my ever-loyal Swart." He glanced at his wrists that still bore the imprint of glass trinkets. "The effect of the talismans persists, you see, for some time after the devices themselves have absented, if one has had time to deepen their influence."

Soorkrul raised his face to receive the swirling yellow leaves of autumn, yellow like gold, ruddy like blood. A cackle of joy escaped his throat. "But now I have you back, my gila of the wilds. And how wild you were when my employers first delivered you to me those scant years ago to be trained in the arts of love before assigning you to the harem of that oaf Numsenmur."

"Oaf?" Crestal's face too was upraised, receiving the yellow and scarlet that dropped from the enormous boles of forest trees, the topmost lost to view. "My lord Numsenmur was harsh, but he was in no sense an oaf. He became king of Ven, something you attempted but failed."

The prisms reshuffled and focused on Crestal like the sharpening of a knife. "It is not for the likes of you, failed assassin and sex slave that you are, to pass judgment on your betters." A grin spread. "Need I mention how I could scarce restrain your enthusiasm when you were first given to me. I could hardly persuade you to stay clothed in the time we had together."

Crestal dropped her gaze to the leaf-meshed forest floor. "I am ashamed."

"Yes?" The cackle turned haughty. "So, this is what your time with Flores has done to you. Intransigence. Ingratitude. My careful training and bedroom instruction gone to nought. Though I dare say that it came in handy when you desired to please your new lord."

She continued hiding her face.

"I thought thus. Surely you know by now that you cannot hide anything from me, Soorkrul of the Light, Soorkrul of the Revelations. I have infused crowds with my visions!" He raised his arms to embrace the still falling leaves. "Bracelets or no, none can resist the power of our Order, which stretches from our center in Klopus like the tentacles of a goliath. Now you must be patient, my little eager one. I will in time reward you again with a chance to show what you still know, once I return you to the place of your childhood."

"You will allow me to return to my own land? The land of gilas?"

A mocking expression took hold of the prismed visage. "Among the Mok-sa? I think not, little one. They were aware from the start that you came into our hands. They do not wish you back."

A tear coursed one of her cheeks.

"So, you see, you have no one but me, your chief benefactor, not that slow cripple Flores of the Turlicum who left you to rot while he pursued another gila across the wilds of the world, only to take you up again when he could no longer possess what he truly wished."

"I do not believe you." Crestal's auburn hair, interspersed with blond strands, glazed with yellow. From between hoary tree limbs, sunrays erupted and bathed her head like an aureole as if the gods were selecting her for special favor, the yellow of her hair melding with the yellow of the sunrays.

"It matters not. You shall ride contained the rest of the way, however, like it or no, when the rest of my expedition arrives, and they shall meet us at this bend in the Hedronmas as per our arrangement. Flores has killed many of us. But the Order has many more. You shall be placed in a box such you are already long familiar with, and you shall be transported in secret thus to Klopus, away from the prying eyes of the stupid people of this world, who need the Order to preserve them from heresy. More than a box...a royal palanquin."

More tears flowed. "I want it not."

"You will ride contained as befitting one with your potential." Soorkrul gazed down at Crestal, who refused to meet his gaze. "Have you still...your protuberances?"

A brief nod followed. "They are almost gone."

"Then the Turlicum does not suspect your true nature?"

A brief shake of her head.

"That is good. You can never fulfill what was intended for you by your Mok-sa, just as you did not fulfill what I intended for you when I delivered you to Numsenmur, and you failed to administer the poison to Numsenmur as I had trained you to do."

For once she defied her abductor. "I am not a murderer! Even of true murderers like Numsenmur."

Soorkrul snorted. "Such delicate sensibilities in one so young. So innocent. And so helpless, having fallen into my hands alone to do with as I please. But it matters not. Numsenmur is gone; he long lies in the Eye of Vensor."

She glanced down again. "Only traces of my bumps remain. Flores never noticed. Neither did Numsenmur, who had never seen a woman before me, so knew not what to expect."

"Who is there who could guess? Who is there in the world who could conceive of the plans of the gods? Of the content of the Thirteenth Revelation? As fast as one comprehends divine Nature, Vensor and the other deities of the Urlis spin new webs of fact and fancy always just beyond one's ken, hidden behind Nature's Veil. That is why only the unconscious can apprehend the true face of God." Soorkrul smiled at the heavens. "Only the Order, and I alone within it, have been chosen by the predestination of the fates to receive their special knowledge. Chosen from before we were spawned in the temples of queens. Just as you, dear Crestal, were chosen for your role before your nuptial act. Just as more like you will follow upon the next Flight."

Crestal's shoulders hunched as if remembering something long suppressed.

Limbs snapped as of leafy boughs giving way before weighty intrusions. Huge lyarts appeared from the depth of the forest, upthrust tusks threatening harm to any unfamiliars who might stray within their reach. The pair of beasts hauled a four-wheeled wagon with shocked wooden wheels to absorb jolts, a familiar wooden box within the wagon, copper bands sealing it shut but for a series of breathing holes along its sides.

A score of slavers escorted the contrivance, their dour expressions on their smooth faces betraying a concern that even here in a secret place far from the recent pyrrhic encounter with the Lord of the Turlicum, the Simet-trained warlord might surprise them as their comrades had earlier surprised him. Comrades now deceased. Several glanced skyward, concerned that malkop-vultures might have traced their progress thus revealing their vulnerable position to the avenging Turlicum. Green boughs covered their view, however, no trace of sky visible among the vast verdant mansions except for occasional stray sunbeams.

Soorkrul adjusted the dark robe that covered most of his body. He spoke to the newcomers as one used to quick obedience. "Open the chamber. Place within food and drink, enough for a week for one. Put the Mok woman inside, then seal the crate for final delivery to the Elders of the Order. Look with care—but see nothing. If ought learns what this crate contains, that will go ill for its escort."

The slavers exchanged apprehensive glances. There was no escort but them. Without delay, they pried open the container. Then they laid hands on Crestal, who moaned and cried as they placed her within, uselessly, and they finally resealed the copper bands about the box.

"She may not exit until we arrive in Klopus. Listen to her breathing at all times. If she suffers harm during the trip, that too will not go lightly with you."

"Yes, Sobol." Whipping the lyarts, the slavers turned the cart around and set out through the forest, their master well-guarded in the center of the little expedition.

Soorkrul smiled as he prodded his grey-skinned reven, guiding its progress through the bowers by means of the rawhide reins. "Sobol," he said to himself. "It is good that my reputation goes before me."

No more words came as the forest swallowed them up.

CHAPTER 6

A fter the Fells of Sish, the Suma expanded and the ripple between the waves grew even less visible to the casual who may happen to observe it. With leaves and limbs and a fresh tasty breeze of cool weather whipping the surface of the river, every boat and canoe that passed over its white-tipped waves was guided by happy sailors and pilots, smiling and invigorated by the gentle lapping of clean wind on cheeks despite the increased hazard of the swirling waters.

The invisible paddles dipped. Macius stared as he pushed his canoe forward as noiselessly as possible, still not quite certain that the newly acquired devices on his wrists had finally, after so many years of effort that took him across half the world, become his and his alone. Still not quite certain that they indeed cast a cloak of illusion about him, though he had seen many times the truth of this in the hands of others.

His mind wandered. Usually as ordered and disciplined as a Simet warrior, Macius, the thief from the voluble seaport of Vaw, a spawn of Vaw's queen, and himself an initiate in the Cult of the Living Kot, though only an initiate of the first level, allowed the image of a malkop to come to mind.

Before seconds had passed, the occupants of two sizable boats passing alongside his pirogue halted their paddling and stopped to stare with open mouths at Macius in his little boat.

Macius paused. What could be the problem? Frantically he felt for his bracelets—three were still snug on each wrist and—so far as he could tell—there was no salt or salt-water in the vicinity that might neutralize their powers as he had done to Soorkrul.

But they continued to stare. One of the larger boats changed course as a rough-looking sailor leaned on the rudder and the men laid into their paddles, outrage and anger darkening some faces, wonder and lust brightening the faces of others. All were eager to close with his little canoe.

What indeed? Macius chanced to glance at the swamped waves beside his canoe and for a brief moment they stilled. In that moment, he glimpsed what could never be—a beautiful denizen of the skies, blond hair flowing down over a pouting, red-lipped mouth and pendulous breasts of a gila while it pulled two oars fixed to either wale, two vast wings catching the wind alongside like sails—an image to attract the stares of crowds.

So, he had not yet mastered the bracelets. To master the bracelets, one must first master one's mind. That was the difficulty. Quickly he pictured in his head calm waters and a minor ripple among ripples and the image of the malkops instantly vanished to be replaced by empty river water.

The pair of boats braked as those rowing and paddling applied themselves to halt their progress. The sailors peered about as if they had lost sight of the source of their interest. Half looked skyward, the logical place to find a malkop, but none were visible. The others thrust oars outward as if to touch something they could no longer see, though the suns shone brightly on them all.

Macius quietly paddled away—the bracelets once again projected only illusion. Proximity was dangerous. Anyone contacting his little canoe would immediately discover that the illusion was only a matter of sight.

By afternoon, Macius had rowed and paddled far upstream, once more leaving no trace of his passing except the occasional ripple of water and dip of an invisible oar beside him.

Days passed.

Bypassing the city of Tes, destroyed in the recent fighting, but already recovering as its queen resumed her reproduction, Macius found the fork in the Suma that led northwest.

A familiar path.

More days passed, then he came to the port serving the Mines of Maanus, where imperial Ven put the bulk of its prisoners of war to labor mining corta for its irsrem industry of tear-glass. Macius raised an eyebrow as he slowly paddled away from the unfortunate scene, with the Maanus peaks commanding a view for miles about—the eyebrow a tell betraying intense stirrings of emotion within Macius as if he had had experiences in that matter as well. The blockhouse guarding the port was again housed by alert imperial soldiery of Ven—now that a new queen was in Ven and the Calling for Sons had resumed.

Further days elapsed. And on the right, he passed an enormous cave-like grotto where a gush of water erupted to join the river, indicating a deep spring somewhere lost in the dark interior. The water flow was deep enough to accommodate boats much larger than his little canoe, and by the entrance, Macius glimpsed pornographic iconography carved and implanted to warn others of the nature of the grotto's owner. He pursed his lips, and focusing his mind more than ever on the image of simple river water, he paddled hurriedly away from this distant outpost of the Guildmaster of Ven and Soorkrul's brutal slavers.

A large rocky crest appeared. Then he passed a wide-open glade that was covered by torn remains of tents and in the center rose a gigantic pile of ashes such as the victors in a battle who were still angry at the behavior of their enemy sometimes piled up the vanquished dead and burned them to prevent the malkops from taking their souls to Vensor's Eye. Malicious treatment unjustified by civilized warriors, Macius thought. A single glance sufficed for him to conclude that nothing remained of the struggle worth his time and effort to pilfer.

Adjoining one side of the glade loomed a vertical cliff with a single large scutate door at its base made of what appeared to be pure irsrem. Such a door must lead to a larger complex of tunnels beneath the rocky crest, and Macius realized that the door and the tunnels must exit through the grotto he had recently glimpsed. The field of burned dead must be but another of the evil deeds of Soorkrul the Eunuch Lord and his underlings. Who knew why the Lord would trouble himself with an outpost so distant from Ven when the only city in this part of Maalstrom was the imperial city of Tumset? Nothing clean or legitimate, he concluded. He paddled on.

Another week and Macius had exhausted the small store of meat and grain the previous owner had left under a cross-plank and he felt the need to find more nutrition and fresher water than that offered by the river. At last, far removed from all settlements and all signs of civilization, Macius decided to risk a landing, now that he was away from all signs of the Eunuch Lord and the long arm of the city of Ven, and coming closer to his destination. Here, the river Suma, or rather this one tributary of it, had shrunk to the size of a brook no more than twenty feet across but still deep enough for him since the little pirogue he possessed required no more than two feet of water to remain buoyant.

Around Macius, the steep forests rose, glades no longer interspersed to relieve the eye from becoming lost in its green hirsute tangles. In its midst he thought he glimpsed fur-encompassed eyes, and an occasional remote hoot echoed as of arboreal clans warning this stranger not to transgress. Five-armed spider monkeys, Macius nodded. He had seen and heard them before. Best to avoid them, but now that he possessed 'the items', he could be the master of all the denizens of the forest and need have no fear of a repeat of his previous naked demarche in this jungle realm.

Fresh water he found. And focusing his mind on the

image of an empty breeze, he learned that he could approach one of the many fat rodents without alerting them and with a quick dagger to the throat soon was cooking their flesh over an open pit. Incomparably easier than bothering with time-consuming traps.

Time he did not have. Not if he was to be certain to anticipate whom he expected.

Salting away extra seared flesh, he packed his wallet and set out inland, away from the brook and his beached pirogue, now covered by leafy limbs. His boots consumed the miles along varying forest paths, his way circuitous where no paths existed.

The weather finally broke as the full weight of late autumn came over Maalstrom, every latitude the same on this world without polar eccentricities, solstices, or equinoxes, the suns alone causing the seasons by merging or divagating, all influenced by the Eye.

A storm broke as cold settled over the forest and still Macius plodded on, only salted meat and his dagger and small swigs of water granting him life in this death-dealing wilderness. Yet he was no longer helpless, as before when he had first traveled this long road in pursuit of the owner of the bracelets. Following that day long past when he had set foot on the Island of the Sun-God and witnessed from concealment Yezd commandeer a malkop in the valley of fruit trees within the crystal pyramid, and watched Yezd remove the talismans and count them to the number seven and wash them in the orchard stream.

And he had heard Yezd—he of the one yellow eye and the one blue eye—mumble to himself in frustration about his castle in the forest, and Yezd had replaced the items on his wrists and with a single voice had reasserted his mastery over the malkop and forced it to fly him to the glass city in the clouds where Yezd was lost to sight.

Then it was that Macius had conceived his life's purpose: Ignore the treasures he had found. Leave the Sun-

God's island. Travel to Ven. Inquire about Yezd. Find his castle. And infiltrate the castle in order not only to learn the secret of this greatest of treasures—Yezd's bracelets of tear-glass—but to steal them for himself and force a malkop to take *him*, Macius, to the high city in the clouds instead of the red-robed Yezd.

Now he was finally back. Before his steady gaze, his studied contemplation, from the cover of a net of red-leaved bowers even now detaching to fall in droves around his booted feet, Macius looked through a descending white mist upon the same grey manor he had visited in what seemed eons ago—the castle with the heavy doubled gate decorated with carven images of the god of fire, Atasan, still cracked open as he had left it the year previous when he had departed, leaving Flores and his companions to their own devices.

The open ground before the gate even still bore the remains of one of the beast-like men whom Flores had killed when he had rescued Macius, its white bones turning to dross. It was then that Macius had lost the bracelets after attaching them to the ankle of a fleeing malkop and cutting the chain that had held it captive, and the beast-men whom Yezd had assigned to guard the castle had then kept Macius a prisoner within it.

But now Macius had got the talismans back, and it was he, and not Yezd, who now had the power to assign guards to the castle. But in guards Macius had no interest. Who was this man called Yezd? From where did he hail? What was his interest in visiting the malkops' city in the clouds? Macius had learned none of this in his previous demarche. And most important: was Yezd capable of constructing more of the bracelets? Yezd had but one more talisman, this Macius knew, for their number was only seven. But what if Yezd could produce more of the talismans, more of the items of which only seven had sufficed for Soorkrul to command the entire city of Ven and its three valleys and turn whomever he pleased into beast-men.

In answer to all these questions, Macius resolved not to reveal himself, but to watch and wait and listen. It was possible to infiltrate and only pretend to be under the control of the items—this Macius knew because he had done that. But this time, if Yezd were to discover him as he had discovered Macius before, it would be Macius casting the spell, not Yezd. If Macius chose to do so, who knew what secrets the red-robed scribe might reveal in such circumstance? On the other hand, who knew what the results might be if Yezd with his one talisman chose to resist Macius with his six?

It was best not to risk it.

Wrapping his mind in the image of a gentle breeze, Macius stepped from the shelter of the golden boughs and strode unhurriedly across the open neglected plaza to the chateau's open gate. Poking his head through with care, he quickly assured himself that the place had no residents. No longer did men roam the grounds, believing themselves to be beasts while under the control of Yezd. No longer did Yezd, he of the one blue eye and the discordant yellow eye, conduct experiments on malkops and men, sometimes with harsh results.

No smoke rose from the main building. No howls from the barns and adjoinments beyond. There was no sign of life anywhere within the corroded crenelated walls, as none amidst the open neglected fields overgrown with weeds and worts.

Macius ventured within the open gate. Having already decided on his plan of deceit—and deceit was ever his preferred approach, contrary to the forced solutions preferred by Simet nobles—he turned to the right and located the stairwell that led round to the third story where he entered a long not-overly-wide chamber with many windows that overlooked both the courtyard within and the open plaza without.

It was the perfect place to stand and watch and plan.

Yezd, the red-robed maker of underwater gills that enabled men to swim beneath the sea and of bracelets of glass that enabled men to deceive and command each other and even fly through the sky, would eventually come.

Of that, Macius had no doubt.

CHAPTER 7

Retracing his steps back to the forest glade where he had encountered the Swifters' net, Flores was relieved to find his new 'Tha', his new loyal reven, still in the vicinity. Of course, it did not respond at once to his friendly calls—after all, it was not raised as his own. But in time, while Flores became increasingly frustrated with impatience, the animal did come close and the Turlicum was able to take the reins and feed the beast fresh redentine and spit on its gills. Finally, he was again mounted, with Nedelroc sheathed on one side and a short glass rapier on the other. The rapier was not long enough to execute a cabré in combat, but this reven responded only reluctantly to the tugs and spurs that should induce that in any combat-trained Simet reven. I must work to improve this, Flores thought.

He spurred the beast forward.

As the climate grew colder, and mist began to fall, he still made his way northeastward, paralleling the trend of the Hedronmas. This much the reven seemed to know, and Flores having no other guide, let the animal proceed. Klopus was ahead, somewhere near the headwaters of the river. And the land of Mok-sa, where Vensor women lived supposedly in the open, in defiance of the planet-wide prohibition on women imposed by the male-only cities of Vensor warriors. The ancient rule was: all females when found must be delivered unharmed to the Sacred Temple of one's own city. How did the Mok-sa manage to defy this universal rule of the god Vensor and live otherwise? Crestal had been unable to explain in detail—now she had been abducted by Flores' most intransigent enemy.

Once more Flores found himself penetrating woody arcades, bizarre forms of life passing overhead and around as if he indeed was the freak that Swift of Foot had claimed. Isia centipedes crept on the ground. Spider monkeys sped overhead. Predatory ros-na coughed in the distance, causing Flores' reven to shudder at the sound of its ancient foe.

Along the riverbank, wild herds of reven-na slithered into the water upon sight of Flores, his own mount snaking its neck as if showing a desire to join its cousins. Once, Flores even caught sight of a band of mounted Vensor-sa on the far side of the river, beards and filets on their foreheads, signaling their affiliation with the city of Neset, the traditional foes of Ven, and whose king had recently occupied Ven and slaughtered its people, even murdered its queen inside Ven's own Temple. Flores retreated into the forest. He had no quarrel with Neset-sa now. To be seen by them would mean only needless risk.

Northeast and northeast he traveled. The remains of the torn tent he had brought and which was serving to protect him by night, he found he had to wear about him like a cloak by day to weather the cold. Still the reven marched on, guided only by its inherent homing instinct, its clawed paws mastering every obstacle.

The suns had merged and one day Flores awoke and saw that the suns had once more begun to divagate, the edges of two disks again discernible. A week later the short Maalstrom winter began to clear and the first shoots of a verdant spring to erupt from the earth.

The landscape had been flat though filled with thick forest, now it grew hilly, ridge after ridge rising before Flores and his mount, causing new delays, but a relief to both eye and ear as echoes ranged through narrow valleys spread with hibiscus and lavender, the reven easily managing the rocky scapes that became more numerous.

How much time had passed since the bloody ambush in the wilds? Late autumn had become winter and winter now gave way to early spring. The land came alive, bursting with life on all sides, every valley, even the crest of each ridge, exploding with purple and yellow flowers. Birds of all types swarmed the horizons to consume the cornucopia that Vensor and His twin Vensed had released on their forever insufficiently grateful subjects.

One afternoon as Flores climbed a narrowing path in a rising valley encompassed by sheer cliffs, a new shape came suddenly into view, aloft on wide wings.

Flores froze.

Such an image could not be. No such creature could live and breathe on Maalstrom. Everything he had ever seen or believed to be true was contradicted by this new revelation.

The creature was no bird. Neither was it malkop, though it bore all the essential traits of the latter. The newcomer boasted yellow blondish hair but mixed with darker strands, something never found among malkops whose hair was always sheer blond; the newcomer's feminine face had lips wine-dark red; a mature woman's body entirely nude with globular breasts announcing imminent reproduction, with narrow waist, and long lithe but eminently strong legs with bare feet. All was held aloft by gigantic bright wings entirely free of fur or feathers—glabrous and near transparent while true malkops had brown wings with traces of feathers, small but visible up close. Malkops always clothed their genitals with rope loincloths. This new creature of the sky had no such modesty but flew with breasts and genitals exposed, heedless of its effect on land dwellers. Or intending to arouse to acts such as malkops rarely evoke?

Flores shook his head to clear his eyes and empty his mind. What did this disturbing manifestation portend? For what conceivable purpose could this creature's nudity serve? To see a malkop divested of its brown loincloth was blasphemous among Vensor-sa. And among Vensor-sa, reproduction was strictly limited to one queen per city.

Before Flores could sort out the least of his confusion, three more bird-like creatures dropped out of the sky like eagles and fell upon the newcomer. In seconds too short to measure, three malkops—unmistakable in their distinctness from the newcomer—collided in air with the nude figure and unleashed a savage attack.

Claws sprang from the thin fingers of the malkops and ripped the other's flesh in shreds, causing blood to burst into clouds of scarlet, the newcomer seeming to have no defense against their assault. No claws emerged from the newcomer, akin to the malkops though the creature seemed. And when the malkops finished their harsh deed by opening their mouths and emitting their unique strands of white foam that hissed and burned their victim, no such acidic strands came from the victim, who responded—to Flores' great surprise— only by screaming and crying. Malkops have no speech, he recalled, not even the capacity for a groan, and could emit only insect-like clicks. But the malkops remained entirely silent throughout their calculated murder while their victim screeched in pain.

Briefly, the sky was filled with a complicated tangle of enormous wings as the newcomer desperately sought to flap away to save its life. To no avail. In moments after the arrival of the three malkops, the flyer with the smooth translucent wings collapsed from the sky and plunged into the valley. Its body hit the pitched side of an escarpment and tumbled over, coming to rest by the streamlet at the bottom of the gorge not far from Flores, having left a wide trail of red blood up the side of the ridge.

As Flores stared open-mouthed, the three assassins flew casually away, seemingly satisfied with their bloody deed and they soon vanished across the nearest ridge, not bothering to retrieve the body of their victim. Flores had once engaged in combat with malkops and knew their techniques, but this was something different, this was murder.

Flores calmed the nervousness in his reven and slowly urged it forward to view the results of the attack. Not ten feet distant lay the ruined remnants of what moments before had been a living, breathing, even beautiful image of a gila although kept aloft by huge insect-like wings. Now all that was left was a ripped broken shell, even the newcomer's gorgeous face disfigured.

It took Flores no more than a few seconds to ascertain that no life remained.

"Hoom," he muttered. He spurred his mount up the track. Let the gods sort out conflicts among gods, he thought. Mortals can do no more than sacrifice to the Sun-God Vensor and hope He hears their pleas. But even Vensor, as Flores had learned, was deaf and dumb, and in the right circumstances even a mere mortal like Flores could invade His heaven and rob Him and pull His beard in the bargain. Such did Macius teach him before the enigmatic thief had vanished.

Up Flores climbed, he and Tha-two, as he had begun to think of his new mount. The crags grew taller, the little rift valleys steeper, and he lost track of the Hedronmas. The clouds of winter had given way to a clear cloud-billowing firmament, arousing an expansive mood, and he soon forgot the strange murder he had witnessed among Vensor's denizens of the welkin.

The third day he spied a strip of rawhide such as men might use during travel. Pausing, he dismounted and examined it closely. His brows rose. *Yesss.* The style employed by slavers of the Eunuch Order to contain their glass or iron darts. Flores nodded. He must be on the very track of Soorkrul and Crestal, and from the look of the well-padded path, they must be accompanied by a growing escort. Swift of Foot had not seized them after all.

He had best watch for an ambush—yet make haste, for the closer they came to their capital of Klopus, the less would be any opportunities for Flores to overtake them and free his mate.

Watching each step of his reven closely, he tried to keep one eye on the ground and the other on the sky in case another winged gila should appear and evoke another lynching in the air by the malkops. Afternoon came and Flores continued to climb a path that increasingly narrowed as he crossed another ridge. The swiftly lengthening shadows portended imminent night and Flores felt the need to hurry his pace when he sighted a brown lump beside his path.

Reining in Tha-two, Flores peered up the ridges on either side for sudden attacks by highwaymen or a predatory ros eager to sink its bone-bare dagger-like hook into red flesh. Detecting nothing, he edged his mount forward until he could peer down upon the lump.

"Shoom," he muttered. "A child."

The lump took on the traits of a small boy of perhaps six short Maalstrom years—deceased as was plain from how his face was deeply buried in mud. Wearing only a loincloth, the body of the boy showed between crisscrossed tattoos several injuries that must have been lethal. Beside it lay a fire-hardened spear with an iron point and alongside it lay a broken bow and small quiver but no arrows. Whoever, or whatever, had ended the boy's life, he had, at least, first emptied his quiver.

A harsh world, Flores reflected, that sends infants into the wild with no more than sharp sticks for protection. We of Ven embrace our infants at the Calling for Sons of the Temple and adopt them into our clans. What would be the sense in sending our next generation beyond the city to quickly die?

Prodding his reven forward, he passed the boy's body and attempted to clear his mind of the tragedy. Around the next rocky stalagmite, he jerked the animal back. In a clearing lay a dozen more infant corpses. All males, all tattooed, some boasting feathers—and all dead. From the vicious wounds on their bodies, it was clear they had been cornered on the path and massacred by some force of military strength, perhaps grown men. Flores nodded. Harsh is too weak a word. Pitiless and brutal were closer.

Glancing skyward, he noted an approaching swarm of malkops, eager to fulfill their eternal function of collecting the dead. They would not descend until Flores and his mount had moved far off. He shrugged again. They would be flown to the Eye of Vensor—an actual place on this brutal world, he recalled, where the malkops and Atasan jealously defended their island from intruders such as Flores. This too was out of the hands of mortals and in the hands of the gods.

Once more he tried to purge his mind of the atrocity, which could only delay and embarrass him in his goal. Cresting one more ridge, Flores paused at the edge, for suddenly the land opened upon meadows and groves of tall trees that grew thicker along his right, where, from the gatherings of flocks of birds and a constant shimmering, he concluded he had relocated the river. But he dared not cross until he ascertained what else lay before him.

In the distance, he sighted what appeared to be a disturbance on the fields and as he peered beneath a cupped hand he made out a caravan of dozens of men and lyarts, one pulling a box in a wagon. Could this be his target? Had he been successful in his long pursuit over so many months, to have simultaneously caught up with Soorkrul and his stolen consort at the same moment as arriving at the Eunuch Lord's legendary capital?

He stepped closer along the path, the better to see.

Without warning, a net sprang from the ground, erected by spring-loaded jambs. Before Flores could reach his dagger or axe, the net twisted about him and he fell flat on the ground, wrapped more tightly than a night spider's web-shrouded dinner. Indeed, his eye wandered to crevices and cracks in the scarpments about him as if the loathsome creatures would come creeping from their burrows.

None came. Rather he sighted a pair of reven-mounted warriors hopping in his direction, the riders clinging to the sinuous necks as they hurried their mounts at top speed.

There was nothing to be done but await their untender mercies.

"Damn myself for a fool."

Confirming his worst suspicions, the riders bore the accoutrements of Soorkrul's slavedrivers with crossed leather bands, sheathed darts, and leather skirts burdened by swords and small shields.

As they neared, one dismounted and came close to Flores. "Another slave for our masters," he sneered. "And this one will cost us nothing, not even one silver mir." Laughing, he waved to the far caravan and three more slavers hopped their reven-na over and soon Flores found himself lifted while still wrapped in the net.

"Beware, slavers," Flores said coldly. "I am familiar with your trick."

"Trick?" They laughed. "You think you have a key to our cage?"

"Behold. With a simple stretch of my limbs, I will break these bonds. Then watch for your lives, for I shall nourish the earth with your vitals."

With that, Flores stood firmly and with a cold grin exerted his strength against the simple strands, which to all appearances were precisely the same as the net cast over him by the Swift of Foot.

Nothing happened. Flores grunted and tried again. Still no result. "It seems these strands are of something stronger than what the Swift of Foot employ. Just wait, slavers. I'll wipe the dirt with your bodies yet."

Now pushing against his bonds with his full strength, Flores grunted and groaned and the veins on his neck swelled and sweat flowed down his cheeks. The bonds gave not an inch.

"Swift of Foot, you said?" One of the slavers chortled. Glancing at his comrades, he added, "Yes, I have heard those cowardly vagabonds of the prairies have tried copying us in this matter. But they should know not to try to be like their betters. When we see them, we have only to shout and those scum flee like frightened rabbits. Now come along, stranger. We are bringing a new crop of slaves for our training school and there is but one lesson that you must first learn. Do as you are told! Now hurry. We are still in time for the next Flight."

With that, he uncurled a whip and lay its metal-studded tip upon Flores' skin, only the iron-hard bands encompassing him preventing it from drawing blood. With no more ceremony, they loosened the bands around his legs and attached a thick rope around his neck, then with a harsh yank forced him to walk behind a mounted reven, which was not inclined to slow its pace for him.

His own mount, far from bolting, seemed happy to have finally arrived at its home, and trotted alongside the other reven-na, taking no more heed of its former master and adding one more small indignity to his situation.

In a few minutes—mercifully short minutes to Flores' relief—they came to the caravan and Flores was chained to a column of two dozen similarly enslaved Vensor-sa, and his bands were quickly and efficiently removed. He could only note with regret that this was far from the first time he had experienced such degradation. At least, he thought with some consolation, they were not likely to simply execute him. Every Vensor city had need of strong warriors so long as they accepted the status of permanent slave, and Klopus could be no different in that regard.

Chained to the slave queue, he suddenly noted that not all the slaves were adults—at the end of the queue struggled along a dozen infants who seemed mirror images of the slaughtered children over the ridge. So, it was these slavedrivers of Klopus who had done the evil deed. He rubber-necked to see if the prisoned boys cried or begged for mercy. Not a one as he could tell. On the contrary, all dozen seemed to walk with savage miens as might befit far older men, already adapting to their new life.

Something else helped to raise his shattered spirit. In the middle of the caravan, two lyarts hauled a wagon with a sealed box in its bed. He had seen such before. This box may contain his lost consort, Crestal. But try as he might, straining his neck to see over the others, as he was whipped to keep pace when the caravan resumed movement, he could not see Soorkrul. And since he could not see through wood, he could not verify that Crestal lay within the container in the wagon. If only he still possessed the bracelets—how easy it would be to cast illusions on all he met and go where he willed. But the jewels had mysteriously vanished.

Ahead loomed the high city wall of the fabled city of Klopus. He had heard of the place for his entire life, but as it was considered impious in Ven, as in every Vensor city, to question their religion or the eunuchs who were its chief administrators, it had never occurred to him to challenge its power or send an expedition to investigate this far city. Now he was to see it up close and personal, and from the worst possible vantage point. And, perhaps worst of all...from the point of view of a declared heretic who had taken a prohibited gila for wife.

Maybe this was not the best time to confess his heresy, he thought. And just maybe it was best if Soorkrul not see him, as Flores could not see Soorkrul. With that thought, Flores stopped straining to catch sight of his enemy, and for the first time since he had departed Ven, he lowered his head and leaned forward as if to shrink. Were Soorkrul to catch sight of him now, his life would be over in seconds. Not even the prospect of Crestal, perhaps sighting him through holes in the side of the container, brightened his mood, though he had never come close enough to be recognized by anyone who might be in that sealed box.

So, Flores walked, and sulked, and smoldered for the moment that his captors might lower their guard. This accursed city would best not allow a weapon in his reach again, or he would teach it a lesson it would not soon forget.

CHAPTER 8

The city gate drew near, and the usual decorations that always accompanied the eunuchs of Maalstrom came into view: pornographic iconalia consisting of mostly golden barbells, twin like the suns, with a silver phallus, framing the city gate, other symbols such as artistically intertwined phalluses set in chalcedony and onyx supervening overhead on the vast stone lintel in the style of eunuchs, such as was found in every Vensor city's House of Prostitution.

The little caravan passed through the gate under the watchful eye of a half-score of the usual dark slavers, their hands on metal-studded whips and poniards, the guards strutting about to caution the new crop of slaves not to resist their appointed fate.

Inside the gate, a great plaza opened up and Flores was surprised to see that his caravan was but the smallest and most recent in a long series of such and he began to wonder from where such a large traffic could come since the eunuchs' caravans that he had seen arrive in Ven from distant Klopus had always been few and rare.

"Driver, good sir," he ventured while still chained with the rest of his caravan and eyeing the many chained gangs accompanying the other caravans, some of which also included groups of chained boy-warriors. "Where have these unfortunates come from?"

The nearest slavedriver stared at him with round eyes like his question was a personal insult. "How can anyone be so stupid as not to know that our holy temple of Klopus serves the entire world. There is no part of Maalstrom that does not fall down in worship of the Oracle's leadership. And who gave you permission to speak!" With that, he lashed out with his whip and Flores for the first time felt the metal stud, blood springing from one shoulder where the tip touched. He grimaced and closed his mouth.

Well into the open plaza inside the city walls, Flores saw that the caravan nearest him was not only larger than his caravan with many more captives, both boys and adults, chained in queue, but also had several large and heavy four-wheeled wagons, some loaded with ingots of gold and silver, and still others loaded with stacks of cured lyart hides and a selection of irsrem and iron weapons tossed on top, all open to inspection as if the eunuch owners had no concern that anyone under their supervision would dare pilfer.

What punishments must they administer to persuade commoners, desperate and hungry as they must be, to refrain from violating the eunuchs' rules? Flores wondered in silence. He sighted a worker—plainly not a slavedriver, but merely one of the many laborers who came to assist—who was missing a hand. Harsh, but effective, crossed Flores' mind. Only one such highly visible unfortunate was enough to persuade the rest not to risk the same by breaking the eunuchs' rules by attempting to steal.

Under the direction of more slavers, laborers surrounded one of the larger wagons and hurried to onload open crates filled with heavy hides and iron swords brought from an adjacent warehouse, and Flores realized that the wagons had just arrived in Klopus and were being readied as if to leave for parts unknown.

As a clutch of laborers carried another open crate from the warehouse, and with a great struggle attempted to place it in a wagon while a pair of slavedrivers whipped and cursed them, one of the lyarts drawing the wagon shied and jerked the wagon forward, causing the crate to slip off the wagon. Before the slaves could halt its slide, the crate fell full on one of the slavedrivers who fell pinned beneath.

His screech rang across the plaza.

While slavers hastened to come to the aid of their comrade, a sudden thought hit Flores. Without hesitation, he hissed to the dozen chained captives around him: "Follow my lead. I will explain later." With that, he leaped forward, dragging them after him, and to his surprise as much as theirs, they cooperated and followed him in a line until he stood by the crate where slaves and slavedrivers were trying to lift the heavy crate off their comrade.

"One side," Flores called in the commanding voice of a Simet warrior and life-long chief of the Turlicum, the aristocratic Clan of the Reven, as one used to being obeyed. The drivers stepped back, they too surprised at their own instinctual reaction.

Flores shoved a slaver aside, then, bending over and squatting, Flores exerted his full strength beneath the heavy crate and, at once, dislodged one side from the stricken slavedriver. His comrades pulled him to safety.

If Flores expected thanks or a reward for his act, however, he was soon disabused. More metal tips stung his skin and a bruising club smacked square into his face, causing Flores to fall to one side, dragging half the queue down upon him.

"No one told you to break out of line, slave! You have thrown all our operations into chaos just before the annual Flight of the Mok-sa when we are hurrying to prepare for it."

The slavedriver whom he had rescued, however, barked between groans at his comrades while two other slavers raised the injured man up. He limped on his wrenched leg. "Stop. Let this slave be. And his companions. He saved me from having two broken limbs instead of just one. By Vensor, this slave is stronger than the lot of you. He will be useful not just for laboring, but for the upcoming Games."

Apparently outranking the other slavers, the one whom Flores had rescued was instantly obeyed, and the beatings and whippings halted, though the one he had pushed aside continued to glare.

"Unchain this man," said the man with the broken leg. "We need his muscles to finish loading these crates. Moreover, I want him tended by the physician."

The other slavedrivers nodded and unchained Flores. Standing him up, now free of his chains, it was clear that the club had done much harm to his face as his face was swelling rapidly and shedding blood and fluid. Luckily, he could still see, and under the pitiless direction of his new masters, he found he had no choice but to resume helping the laborers in their hard labor, his helpfulness having benefited him nothing.

A plain-dressed Vensor approached with a leather sack at his side. "Hold, stranger, while I inspect your wound." The man peered and prodded and at length he extracted a substance from his bag and smeared it on Flores' face. The physician sighed. "I fear this may take some time to heal, slave. That was brave but foolish. Still, you happened to save the life of Klep, an influential adjutant who was just promoted and was helping the slaves only from former habit. Was that your plan?" The physician stared into Flores' eyes.

Flores was unable to stare back. Did he indeed have a plan in his foolish act? he wondered.

"On the other hand, you embarrassed Romos by shoving him—the one who clubbed you. He will not soon forget your deed. He is not one to forget a slight. I advise you to watch yourself around him. Meantime, you will need a cover to assist in your healing, else you will be scarred for the remainder of your life. Others here would not care..." he glanced at Romos, "but I, Telemer, at least, think of such things."

Flores nodded, still frowning. Under the haughty stares of the eunuchs' slavedrivers, he stood quietly while the physician pulled a stretch of leather from his bag and cut two holes to allow for eyesight and another for his mouth. Cutting away most of Flores' hair till his face and skull were shaven, Telemer applied a linen bandage then wrapped the leather around Flores' skull and tied it in back with a strip of hide.

The physician stood back to admire his handiwork. "That will do for you, my friend. I will come to change and clean this bandage soon. Meantime, try not to sweat." The physician turned, and without a backward glance, walked away.

Just how Telemer proposed that Flores should refrain from sweating, Flores could not imagine, as the slavers about him motioned for him at once to resume laboring by means of threatening motions of their whips and clubs. Not wishing more bruises and leather coverings, Flores resumed work. At least he was no longer chained.

Not all the crates in the plaza contained irsrem rapiers and iron swords. Some of the crates—the smaller ones within wagons drawn by reven-na instead of lumbering lyarts—were also open to the air, but seemed to hold large bladders of some fungible material that Flores was unable to make out from his viewpoint, occupied as he was with bending, lifting, and loading more crates into the wide low transport he was tasked with.

Still other wagons were drawn up in a row of their own across the plaza, he noted. These seemed to be the focus of special attention by the slavers, and for the first time since he had passed through the city gates, he spied several of the eunuchs who governed the city, if all he had heard about Klopus was true.

Two were men of moderate height, clothed in dark compassing robes that concealed all but shaven head and hands, the low hems of their garments seeming to scrape the dirt beneath their feet. Unlike their armed slavedriver servants, the eunuchs seemed to entirely lack any sort of weapon. But, of course, as Flores reminded himself, their powers lay not in steel or tear-glass but in their supervision of Maalstrom's universal religion, the fanatical worship of the Sun-God Vensor, a cult that even Flores, after all he had seen, could not purge himself of.

I too pray to Vensor, he thought, but I am different from these eunuchs. They supervise houses of male prostitution in every Vensor city, like an animal cult, but when it comes to fighting like true men, they send out their minions, their bandoleer-wearing slavers, and promise them salvation to encourage them to massacre and enslave the eunuchs' enemies—even small children as I just discovered. They even trick acolytes into staring at the suns until they become blind, while their top-ranked eunuchs find excuses to remain indoors and sip wine.

Such was Soorkrul.

But where was the Eunuch Lord?

With all his activity, Flores realized that Soorkrul had not been part of the caravan that had brought Flores into the city, after all. And now, pausing in his labor momentarily to stand tall and throw his gaze over the length of the plaza, he concluded that Soorkrul was nowhere to be seen, that if the Eunuch Lord had recently entered the plaza, he had already entered the city proper, where buildings and warehouses multiplied, which meant that Crestal, too, had left the plaza.

It was just as well. Else he had already been discovered and an axe even now would be descending to sever his neck.

Still, his new mask—painful though it was—might serve to protect his identity for a time in this city of devils, at least until he could find a way to break free and steal back what had been stolen from him.

While Flores smoldered in silence, the activity around the smaller wagons, the ones pulled by reven-na and containing boxes the approximate size of double coffins, calmed. Several slavers gazed skyward toward the east as if expecting to glimpse something of importance, then returned to hammering boxes and crates and inspecting them.

What could they possibly expect to find in the sky? Flores asked himself between hauling more crates. Did they expect to deliver to Vensor the many weapons Flores had loaded in exchange for whatever it was they expected to see in His cloudy realm?

"I have seen much," Flores muttered under his breath, "but nothing yet able to hurl metal to the clouds." He grinned through the pain and kept working.

At length, the short Maalstrom day bled away, its clean duskline speeding across the plaza like a flock of swallows, casting the city in sudden shadow enpaled by the corpse-like whiteness emanating from the moon god Nantifus, the occasional towers throwing whorls and trapezoids one upon another till they faded into the blackness of night. Lamps erupted across the city as its denizens lit oil-fuel in their many glass lanterns.

Finally, the slaves were allowed to cease work. Several collapsed on the cobblestoned sward but were instantly prodded back to their feet by angry drivers, where they were made to stand in line to be counted. They were chained in a queue and herded by the light of portable lamps to a low warehouse that adjoined the plaza, and as Flores entered, in his turn, he found the warehouse was a barracks. Here the men were unchained one at a time and finally directed to a series of billets of poorly maintained wood where they could lie upon dirty lyart hides until their labor was again required. Far too exhausted to examine their new surroundings closely, the slaves collapsed and fell into a deep sleep, Flores included.

The eight-hour Maalstrom night passed swiftly as a diving eagle, and Flores jerked awake. At first, he thought he was asleep in the forest, dreaming evil dreams. But the loud clang that had stirred him repeated.

Sitting up, he rubbed his eyes and focused on a brace of bandoleered slavedrivers by the front entrance, clanging a rusted copper bell.

The doors opened up on a bright sunlit day.

"Back to work, scum of Talen! You may not indulge

your laziness in our sacred precincts of Vensor." One of the slavers pointed to a metal vat just outside the door. "Take what meat you can from this pit on your way to work. It will be removed in two minutes."

That worked to get the mass of hungry slaves out of their rickety beds and on their feet. The ones near the entrance rushed to grab what they could of the remains and refuse of slaughtered reven and lyart. As the last slaves exited, they found nothing left but claws and wings of rumna. Those quickest to seek their beds the prior night found the least to eat.

Flores managed to snatch part of a rum wing, and as he gnawed a bone, wondered if it might belong to Swift of Foot. If so, he had not been swift enough. A quick inspection of the end of the wing proved it did not end in a hand, though, so with a sigh, Flores continued to gnaw in a futile attempt to satisfy his hunger.

Outside, the slaves were arranged once more in line and counted. The boy warriors had been moved to a different barracks the night before and now Flores glimpsed them being led to some other destination—still proud, still haughty, despite their fate. Even embracing it from the way they stared admiringly at their new city.

More wains and wagons rolled into the main city gate, but the Turlicum's attention was drawn to several men approaching. One was tall and strong and bore scars as from many instances of combat. Unlike the other slavedrivers, not only were the bandoleers of this one loaded with iron-banded glass and iron darts, but at his side was a four-foot glass rapier, not merely a dagger. A soldier, Flores reflected, not just a cowardly slaver.

By his side walked one of the elite, a dark-robed eunuch whose robe was edged in squares of red thread. His shaven skull overlooked a smoothly-shaven face of calm expression, another who was as used to quick obedience in others as was Flores.

Escorted by a clutch of the usual slavedrivers, the pair walked the length of the queue, inspecting each slave as if seeking something in particular, though Flores noted that they did not examine their persons, but seemed more interested in less obvious traits.

They came to Flores. One of the lower-ranked slavedrivers thrust a curled whip in Flores' face. "Turn your head, slave." Flores was slow in obeying. The whip promptly uncurled and the slavedriver raised his hand to lay its rawhide on Flores' exposed flank.

Before Flores knew what he was doing, he thrust out an arm and grabbed the man by his neck—he lifted the slavedriver off the ground. Only then did Flores recognize Romos, the one whom he had embarrassed the previous day.

"Try lashing me again, Romos, and you will rest in the Eye of Vensor within the minute." Flores grimly spat this out, then with both arms shook Romos like a rat.

A glass rapier pricked Flores' side. "Lower him, slave! Placing hands on a citizen of Klopus is a grave offense." The tall slaver spoke.

With a smirk, Flores lowered Romos, who stood shaking, his knees trembling with fear.

The eunuch in red-threaded robe pointed to Flores. "This one."

Romos continued to shake. He expostulated, "This scum lays his hands on me—and you let him live?"

"We need such as he."

"This incompetent surly slave? He is who you want? Surely you can find others for the Games besides this low criminal who cannot obey his betters." Romos' knees still shook.

The eunuch turned his gaze on Romos. "Can you name one?" He smiled and passed his eyes down the queue over the other new slaves. "I see no other athletes among this crop. Are you, Romos, volunteering to take this slave's place in the arena when the crowd shouts for more?"

Romos fell silent. "No, Selem. I do not." He lowered his gaze.

"I thought not." The eunuch stared at Romos. "You have raised your voice to an Elect. Perform your obeisance." He held out a finger with a red ring and Romos hesitated, then dropped clumsily to one knee.

Flores watched Romos' lips wrinkle in suppressed frustration.

With darkened face, Romos kissed the red ring, then stood again.

Not too humiliating, Flores thought, his own lips smirking. Thus do these Eunuch Lords demonstrate their power—just like Soorkrul. Perhaps I should refrain from lifting and tossing Selem also. For now, that is.

Selem turned to the escort of slavers. "Bring this one." He paused. "You have a name?"

Flores swallowed. He had not thought of this before he laid hands on Romos. Before he could plan a suitable cover, he blurted out, "Isav. Of the city of Lesel."

"Lesel," the eunuch repeated. "That city is far. We only rarely do business with them. Too bad you are not from Ven. We have great need of men familiar with Ven since the recent king of that place caused us such mischief. Our colleague Soorkrul, who has just returned from there, wants his head. The whole of Klopus is in a tizzy over what that wretched king has done to the true religion, not only in Ven, but if tales be true, even unto the very Island of the Sun-God where Vensor Himself dwells. There can be no greater sacrilege."

Flores eyed the ground. If only he could speak his mind.

"Now come along. The city is hurrying to meet our schedule. The Games must be ready for when the Flight occurs, and that will happen within three days."

Flores wondered again what this Flight could be that the eunuchs were anticipating with such excitement. And now he had something else to wonder about: just what

Games this Selem meant. The only games Flores knew of involved the training of reven-na for battle, or bedroom games taught him by his energetic partner, Crestal. No other games held any interest for him.

Enslaved but unchained, Flores walked with his leather-bound head high as he accompanied Selem and his slaver escort under the burning glare of Romos and the growing heat of the quickly splitting twin suns on Vensor's Maalstrom, pale images of its five colorful moons soaring above.

CHAPTER 9

No living person ever felt such joy as the dark-skinned man with amphibian features who lurked on the third level of a certain spare fortress-cum-chateau ensconced between two bluffs far from the headwaters of the river Suma. Below him and across an open field, interspersed with weeds and worts and barely visible in the twinkling cloud-driven sunlight, a smudge had appeared.

More than a smudge. An image like the vibrating beat of a quivering star separated hesitantly from the trees that bordered the field. For one moment, the star pulsed, projecting a pinpoint of dull light, then morphed into a maelstrom of images. Macius stared, unable to comprehend, but each image that passed before his gaze like a kaleidoscope fell into his prodigious memory, each marked and filed to be recalled when and if he ever saw their like again.

Frames of mysterious machines; faces of people whom he knew to be long deceased, such as the brutal kings Numsenmur and Nesos; Ven's former king, Sir Ust, who had mysteriously disappeared before the ruling Simet-sa nobility could dethrone him; even the incomparably incompetent Sendas of the Molersal.

All dead. Yet here they lived.

More images flashed in the shadow of the grove. A huge metallic tube, one end of which had sunk into a morass while insects flew about. A hornet of impossible size with exaggerated antennae. Flocks of malkops whirring about a gigantic black pillar. And—most unlikely of all—a series of figures that could only be living gilas—women whose faces were entirely unfamiliar to Macius, though he had accompanied two of those rare creatures for months in the wild. Where could the visitor have seen them, except in the place that Crestal had described: her native Land of Mok-sa, the land where gilas lived.

The images flashed one upon another until they merged into a blur.

They came suddenly to a halt.

The visitor stepped into the sunlight, and nothing more could be seen but a slight distortion in the glittering sunrays of early spring, much as Macius himself had willed nothing more be seen than a ripple in the water of the Suma. Only one circumstance existed to explain what Macius saw.

Yezd had come.

The weeks of patient waiting had at last paid off, for the red-robed erstwhile scribe of Ven, the most scribal of Ven's entire scribal guild and famous throughout the imperial city for his skills, had finally come to claim his own, or to prepare some alternative for losing six of his seven bracelets should he be unable to reclaim them.

Macius rubbed his wrist. Again, as he had done one hundred times each day, he counted six of the glass irsrem devices. Gazing across the field, he watched the seventh in the hands of their maker, Yezd the scribe, the maker of miracles.

The thief let his gaze fall about the room, again as he had done a hundred times each day in anticipation of this moment. The several tables where Yezd had dissected malkops were long bare, only bones remaining. The rings set in the floor where Yezd had chained living malkops while he experimented on them remained firm. Even the rusted axe that Macius had used to sever the chain, which had enabled a frightened malkop to fly out the window with Yezd's seven bracelets tied to its ankle was still here, an epochal event because it scattered the powerful devices across the face of Maalstrom for the unwary to discover.

Could there be more of the devices hidden in some cubby within Yezd's castle? This was the chief reason why Macius was certain Yezd would return. His own searches had yielded nothing. Only the scribe himself would know where, or if more bracelets truly resided in some hidden cache.

The disturbance in the field drew closer. No more than a convection in the wind, nothing that any observer would have cause to look at twice. As it came nearer to the chateau's front gates that stood invitingly ajar, the disturbance seemed to pause as if the visitor weighed something unknown in its mind, or attempted to lay to rest some doubt. Macius withdrew from the window. To be discovered now would throw away a near lifetime of effort.

The visitor resumed. Resting momentarily before the carven image of the God of fire, Atasan, he touched the flexible jaw as if performing some ritual, then passed through the gate.

Macius retreated to the far southerly corner of the room. Focusing his mind entirely on the shadows that hugged the corners, he blocked every thought from intruding, even forgetting the dagger in his belt. His preferred solutions were stealth and silence, not the drawing of blood. Only his disciplined mind and the luck of the blue god Gethos could bring the success he craved.

Quiet steps sounded on the stairwell whose entrance lay just inside the gate. Yezd learns as fast as I, thought Macius. He enters like a breeze, not bothering to close the gate, and now climbs the stairs as if he were the thief, and not I.

The quiet steps grew gradually louder, unable to achieve complete silence due to the crunching of pebbles that the months had strewn in the stairwell—among the acorns that Macius himself had laid.

The steps paused.

Then resumed.

Again paused.

Again resumed.

Macius had no more doubt now whose mind lay behind the swirling chaos that had crossed the open field. Cautious to the last. Just when Macius felt he could no longer maintain the focus of his brain while hammering back the host of emotions and thoughts that struggled to intrude, a darker shadow impinged on the threshold at the far end of the chamber.

The shadow stepped cautiously into the room as if it trusted its own senses as little as it trusted that others would not sense it. Something glinted within the shadow. Beside Macius, a rectangle of dull light set in the wall flickered to life.

Macius almost sprang from his cover in surprise. He did not recall this device from his previous demarche—but he instantly regained control. Best to wait and watch— always best to wait and watch.

The rectangular panel glowed and shimmered and hummed as if Vensor's own sunrays radiated through the room in search of intruders. In a minute, the humming stopped and the panel grew dark.

The shadow by the northern entrance, the only entrance or exit from the room, took form and revealed itself to be an old man. He gazed out the wide windows at the sun-drenched neglected fields below, once planted with rich crops, now long returned to wilderness.

"So, I remain alone as I hoped," the visitor spoke under his breath to no one but himself. "Not even the bane of my life has followed me."

His one yellow eye in eternal conflict with his blue eye, his sere skin bespoke of mysterious methods of preservation, ancientness settled on his features rendering him a fossil from antediluvian epochs that somehow maintained suppleness and breath. His body bore a simple lyart-hide skirt common among all Vensor-sa overlying linen trousers and hide boots and topped by a shaggy vest of vok-skin to keep away the cold, though Macius wondered, watching from his secret aerie, if Yezd ever felt actual cold or heat. Who knew how many years had passed since the old man had first taken breath, that dweller in blue pools and green mansions? A single glance from the smooth-faced Yezd convinced Macius that the ancient barrow of his skull had still time to endure, still years inexplicably granted him by the gods.

Macius felt envy. Not of the years—all mortals must die and the only thing that mattered was what heroic deed one might achieve before the end came, not the pointless ticking of how many years may pass—but of what Macius was now absolutely certain Yezd possessed: the last remaining irsrem jewel. The one remaining bracelet, the glittering ring of glass that enabled Yezd to cast a shadowy veil about him whenever he willed.

The thief stared at Yezd's wrists but could not see the device. That meant little, as the jewel remained always transparent unless in direct sunlight, only then might it gleam as if inviting passersby to unguessed pleasure.

Yezd crossed the room, and turning his back to where Macius skulked in his self-created shadow, he touched a switch on the wall and the whole room burst into bright light, shocking Macius as much as the panel that shimmered by his side. What manner of magic was this? Only oil-burning lamps had ever given forth light in the experience of the thief's short life.

Yet still Macius stood and stared, unmoving, his mind pure, the image he cast entirely transparent to all but those whom the gods grant the ability to see, casting to Gethos his fate should the bright lights betray him.

They did not.

Yezd turned about and let his gaze wander about the brightly lit chamber in what was now merely casual inspection and his mismatched eyes did not so much as pause when they came to Macius in his corner. Paused not, and moved on.

Macius allowed the merest of breaths to pass his lips. For breathe he must, bracelet or no.

But Yezd only relaxed more and proceeded to move about the room, rifling through drawers and pawing through wooden crates filled with dusty appurtenances of unclear design.

"None," he whispered. "Not the barest of elements for what I need. How am I to make it to the Eye after losing my sole method of transport? Even the gills have failed—stolen by that Turlicum and his henchmen the very day I completed them. Then for that miscreant Flores to lose the precious items to Sendas—of all people who might have guessed their true power, that utter fool, Sendas. And finally, to that beastly eunuch, Soorkrul, who could think of nothing but to make himself a living god on earth. Now the bracelets are lost for good. Who knows who wears the jewels now? And where? Only time can reveal them—likely from an unguessed quarter once they fall into the hands of some unwashed peasant who will hand over the keys to the universe to spend a night with some ignorant eunuch or secret gila. Thus, this tangled planet turns on its axis."

Macius briefly touched the six devices around his own wrists, still maintaining the studied image of nothingness implanted in his mind. How near, yet how far.

"Still," Yezd continued muttering to himself, "I must report all that has occurred on this planet, how our plans went awry so very long ago. I have seen the Eye but not yet spoken, and now I cannot even return to the pyramid. I must report to my Chaldean colleagues how correct they were in their calculations but how wrong they were in the expected results—all due to a lowly insect. They did not anticipate that. At least there still remains Land's End and the backdoor entry into the pyramid."

Standing in the corner of the long rectangular chamber, Macius absorbed all Yezd said, all he heard: I myself saw

Yezd arrive on the Island of the Sun-God on the back of a malkop inside the pyramid of the malkop-selks. But what was this talk about Chaldeans and insects? Best to wait—and watch, as always.

Outside, from the forest, rose a single howling cough as from the throat of a beast. Yezd stepped to the window and glanced out and seemed to shiver—the first vulnerable reaction that Macius had ever seen from his former master. Yezd touched his wrist and the twisting maelstrom returned, hiding the scribe's face while still betraying his location.

Macius thought, might there be more roving beast-men somewhere near the chateau? One of Yezd's former slaves performing its former duty? Flores and I dispatched all we found more than a year ago. Could any still remain and pose a threat to their former master, causing him to shiver, now that he has lost the means to control them?

A quickening of the maelstrom beside the window signaled to Macius: yes. Even Yezd, it seems, could feel fear. Even the master of devices was uncertain without his gewgaws.

The maelstrom devolved into a sprite and Yezd reappeared.

"But one place on Maalstrom remains that still possesses the elements I need to fulfill the mission imparted me by my colleagues—'Source', which remains still with the engineer of Klopus. Enough time have I wasted in this wilderness. Before, I needed only privacy, hence I selected this remote pile of bricks for my experiments. But that time is over. Now I need assistance from the only one left who can give it, else I may end my days marooned in this world, an unlamented victim of a filthy swamp."

With that, Yezd the Chaldean flicked off the wall switch to again plunge the room into shadow. He spun his web of invisibility about himself once more and descended the stairs. As Yezd crossed the field heading east, Macius cautiously peeked one eye out the window and watched a minuscule distortion in the tan and brown weeds of the fields progress until lost to the thief's sight.

"No need to hurry," Macius said aloud, speaking for the first time in weeks. "It is well-known that Klopus lies near the headwaters of the Hedronmas. But how might I locate this thing called 'Source'? And what in all of Maalstrom is an 'engineer'? And what could any of this have to do with swamps?"

He shrugged and sat, and pulling a thumb of salted vok from his pack, he ate. With his jewels and his little canoe, he should have little trouble finding the cultic center of Maalstrom's far-flung Eunuch Guild.

CHAPTER 10

T he pink flesh stretched in a frown. "Speak clearly, Ambassador. I have less patience than the deaf and senile. And if you dare to strew sticks and cloth at my feet, as you did when that senile King Kot was on this throne, your city shall suffer a dire fate."

Initiate of the cult of the Golden Cyclops and the Eternal Whirling Sceptre, Fish of the fecund wharves of the maritime city of Vaw, let a ham-like fist fall on the arm of the new obsidian throne recently installed by his new vizier. King Kot's old throne lay beside it, a heap of broken sticks and shredded cloth.

The Ambassador, Redemer, bent low. "You may accomplish that, Fi—"

The new king erupted with an ear-splitting roar. "*King,* you fool! Do you think to come here and display disrespect to your betters? I am the new king of Vaw, and I rule in my proper name, Cetus of the Xolotl clan, not my familiar name of 'Fish'. You must learn this if you wish to remain ambassador to my city."

"As you say. However, King Kot came to an agreement with our city, O King...Cetus." The ambassador peered upward from his lowered brow. "Now you wish to change things to our detriment."

A fuse seemed to light beneath Fish's skin. It changed from pink to purple, then white. Mens laid a hand on Fish's forearm, and Fish glared sullenly at his vizier and at the hand until Mens removed it.

Mens turned his gaze on Redemer. "Might I suggest a new line of action, Good Ambassador," Mens said in a calm but strong voice. "One more rational and at the same time more in line with the will of our God, the Twin Brother in Heaven, Vensed, who has heretofore been ignored by a certain heretical cult common to the mainland."

Dressed in sumptuous shining eel-skin as befitting a delegate from one maritime city to another, Redemer stood straight, his eyes showing white all round in surprise. "Begging the pardon of Your Highness and His vizier, might I not have heard things entirely correctly?"

"I am certain you heard correctly, Ambassador. Contrary to before, all in the city of Vaw now possess good hearing. We have no need to repeat or shout for the benefit of a deaf king."

Redemer blinked. "As you say. Though, could you have really meant to say 'Vensor' and not 'Vensed'?"

"*Vensed* I said, Good Ambassador. And Vensed I meant. No need to take alarm or be offended. Let your religion be yours and our religion be ours...until you learn the truth of our belief, which you have only a short time to do."

"I think all the gods may take issue with what you say." Redemer looked both alarmed and offended.

"Vensed is the greatest of gods, Good Redemer! He shall put them all in their place if it be His will, just as our powerful city of Vaw—the seat of Vensed's voice on Maalstrom—shall put other cities in their place should they themselves take issue with the greatest of truths."

Redemer no longer knew what to say. He peered about in subtle fashion as if he had somehow wandered into a house of the mad.

Mens continued. "Vaw has fully recovered from its former ventures. All is now in order. All is now prepared. Our treasury is filled, and our fleet the strongest in all the oceans. Other cities may keep their religion so long as they formally acknowledge the sublime Truth, the supremacy of the eternal God Vensed...instead of Vensor." Mens glanced at Fish.

The new king of Vaw squatted on his throne gripping the throne-arms while switching glares between Mens and Redemer, still striving to squelch his fierce emotions.

The vizier looked back to the ambassador, who came from a minor port, Verlaw, southeast of Vaw and across much ocean, a former colony from the latter city. "The new throne of Vaw, under King Cetus of the Xolotl clan, Emperor of the world-spanning city of Vaw, First Initiate of the Cult of the living Cetus, slave to the Golden Cyclops and Her Eternal Sceptre, sole wearer of the purple cap, requires obeisance from all other cities, including your town of Verlaw. All of the distant ports of the whole ocean are bending their necks to Vaw even as we speak."

"Have you forgotten, O Vizier..." the ambassador spoke carefully, "and I mean no disrespect...that our beleaguered town keeps the best essence flowing to Vaw while at the same time keeps the violent draks in check? Your city produces no essence as other cities do, but our town delivers essence of the highest quality. Were the draks to conquer our city, no more essence would flow to Vaw."

"We have forgotten naught, Redemer," Mens replied. "Your city demands much silver mir and gold in exchange for your essence. But, you see, we have discovered its source. And we have learned there is a new way onto the Holy Island of Vensed, where lies more treasure than can be found in all the rest of Maalstrom. Once we implement my..." Mens glanced quickly at Fish who still frowned at everyone. "I mean *our* plans...Verlaw and its queen shall benefit as much if not more from the new world-encompassing Empire of Vaw under the tutelage of our God Vensed, as He has spelled out for us in His Book of Zeyd."

"You do not mean one of the many learned Compendia from the ancient and learned city of Ven, such as the Compendium of Sidros? The Book of Zeyd is rumored to be...how shall I venture to suggest...a myth?"

"No, indeed, Redemer!" For the first time, Mens too

grew angry. "Some of the holy passages from the Book of Zeyd prosper within the walls of this palace. And Vensed has revealed that the remainder are to be found on the Holy Island of Vensed, which we hope to recover for the benefit of an ungrateful Humanity. Even for the benefit of ungrateful Vensed-sa like yourself. And even as we compensate ourselves for our many efforts."

"You mean, Vensor-sa—"

"Do not test my..." Again Mens glanced at Fish, who fumed even more. "I mean *our* patience, Redemer. We do not speak the words Vensor-sa here, but only Vensed-sa, as we are the offspring of a different god, a different religion, indeed a different queen from time immemorial—She of the shining madness of the divine."

Redemer shook his head. He caught himself, and like all good diplomats, lowered his gaze and nodded. "As you wish, O Good Mens. I am sure that the god...*Vensed* beams his yellow pleasure down on both Vaw and Verlaw and on Vaw's new king Cetus of the Xolotl clan, First Initiate of the Cyclops and Her Eternal Whirling Sceptre. May I formally submit Verlaw's request to ally itself with Vaw under Vaw's beneficial rule? Our latest delivery of essence has been completed and my city has great need of Vaw's support against the continuing drak raids."

Mens smiled. Fish still smoldered, despite what had just been accomplished by his vizier.

"Acknowledged. And accepted," Mens said. "You may expect a Vaw garrison to bolster your defenses versus the barbarian draks as substitution for our usual payment of gold and silver. You shall soon have no more cause to fear Sloter."

With that, Redemer, ambassador of the small and beleaguered port of Verlaw, lowered his head and backed out of the throne room.

Once he had gone and Fish and Mens were alone except for a coterie of irsrem-armed guardsmen, Fish raised one hand, and turning on his vizier, struck him across the face with an open palm.

As Mens' cheek turned pink to match the pink of Fish's cheek, the vizier staggered backward. "Fi—" he blurted, for once taken entirely by surprise.

"That is 'King Cetus', Mens! And do not interrupt me again, especially in the presence of fools sent to Vaw by dumpy little towns like Verlaw that no one cares about. Count yourself lucky that I choose not to clench my fist. You interfered once before with me and I put you and your yammering in your place. Do not force me to put you in your place again."

Mens blinked. He swallowed and glanced at the soldiers that stood in the palace room, several of whom were frowning at what they had just witnessed. Mens raised a hand with an almost effeminate turn of wrist to signal the next item on the royal agenda. "It is time...*King Cetus*...for the ritual."

"So it is, Mens. But I will only spare the time because you have promised to crown me with the purple."

"Indeed, O King. You must receive the purple or the people will not accept you."

"Once they have accepted me, I will have no more patience for such nonsense as today. Now, let's go."

Fish rose from his throne and for a moment none other in the throne room moved. The soldiers rested eyes on Mens, many still frowning.

The vizier nodded and the soldiers moved, formed an escort for the king and for their new ecclesiastical pope and head of Vaw's Committee of Public Safety—Mens.

Striding out of the palace, the royal retinue passed a series of large boxes lining the plaza, levels of the maritime city descending both below to an arc adjoining seaside and above to a smaller arc that centered about the island's volcanic peak.

As the band passed the boxes, which had no windows to break the monotony of their placid surface, vague sounds arose from within. One guard cocked his head to listen better.

"Give no attention," Mens instructed him. "None of what passes within is of any concern to us pious warriors of God. Only Atasan concerns himself with heretics."

Fish did not cast a glance at the boxes, but, elbowing those too slow to stand aside, hurried up the terraced slope past shops and barracks and the usual institutions of every Vensor city, though now rechristened Vensed since the advent of the cult that the philosopher Mens had brought. A new wrinkle, a new cult, a new head of state, and new punishments for the wicked.

The suns were sinking swiftly, and as the shadows of night gathered beneath the brown moon Talen, a gong announced the imminent celebration. Around the little band, more people collected: all male, and all bearing skull caps of various colors with eel-skin capes to match. Most were florid green, fewer were marine blue, fewer still wore yellow— with many subtle shades denoting a strict hierarchy of privilege.

Lofty steps led into the very heart of the mountain and the royal retinue climbed the winding flight of steps reserved for the higher orders—the green or blue-capped populace ascending by several other stairsteps.

The retinue arrived at last at a split in the side of the ancient volcanic crater where, by the light of many torches, they filed through the gap past vertical cliffs that joined above, until once inside and once more open to the sky, several items became visible, forming the focus of a broad amphitheater constructed into the sides of the volcanic crater and a verdant plateau that overlooked it.

First was a rusted black-red hulk of iron and steel that had lodged in the crater at some time lost to history, for what purpose and by whom none could say. The body of the hulk was elongated but fatter at one end than the other. Attached to the top was a contrivance of mysterious purpose consisting of several huge sword-like blades of hardened steel that had managed to survive the ages, and over these blades poured a stream from a lake on the plateau, the force of the water turning the blades in a circle that never slowed and never increased but never stopped. The interior of the rusted hulk was open and occupied by ancient, corroded seats apparently designed for people though now empty.

The second item, on a squarish stage of coal-grey pumice, rested another obsidian throne such as stood in the king's palace. Here, the royal delegation halted and Mens invited Fish to sit, his flabby limbs of inexplicable strength occupying the black glassy landscape that in living memory had known only the expired dynasty of Kot. Mens produced a purple cap, and in the presence of the growing multitude, placed it on the head of Fish—royal purple, which none but the highest Initiate may wear, the topmost sacerdote of the Cult of the Living Cetus, King Cetus himself.

"Men of Vaw," Mens called to the populace. "Give obeisance to the one hundredth Master of the Whirling Sceptre, your King placed over you by your God Vensed in the service of the Golden Cyclops." Fish's pink-lined gills worked with pleasure as if he were still submerged in the water of spawning, and his bullet head split into a wide grin as the corners of his extraordinarily wide mouth traveled the breadth of his jaw like the tendrils of some underwater plant, showing rows of teeth one might expect to find in a predator of the deep, Mens himself drawing back a step due to the possibility of a fate more lethal than a slap.

"Let the ceremony begin." Mens called, his voice echoing off the rocky sides of the amphitheater.

CHAPTER 11

The woes that smote in ancient days
The seed of the perfect Mok-sa,
Who perished long ago with grief on grief,
Still falling. Nor does this age rescue that,
But fastened on them like ill luck,
This blood-stained growth
Of those that reign below
Spread still relentlessly
With maddened speech and frenzied rage of heart.

Flores, son of Sumvensor, Flores of the many devices, Lord of the ancient House of Turlicum, the Reven Clan of the city of Ven, did his best to ignore the growing pain in his face caused by the temporary leather covering tied about his head. He rubbed his temple in a futile effort to relieve an itch. Despite the vague rewards promised to the victors in the Games by the eunuch Selem and the soldier companion who escorted him, a smoldering anger grew within. Combat he was promised. Combat he wished as the only release his blood-drenched soul now craved.

Crossing the wagon-freighted plaza, they strode up a long avenue flanked by more barracks and a taller structure with high arched windows of expensive genuine glass, dyed with the colors of the moons, its entrances blocked by more weaponed slavers. His curiosity aroused, Flores glanced at the building and its high windows.

"Do not stare," one of the slavers said to him. "That is only for the Elect. Slaves like you may not even look at that place."

As they passed, Flores saw from the corner of his eye a eunuch in black robe enter the front and disappear within.

A few streets later, they came to an even higher wall, one with no windows, this wall curved. Many gates pierced the high wall, and as Flores entered one, he noticed other inhabitants of Klopus entering or departing casually through the others. His nostrils twitched to the familiar smell of ozone.

Once inside, Flores found he was within an oval arena, two hundred yards at its widest. Circumventing the arena were terraces of concrete stands for spectators, now mostly empty.

The open agora was peopled not only by slavers but by a score of slaves and another score of the child-warriors recently recruited—or abducted—by the slavedrivers of Klopus whose greed for new blood seemed great. Laborers, slaves, and slavers alike were sprinkled among the audience seats, though no gila-women in the universal custom of Vensor-sa, who, favored by Vensor from the sins of natural order common to all other forms of life, were exclusively male, as evidenced by the fact that no Vensor-sa possessed a navel, the universal sign of Atasan, the sign of animal birth.

The main attraction for Flores was a series of posts and stolid bulky panels constructed of rorewood and displaying divers weapons. At least a dozen men thrust and parried with four-foot irsrem rapiers and stubby iron swords, while the warriors attempted to block their opponents with small round shields. Under the watchful eyes of a half-dozen trainers, none paused in their military exercises as Flores came up. The stench of ozone filled the air as the sparking of charged irsrem was stirred by the ritual of Atasan, the ritual of combat.

"Select a weapon from there," the soldier who accompanied Flores said to him, "then wait here for your turn. Doubtless you will have a thing or two to learn from us soldiers of Klopus, who are the best fighters in the world."

He pointed at the paneled portable wall where hung a plethora of weapons, ignoring the scabbarded rapier at his side.

The thought crossed Flores' mind: the best fighters in the world? More than once have I watered Maalstrom with the blood of these slavers. I would do so again, but not now. Not yet.

Selem the eunuch approached. Flores took a step, but Selem stopped him. "Wait." The eunuch turned to the soldier by his side. "This one is large, Frelek." Selem pointed at Flores. "Give him a simple sword so he has no special advantage, then have him engage the others."

Frelek nodded. "As you say, Elect. But should he compete so soon? Perhaps he cannot see well through his mask. It would be a waste were he to die a dog's death the very day he begins his training."

Selem leveled a steady gaze at Flores. "He sees well enough. See how his eyes glare at me and at Romos through the eyeholes? This one wishes to fight."

Romos stood and stared down, as it were, at Flores, his arms folded, a smile on his face in anticipation of the coming humiliation of this impudent slave called *Isav*.

Frelek nodded again and turned to Flores. "That sword hanging at the end. Take that one."

Flores nodded briefly, his leather mask becoming more and more an irritant. Stepping to the nearest panel, he took up the iron sword with his right hand as a pair of slavers guarding the panel watched. He spun the blade in the air. A good weight, evenly distributed, even if iron was less than honorable for a trained Simet warrior, who should prefer irsrem, the glass that the gods prefer in their own ethereal combats. But iron was appropriate enough for one whose only desire was carnage.

"Look, Frelek," the eunuch said. "You cannot hold back this one's enthusiasm. I sense a thirst for more than practice."

"We shall train him with care, my lord. Have no fear that

we shall let harm come to him."

"That is not quite what I meant..."

Frelek shrugged. He turned to Flores. "This way, slave."

Flores stepped toward the other gladiators.

Frelek called to one of the slavers engaged in practice. "Cross swords with the new man, Grol. Let us see if he can defend himself. But do not injure him."

Showing no caution, Grol stepped close to Flores. Before any could intervene, he thrust suddenly at Flores with a long iron blade, aiming for the gap between Flores' right sword arm and his side. If Flores failed to counter, he would have a slice in his skin to remind him not to be so slow in defending himself.

Expecting just such a dishonorable act from a slaver, Flores parried it with a flash and thrust his own sword into Grol's quadricep.

The slaver let out a howl and dropped his weapon. He rolled on the ground beneath the widening eyes of Frelek, Selem, and the others, including a still angry Romos who watched chagrined, increasingly intimidated by the large slave with the leather head-covering and smoldering eyes.

Selem the eunuch pursed his lips. "As I was saying..."

"Slave," Frelek yelled, "we do not injure here! Refrain from harmful blows until you are trained and released to the Games. Have you no sense? You have only today and tomorrow to prepare before going head-to-head with trained killers."

Flores pointed with his blade at Grol, still rolling in pain. "This one is not worthy."

The trainer's eyes grew large. "You think you are better than Grol?" Frelek barked. "He has bested many men better than you. Just for that, for your hubris, I am selecting one of our champions for you to joust with since you are so eager to feel a blade cut your own skin."

Romos interrupted to sneer. "I for one cannot wait to see if this slave's skin is as sensitive as others."

A larger slaver whose legs were covered by leather pads but his chest bared, strode casually up to Flores.

"Coralanus, do not harm the new man," Frelek said. "Just give him a taste of what he can expect when we put him in the arena day after tomorrow."

Coralanus smiled, and pulling an irsrem blade from his scabbard, he swung it about as if knitting a net between him and Flores, the blade charging with the energy of his emotion.

Flores ignored his every move but stood silently, his iron sword clutched in his right hand poised erect but angled between them.

After a minute, Coralanus pretended to thrust at the same spot that Grol had aimed at but switched at the last moment and thrust at the gap between Flores' left arm and his side.

Without attempting to parry the thrust at his right side, which Flores knew would be a feint, he promptly parried the thrust at his left side. With an explosion of sparks and ozone, the gladiator's rapier went spinning in the air.

Flores stomped Coralanus on his chest with the bottom of one foot—the slaver fell to the ground where Flores brought his sword down over the man's neck.

All in the arena halted to stare and many of the spectators rose and put flat palms over their foreheads the better to see.

"Halt, slave! Do not kill Coralanus!" Frelek shouted in confusion and surprise. "He may well be assigned to face you."

The Turlicum drew his blade slowly across Coralanus' neck, not injuring him but giving him a shallow cut that did no harm but bled. Two down. More to come. Flores felt the pain inside ease.

"There is indeed something special about this man," Selem the eunuch said. "I could almost swear we are watching a Simet trained warrior at work. A Simet from distant Lesel, whose name is Isav—or so he says." Selem peered deeper. "If any of what this man told us is true."

The Turlicum twitched. It would not be best to go so far so soon.

"He fights dishonorably, Lord Selem," said Frelek. "How can I teach such a one the proper rules of combat?"

"I have a feeling that if you give him irsrem, he would fight even better than with iron." Selem turned his shaven head towards Flores and peered as if reading something invisible. "Are you sure he is not teaching you, Frelek, instead of the other way around?"

Flores thrust the iron sword into the dirt between cobblestones where the energy transferred from the irsrem rapier passed into the ground, and he stood silently, arms folded.

"I will pair him with several others on the field and attempt again to train him." Frelek looked to several gladiators who had halted their own practice to watch. "Who wishes to go against this man next?"

They exchanged glances and each minced a step back.

"What? In a few moments this stranger has intimidated the lot of you?"

Without saying anything, they blinked.

"Must I assign one of the children to challenge this slave? Maybe one of you would recover his manliness then."

Flores interrupted. "Do not embarrass your eunuch lord, Frelek. I see no reason to bring shame on Klopus by slaughtering your infants."

Frelek looked like he might burst a blood vessel.

"He is right, Frelek," Selem said. "Do not bring such shame on our city. You would only waste youthful lives which shall be useful to us when they have grown." Selem continued to stare at Flores. "I believe that this one will not hesitate to kill anyone with a weapon who challenges him." He took a breath. "No more training is needed for him today. This one was ready for the Games the moment he entered the city gate. Promote him to second-class swordsman and give him the benefits of that status, including housing him in the swordsmen-in-training barracks. We shall resume his training tomorrow."

Frelek fumed as hotly as Romos, but neither dared anger one of the lords of Klopus, one of the Elect, whose word was law.

Bending low, Frelek suppressed his frustration and proceeded to lead Flores out of the arena, this time unchained.

As they departed, and Selem the eunuch walked away in a different direction, Romos glared surreptitiously at Flores' shrinking back until the Turlicum had vanished. Stepping to Grol, he whispered something in private.

When the divine moon Tumsenet arrived, spreading its verdant cloak over the city, Flores sat on a bunk in a different barracks from before, his second residence in two days. This one was a decided improvement. Though all of the bunk beds were open and lacking privacy, none of the inhabitants were chained, and dinner was actually rolled into the barracks and served, and there was enough fresh lyart meat to repair muscles strained by the day's practice. He had no more concern of going to sleep here with an empty stomach, nor would he be driven out at dawn like cattle to perform menial labor.

He was coming up in the world.

As soon as he finished his meal, Telemer the physician entered the barrack to change his leather mask. A slave accompanied Telemer with a vat of clean water and soap.

"Let's see what the gods have wrought for us, my friend," Telemer said, removing the sewed leather. With a subtle glance at the other gladiators in the room, Flores turned his face toward the wall.

"No need to be shy about your injury, second-class swordsman. You should be proud that you were promoted. And it is good that you show an interest in your new work.

But hold off, I beg you. The last thing you need at this time..." Telemer washed Flores' face with care, "is for you to sweat and bleed, or even worse, receive another blow that might make repair impossible. I know. I have seen this kind of thing before. Your face looks good compared to yesterday, but be careful, my friend."

Flores nodded as Telemer finished cleaning his wound, but kept his face turned to the wall. It was not shyness that kept his face turned. At least a dozen of the score of gladiators in training stood about, staring at Flores as Telemer worked on him. Without his mask, who knew whether he might be recognized and what the consequences might be?

As Telemer covered Flores' skull with a new mask—this one with the eyes and mouth more precisely excised—several young boys approached. Flores glimpsed extensive tattoos such as were common to all Vensor-sa. In other Vensor cities, tattoos signaled membership in a feudal clan run by aristocratic Simet-sa, and the tattoos were exclusively images of a clan's totem animals. Here in Klopus, however, the cultic capital of eunuchs, who excel only in providing sexual services to those Vensor-sa who feel the need, what could be the subject of their tattoos?

To Flores' surprise, the boys had none of the sexual symbolism such as were mounted on the city gate, but rather images of insects. Specifically, something very much like ants. Flores could not quite make out what was meant and decided to learn from them what he could.

Adjusting his new mask, he asked, "I have seen your kind driven into Klopus as slaves and now here you are in training for the Games, plainly akin to those I saw enslaved only two days ago. Do you feel no loyalty to the city of your ancestors?"

They looked at each other with surprise.

"Loyalty? What do you mean?" Their surprise seemed not to pass.

"Why, I mean willingness to give your lives for the city of your ancestors, the city of your clan. Surely you have sworn to the gods that you will fight to the death for the city of your birth, as our god Vensor intended for Vensor-sa."

This only brought more expressions of confusion and wonder from the boys. "Whatever do you mean?"

"You do not understand me?"

"Oh, we understand your language. But your ideas are strange, stranger."

They again exchanged puzzled looks. "It is our destiny to come to Klopus. It is our destiny to labor for the Guild as slaves, or if we manage to rise in rank, to train as warriors to defend Klopus. We have known this from our moment of spawning. What else can we do?"

"You can defend your city of spawning."

"Our city of spawning does not want us. That is why we were expelled. The city of Vedeg, which they call the land of Mok-sa, allows no males past the age of three months. Only gilas live there. And we are not gilas."

It was Flores' turn to be puzzled. "I do not understand."

"And because we do not like mushrooms."

"Mushrooms!"

"Those Mok-sa gilas do not eat meat, but only mushrooms. We are men, warriors. We want to eat meat. We cannot live on mushrooms. We are happy to be here."

Flores omitted commenting that these 'warriors' were not more than a couple of years old, though growing swiftly in the manner of all Vensor-sa, taking up arms but a few months after spawning. "But I saw others of your kind slaughtered in the wilderness. Are you not aware that they were killed by slavers from Klopus?"

They shrugged. "Some of our comrades prefer the wilds. Hunting, killing and eating animals. There are many of us who are expelled by Vedeg. If the Klopans do not kill some of us, our numbers would soon overrun the world. Someone has to thin our ranks. Everybody knows that."

Flores furrowed his brows in thought. "But why here? Why Klopus? Perhaps there are cities that might accept you. Most Vensor cities, of course, would not since they live or die strictly by their own kin, defending their own Temple in the name of our Father Vensor."

"No, we prefer Klopus. Only Klopus has the Oracle."

"Oracle?" Flores was beginning to feel uneasy at having lived his entire life in the same city of Ven as the Eunuch Lord, Soorkrul, yet not knowing anything about the eunuchs' guild or where they recruited their many fanatical slave soldiers.

The boys shrugged again at this. "The Oracle is here in Klopus. That's all we know about that." They drifted off where one of their number was throwing dice.

A pair of grown men took their place.

"We heard your question, comrade. The boys are new, they know little about our holy city."

"Yes?"

"Our Oracle is the tongue of the divine, he speaks the Word of God."

"Your Oracle is a person?"

"Indeed, he is favored by Vensor with the very thoughts of the divine which he reveals to us when Vensor directs him to favor us."

Images of the corrupt priestesses of Vensa dispensing orders of their queen through Vensa's golden statue in Ven flashed across Flores' mind, and the utterances of green-scaled Atasan in his irsrem hive at the end of the world. It seemed the Word of God had many tongues in many places, not all of them honest, and not all of them like Vensor-sa, whatever that term may finally mean. Flores was beginning to wonder if the term 'Vensor' meant anything at all.

"There is a Temple in Klopus. On the east edge of the city lies a vast building that surrounds it. Our Temple is a cave of metal. No one enters but the Oracle himself. We have never been there. We are not permitted."

"And the Oracle is..."

"The head of the Guild. The highest eunuch of all."

"You have seen him?"

"Not us, by Vensor. But if we survive our training, we shall. He confers the honors on all gladiators who move up in their training. You have been selected for the Games day after tomorrow, a rare honor for one so new. If you survive, then you shall see him yourself."

The Turlicum slowly nodded. Wheels within wheels.

"But we have heard something else."

"Oh?"

"If you injure another partner tomorrow, they will demote you back to slave status and you will live out your life at hard labor."

"You don't say."

"We heard this from Selem himself." The pair nodded to each other. "And there is more."

Flores listened, wide alert.

"You may not injure another, but Romos has bribed someone from another barracks, a blooded gladiator, to injure you. We do not approve of such. So, watch yourself tomorrow. You did not hear this from us."

"Thank you for letting me know, comrades. I shall be careful tomorrow. I await the Games to act."

They exchanged glances and shrugged.

"By the way, comrades, I am certain I saw a gila in the plaza when I was first privileged to enter the service of Klopus. Where might one see such a despised animal again in our fair city?"

They shrank back and looked at each other with furrowed brows.

"We may not speak of such. No one can because traffic with the creatures of Atasan is forbidden, as everyone knows." One looked back to Flores. "But things occur in the Hall of the Elect that are hidden from all, things no one is allowed to discuss. If you are smart, you will avoid that place and never mention those...*entities* again. Even if you see one." The pair unconsciously glanced up as if they had heard something on the roof. "When they are found, they are turned over at once to the Elect to do with what they will."

"How can I avoid the Hall if I do not know where it is?"

"Everyone knows that place. The high-walled building flanking the main avenue which you doubtless saw when you were brought to your first barracks. The place with the high arched, beautifully dyed windows. Now erase that from your mind." The gladiator glanced at his comrade. "And erase us too. We never spoke."

With that, the pair walked nervously away.

CHAPTER 12

E arly morning came and a group of slavers unlocked Flores' barracks and entered.

"Let's go, swordsmen. Today your training really begins. Do not disobey and do not disappoint. Your every move will be watched. There will be a break for food at noon—if you live that long." One of them laughed at his joke.

Throwing on his tunic, Flores joined the others and twenty second-class swordsmen in training, of all ages, headed out the door for the arena in hopes of becoming first-class swordsmen—hoping to keep breathing and eating regularly, if nothing more.

His escorts were unfamiliar to him, but once the trainees found their usual places in the center of the arena, Flores noticed Frelek, Romos, Coralanus, and even Grol present, the last limping a good bit with a determined scowl on his face. For the first time, he noticed in the stands what appeared to be a portion of seats reserved for eunuchs, for not only did Selem enter and sit there but several more of the rulers of Klopus, all with shaved heads and piercing eyes and dressed in their usual encompassing cloth robes with red threaded hems. Their eyes seemed rarely to wander away from Flores.

There—another entered. Flores' gaze narrowed to a slit. Soorkrul had come, he of the prismed features. The representative of the Eunuch Guild in Ven seemed not to recognize Flores, which, for a moment, puzzled the Turlicum. Then he recalled that he wore a leather mask that no one could see through. Best not to heal too quickly if his mortal foe was watching.

Frelek and Romos set to arranging matches between the other trainees, some with each other, others with more experienced gladiators. None with 'blooded' gladiators, however, several of whom stood together in a clump, evaluating the newcomers.

For a time, the matches proceeded, and the clacking of swords and rapiers versus each other or against small shields resounded through the seats of the arena, the smell of ozone already spreading. Flores was left standing by the weapons panel without instructions, his eyes wandering over the growing number of spectators, and especially over the eunuchs whose eyes seemed to focus on him.

Was something up? Perhaps the warning he had received the previous night was accurate and everyone had been informed but him.

One glance at Romos, who glared at Flores with undiminished anger, and at Grol who glared with even hotter hatred, confirmed that more than extra care was in order if he wished to survive the day.

"You," Frelek pointed a poniard-like dagger at Flores. "Take up a rapier and approach."

Flores nodded. Selecting a four-foot glass blade, he stepped to Frelek.

"You may begin with Streker. Cross blades so we may see what you can do." The trainer locked his eyes on Flores. "And no funny business!"

The Turlicum nodded, glancing away so the extent of his own anger and thirst for revenge should not show.

The pair faced each other and Flores quickly sized up his opponent as a novice, clear from the hesitancy in his eyes. Flores slowly swung his rapier to see what Streker would do and not to frighten the man.

Streker stepped back, hesitancy giving way to fear. He took a breath then swung his own rapier to contact Flores' weapon. No sparks resulted as neither rapier had yet charged, evidence that strong emotions had not yet taken hold.

They crossed swords several times more, and though Flores soon tired of the pointless exchange, he kept up the charade, conscious that a demonstration of his Simet training now would destroy the plan he was starting to form.

Streker seemed to gain confidence and Frelek watched both approvingly. After perhaps five minutes of the kabuki performance, the trainee struck out in an attempt to penetrate Flores' defense and throw him off balance.

Flores smiled. Pointing his own sword as if to parry, Flores suddenly dropped his weapon on the ground and stumbled.

A dozen men halted and stared.

"What was that, Isav? What is wrong with you?"

"Nothing, Frelek. I thought I felt a stone in my shoe. That is all."

The trainer let his breath out. "Do you wish to examine your foot?"

"No, Frelek. It has passed."

Frelek shook his head. "Then resume. But enough with that opponent. It is time for you to engage someone more experienced. You have much to learn if we are to put you in the Games tomorrow. With Grol out of the running, we have need of you."

Grol watched snidely from one side but managed to let a half-smile cross his lips as he exchanged glances with Romos.

"Aquilus, iron sword on iron sword."

The new fighter approached Flores as he switched out his irsrem rapier for an iron sword. The new opponent waited patiently for Flores to take up his sword and step forward.

Aquilus wore both a breastplate and a helmet with two feathered horns. There would be little likelihood of a slave knocking him down with one foot, like Flores had done with Coralanus the previous day.

The fighter came closer to Flores, weaving his sword

laterally. Flores wove his the same, like two chess players fielding pawns. As Flores expected, Aquilus struck out with a feint, followed immediately by another feint, and the Turlicum pretended not to expect either movement but reacted slowly, attempting to parry each but missing.

His opponent briefly smiled as if he had now taken the measure of this new slave with the high reputation. Undeserved, it now seemed.

After ten minutes of successful parrying and thrusting feints that were slapped aside only slowly, Aquilus threw caution to the wind and began hammering Flores from above with repeated blows in the kind of attack one might unleash on a dullard unable to defend himself.

Flores again stumbled, this time falling backward, his sword held aloft in his right hand to repel the blows.

Aquilus laughed aloud and thrust his sword into the ground. He turned to Frelek. "Is this the best this slave can do? What you told me about him was nonsense. He can hardly stand."

The trainers stared at Flores as he regained his feet and stood staring back at them dumbly.

"I wonder now what I was thinking," Frelek said.

"As I said, he is only a dumb brute, born to be a slave," Romos spat. "He has no place in this arena."

"Well, we are far from done with today's practice. Let the next one face him. Achates, it is your turn. See if you can find a warrior in this man's carcass."

"Yes, Frelek." A blooded gladiator stepped forward.

Grol and Romos exchanged their smirks for open smiles as if some new game was up. Achates had not only a similar two-pronged helmet as Aquilus, but breastplate and leather thigh coverlets, and a small round wooden shield on his left arm as well. There would be no repeat of yesterday's humiliations with him.

Taking up a shorter three-foot glass rapier, Achates cautiously closed the distance with Flores, who kept his three-foot iron sword raised. The usual feeling-out followed as each party made subtle moves with their weapons, testing the response of the other. Flores' sword moved more slowly than that of Achates, however, and Flores gave ground, allowing himself seemingly to be outfought and intimidated by a shielded experienced soldier.

Flores had noticed, however, the change in expression on the faces of his enemies and expected something more than play this time. Someone had decided to end his quick comeuppance in Klopus in a permanent fashion.

Back he stepped again while Achates spun a web of razor-sharp irsrem before him, its sharp blade impossible to dull or damage, even when crossed with iron.

He parried.

Stepped back.

Parried again.

Achates pushed him harder and harder, not hammering primitively as Streker had done but continuing to weave and advance, now thrusting with feint after feint, leaving Flores uncertain as to which might be a genuine thrust.

Flores pretended to stumble again, hoping to lure Achates into a premature all-out attack. His opponent did not comply but continued with measured thrusts as one with experience in all the tricks and tactics of personal combat, keeping his eyes always on the eyes of Flores.

Flores retreated step by step across the arena. The other fighters paused to watch until the only clacking to be heard came from Flores and his challenger, the staccatos echoing off the high walls and terraced concrete seats like gunshots. The eunuchs leaned forward to see more clearly, several grasping the railing in front of their seats.

The slavers and trainers all stared, intent on the outcome of what had plainly become more than practice, a combat stench of ozone hanging over the arena, the clearest evidence that the ritual of Atasan had awakened and the emotion of murder charging Achates's irsrem blade, each contact with

Flores' iron spitting several sparks into the air.

A sudden clang resounded from close behind Flores as one of the slavers hammered a small gong. For a fraction of a moment, Flores glanced to one side to see if some danger was coming from behind—

Achates went for the kill.

Spinning his rapier against Flores' sword and spinning it in circles in the air, he accelerated his pushing of Flores backward.

The gladiator slid his blade—stabbed at Flores' face. The blade cut a gash across his mask.

Yet, not collapsing or giving up as any other new fighter would do, Flores brought his own blade down with a blow. Knocking the rapier out of Achates's hand, he slipped it under the warrior's helmet and sent it flying. Then Flores thrust the tip of his sword under the rawhide strips that held Achates's breast plate over one shoulder and cut them. One side of the plate came loose, exposing the heart of Achates, and burdening him with a heavy armor plate that swung about, the plate now useless.

None could tell who was the more embarrassed and humiliated in that moment: Achates who was Flores' intended assassin, Grol who stared open-mouthed, or Romos whose eyes grew white with shock.

At that moment, Flores stumbled again over his feet, falling backward on the cobblestones and dropping his sword where he lay almost flat.

Achates immediately recovered his courage, and snapping up his rapier, rushed to Flores to finish him off while holding his bulky breastplate in place with one hand.

Flores rolled to grab his own blade.

Frelek managed to blurt, "Hold! Enough, Achates! Enough, Isav! No more, the two of you."

Achates leveled a cold glare on Frelek but obeyed and lowered his blade. With a quick turn he walked away, cursing under his breath, and he threw his breastplate aside.

Selem the eunuch came up. "Well, Frelek. It seems the mystery about this man deepens. I still think there is more to this one than meets the eye. Do you still doubt my opinion?"

Frelek bowed his head. "I would never doubt your opinion, my lord. But—"

"Someone it seems agrees with my suspicion." Selem interrupted and let his gaze go down the line of warriors and trainees, where the conspirators blinked, exuding sweat. "No matter." He looked at Flores, who continued to sit motionless, his sword lying on the grass. "Promote Isav to first-class swordsman and make sure he is ready for tomorrow's Games."

"But, my lord," Frelek stammered, "I—I have come to the conclusion that this man is quite stupid. His victories are due to mere chance. See how he squats even now with his rump on the ground."

"Stupid or not, he has a strong arm and knows his weapons. He will be useful tomorrow, especially since Grol is out of action. Have Telemer see to his face. And I hope for your sake he has not been harmed." Selem nodded knowingly. "Perhaps you are right and he wins by mere chance. On the other hand, perhaps there has never been anything wrong with his feet. Tomorrow we shall find out. If the former, he will not survive the day. If the latter..."

"As you say, Selem." Frelek bowed low.

As Flores was led back to his barracks, he let a long glance linger over the stand where the other eunuchs gazed back at him. As the other fighters in the arena mobbed each other and chattered about what they had just witnessed from the unpredictable newcomer, Flores watched Soorkrul closely. Was that a sly look on his face, or simply the suns in his eyes? The other eunuchs were looking up, and one last glance revealed the usual distant forms of malkops overhead, already gathering for whatever may ensue on the morrow.

* * *

That night, Telemer again visited Flores but this time in a new barracks, his third home in only three days—the barracks for first-class swordsmen. Quite an honor for one so stupid, Flores smiled to himself.

In a semi-private room partially shielded from the eyes of the other first-class swordsmen, the physician once again removed the mask, helped by his assistant who again washed his wound.

"Thank Vensor you refrained from any recklessness today and that this tear in your mask did not reach your skin. Achates is skilled and has no mercy. Given the opportunity, he would have clubbed you worse than Romos did. Then there would be little I could do to help you."

"Maybe matters were not quite so dire as you suppose, physician."

Telemer gazed at Flores. "They say you are a stupid person who got lucky. And what you just said sounds like something a stupid person would say. But there is more to fighting than you realize, my friend. I say this as a friendly voice to one new to crossing swords with true warriors. Be patient, would-be warrior, and I beg you to be careful. It will take time before you can hope to hold your own against the warriors of Klopus, assuming you survive the Games in the morning." He looked down his nose at Flores and shook his head. "Not everyone will."

"As you say, Telemer. I will try to be careful tomorrow. But I grow tired of sitting on my rump while others laugh. That is not my nature."

Telemer shrugged. "As you say, friend. It is your funeral, not mine." He pulled a new mask out of his bag, a smaller one that covered only half his face, and made to place it on Flores' face.

Flores pushed it away. "I prefer the other, physician."

Furrowed brows. "Why, for Vensor's sake? This one is less cumbersome. And it has larger eyes for you to see better."

"I have my reasons. Let's just say I am sentimental and don't like change. Can you put back on the larger mask with the rip on one side?"

Shrugging, Telemer directed his assistant to rinse, scrub, and dry it, and then Telemer put the former mask back on. "If this is what you want. It must come off in a week in any event."

Flores noticed something familiar about the leather. "By the way, Telemer. From the greyish-brown tint and sheen, could this leather be from a reven?"

The physician inspected it. "I believe so. The color matches."

"I wonder if you might have one of the paws of the dead reven nearby? And rawhide strips? The lace on one of my boots is shredding. And a small shiv, perhaps?"

The doctor blinked and glanced about as if he had just been asked to help a prisoner escape. "Perhaps. But why, for Vensor's sake? Do you plan to take up knitting?" He laughed loudly.

"Sentimental things only, Telemer. That is all. If I am to die tomorrow, I would like to embrace something that I used to hold dear."

A moment and Telemer nodded. "I will see what I can find, my friend. Though I am sorry to say that this sounds very much like the last meal of one condemned."

"It may be."

The doctor rose, and with his assistant pushing their cart, he feigned a Klopan military salute, level hand drawn over chest. "I must take my leave now, my would-be warrior. This night is the Eve of the Flight as the whole city is preparing to receive our guests, and the Games are being held in celebration of the event. The eunuch lords are already gathering in the Hall of the Elect for their own ceremony, and the streets are being cleared of traffic and pedestrians as a curfew goes in place tonight in observance of the holiday. I shall see you, no doubt, on the field of battle early in the morn."

He smiled, and as he walked, he called out to the other swordsmen lounging and lost in thought in their own semi-private rooms, "Love is in the air, my lovelies! Love is in the air!" In another minute, they passed through the exit, motioning to the armed gate-guards who were always present to prevent last-minute doubts turning into panicked desertion among the scheduled fighters.

Despite the pain that still radiated from his face, Flores puckered it in puzzlement under his mask. What had Telemer meant by 'our guests'? And what did he mean by 'love is in the air'? How could love exist anywhere in this vicious city that massacres children, holds lethal gladiatorial games, and mutilates slaves for the simplest offenses?

An idea occurred.

Scanning the rest of the barracks to see if any of the other trainees were taking an interest in him, and concluding that none were, given the exertions of the day and their apparent concern over what might happen to them next morning, Flores stood and stretched as if preparing to sleep.

Closing his curtains to enhance his privacy, he left them closed but walked to the end of the hall as if to tend to his bodily needs. Here were more semi-private cubicles, another decided improvement over the wide-open rest area of the second-class swordsmen of the previous barracks, which had had no privacy.

Pretending to confine himself for his private business, he instead looked up. A thin wood panel served as a ceiling and Flores quickly made his decision. Climbing up, he removed the panel and found himself in a broad attic partially lit in various interstices by oil lamps from the barracks below. Another panel appeared overhead. Sliding it open, Flores stepped onto the roof of the trainees' building, open to the sky.

A brisk wind blew scud to the light of three moons, Nvediteg chasing clouds, brown Talen crawling its slow pace across the firmament, and Gethos the god of fortune casting swiftly moving blue shadows that merged with blackness in every crevice and corner.

He would not get better weather, or a second opportunity to learn what he wished to learn before the Flight—whatever exactly that entailed—would happen. He must find Crestal. And his best chance of locating her was to find the Hall of the Elect.

The wind cooled his cheek through the open rip in his mask, which he began to think of as part of him, his divine protection, something he must not lose while he remained within the city walls. Blue and brown caressed his eyes and made him glad he was alive in this world of beauty and pain, despite all the slaughter and cruelty that the gods saw fit to inflict.

Sliding down one side of the building, he pieced his way slowly towards the Hall, pausing in shadow whenever some other shadow seemed to pass by, clenching his hands when he seemed about to be discovered.

Once, several workmen hurried past, hauling a laden cart and peering furtively about as if concerned to be seen on the street past the holiday curfew and perhaps losing a body part as punishment.

Flores resumed his stealthy pace.

He sucked a breath and froze. From around a corner two eunuchs in their usual black robes loomed out of the darkness and walked quickly past. Intent on their mission, they stared straight and pressed on, almost stepping on Flores' foot as they went.

Flores breathed again. What better way to locate the Hall in this dead of night? He followed.

Minutes later, Flores sighted the building with the high arched and dyed glass windows, seemingly the only building that had windows of any sort, and watching from a pitch-black corner, Flores saw the two eunuchs approach the front entrance, climb the steps, and the armed gate-guards open the doors for them to pass inside. More eunuchs entered behind them, and even more arrived until Flores surmised that all the Elect in the city must be there.

What to do next?

For a while, Flores skulked in his black and blue-shadowed corner, wondering just how he could glimpse what was elapsing inside and maybe catch sight of Crestal. Dare he move? He dared not, as it could be only a matter of minutes before someone caught him loitering on the street.

He must circumvent the structure and see if he could find an unguarded way inside. Unlikely, but he would not know unless he tried.

A cloudbank threw the street into complete blackness and Flores took his chance. Crossing the wide street swiftly, he snuck around the building to the back where a quick inspection proved no other entrances existed.

He was chagrined. But then he sighted several large sheds for utility and storage, and crates and receptacles for trash. With a single glance to ensure no one watched, he climbed upon a shed as quickly and noiselessly as possible, and from there climbed onto the roof. Perhaps this place had an attic like his barracks.

For a moment he paused—from somewhere came a faint sound like a high treble. What could that be? Flores shrugged. A mere sound could not stop him now.

The back wall was as high as the wall facing the street and it was not easy for him to ascend to its top, but once there he found that the roof was considerably lower and he had but to drop down to gain its surface and benefit from the shadows that the high encompassing wall threw. Here he could explore without fear of discovery from the street.

To his surprise, he found that the roof itself had skylights of the same beautifully dyed glass as the windows on the front and sides of the building.

He took a cautious step forward and again paused—the sound was louder, now a loud buzz. He stepped forward and realized the buzzing came from several places on the roof adjacent to the skylights where free-standing metal sheaves seemed to cover several small apertures.

Suddenly, a swarm of hornets burst from the apertures. Briefly they circled Flores, then sped away followed by another swarm that flew out of the night and entered the apertures, which Flores concluded were flues leading into the depths of the building. But why these common leroo-sa wasps would inhabit the Hall of the murderous eunuchs, he could only speculate. Their sting was painless, he knew, and had only one use on Maalstrom, but surely eunuchs would have no use for them, since their sting was only useful to gilas.

He ignored the insects.

Flores stepped forward and his eyes focused on a fragment of clear crystal, and he caught his breath at what it revealed inside the Hall of the Eunuch Elect, the most sacred sanctuary of the fabulous city of Klopus, home of the notorious slavers and whoremongers that afflicted all Maalstrom with their bizarre cult.

At one end of a wide chamber rested a large altar-like throne of gold and silver inlaid with lapis lazuli and studded with rubies and diamonds. On the throne sat a gnarled and wrinkled eunuch who was so aged that even his black robe could not hide the fact that he could not have much longer to live, though some strange source of life seemed to animate his grey face. His face, clearly visible even at this height, seemed somehow alien to the other eunuchs, and Flores could not figure why such a difference might exist.

Around the throne of the Oracle of Klopus, as Flores concluded he must be, loitered the two eunuchs whom Flores had followed, standing on either side and stroking and fawning over him like the lowliest of servants, pushing drinks and sweetmeats into his hands whenever an empty palm was shown.

Along the sides of the great hall, idols of the gods were

inbuilt to the gypsumed walls intermixed with pornographic sculptures: Nvediteg the storm god hurled thunder and lightning, the latter glittering with rare gems; the mountain god Nantifus with convincing images of death and disease; brown Talen displaying his claws and reptilian tail; Tumsenet the forest god, his green exudence portrayed by green tesserae, roots sunk into the floor; Gethos the lucky god of the seas, dorsal fin above slanted eyes; and, as always to be found among the eunuchs, salacious versions of the Sun-God Vensor with the double suns appearing as male testicles and a monstrous erect yellow lingam overarching the chamber, shining to the light of many torches and lamps. Between each idol stood spheres of irsrem on pedestals of chalcedony and onyx fringed with silvered filigree—at least a dozen in the chamber—hives of leroo-sa hornets glowing in various stages of excitement, ranging from orange and blue to green and violet.

But what was transpiring on the floor of the chamber absorbed Flores' gaze more than the walls or the chief eunuch's altar or the eunuchs' obsession with hornets. He glimpsed a king's ransom of luxurious goods and sacrificial offerings such as he had only seen in the treasure rooms of Vensa in the forbidden Temple of Ven. Strewn about seemingly carelessly on low tables, or even tossed on the carpeted floor, were dunmelons from far cities, baskets of grain of ses, broiled flesh of reven and lyart, expensive karakul of vok-sheep employed casually as throw rugs, and richly inlaid rapiers lay about with steel blades worked with agate and amethyst. Everything the wealthy and privileged might desire sat within the chamber in abundance. Flores thought, there need be no fear that the soldiers of Klopus might miss a payday if the city were indeed this rich.

Yet his eyes were not done with wonder. Upon lounges and couches scattered from end to end of the chamber, rested the Elect themselves, whose merest word was law. In turn, they stood to stroke and hug the hives, the insects buzzing about the chamber seemingly at will before exiting the flues only to soon return.

On the couches themselves, however, reclined the core of the celebration, the prize of the evening.

No one was ever more shocked than was Flores at the moment he discerned who lay upon the makeshift lounges: two dozen at least of gilas—women entirely unclothed, lying open to the advances of the eunuchs, including, as Flores was again shocked to see, Soorkrul of the Light of Ven. The bodies of the eunuchs were also devoid of clothing, a sight that Flores had never witnessed despite a lifetime of seeing them walk the streets of his home city.

Flores was shocked even more to realize that the 'eunuchs'—despite how they portrayed themselves—were not eunuchs at all, but males as fully functional as any male child of Vensor. Lying upon gila after gila—who were all smiling, all receptive to their amorous advances—each eunuch released his masculine urge without hesitation and apparently without guilt. Despite the image they portrayed to the world, here in their capital, none of the Elect were emasculated, none were blind.

Flores recoiled and tried to put his mind back in order. Thus, the city of Klopus endured. Teaching male whoredom to the common masculine rabble of every Vensor city on Maalstrom, and murdering anyone found harboring a gila, they themselves, it was now clear, regularly held orgies with the forbidden sex in their own capital city, in the privacy of their own Hall of the Elect, far from the prying eyes of the scattered settlements of their deceived worshipers, and they themselves were not eunuchs at all.

While Flores watched, his mouth open, he saw a wasp land on the arm of one of the gilas in the midst of sexual contact with a eunuch. The wasp stung her on the arm without the woman noticing. That must be the Elects' purpose in including the insects.

Flores raised his head again as more insects swarmed

about the flues. This was how the eunuchs maintained their monopoly. This was how they kept their power. As Flores had already learned, the sting of the leroo conferred immunity from pregnancy, therefore each gila he saw below could not become pregnant no matter how often the eunuchs toyed with her, so long as she received the sting of the hornet periodically.

But where did these gilas come from? And above all, was his beloved Crestal among them? Flores peered through the slender glass fragment, searching in desperation for the familiar lovely face with its blond and brunette strands intermixed and its amber eyes tinged with a green of the most fabulous emerald beauty, the eyes that had captured him the moment he glimpsed her in the moonlit tower so long ago with the efflorescent suns glowing about her head like a crown. If she should be below, not the entire soldiery of Klopus would prevent him from crashing through the roof and slaughtering every soul in that evil chamber.

But he saw no sign of her. These women were others, though a few appeared similar in form to Crestal—yet another mystery.

Quite a cute arrangement, Flores thought. The eunuchs—he felt he could not cease using the term despite their deception—had no need of a queen to replenish their numbers because they obtained all the warriors they needed from some other source. That made Klopus a parasite city ruled by a global race of parasites that had spread their cult across Maalstrom by lies.

Had he seen enough? Crestal was not there, although Soorkrul was, crawling eagerly onto the body of woman after woman as they lay on their couches, taking turns with his colleagues.

Flores was about to tear his eyes away from the scene when a new development thrust itself on his exploding brain.

Soorkrul stood, exposing his nudity, and while Flores stared full upon his face, he realized some alteration had taken place about the eunuch's eyes. Where before, Soorkrul's eyes had been normal in every way, as human as any other Vensor on Maalstrom, Flores now perceived that the eunuch's eyes seemed to have somehow split, the pupils replaced by several facets. Silvery scarlet reflected off each facet and he realized that his enemy's eyes had become compound as if imitating the ommatidia of the hornets' eyes, not protruding like the compound eyes of true insects, but inlaid like two small skeins of red-silver nets. Soorkrul approached another receptive woman, and descending, mounted her, the woman gazing deep into his faceted orbs as if nothing were out of sort, indeed as if his insect stare were as entrancing as any lover's gaze.

All about Soorkrul, each eunuch's eyes had similarly transformed, their ruddy facets glittering to reflect the many torches and lamps within the chamber—except the Oracle himself, as Flores noted. Only the ancient relic upon the throne continued to stare upon his underlings with entirely human eyes and an entirely human smile.

Flores breathed deep to regain control. He had seen all he wished. No more did he wish to see, no more did he wish to learn. He did not even care from where these insect predators obtained their female prey, or why they felt impelled to engage in an act that could in no way lead to reproduction, though Flores had never questioned it when he himself had helped administer the sting of the leroo to his own Crestal at her own insistence, or why his own father had kept a hornet hive in his own clan chateau. He shook his head. There was much about his world of Maalstrom—and even about his beloved Crestal—that he still did not understand.

It was time to go. Brushing aside the clouds of excited hornets, he leaped to grasp the top of the retaining wall on one side of the Hall and he pulled himself up. He dropped to the receptacles in the back, and hugging the corners, began to make his way back to his barracks when a sudden shadow rose before him, a darker patch among dark patches, a patch that moved like nothing inanimate could. But what could move like a ghost among shadows, near invisible in the night? What would wish to?

Occasional dull glints seemed to flash within the shadow and Flores froze with his eyes fixed on the patch. At once, the patch froze, too, and the glints ceased, becoming once more a mere darker patch among dark patches. Flores shook his head. The shocks that his mind had received tonight were making him see things.

Walking casually like a stupid trainee who had simply lost his way, he retraced his path to the barracks, fortunately without discovery. Scrambling to the roof, he descended into the attic and lowered himself back into the rest area.

As he entered his semi-cubicle, he beheld on his bed a reven paw fringed with claws, together with several strips of rawhide. Ignoring his boots, he took up the half-mask that Telemer had left behind and Flores pieced the claws onto the mask using the small metal shiv. Then he added to the top a vertical wave of brown vok-hair that he took from his bedding. When he was done, he lay down to snatch some much-needed sleep. The morrow may at last bring some surprises to others besides himself.

CHAPTER 13

The amphitheater of Vaw gradually filled as every adult male in the city took his place, having donned their assigned caps and left all weapons in the city below.

Mens turned to the audience, having assured himself that the time was ripe. "Initiates of the Cult of the Living Cetus," he called, the carven sides of the amphitheater serving to well-amplify his voice. "Slaves of the Eternal Whirling Sceptre. It is time to renew our ancient bond and pledge our loyalty to the mother of us all, the Golden Cyclops."

From the midst of the crowd, more soldiers appeared, dragging an aged man. Propping him up on the coal-grey stage, they bound his grey-bearded mouth with cloth.

Mens looked at the prisoner and called out, "Who comes?"

The assemblage replied with the required response, "A poor blind beggar who seeks entrance."

"Who goes?"

"A rich seeing man who has betrayed his comrades."

"What is our purpose?"

"To transmute God's Word to flesh."

"What is the law?"

"Man with man."

"What is the lawbreaker?"

"Fortuna, Hap, and Cetus."

"What is the punishment?"

"To broach with Chaos."

And so it went. An hour passed and finally the recitation

came to an end. The old man almost collapsed and was at last offered a rickety chair to sit on, which he quickly did, his arms still bound before him.

The stream that poured down from the darkening plateau and turned the steel blades on their axis without pause did not flow upon the stage but into a cleft in the crater behind the rusted hulk, and when the ceremony was finally done and the audience returning to their homes, the royal retinue, accompanied by the bound man, entered the cleft. Here they found a rough incline that led perceptibly down, paralleling the flowing stream.

For a great distance the incline led down until the retinue arrived at a balcony with a high railing that overlooked a watery grotto, constantly refreshed by the flow. Raw stone rose about the grotto, flanked by stalactites, and arched to join overhead. The grotto led to other grottos deep inside the rocky outgrowth upon which the city of Vaw was built, redolent with salty air from the sea. The black pool shimmered with torchlight as Fish, Mens, the prisoner, and their armed guards lined the railing.

"Look well, old man," Fish spat, the sounds from his barreled chest echoing through the chamber. "For none ever escape the Doom, as you yourself well know."

Only a grunt answered.

Fish raised his voice. "Remove his gag."

Slow to obey their new king, whose anger and caprice were legendary in the city, the soldiers glanced at Mens. The vizier nodded. They quickly removed the gag.

"Hack!" The aged vocal cords took life like a motor long dead but unexpectedly reviving. He coughed, his entire body shaking. "Heh. That is what you expect to happen, you wretch? This is what you think to do with me, you pompous ingrate, Mens? You flatulent corpse, you Squawk?"

"Take care, Kot," Fish yelled. "You no longer have this city in the palm of your hand as before when you brought us all to the brink of ruin. I can now crush you with these hands as I do this puny stone." Fish took up a lump of pumice, and with little effort, squeezed the rocky lump into shards, seeking to intimidate Kot with a harsh stare.

"Eh? What was that?" Kot ignored Fish and rattled on. "Does my pathetic Squawk wish to speak? I give no such permission to him. Nor to my treasonous vizier, Mens."

"I have never been treasonous to anyone, Kot," Mens said.

"What's that? You have no seasoning? No one cares how you prepare your meals, Mens."

"That is not what I said, Kot—"

"You are not sad either? You well should be after what you have done to me. Now what have you done with my throne, you lousy traitor?" Kot danced from one foot to the other. "I even allowed you to reside in my very own palace in a sweetly darkened room unbothered by windows or light so you could devise how you can finally pay me back the many vast loans I made you."

"I paid back all of those—"

Before any could intervene, Kot struck out with his bound hands and punched Mens in his throat.

Mens jerked back, coughing. Missing the railing, he lurched over it and plunged into the vast black pool beneath.

As Fish and the guards stared open-mouthed, Kot peered over the edge, gloating. "Ha! You never paid me one cent on the seventeen mir I loaned you five years back. Now this is how you treat me? You condemn me to the Doom! To be torn apart by the Cyclops! Me, your benefactor, your king and protecter."

A low guttural moan echoed through the grotto from an adjoining passage. Ripples of water grew into waves as a huge shadow emerged from the passage.

Standing up in the waist-deep pool, Mens turned his gaze toward the shadow.

"It first strips what it plans to kill," Kot yelled down from the parapet. "Ha-ha! Where is your advice now, filthy

Mens? Once the Cyclops deals with you, I shall deal with that blowhard, Fish. Watch now. She comes!"

Behind Mens, the vast shadow emerged into the torchlight, taking the shape of a monstrous slug of orange-golden hue. Lurching its tons of flesh forward one step at a time on small arms and legs, it showed its face.

Horror and disgust seized the retinue, even Fish recoiling from the image of Vaw's queen, its cultic goddess. A minuscule human-like head bobbed like a seal as it progressed, one epicanthic eye focusing, the other a jagged ruin where some object had blinded it long ago.

Suddenly, a second body fell into the water. It landed beside Mens.

Fish shouted, "Can you hear that, Kot? I said there will be no more confusion in my city...the city of Cetus! Vaw is no longer the city of Kot!" Fish guffawed while clinging to the railing, his body shaking, his stupefied guards looking on.

"But, sire," one guard asked. "What of the grand vizier?"

Fish had not thought that far ahead when he threw Kot into the drink. Now he frowned in confusion, his wide lips splitting his skull like a hatchet. "Oh yes. My vizier Mens..."

Two guards leaned over the rail and made as if to extend their rapiers handle-first to enable Mens to crawl out—the vizier ignored them but continued to stare calmly up at the Cyclops as its vast shadow loomed.

The slug-queen let loose a bellow that shook the grotto, belying its tiny head. It lurched forward another yard, towering its flesh over the two luckless men in the pool marked by Providence to be the evening's sacrifices.

Fixing her one good eye on Mens, the queen opened her mouth as if to consume Mens and Kot, raised both arms to tear them apart.

From the black shining water, Mens swung one arm in a half-circle over his head, then let his arms rest by his sides.

The slug halted. Squinting at Mens as if it truly saw him for the first time, Vaw's queen slowly lowered its bulk so it no longer towered overhead.

"Morla," Mens said with calm. "You may come out of your spell. Your children wish to worship their Mother."

Inhaling a deep breath, the slug-like queen of Vaw dropped its eye guiltily to the surface of the pool. "My children... Where are my children? Is it you, my beloved?"

"Indeed, it is, O Queen. We have come to adore our Mother, to thank Her for Her endless sacrifices, for Her efforts in granting us the life we so treasure."

"My beloved. I cannot see you well. Is it truly you, my children?"

"We are here, Morla. We are listening."

The slug groaned. Then said, "Of all the regrowth my kind are capable of, the one thing still forbidden me is to regrow my eye, pierced by a blade one harsh evening across the world when I seized the whirling sceptre and found this island with its crater, then became marooned and was not able to leave again."

"We all give our bountiful thanks to you for your pain and devotions, O Queen."

"When the mood comes upon me, my children, I cannot help myself. A madness seizes me and I know not what I do. Can you inform me of what I do when I am under the spell? Can you explain to me why I am sometimes possessed in this evil fashion?" A great tear descended one yellow-orange cheek. "Do you forgive me, my children? I beg you to forgive me."

Mens cast a subtle glance up at Fish where the new king of Vaw stared down, still frowning, one arm massaging the other where Morla had torn him limb from limb the prior year, before his axolotl blood derived from his mother, Morla herself, had rescued him. Forgiveness was not in the makeup of this Cetus, though even he knew that it was not possible to allow harm to come to the queen of the city, the source of every egg that spawns, the beating heart of Vaw.

"How can you ask, my Queen?" Mens let his most beneficent expression shine on Morla. "Your children are ever loving, ever grateful. Your children forgive you all and everything. Morla of the city of Vaw is the definition of justice and mercy."

"For you, my children—"

"Do you believe you have the strength now to return to your Sacred Spring and resume your divine creation, beloved Morla? Your children wait with open hearts and open hands to welcome your efforts."

The minuscule head nodded. "Yes. You are kind. You are understanding. I will return to my holy task, which I know better than all should never be interrupted."

"Go with our blessing, Mother. Bless us with more offspring."

With that, the vast slug laboriously turned about, and yard by yard, crawled up the side passage until it was gone.

The guards again lowered their rapiers handle-first and Mens scrambled up across the railing with their assistance.

Fish let his gaze wander over Mens, assuring himself that his vizier was still with the living. The Cetus rubbed his head, puzzled. "In all living memory, no one has ever escaped the Doom, but all that we condemned have been torn to pieces by this queen, excepting only that wretched criminal, Flores of Ven."

"Her mood shall return. It would not be wise for any but condemned criminals to fall into this vat hereafter."

"Yes, Mens. Only you and Kot were spared today."

"Kot?" Mens peered into the water. "But where is he?"

Furrowed brows on all sides, Mens, Fish, and the entire retinue stared into the deep but could detect no trace of the former king of Vaw.

"Where has he gone?" Fish rumbled, his pink glabrous face pucked with worry.

CHAPTER 14

They came for Flores and his companions soon after dawn, a half dozen slavers in plain accouterage, slick rapiers with handles of rosy rorewood and green sercotrope, poised to bolster the courage of the hesitant. Though the contestants were first-class swordsmen, the commitment of a player may always grow thin when finally faced with a determined opponent bent on ending one's life. Not all players become gladiators—the blood of a blooded gladiator, after all, was not his own.

Flores had no such emotion. Indeed, he had no emotion at all—but one. One which he felt it best not to think, much less voice or act upon. Now was still not the time.

Hurried forward with level glares and unfurled whips that cracked the air, the first-class trainees ran to the arena where they were herded to one end of the oval amphitheater close to the high panels where the assortment of death-dealing engines still hung. Flores noted that none of the instruments had been changed or switched. He nodded—that was good.

To his surprise, the other end of the amphitheater soon filled with several dozen of the boys from the second-class swordsmen's barracks, the would-be warriors, along with a new collection of boys of many ages, who could only have come from a fresh batch recruited recently—or abducted—from the wilds. They milled about in poor order while several young men of Klopus shouted instructions at them, which were mostly ignored.

The stands were filling rapidly with citizens of the city, who, if the citizens of Klopus were anything like those of his home city of Ven, would not be satisfied without the spilling of gore. Natural born killers, Flores reflected, such is the angry soul that Vensor has infused in us all. The children of Vensor accept nothing less than ultimate victory. Even the dead do not rest but go to the Eye of Vensor where his soul resumes the deadly struggle on merely a new plain, the plain of Heaven—even though, as Flores had learned, there is no heaven but only HeavenHell.

The slavers made his barrack comrades stand in two rows and Flores stood at attention in the second line. He felt an indescribable urge to remove his mask and scratch his face like a madman, and against his physician's advice, he jammed his finger under the leather surface repeatedly to relieve a growing itch. Soon he would have no need.

When he focused again, he perceived that the special boxes for the Elect had filled with eunuchs—to Flores' relief, their insect eyes had returned to normal and they were once more clothed—and some even had their favorite gilas sitting beside them, they too now clothed in ugly black garments. So much for keeping their illicit relations a secret, he mused. They must be very confident of their power that they would display their violations of their own cultic laws so openly. Peering through his eye-patches, Flores frowned.

Crestal was still missing.

No matter. This day would best not be witnessed by the faint of heart.

The spectators came hurrying in—a much greater number than Flores had supposed might populate this distant city of doubtful economy—and they soon filled most of the benches. When the ground-level boxes of the Elect had filled, the exits were blocked by wooden barricades, the first Flores had seen. Armed guards manned these, too. So, Flores concluded, the Elect indeed meant to fulfill their goal of 'thinning the ranks' while they selected only the best for their soldiery. They clearly expected only the better trainees to survive this day.

Again, no matter. Flores set his lips at an angle between wrath and smirk. At a whistle from a referee, a group of men standing close to the boys' ranks blew flutes and crashed cymbals and a rattle of drums soon rumbled across the field to merry tunes from the little musical band.

He heard hissing, and turning his gaze, his eyes saw several reven-na taking positions behind the largest stolid weapons panel, the animals already saddled for mounted jousts. Another surprise. Flores had not supposed that the slavers of Klopus undertook this Simet activity.

From the festive nature of the scene, Flores might have supposed it was nothing more than one of the many festivals that any Vensor city held to entertain the masses and keep them compliant and grateful for the munificence of their feudal masters.

One element, however, was distinctly different from what Flores felt he might expect from either a festival or a staged combat: every few moments, the spectators gazed skyward as if expecting something altogether miraculous to appear, though nothing was to be seen but malkops.

Once more, Flores wondered: Just what was this Flight that everyone expected? What, or who, was to fly, since there was nothing special about the blonde acolytes of Vensor waiting to retrieve the dead? He shrugged again. It was nothing to him. Only the fulfillment of his plans mattered. He himself had no destiny but a red-streaked deliverance to his reward: eternal combat in the Eye of Vensor.

Pointing to the lines of boys, the slavers yelled for them also to form two rows. They obeyed but still milled about, confused or stubborn, and still devoid of weaponry.

A large man decked out in bandoleers with glass darts and a coiled whip, upon a nod from the Elect in their box, shouted: "Vensor! Hear your children! Accept the efforts of your Elect for your eternal glory. Open the Games!"

So, these Klopans did have some sense of ceremony, Flores noted. And he noted cynically that the announcer recognized only the efforts of the eunuchs, and that no animal blood had been spilled in dedication, contrary to the custom prevailing in most Vensor cities when beginning a festival typically required the sacrifice of either a lyart or several voks. A murmur spread through the spectator benches, from the many scars visible, many of whom were clearly survivors of previous Games.

Two large carts rolled between the lines and the boys' jailers-cum-advisors distributed a collection of weapons among them, choosing them one by one and handing them over to the tattooed children, some still sporting crested headgear that they had fashioned for themselves in the wilderness to match their self-inked tattoos.

Once they had formed two opposing lines, the referees withdrew. A loud whistle blew. How could anything constructive come of such an incompetent contest, Flores wondered, outrage and disappointment growing within at what he felt certain must ensue.

The bloodletting began. A number of the boys lit out on their own and crossed the line to pierce or slash at their appointed enemy, although all came from the same birth-city, the mystical city of Vedeg. No city loyalty, here, Flores thought, exactly as he had been told by the boys themselves.

Clans emerged from the chaos. Those who had held back organized themselves by clan tattoos and fell upon the disorganized stragglers in bulk, soon dominating the fight. The small bodies rapidly fell and more were injured, until the grass of that corner of the amphitheater was soaked in blood.

Yet all was not done. The trainers intervened. Rushing in with rapiers and small buckler shields, they identified the ringleaders of the several clans that had spontaneously organized—they struck the little clan leaders dead. The only leaders allowed in Klopus, apparently, were the trainers themselves.

The groups soon fell apart and combat devolved among

individuals, who struck and mutilated and screamed and shouted their childlike war cries until no more than a dozen remained—all blooded.

A whistle blew.

The fighting halted. The trainers rushed to the survivors and with triumphant grins raised the right arm of each survivor high. "Klopus has a new entering body of cadets."

The surviving boys shouted happily, and under their guides' direction, executed all wounded who held back or who lay on the turf. Victory wreaths were placed on the head of each surviving boy, who danced with pride as the spectators stood and whistled and clapped encouragement, leaving the blood on their hands to dry of its own accord.

Quite the method for producing killers who hold no other thought than victory or death, Flores nodded. No wonder they came at me in the forest, fighting to the very last. Yet I have made cowards of even such warriors as this bestial city produces.

While the small corpses were hauled off the field and dumped outside the walls for the malkops to snatch so as not to interrupt the Games, a group of trainers came up to the second-class swordsmen. Here the trainers were more particular and more careful, handing out rapiers and iron swords and iron-crowned spears with a certain delicateness and taking care not to turn their backs on the would-be warriors. Walking backward, they motioned their students to separate and pair off until a dozen pairs of gladiators faced each other on the field.

The whistle blew.

A half hour passed as the various couples thrust and parried. Flores noted that none of these combatants allowed their eyes to stray skyward even as malkops could be seen flying up beyond the far wall with the corpses of boys in their arms. Apparently, what may transpire in the heavens was to them considerably less important than what was occurring on the mortal plane.

Several men fell in quick succession: one transfixed by an iron-shod spear and grimly driven down; another cloven down the breast by a halberd; a third losing his rapier when he glanced to see what had happened to a comrade and was promptly pierced through the heart by his opponent.

Again, the spectators applauded.

Apparently, not so eager to waste the lives of qualified soon-to-be-warriors as they were with the lives of untrained unruly children, the Elect who supervised—Selem and another eunuch—signaled an end to the second-class contest and bid them return their weapons and retreat from the center of the arena.

Selem and the other Elect looked to the first-class swordsmen, but not before once again scanning the skies for what Flores assumed must be signs of the imminent Flight, in honor of which the Games themselves were being held. Ignoring the winged malkops, the pair stared particularly toward the eastern horizon, Flores noted, as the divagated Suns of springtime grazed noon and began their swift descent to the west. No more than three hours of daylight remained. The Turlicum noticed broaching the east horizon a shining lump like an oversized star or an undernourished moon. Yet Maalstrom's moons were accounted for, they too making their first pale appearance amid the spreading shadows of the far horizon.

The blooded gladiatorial trainers motioned with rapiers and whips for the second-class aspirants to take up positions again in two lines. Flores took his place in the second line. At first, he wondered how he was to be expected to fight since the first-class cohort had been given no weapons, and the stolid panel pendent with engines of death was now out of reach of him and his comrades. Then he saw that slaves were dragging the same pair of wagons as before and soon the trainers again distributed weapons among the combatants as they had done with the decimated children.

This was not what he had expected. And was not at all

welcome. He would have to plan again.

Romos and Grol came near and directed the wagon to pause, and with some nervousness they selected the weapon they wished Flores to wield that day—an iron-shod shaft. Flores frowned as he accepted the device. Weighing it in his hand, he immediately concluded that he was once more being set up, and his suspicion was confirmed by their ill-concealed smiles as they proceeded to give out more weapons to the others, happy that Flores had cooperated. Flores had no doubt that the iron would crumble quickly once combat began, while his opponent, he saw, was armed with indestructible irsrem.

Flores did not recognize his opponent and suspected the man had been somehow slipped into the ranks as a ringer just to fight him. From the man's grin, it was clear he believed Flores would be an easy mark, and from Flores' own performance the previous day Flores did not wonder at this, needing no whispering between Romos and Grol for him to think this.

Two score blooded armed warriors approached and formed an encompassing square of buckler shields around the cohort of first-class swordsmen in training. They were to have no opportunity to avoid their fate as determined by the Elect who continued to stare haughtily from their raised box among the benches. Were their gilas staring just as haughtily? Flores could almost swear, though he had to admit that the scarcity of these almost mythical creatures on Maalstrom lent an aura of inscrutability to their unfamiliar features.

Once again, the drums rattled, sending their deep rumble across the field. The flutes repeated, followed by a clash of cymbals. And with a louder shriller whistle, the latest episode of the Games began.

The trainers hurried backward to the shield wall, uncoiling their whips in case one of the fighters disgraced himself by showing reluctance to fight. Some of the Elect stood and leaned the better to see, and once again Flores felt that he garnered more interest than the other fighters, especially from Selem who hovered near, apparently the main organizer of the Games. His enemies Romos and Grol stood watching with folded arms, triumphant but still nervous, with Aquilus, Achates, Coralanus, even Streker, watching with coldness from the ranks of the square guarding the combatants.

Not yet, thought Flores. Still not yet.

His latest opponent wore leather coverlets over his quadriceps and a leather corselet over his chest. He weaved a rorewood-banded irsrem sword between them and stepped closer, seeking some opening in Flores' defense.

The Turlicum had no defense but his iron-shod spear and wove it before him, seeking to leave no opening.

"Don't waste time, Furselim," Frelek yelled. "You'll be needed when the Flight comes."

Flores' opponent paused, nodded. He resumed, now advancing on Flores as if expecting him to fall on the ground as before.

Flores stepped back—Furselim promptly stabbed, seeking to pierce his victim's unprotected bared chest.

None objected at this clear attempt to end his life. Selem and Frelek just calmly watched.

But Flores did not slip. Instead, he spun on one bent knee, then jammed his point into Furselim's ankle.

The blooded gladiator collapsed, blood running.

Yanking free his spear, Flores buried it in Furselim's bare neck. The rest of the man's blood gushed into the grass.

A dozen pairs of eyes widened in disappointment. But some spectators in the stands clapped.

One man was only one man, however. With a nod from Selem, Frelek called, "Achates. See what you can do with this slave."

Eagerly, Achates stepped forward, grinning as if hoping to even his score with Flores. Learning from his previous encounter, the gladiator this time wore an expensive chainmail shirt of woven irsrem platelets with golden irsrem armor over his thighs. There would be no sliced rawhide loosening his breast plate this day.

Before he could close with Flores, the Turlicum had already snatched up Furselim's rapier, and as Achates advanced upon him, he crossed swords with the gladiator overhead, creating a wash of sparks to spill onto the man's face. Sensing what was coming, Achates stepped back only to see Flores open up a long gash in his forearm. The gladiator lost his grip and his iron sword fell to the ground.

Helpless, he paled.

"Fight him, Achates!" Frelek motioned to Romos, who threw another sword at him. Achates caught it. It too fell to the ground.

"No, Isav!" Frelek yelled. He glanced behind as Selem approached, concern on his face.

Flores let his helpless opponent stand motionless for a moment as he stepped over to the panel and put on a buckler and selected an axe and hung a sheathed dagger on his loincloth. There would be no more tampered weapons.

He approached Achates. The man stood, too petrified to retreat.

"I said no, Isav!" Frelek again yelled.

"These are the 'warriors' you expect a Simet warrior to fight?" Flores said.

Selem and Frelek exchanged stares.

Flores placed his rapier on his opponent's neck. "On your knees."

Achates had no choice but to obey. All other combats in the arena paused as all fighters turned to stare.

Romos yelled out, "Stand up, Achates! Do not disgrace yourself and your city."

The gladiator turned a sickly look on Romos.

"Your city is already a disgrace," Flores called out. "I am here to bring your ilk closer to Vensor." With that, he pierced the side of Achates so he fell flat where he rolled in pain, though apparently had not suffered a mortal thrust.

Frelek stepped close to Flores. "You go too far, slave."

The Turlicum swung his rapier in the air.

Frelek paled and lurched backward.

Flores snorted. "Are these Games of yours only for show? Or should a Simet warrior teach you true combat?"

Selem intervened. "Simet indeed. As I surmised. Of what city may I ask?"

"I will let you guess...from the number of your dead."

His onlookers frowned.

"Coralanus. Take him. No more toying with this slave's insolence. Even if he is a Simet."

Coralanus hesitated but, hardened to hard deeds and unwilling to defy an order from those who held his life in their hands, he inhaled a deep breath and immediately closed with his enemy. Holding a six-foot spear with buckler and rapier, he jabbed at his opponent's feet and face, his own eyes perceiving only the smooth landscape of leather with the one three-inch rip covering his enemy's face.

A clash of irsrem on irsrem resounded across the arena and once again the combatants halted their contests to stare at Flores while slaves dragged the dead away for the malkops.

Buckler pitched against buckler and Coralanus attempted to push Flores back to slip and fall as before. Instead, Flores slipped his buckler onto the other's spear and used the leverage to flip him up and on one side.

"To Vensor," Flores muttered. His rapier pierced the man's heart.

With a yelp, Coralanus flopped and splayed on the ground.

The gladiators sucked their breath—the spectators in the stands jumped up and madly applauded.

"Streker. Romos. Grol. Anyone. I want this man taken down," Frelek yelled.

Selem stepped back as the contest became increasingly lethal.

Grol poured sweat from his face and turned his eyes away; Romos did the same. Streker looked at his companions with contempt and snatched up rapier and dagger and rushed forward to end Flores' life.

In moments, he fell face forward on the grass as his lifeblood poured from his neck.

The stands applauded louder.

Passing their gaze over the spectators, and clearly concerned at the impudent slave's growing popularity, Frelek waved his outraged trainers back and sent several more blooded gladiators in to finish Flores off.

The first fell with a thrust to the neck. The second collapsed as Flores' axe split his skull.

"Enough," Frelek called. "Seal the square."

The warriors exchanged worried glances.

"Are you certain, Frelek?" one asked. "If the fence should fail, then the city..."

Frelek turned to Selem for confirmation. The eunuch's face was also contracted with worry, and Selem nodded: Do it now. Selem and Frelek both glanced upward again. The time for Flight was closer. The Games must finish.

"Seal the square," Frelek repeated, and a host of slaves dragged in eight-foot-high sections of steel chainlink fence, sealing off an area around Flores.

Staring at the proceedings with contempt, he waited calmly for whatever device his captors had conceived to try to recover some of their self-respect at having been stymied by a single foreign slave. Across the arena, more eunuchs arrived at their dedicated boxes, including one who was different, one carried in a litter of eight brawny slaves. Flores recognized the Oracle. Flores must indeed have stirred up the city; murmurs rose from the populace as the eunuchs took their seats.

When the sections of chainlink fence were in place and

bulwarks stabbed into the ground with generous stretches of rope to hold all in place, and Flores surrounded alone within, he perceived one large wagon trundle through a gate, drawn by four large lyarts that twitched as they approached as if from nervousness. The wagon carried a long narrow container, sealed as tightly as the gilas that the Elect sold to corrupt Vensor-sa in their cities scattered across Maalstrom.

The Turlicum glanced around to see what resources he may have for whatever was being arrayed against him—his rapier, buckler, and spear, and his hidden dagger. Behind him, firm wooden paneling rose almost vertically six feet high and still hung with various weapons, the sections of fence connecting to either side of the panel to form a perfect imprisoning circle. At least his tormentors did not intend to deny him the defenses of a warrior, though it was perhaps only the growing murmurs from the crowd that impelled them to this.

The wagon came near and a section of fencing opposite Flores briefly opened and a score of slaves hastily dragged the oblong box within, then hurried out of the circle as the fence was replaced. Two score of warriors, slaves, and even the newly graduated boys gripped the sections to ensure they remained in place, ensuring that Flores would have no place to flee.

A rope pulled and one end of the box fell flat. For one moment, Flores saw nothing within, the interior bathed in darkness. Then a smell struck his nostrils—a familiar smell, one he could never forget. Memories rushed upon him: first when he was a child and a prehensile paw sank its claws into his right wrist, partially crippling it and requiring years of effort before he could finally train the scar tissue to obey and hold a sword.

Second, a more recent episode when he was trapped beneath the refuge and fortress of Soorkrul in the far western wilderness and the slaver Malag had unleashed tormentor after tormentor upon him in desperate efforts to end his life before rescuing Amina.

Now the same sickly sweet stench overwhelmed him again, and the source of the stench slipped quietly out of the box.

A predatory ros of the wild forests paused and turned its bony skull with the one hawkish beak from side to side as it searched for its accustomed verdant forest. Finding no covering leaves to hide in, but its eyes catching sight of its hated two-legged enemy, it gripped the grassy floor and unleashed a shattering roar.

Frightened, the crowd jumped to their feet. What if the fence were to fall? Many looked behind as if seeking nearby exits.

So this was the eunuchs' last card, Flores thought. Having failed with all else, they now sought to rip his flesh with beak and claw as they had ripped his leather mask. He crouched to receive the beast's charge which he knew would momently come.

He barely had time to crouch when the animal sighted him, and as the one enemy close enough to fall beneath its talons, it immediately launched itself at Flores in a terrific leap.

The crowd sucked its breath.

The leap was too quick for Flores to position his spear and the beast fell full upon him. Flores could almost feel Romos and Grol grin with triumph at his imminent death. Also, too quick for him to respond with his rapier, he dropped both weapons. Gripping the flesh-naked beak with both hands and holding it shut, Flores and the animal rolled together, the beast's claws ripping grass as they missed Flores' flank.

One paw struck home, and Flores' blood erupted spraying the air. The crowd yelled.

Rolling toward the panel with its supply of weapons, Flores came to his knees and desperately held the trap-jaw shut with both hands while squirming to avoid more contact with the capable prehensile paws. At last, he managed to lift the beast in the air by its jaw and fling it away.

It alighted and sprang again.

His rapier and spear too distant to retrieve, and the panel still too far back to offer any alternative, Flores slipped the shiv from his loincloth. As the beast landed, he jammed the shiv into its lower jaw, clamping those sharp teeth together.

The animal rolled and spun in pain.

Flores had only seconds before it would free itself and come again. He turned and launched himself at the panel. With hardly a moment to think, he snatched up a ball and chain attached to a length of steel-like rorewood.

Dislodging the shiv, it leaped.

The Turlicum spun the ball—missed.

The ros bowled him over. With both legs, he thrust the animal into the air, turned and climbed the panel, sending swords and shafts and shields tumbling to the ground in an avalanche.

The clattering of steel and glass caused the ros to hesitate. Which way was his prey? It sighted him clambering to the top of the largest weapons panel.

Flores gripped the ball and chain, for a second taking in the panorama—the eunuchs were standing to a man, excepting only the Oracle, though he too seemed interested in the outcome.

At that moment, for the first time since he had entered the city of Klopus, Flores saw Crestal. She stood beside Soorkrul among the eunuchs and she stared straight at Flores. But her expression was dull, even uninterested.

His ego deflated. After all the risks he had run, after all the efforts he had expended, after all the men he had murdered just to rescue her—she was not interested whether he lived or died?

Well, perhaps I no longer care either, he thought.

The animal leaped again—straight up the panel where one clawed paw ripped at his boot.

Flores smiled. There was one sure way to finish a ros—and he had it. Bringing down the spiked ball direct on the forward spine of the animal, the ball snapped the animal's spine with a loud crack, at once depriving all four vicious paws of life.

The beast fell to the ground. It slithered and spun in vain attempts to resume its movements and end the life of its prey. In less than a minute, however, its eyes glazed and it ceased moving and its breathing ended.

The stands erupted. "Isav! Isav!" To the chagrin of the Elect, who mostly frowned, the spectators jumped and cheered, hugging each other and throwing items in the air in celebration of the latest champion of the Games.

Selem drilled Frelek with his eyes. "Now, or you'll be next," Selem growled.

The chief trainer of Klopus' gladiators turned to his trainers and trainees. "Bring that man down, the lot of you. I want him alive and on his knees before the Elect with no more delays."

"Before the jousts, Frelek?" They glanced at the several pairs of reven-na, waiting patiently on the side, their sinuous long necks rippling in fright, reacting to the smell of a predatory ros nearby.

"Now, by God! I said now!"

Exchanging glances, the fighters threw the fencing down and moved in a mob to the panel where Flores remained perched, six feet above the fray. One hand gripping the ball and chain, the other snapping up a rapier as he bent down, he straightened again. He reflected on another ancient principle of combat: when one's opponent is making a mistake, do not interrupt him—now was the time to interrupt. As the best warriors of Klopus surrounded the panel, Flores ripped off his mask.

At once, two faces in the stands burst in wonder and surprise.

"Flores?" Crestal smiled.

"Flores," Soorkrul hissed. "Even here? That mask..."

The Turlicum pulled his half-mask out and placed it on his head, his ancient clan insignia of a flayed reven paw arching down beneath a luxurious plume of vok-hair. He raised his eyes to the now rapidly darkening sky. Above the horizon, the cone of a blue comet burned brightly. Below it, Flores locked on a series of chiaroscuro objects flashing piebald, rapidly growing in size like furies from a nether world.

He raised his rapier.

"Vensor! Accept this blood in sacrifice to the warriors of Heaven!" With that, he launched himself into the center of the mob.

CHAPTER 15

T he aged crone stepped forward with caution, helped to stand erect by a coterie of women, strong, healthy with youth and vigorous blood. The sere skin of the old woman, monument to mysterious processes defying nature's order, contrasted with the eager shining faces of her helpers. They guided her progress with care, the affection of daughters for a progenitor of old, eternal as the stars.

Her aged voice rose above the excitement that had seized the chamber. "Take care, blood of my blood. Heed the advice from ancient times, gathered at the cost of endless lives. Do not take flight before the appointed time."

"Yes, Mother," the dozen girls spoke as one. "But several have already flown."

"To their peril, the fate of those who listen not." Her withered arm swung wide over a broad chamber filling with eager girls, muscled protuberances giving air to iridescent wings stirring the air in the light of a score of oil-lamps. "Take heed, my blood," she called. "The comet has appeared. But wait for the harsh wind to spread your seed across the world. I cannot advise on which direction to favor. Providence and Mother Maalstrom roll our dice and favor only the select few from our numbers."

The winged girls poised, impatient as children. The gods in their wisdom and beneficence made their blood to boil, their minds to flame with desire for their destined fate, whatever outcome may result, blissfully disregarding the risk. Their wings fluttered the stale air, long walled off by a series of perpetually closed gates that for their entire lives had shut out the colony-destroying predators of the outside world.

Sunrays peeked through a lofty gap in the ceiling, reflecting many leaves carried on the wind.

Mother nodded.

The gates flung open. The chamber of nude women rushed to the exits, and climbing to the highest peaks and scarps of their craggy city, they took to flight, their numbers vast, embracing the wind in tumult.

In less than a half hour, the city of the Mok-sa had fulfilled its sacred duties and a horde of neutered women, workers not blessed with wings, with uninspiring faces and clothed in simple tunics, returned to their unrequited labors and escorted Mother past underground chambers of endless heaving reproduction and back to her guarded refuge where she resumed her fruitless study of the primordial curse of the Mok-sa. She sighed. "Mayhaps one of my blood will at last succeed where all of my efforts have failed."

* * *

The Lord of the Turlicum, his vok-crest flying, landed amid the howling mob with a thud. Near a dozen were crushed or sent rolling to come to a stop, flattened. Slicing the calves of a half-dozen more, Flores rolled with the rest and came to his feet behind several who peered about, having lost sight of their enemy. Before their eyes lit on him, a spiked steel ball ended their lives in rapid succession, brains flinging across the yard to shock and dismay the others.

Flores rammed through their ranks, laying the Klopan fighters low with each step, each step accompanied by a swing of the ball and chain backed by powerful muscles. Iron swords raised in desperate defense snapped. Irsrem rapiers spun freely in the air. Helmets ripped off skulls and skidded in the dust. Before Flores knew it, the arena was awash in more blood than the remote clearing in the distant forest where he annihilated Soorkrul's entire expedition of warriors.

Overhead, loops of darkness swelled, throwing the armed mob into greater confusion as they hesitated to discern friend from enemy. Flores, however, had no such burden—all he saw were enemies. All he saw fell to his vengeance.

Two gladiators collapsed behind his enormous blows and opened a gap. Romos appeared, standing with sweaty face, his eyes shifting nervously between his masters who loudly egged their warriors on and fear of encountering the avenging demon who was throwing ever greater numbers of Klopan soldiery into chaos.

Flores caught a second-class warrior from behind, snatched a heavy iron dart from the warrior's bandoleer and flung it.

Romos clutched his throat and fell on his knees. Grol glanced once at his friend and turned and limped away as fast as his injured leg permitted. A second dart landed between his shoulder blades and he face-planted in the dirt.

The Turlicum had a single glance of the eunuch Selem hurrying off the field towards the spectator boxes of the Elect—then the ranks of his enemies closed about him again.

Crushing two more skulls—and abruptly cutting off their angry shouting—Flores tumbled as the spiked ball tore loose from its chain. Swords spun in the empty air that Flores had occupied.

A trainer swung an axe—cleft the spine of a companion—Flores severed the trainer's arm and snatched the axe for himself. A moment's glance and his heart beat faster—the axe was his very own Nebelroc, now returned to its master.

More ranks of outraged warriors and would-be gladiators closed in, even a dozen of the recently recruited boys, now all blooded. Flores made no distinction but his axe found trimming the boys' necks as easy as a scythe trims wheat, their bodies falling beneath the older warriors and tripping them.

The fight became a slaughter, and the slaughter became a massacre as the bravest soon fell dead while the more hesitant failed to press forward.

Frelek managed to make his shouting heard over the din and carnage. "Bring the reven-na! Drive him down with our mounts!" Several heard Frelek and leaped on two reven-na. Frelek himself took a third.

As the three spurred their amphibious beasts toward Flores, the Klopan warriors parted—Flores took advantage and rushed the panel where he climbed to the top, sheathing the axe as he climbed for rapier and dagger. Before Frelek knew what was happening, Flores had again leaped and landed on top of the sputtering trainer.

His dagger did the job, and Frelek fell moaning from his saddle.

Flores dug his own booted heels into the sides of the sinuous animal and rode down more Klopans.

A helmeted soldier—from his skill neither a slave trainer nor a would-be gladiator—rode his mount straight at Flores. The Turlicum noted in a flash how his newest opponent eyed Flores' right hand, planning an opening move in the traditional mounted combat peculiar to trained Simet-sa. The Klopan propelled to ram Flores' beast and shock his enemy.

But Flores reflexed, jerking his beast backward. Flores pivoted the beast rightward.

His enemy saw what he perceived to be an error and smiled. He spurred his beast again, rising on its hind legs to cabré and raising his rapier and angling it down to attack Flores on his unprotected left side and lever Flores from his saddle.

Flores stood his ground. As the warrior's beast descended, the man watched in dismay as Flores uncrossed his hands so that the rapier that had appeared to be encumbered in his right hand, was now displayed in his left. Too late to stop the downward rush of his cabré, the warrior was driven onto Flores' blade and fell to the ground in an explosion of gore, the long neck of his mount twisting to gaze in perplexity at the river of blood flowing down its side.

A pike drove at Flores from the third reven, opening a cut down his side, but missing a clean thrust. Flores yanked it away from the warrior and cabréd his new mount onto the other, crushing his opponent.

With that, Flores broke free of the lynch mob as angry Klopans pursued him about the arena, despite the howls of admiration emanating from the spectator stands. Fewer warriors seemed interested in killing him, however, as darkness flowed over the amphitheater, throwing a blanket of blackish-green mixed with patches of pale whiteness from the moons Tumsenet and Nantifus.

Having broken free of the crowd, Flores rushed his new mount to the now shadowy box of the Elect—nothing peaceful remained in his squirming brain regarding those who pulled the strings in this accursed city.

He halted. The box was empty. No eunuch was either in the stands or anywhere else in the amphitheater, though the growing shadows could have hidden hosts.

A welter of cries pealed from the Klopans as they raised their faces to the dusky sky. "The Flight! The Flight!"

Flores lifted his gaze.

From the stretch of starry blackness below the prophesying cone of the comet, the airy darker blotches took shape—swarmed over the arena and the city, numberless as locusts.

In response, cries arose from the remaining Klopans, "Follow them! Seize all that alight!"

Hero of ancient Ven, explorer of wildernesses and oceans vast, he who had challenged Atasan himself in his high fastness, stared in confusion at what could not be. Yet he had seen it before.

Hundreds of gilas—devoid of clothing—flapped translucent wings invisible but for their iridescence, their blond hair mixed with darker auburn streaming gloriously in the wind, their keen faces flush with excitement and eager for a hoped-for future as each glided lower peering for some niche in which to alight, heedless of the danger posed by knots of Klopan soldiery intent on snatching them.

As Flores on his mount stared in stunned silence at this latest effusion of the mysterious tangle of life on Maalstrom, a body dropped at his feet with a thud. His furrowed eyes made out a nude male, similarly winged as the females, but with inset compound eyes like the Elect and outsized genitals. Having mated, its short life was done. Its body broken, its multi-faceted eyes closed and it ceased breathing.

Another body crashed close by. The gila was a bloody ruin clawed by predators. Flores glimpsed two malkops flying aloft to attack and kill more of their ancestral rivals. But there were too many for even the growing number of malkops to intercept, the timing of the Flight overwhelming them with sheer numbers.

On the ground, bands of Klopan warriors rushed to and fro as several gilas landed in the arena or among the spectators' bleachers, and the warriors immediately cut their wings and placed them in chains before hauling them away—without resistance, Flores noticed, as if the gilas realized this fate was far from the worst that could happen.

One of the warrior bands focused on Flores, and with an explosion of anger, pursued him again. Done with his fruitless examining of the amphitheater's benches, he yanked the animal's reins and hopped toward one of the arena's exits.

A thick blanket of darkness covered all but a thicker sprinkle of stars and the two looming moons above and scattered sparks below as irsrem flashed in combat.

Several boy gladiators tried to block the exit. Flores barreled through, his rapier leaving two without a limb—

their companions would execute them before the night was over as the Elect of Klopus had no time for tending to the disabled. Not when the supply of boys was as endless as the number of gilas flying above.

Spurring his reven through the streets, Flores found himself on the same cavalcade as led to the Hall of the Elect. He had but one chance to complete his goal and find Crestal, his own gila of choice. About him, more gilas landed—some voluntarily as if none had warned them to steer clear of the city—these were promptly taken, their wings clipped, and escorted to the Hall. Flores saw one taken inside.

If a gila existed somewhere in the city of Klopus, but Flores was unable to find her, the logical best place to search was the Hall of the Elect. Even if he had already looked but not seen her.

A flash of iridescence caught his gaze—a gila crashed onto the roof of the Hall. Glass rebounded, rainbows glinting, and shards collapsed into the interior.

There could be no better time.

Flores ran his reven up the short flight of steps directly to the Hall's front entrance. Before the guards could block him, Flores cut them down—'best soldiers in the world', Flores snorted. He did not hesitate but propelled his mount through several antechambers and sprang into the main naos where leroo-sa and their hives dwelt among the images of the Urlis, the Brotherhood of gods.

His surmise was correct. A score of Elect froze from their inspection of newly arrived specimens for their harem; more Elect and bound gilas arrived from other entrances. Soorkrul himself stood in their midst and glared hatred at Flores—his panic seemingly locking him in place.

At his side stood Crestal. One glance at Flores and her arms raised. Her mouth opened. "You've come!"

Soorkrul turned his angry face on her. He slapped her, triggering a bright crimson flush, and she burst into tears.

Flores exploded. He spurred the beast forward in a

single hop and leaped off his saddle. Soorkrul collapsed under the weight of his body.

Soldiers swarmed into the Hall—Flores slashed and threw them back even as he dragged Soorkrul back on his feet by one hand around his neck.

The eunuch managed to squeeze out, "You think to take me to your prison?"

"No, Soorkrul. I think to take your head on a pike."

Soorkrul paled—struggled.

With a clean swipe of his razored-rapier blade on its polished rorewood handle, Flores cleaved the eunuch's neck from shoulder to clavicle, sending his surprised face tumbling high in the air to finally land, clumping at the feet of his comrades and guardsmen.

All halted in shock as Soorkrul's corpse drenched the inviolate marbled floor in red blood.

All but the thing on the throne, the aged Oracle, who was still well protected by a half-dozen specially trained protectors, the elite of Klopan elite. Flores had no personal quarrel with the Oracle—he hurried to embrace Crestal, taking advantage of this opportunity while the rest of the room contemplated the death of Soorkrul, one of the holy Elect, in their very own sanctuary.

The wall opened. The throne moved silently backwards into the wall. The wall returned with an audible click. The Oracle was gone.

"Flores my love!"

The Turlicum snatched Crestal up and plopped her on the reven.

"We have this one chance from Gethos. We must fly now or join Soorkrul in death." As dozens of Klopan warriors flooded into the chamber to avenge the sacrilege inflicted on their holy sanctuary by the Ven heretic, Flores grabbed a pike, and with one hand, stuck Soorkrul's severed head on it. Leaping on the reven, he gave it a kick and sent the beast pell-mell through the melee, through the front entrance, and onto the confused street, holding the crowned pike aloft for all to see, his harsh victory cry echoing off the walls.

In minutes, Flores and Crestal sped their way through the still chaotic scene of Klopans snatching gilas wherever they landed and killing any who resisted, Flores as devoted to his nightmarish goal as Nantifus the bringer of disease, the god's moon sailing above the silvery streets even now as harsh witness. Bounding through the streets, Flores' axe cut down every ghostly figure that emerged to block his way, his lungs expelling loud cries of triumph that echoed through the city, Soorkrul's head bobbing on its pike.

They found the main city gate. The gate stood open as Klopans departed in great numbers to scour the country in all directions for more of their Elect's favorite prey. Where they could not follow, and it seemed the gilas from the land of Mok-sa seemed intent on flying to greater distances, the Klopans produced bows and sent arrows into the sky to bring down still more, matching the number murdered by the malkops.

At the entrance, Flores jammed the pike butt-first into the ground, leaving Soorkrul's head to glower, his glowering insect eyes frozen in death.

He spurred the reven forward, and as the night deepened and the pursuit and the slaughter moved out of the city and into the western countryside, Flores spurred his reven ever harder eastward, Crestal mounted behind. They must be far from Klopus before the suns broke again.

CHAPTER 16

Inside the city of Klopus, a low wall encompassed a stretch of park boasting deciduous trees and pleasant fields of grass tended by slow-moving slaves with scythes. Two hundred meters inside the park rose another wall, this one markedly higher. Its face was plain, concreted, devoid of handholds, and no plant growth was permitted on the empty concrete plain that circled the second high wall. The second wall marched in a broad oval. All was encompassed by the equally high crenelated ramparts of the city itself.

With the split suns bright overhead, the Oracle of Klopus approached the high inner wall atop a palanquin carried by eight muscular slaves and his usual half-dozen elite guards. In response to some obscure movement of the Oracle's hands, a section of the high wall dislodged from the wall's outer surface and pulled back into the depths of this citadel within Klopus.

The Oracle's palanquin entered. The hall that had opened before the retinue stretched deep into the citadel. When they came to the end, the aged eunuch on the palanquin motioned that his slaves lower the litter. He stepped off and stood.

He stared back down the empty corridor now bathed in shadow. A minute passed while the Oracle stood and stared. Finally, he motioned his retinue to move out of the hallway and stand entirely inside the sanctuary. The Oracle made another obscure movement with one hand and the portion of wall reappeared from a side receptacle, moved back into the hallway, and proceeded up the corridor until it clicked back into its original position.

His retinue exchanged nervous glances and attempted to read their master's mood in his sloe-angled eyes, the eyes with the epicanthic fold.

"You will wait here as usual," the Oracle said. Turning, he opened a massive door by obscure means with his hands and passed through. Again, he waited a minute as if he expected some other to follow. But none did and he finally shut the door behind him.

The Oracle stared upward at a great steel behemoth several hundred meters in length and a hundred meters high, the behemoth cast in piebald shadow by overhead nets and a mesh of rorewood serving as a roof. Like an enormous bullet, the monster possessed no windows but only a single wide porch-like platform stuck permanently open to allow access to the construction's equally shadowy interior. Both ends of the oblong bullet rested on massive metal props—the props of one end, however, were six degrees off and buried half-way in the endless plain of concrete that underlay the behemoth. Fine-meshed nets hung on the inside of the encircling wall; more nets hung at angles across the vast interior space as if someone had sought to ensure that no foreign bodies, winged or otherwise, might contaminate the interior.

A minute passed while the Oracle stood alone by the open platform. He leaned to one side, silent, but listening.

A gentle breeze brushed his clammy striated cheek and a bright glittering sparked by his side. The glittering materialized into a person, a man as anciently aged as the Oracle.

"So, you return at last, Omega. I had given you up since you last visited." The Oracle leaned to one side.

Omega's one blue eye and one yellow eye focused on the eunuch. "Your wounds—do they still pain you after so much time?"

The eunuch glanced down to where one of his arms had

been reattached after having been severed. "I still live. You were correct in your assessment, Omega. When you found me in the wilds, the extent of my wounds was so great that I thought my body could never be restored." The eunuch smiled. "But the Chaldeans are never wrong."

Yezd sniffed. "There was a time when I myself believed that. But a fall from a rover a thousand feet in the air was not easy even for a Chaldean to repair."

"I am grateful. Though I still wonder what became of those who took the rover and dropped me from on high."

"I am still investigating. I know they founded a city called Ror where Tlata took up residence. Vensa eventually crushed it and had her warriors kill all they found. And you were still recuperating when Vedega returned to Klopus from the wilds, so you may not remember all that happened afterward. She seized the guns from the male lynch mob and turned their guns against them, shooting all the men but you and me and the other remaining engineers and two of the most submissive males. She shot Lamoc Rho-3, who became their leader after Khurko Tau-3 disappeared."

The engineer looked nervous. "It was a close call for me twice over."

Yezd continued. "Who can say who was the harsher? Vensa or Vedega? Your city of Klopus exists only because Vensa's warriors drove out Vedega and her female Mok-sa after their failed attack on Ven."

"You were gone when I finally recovered."

"To avoid Vedega's murderous appetite. Her actions made Khurko look tolerant."

"You should have been here after Vedega left. Vensa's little tattooed savages had never seen an engineer. It did not take long before they were worshipping all us engineers as gods. But we were eunuchs. So Vensa's little primitives worshipped that condition, as well, and spread the Order of the Eunuch Guild to every city on Maalstrom. Some even cut themselves to be more like us, not understanding that on

Earth we discovered that amputation increased one's grasp of mathematics and spatial reasoning when accompanied by special alleles inserted in our DNA and that it was done for no other purpose. We volunteered for the operation so we could become the best engineers and qualify to run a starship."

Yezd nodded, twitching his short white beard.

The engineer went on, "It is amazing how a few demonstrations of gunpowder and electricity can impress the minds of stone-age children. Even centuries later, after all the other engineers have died, leaving only you and me, these savages still worship me as their Oracle, though I am the only true eunuch still living in Klopus. Your fountain-of-youth potion from hornet DNA, which helped me recover from my injuries, was another miracle that impressed them. Now you and I have outlived them all."

"One of the few benefits this planet has given us."

The engineer looked at Yezd again with curiosity. "Did you ever discover what happened to our rover? Or our helicopter?"

"Neither, I am sorry to say. Milo left Ror before Vensa destroyed it, but where he went I never learned. His wives scattered to the ends of this planet and founded cities of their own. As for the helicopter, I know no more than you do—after the injury to her eye, Morla flew the helicopter southwest, to who knows where. She too is likely as dead as Tlata."

The engineer took a breath. "It seems our little colony succeeded by failing. We split into genetic fragments that survive by slaughtering each other but can never wholly exterminate each other because each fragment is close kin to the others and all are interdependent. A recipe for perpetual war ensuring perpetual balance."

Yezd nodded again. "Yes. By colonizing Maalstrom, our Mok-sa brought a calamity to this world. Nature corrected it the only way it knows how, by fragmenting our colony into competing groups. That is how Nature always rewards massive success, by inducing internal collapse that leads eventually to fragmented speciation who compete even while collaborating, like different anthills of the same species." The ill-matched orbs focused on his aged colleague. "But enough reminiscing. I must continue with my mission, my friend. Despite the passage of so much time, I remain unable to communicate with my Chaldeans."

"Your irsrem talismans did not succeed—what you created on your last visit? Your cover completely fooled my guards as you approached."

Yezd snorted again. "They were stolen soon after I crafted them. When I had seven, I was able to coerce a malkop to fly me to the glass pyramid, and I entered the Eye, but I managed only to receive an outdated report from my colleagues. I was unable to send them my own report. And when I returned to my chateau, a petty thief stole all my bracelets, leaving me stranded in that forsaken wilderness for years. I had quite a time tracking down and recovering just the one I now possess." Yezd held up one arm where the light glinted on a silvery glass bauble on his wrist. He quickly lowered it and the bauble became once again invisible.

Yezd let a worried glance pass through the interior as they stood by the massive ship with its platform stuck open at the six-degree angle. "Six missing irsrem rings are loose somewhere in this world, with the energy that powers a starship. The danger lurking in that fact is incalculable."

"You would know about that better than I, Yezd. For you are a Chaldean while I am still just 'engineer number four', a cipher without even a name."

Yezd shrugged. "But you have come up in the world, Number Four. You are now the Oracle. Now, however, to business. To complete my mission, I tried fashioning underwater gills to reach the Island but that project failed also when they, too, were stolen. I wish to try my luck again with more irsrem rings. Otherwise, I fear I can never penetrate the center of the Eye and avoid its guardian and communicate with my colleagues or to finally complete my mission. To create more bracelets, I need the Source. I need crystallized carbon."

The Oracle nodded. "The Source is always open to you." The engineer cast his own concerned glance about him. "But keep in mind my position in Klopus. I may be the Oracle and king of this city, but the passions of my subjects are strong, and the events last night, when that murderous barbarian killed two score of my men and desecrated the front gate, have my whole city in an uproar, which reflects badly on my rule. And if they learn that I have violated my own dictates and the laws of the Eunuch Guild by giving an outsider like you access to Source, they may even turn against me. Some already see no value in being a eunuch, now that only I remain alive from our original eunuch engineers. Accessing Source must be done rarely and discreetly, Omega. To them, Source is black magic and bad luck because the interior comes to life at odd times and lights up. They want me to close its portal and bury it." The engineer peered up the side of the dull, dead behemoth. "And sometimes I agree with them. Our arrival on this planet was so long ago that I myself hardly remember it."

Omega nodded. "I will keep your concerns in mind, Number Four. I will work quickly, as I did before. But I must succeed. I fear what is happening among the remaining Mok-sa, the ones whom Vensa's little soldiers chased out of Klopus, the city that sends its daughters aloft to die in a hundred ways, just for the chance that a few will found another settlement."

The engineer waved one hand and Omega climbed the crooked platform and entered, retracing steps he had first taken one thousand years before when 224 Mok-sa colonists, including 196 hyper-fertile women and 28 virile men had landed on Maalstrom in the starship 'Source', depending on

Yezd and his seven eunuch engineers to help them build their first timid settlement, which they called Klopus after their favorite food—Klopan wheat.

As Yezd entered the dark interior, behind him, a solitary glint flashed once and then vanished.

* * *

Kot drifted below the surface of the water, encased in total darkness. A current carried him farther than he supposed was possible, the black water rescuing his aged and infirm body from the Doom, a fate which he himself had often prescribed for miscreants. The flow took him around a corner of one of the many passages within the system of caverns beneath the elevated crater of Vaw, the crater the outer slopes of which housed the city itself, descending to the great port that attracted reven-towed ships from across the wide green-blue sea.

The once king of Vaw came to the surface and gasped a breath. Quite unable to paddle his limbs, he simply floated, his eyes taking in the signs and details of the rock-lined passage. He could no longer hear the roars of Vaw's queen, Morla. Or the exclamations and speech of his former subjects. Only the lapping of ripples along the sides of the passage.

One side gave way to a tall clear window of hard irsrem—the nether side was an open chamber free of water, lit by a single flaring oil lamp set on a table with chairs, the chamber where he himself used to view Morla and her occasional victims who managed to make it this far before she caught them.

The passage flowed on. It twisted once, then again, and at length became sufficiently shallow that he was able to stand. Kot inspected his body for damage—he found none more than the usual defects of senility and age. Pushing his fatigued thin legs through the brine—salty indicating a substantial backwash from the sea—he came to a small gap gouged in the rocky wall.

Inside rested a boat.

With effort, Kot wrestled the small boat out of the gap and managed to float it on the surface of the water. He climbed in.

Twenty minutes later he rounded a last angle in the stream and his boat slid silently and calmly onto the surface of the ocean. Inspecting the store of food and water that he kept always on board, he covered his face with a small tarp then tied himself firmly to the wales.

"Heh. My foolish subjects think to get rid of me this easily. I will show them...I'll show them all. And especially that brainless blowhard, Squawk, who managed to grow himself new appendages and now has the temerity to call himself 'Cetus, King of Vaw' and thinks he will take my throne."

A wind picked up and Kot settled in as his little boat sped across the waves.

* * *

The high crags beckoned. Pushing the mount to its limit, Flores, together with Crestal clinging firmly and happily to his back, left Klopus and its environs far behind. A bright, cloud-riven day opened up, a trio of gibbous moons showing pallidly on the horizon, shy to show fulsomely. Though they had covered a score of miles since the previous night, occasional gilas still glided overhead, flitting in and out of cloudbanks as they evaded malkops scouting for stragglers. Their fate was no longer Flores' concern.

As the ridges rose one after another and the air grew cooler and more still, Flores finally allowed the animal to slow. Just in time. The reven stumbled. The Turlicum halted and slid off the saddle to inspect and Crestal followed.

"Tha-two," Flores exclaimed. "The very reven that

carried me in pursuit of Soorkrul for the entire last autumn."

"Is that good?" Crestal asked. She stroked and combed her mid-length blond and auburn hair to relieve her nervousness. She glanced back down the path they had followed, the panorama expanding down the plain toward a darker patch that indicated Klopus.

"It means I won't have to train another beast because he already knows me." Petting the reven's neck, Flores spat on its convulsing gills. Its legs quivered.

"We must rest...or rather...Tha-two must rest, if we are ever to make it to see your Mok-sa." He peered ahead. "We must find a scratch in this rocky desert to hide in till tomorrow. It is unlikely our hosts in Klopus will give up on us quickly or easily. Not after I spoiled their fancy celebration and left them such a nice calling card." With a grin, Flores patted the steel blade of Nebelroc. He drew it down from the saddle and cleaned it of Soorkrul.

Crestal stepped close and embraced Flores, reluctant to give up the closeness she had enjoyed while they rode.

"There." Flores pointed up a slope where an overhang lent some shade. "That is where we can park our carcasses. See how the tufts of sercotrope disguise it. We need only make certain the lodgings are unoccupied."

"How familiar this seems," Crestal said, "you and I wandering through a wilderness."

Flores stared at the sky in thought. "Except this time my brain is not inflamed with desire for another, obeying Amina's strange spell."

Crestal coyly smiled. "I want your brain inflamed for me, obeying my spell."

He grabbed her and nuzzled her feminine neck, pulling aside the black enveloping tunic that gilas in Klopus always wore in public. He buried his still bruised face in her blond-auburn hair which had grown to shoulder-length beneath her verdant-amber eyes. "And your brain?"

She laughed aloud. "I was as inflamed for you then as I

am now. But I was too shy to let you know. Would you have listened?"

He shook his head. "I could not. I saw nothing and heard nothing, but what she put in my head. She had plans within plans. And I could see nothing but her ghostly image."

As they spoke, they followed the path up to the cavity. Crestal said, "I was jealous beyond words, Flores. Never allow any gila within you again but me."

"You say that while leading your mate to the Land of Women."

She looked exasperated. "Where else can we find protection? I am from there so they should take me in. Where else can we go?"

"Yet you still cannot tell me much about it."

"It will be easier to show than to tell, Flores."

He let his gaze wander. "That too I have heard before."

Unsaddling Tha-two, Flores let it feed on the tufts of brittle-green sercotrope while Flores thrashed the interior of the cavity to drive away other denizens. None appeared and they relaxed beneath the overhang.

"Admit to me this much, Crestal. You were no child when you left your home, were you?"

She lowered her eyes. "No, Flores. I was more than a child. Much more... You know, of course, that I was Lord Numenmur's consort. Does that tell you enough?"

"Yes. And no. You were not taken by the Guild Order as a child while you were out joyriding on a reven, as you once told me, were you?" Flores drilled her.

She shrank back, eyes riveted to the ground. "Do not make me say it, Flores. I was a slave, a female slave in a land of men. Do not force me to describe my years of humiliation."

Flores sighed. His breath seemed to induce Crestal to shrink further. He reached out and pressed her body close to him until she breathed deeply, relaxing again. "And do not forget what is most important, Flores."

He looked puzzled. He had forgotten.

"We must find a hive of hornets. I must be stung by a leroo soon, or the worst will happen. As I must once a year."

Nodding, Flores said, "The sting of the hornet to avert the worst. Thus, the Elect kept their hives. And Numsenmur. And even my own father. To sting the gilas whom they mated with and kept in secret, since gilas are contraband forbidden to Vensor-sa across the face of Maalstrom."

"Except in the land of Mok-sa. You will see soon, Flores. If we can live just a few more weeks."

"As you say, dear Crestal." He grinned. "Though I confess the vision of so many splendid women in the Hall of the Elect was not something that offended my eyes."

In reaction, she reached slowly down and stroked between Flores' legs, and in another moment, he rolled on top and possessed her as the mad moons swooned overhead, flushed with sacred colors.

CHAPTER 17

The next morning as the suns came up and the partial moons of Tumsenet and Talen gradually vanished, Flores and Crestal stirred. The night had not been cold enough to require a fire, and such would have been risky given the possibility that bands of Klopan soldiery were still hunting for them.

Flores ran his hands over Tha-two to comfort the animal and ensured that its legs no longer shook. With a jerk on its reins, the reven rose on all fours and snaked its long neck, showing its pleasure in having its sides stroked.

Tending to their personal business, the two refugees were soon ready to resume their journey toward the mythical land of women—the only place on Maalstrom where the female sex was not outlawed or enslaved, and Flores still struggled to get used to the idea of soon encountering an entire city of them, in fact, a city where it was men who were outlawed. What would be his reception?

Standing by Tha-two, Flores gazed down the rocky path leading to the plain where Klopus lay. He flattened one hand over his eyes the better to see.

Crestal noticed him stiffen. "What do you see, Flores?" She too gazed.

"Something follows. It has seen us."

She peered. "I see nothing. Are you certain?" She shook her head, gave up.

"A smudge. An hour away. We must try to make that two hours. Where there is one, there will be more."

Their concern relayed to Tha-two and it hissed as if eager to cover more miles. Climbing atop, they hurried the beast farther up the narrow track without pausing to breakfast on edible plants.

Ahead rose a seemingly endless series of ridges and crags separated by high glens and valleys where the suns often failed to shine—to their east, past many miles, a redness stained the horizon, and Flores thought of the fiery blood-red brilliance that emanates from the constellation Atasan, the constellation visible only from the southern hemisphere that shadows all who dare to seek the Eye of Vensor. But this was the northern hemisphere where only the constellation of Barazaggar the eunuch prevailed, which cast no such foreboding color across the sky.

Still, the sky transformed as winds scrambled from the distant south, shedding its rain into each nook of crag and slowing the couple's progress. Rivulets turned into gushing streams and the streams into marshes, which were immediately occupied by gupping frogs and bucking lizards, happy beyond measure at their good fortune as they perched on wet stones and leveled fearless gazes at the two giants urging a third through the muck, devoid of sense.

Finding a drier path higher up along a ridgeline, Flores and Crestal were forced finally to dismount, as Tha-two commenced to quiver like before. They led the beast as quickly as possible—mountain beasts akin to sikes came within a dozen feet and stared uncomprehendingly as the pair struggled, barely able to maintain their footing on the steep slope.

Several days passed. The rain ceased, the air dried, Tha-two picked up its pace again, and at last they came to a V of high cliffs where they might be protected from predators or the elements.

"Thank Vensor for little mercies," Flores muttered.

"If I have to climb one more slope, I'll be shivering worse than Tha." Crestal flopped onto a pile of small stones. "Softer than any pillow in Klopus," she exclaimed with a happy sigh.

"A fire would sure be in order after weathering a week of rain."

She glanced down the path. "Should we?"

"No, we should not. But what do you think? Could anything have followed us after such a soaking? And there are barely enough tubers to feed us. How could a hunting party find enough?"

"I'm for risking it." Before Flores answered, Crestal extracted a flint that Flores had found in Tha-two's saddle and poised to strike a spark from Nebelroc.

He stiffened.

She noticed at once, and she too froze, flint still poised.

"A movement. Something is down the path." He shielded his gaze with a palm.

"But...surely nothing could still follow us. Not through marshes and across mountains... Could they?"

Flores sniffed. "If they did, then they could. Hold off on the fire."

Quietly, she slipped the flint back into the saddle bag.

He continued to stare, focusing, both palms now shielding his eyes.

"There it is. A shimmer of sunlight on irsrem...either a helmet or armor."

"How? How could anyone find us in this tangle of rocks?"

"Only a good tracker could. And that must be what is down below." He turned away. "No time remains. I had hoped to increase the distance between us and whoever that is, but they are clever and persistent. They are closer than before."

Picking Crestal up, he tossed her easily onto the saddle and climbed in front. He snapped the reins and the sinuous neck of the fanged beast arched up and forward and it hurried up the slope, its claws sending dirt and rocks tumbling.

Clambering over another ridgeline, they found the way easier and slid rapidly down until they came again to the path that nature alone had made, nothing rational frequenting where they were going—east where a vermillion sky hovered over perpetual cherry-red flames.

After a day, they paused on the far side of another, higher ridge and Flores peered over the crest to see if anything still followed.

An hour's journey behind them, a smudge crossed the previous ridge. It was immediately hidden in shadow and Flores did not waste time in speculation.

"We must travel faster." He turned to Crestal. "Are you certain we are on the right track to your Mok-sa people?"

She took a breath. "I can't be sure, Flores. I never crossed this area, not even as a child."

He stared at her as if understanding was finally beginning to dawn.

She leaped on Tha-two and Flores led them downward with care to avoid creating an avalanche of loose rock. When they reached the bottom of the slope, he climbed on and they trotted as fast as the animal could manage, to put as much mileage as possible between them and whatever it was that pursued them.

Another day passed. The air grew heated, and somewhere beyond the next ridge or two, a steady molten stream erupted in erratic fountains, reddening the sky.

They halted.

"Where now, Crestal?" Flores asked.

She shook her head in an almost panic. "I don't know. I don't know! I have never set foot here. I only know we must go beyond the flames. There are no flames where the Mok-sa live, there all is quiet and calm and cool."

Flores jerked the reins to halt Tha-two's growing nervousness and bring it back under control. "South. We must go south to circumvent the flames. From what I can see, it seems they lessen in that direction but increase to the north."

Crestal nodded. They turned and set out toward the

south, forced to retrace some of their steps.

The Turlicum became more nervous than the reven, constantly spying out and peering into every bit of shade. As the distance they were required to traverse grew greater, Flores frowned and his hand twitched, feeling the handle of his axe Nebelroc.

He halted.

"This will not work. At this rate we will soon stumble face to face with our pursuers, which we are unlikely to survive. It would be far better for us to arrange an ambush and end their threat in moments."

"If you believe it best, Flores."

Hiding Tha-two around a large boulder, they placed its muzzle over its jaws and induced it to sink level with the ground so as to make no noise. Crestal secreted a dagger in her cassock and hid behind the animal.

Flores crouched between the boulder and a narrow crevice, axe in one hand, rapier in the other with a small sike-hide round shield, his cap of reven talons downturned over his forehead, the top hirsute with vok-tail crests in the ancient style of his aristocratic House. Thus, he waited, his mind finally clear of every worry as he prepared once more to embrace the ritual of Atasan—the only time when he felt truly alive and joyful.

Half an hour passed.

Just when Flores felt his eyes beginning to droop from tension and boredom, he heard a crunch. Around the boulder something had stepped on a pile of leaves and sticks. Another crunch sounded, then several snaps as if a body of soldiers were hurrying forward.

One more snap.

Flores let out a roar and leaped out of his crevice. Exposing his body to whatever was coming, he yelled "Atasan wishes new corpses. Come and meet him!'

Nothing.

Flores peered about, took a step one way, then another,

peered into every slip of shade his eyes could find—and found nothing. No soldiers. No reven-na. No weapons seeking to take his life.

Turning about, he stepped around the boulder.

Here he froze.

Standing silently behind Crestal stood a large warrior in Klopan headgear, Crestal unaware of its presence.

"Crestal! Run!" Flores shouted.

Crestal turned and shrieked. In surprise, she fell clumsily backward over the reven where she ceased moving, unable to escape whatever fate the intruder may have in mind.

The Chief of the Turlicum swung his axe in the air to let the warrior know the battle would not be an easy one for him—he cut the air with his rapier.

The man did not react but stood in total silence, his own rapier still sheathed.

With a rush, Flores jumped to Crestal's side and put one arm about her to drag her to safety when she suddenly yelled.

"Tilsis!"

The warrior removed the Klopan cap and tossed it on the ground. He smiled a broad smile and dropped to one knee with his face lowered.

"Is it...can it really be you?"

Tilsis nodded more deeply and stood again—carefully.

Flores lowered his weapons, and the tension in his body evaporated. "Who could have imagined seeing you in the middle of this forsaken wilderness? However did you get here?"

He touched his mouth—still a mute.

Crestal burst with joy. "My servant from Ven. From the House of Numsenmur. And still unable to speak."

The man evinced a series of hand signals that only Crestal could read. She looked to Flores. "He says that Soorkrul sold him to the Klopans as a slave. After a year, he became a gladiator." She looked back to her former servant.

"Have you left them now? Or are you here to take us back?"

On hearing this, outrage crossed his brow. He stomped the Klopan cap into dirt and spat on it. He spread his hands open with palms up and again dropped to one knee, indicating his continued devotion to his former mistress.

"I still can't believe it," Flores said. He glanced behind Tilsis and again down the trail, looking for the rest of the Klopan hunting party.

"Tilsis, are you alone?" Crestal frowned with worry.

Again he nodded—yes. Withdrawing his rapier—as Flores watched with renewed distrust—Tilsis dropped it, too, as if to say 'No mistress but thou, dear Crestal'. He smiled too at Flores and pointed to his disgorged rapier as proof of his friendliness.

"So, it was none but you following us."

He nodded.

"And no one else pursues us?"

He smiled and nodded again: 'none'. More hand signals to Crestal. A long series of rapid-fire gestures.

"He says he was in the stadium when you fought the gladiators of Klopus. He did not fight you because there was something about you that reminded him of an old friend, and when you revealed yourself by removing your mask, he recognized you. He followed you out the stadium and out the gate. He stole a reven and has followed us ever since though he does not know where we are going or why. He says he has no life without us...that we are the only friends he ever had."

Crestal looked at Flores. "Is that possible?"

"He is here, so it is." Flores called to Tilsis. "A reven? Where?"

He pointed across the adjacent ridge. Gestured it was well tied and waiting.

"So, my old friend. What do you propose to do? We are headed east...to the land of gilas. Heresy and hatred follow us wherever we venture."

Tilsis cocked his head as if contemplating.

Flores smiled. "Are you in? Or will you go back to Klopus?"

The flash of anger again settled on Tilsis' face. Again he stamped on the Klopan cap.

Looking at Crestal, Flores grinned. "I guess that settles it. It seems your gila hosts will have more to deal with than just me."

Flores shook hands with his old comrade, and—to make certain there were no misunderstandings—embraced Crestal and received a passionate kiss from her.

Tilsis did not react, as if he already knew what had occurred in Crestal's heart back in the western wilderness where they had spent so much time together. The servant lapsed into his former role and lay on his back to nap.

"Not so soon, Tilsis," Flores said. "If what you say is true and there are no parties of Klopans pursuing us, then we can afford finally to slow our pace, but leaving your reven across the ridge is taking an unnecessary chance. Can you bring it? Our animal will no doubt welcome sharing its burden."

Tilsis rose to his feet. Tilting his head in agreement, he, at once, scrambled up the sheer face of the ridge and soon disappeared over the top.

Glancing at Crestal, Flores said, "Our friend has lost none of his stealthiness or ability to climb. No one else could have appeared behind us so quietly or tricked me into thinking enemies were before us with just a few thrown rocks."

Soon Tilsis returned riding an amphibious reven that was hardly distinguishable from Tha-two, and after both animals grazed on the few tufts of redentine, the three inspected the saddles and mounted. With hours of daylight yet to go, they set off in search of a detour around the growing heat of the neighboring valley.

This required much time. A week at least passed, and the three exhausted all of the supplies they possessed, and the redentine grass dwindled, and they began to think more and more of fresh fish. Yet there were no more bodies of water. Even the small stream they had followed dried up.

At last, however, it became apparent that they had circumvented the fiery valley and were now traveling east of it and the craggy ridges grew fewer and lower and one day they crossed the last ridge and beheld a wide open plain, a plateau, where herds of lyarts and sikes grazed on plentiful grass beneath a sky perpetually overcast with clouds of ash.

And in the center of the plain washed a large lake, and even as they watched, pods of wild reven-na splashed and caught fish or cud redentine along the muddy edges.

No more welcome a sight could the travelers have imagined. They spurred their mounts down the last slope in a hurry to catch their own fish, for both themselves and their hungry beasts.

The herds gave way, though did not flee, indicating clearly that they had never been hunted in this locale and did not regard the three travelers as predators.

An hour passed, and the three came to the lake. Tha-two was so famished that it snatched several fish in sequence and swallowed them whole, leaving nothing for Flores or Crestal. Tilsis' mount, on the other hand, behaved differently. Tilsis tied a rope around its throat, and when the reven caught a fish, Tilsis tightened the rope to prevent it swallowing and with a backward pull on its reins, induced the beast to release the fish. Doing this twice more, Tilsis was able to feed the lot of them and released the rope so his reven could catch more fish and eat its fill.

No longer concerned about roving bands of slavers, they lit a large campfire and cooked their conquests. Laughter and happiness filled the wide valley, the three finally relaxing, their trials behind them, future tribulations left to the future.

They settled for a long dreamless sleep, the three close together and smiling: Flores and Crestal arm in arm; Tilsis adjacent with his back turned to them and smiling most of all.

When they woke, more than a day and a night had passed. They arose in afternoon and were relieved to see nothing had changed. The lake remained filled with fish and splashing reven-na. The herds of ungulates had returned to graze peacefully not far off, presenting easy opportunities to catch one for dinner. The clouds drifted high overhead in scattered altocumulus sprays. Their own reven-na lay contentedly beside them, staring with curiosity at their wild cousins but giving no indication that they wished to join them.

"Where next, Crestal?" Flores asked, sitting beside her.

"Next?" she replied.

"Yes, where next? Is your city on the other side of this lake? This plain is vast, it will take us many days to bypass it if it lies farther to the east."

She looked at him without comprehending. "It is not to the east, Flores."

Now he looked confused and Tilsis sat up, perplexity on his face, as well.

"Then where, dear wife? How much farther must we travel?"

Crestal stood. "Why, we are there, Flores. We have arrived where I grew up. I remember it well now."

The two men exchanged puzzled stares. Had Crestal lost her reason?

She turned and gazed back at the last crag and pointed at a high tor that thrust out of the crag and presented a flat vertical face. "It is there, Flores. That is their city gate."

Stunned, the men dropped their jaws.

"City? I see nothing but stones and a small spring flowing."

"Pack our animals, Flores. We have but to approach and they will let us in."

Tilsis and Flores glanced at each other again. Tilsis shrugged as if to say 'Let us humor her in her delusion'. They did as she suggested and in another few moments she was leading them and their reven-na toward the rocky tor.

When they came to the vertically flat surface, nothing was visible that might suggest the tor was anything but a natural formation—no signs, no ramparts, no windows. Just blank bare stone.

Crestal picked up a length of dry wood and knocked on the face.

A minute passed.

Just as Flores glanced back to Tilsis with a pitying expression for their dear Crestal's having lost her mind, a sudden grinding filled the air and the face pulled inward on a hidden axis to expose a dark interior.

Too stunned to speak, the men peered.

Crestal walked inside two dozen feet before finally turning and beckoning to them with a smile. A hint of light shone from somewhere up what appeared to be a long corridor. "Bring the reven-na."

They stepped forward, leading the animals who shied but then cooperated.

Fifty feet inside, the gears reversed and the gate slowly cut them off from the outside world with a dull thud.

"This way."

They followed her until they came upon a longer, larger corridor, in fact a veritable city street such as one might encounter in a large imperial capital, with fluted columns flanking each side, and smooth flagstones beneath their feet, and—most surprising—an aqueduct of water for them to quench their thirst at will.

Vertical shafts penetrating the ceiling cast patches of light and brought fresh air onto the avenue so they did not feel confined.

Turning the corner, they came face to face with a dozen people—apparently residents of this strange place.

Crestal raised one hand. "I have returned to my home. My name is Crestal. I request permission to enter, along with these who rescued me and kept me alive in the years I was gone."

Their greeters stepped full into the light of a wide shaft above. They were unmistakably women with smooth faces and shoulder-length hair, though they were not dressed in the dark cassock that Crestal preferred, the kind of cassock that the Guild in Klopus forced all gila-sa to wear when in public. Instead, they wore loose-fitting grey shirts with long sleeves and grey pants to their ankles, their necks and faces entirely uncovered, though they seemed to have no breasts. Appropriate for people who live underground, Flores thought. Their hands, however, stood out as something he had never seen—abnormally large and ending in lethal-looking claws that made traditional weapons unnecessary.

One spoke, "Welcome, Crestal. I do not remember you, but of course all gila-sa who find our civilization are welcome among us. You have nothing to fear. We honor you and your friends here in our city of Grace."

"Thank you—"

"My name is Lorenda. Welcome and make yourself at home. In Grace, everyone is equal." Lorenda glanced at Flores and Tilsis and at their animals whose long necks towered over the women, who nevertheless did not appear nervous in the least. She furrowed her brows. "Everyone civilized, that is. Men, not being civilized, I'm afraid are another matter, and there will be some discussion necessary. What are your companions' names?"

Crestal pointed at her servant. "This is Tilsis. He is mute so cannot answer you."

"Oh. And this one?"

The Turlicum stood straighter and spoke for himself. "I am Flores, Chief of the Turlicum, Reven Clan of the city of Ven, capital of the Three Valleys, and one-time emperor of its vast Empire."

Lorenda shrugged and said nothing but behind her a bright tinkling laugh erupted.

One of the women stepped in front of the others. She was not like the other women but was dressed in a loose-fitting yellow tunic that exposed her legs and arms, her hands were entirely normal, and her tunic barely covered ample breasts. Her face was strikingly beautiful, and she stared at Flores with a calm contemptuous gaze but a gaze somehow mixed with other suppressed longings.

She laughed her bell-like, tinkling laugh again.

"Nara!" Flores exclaimed.

"Yes, Flores. Are you surprised?"

He blurted, "The Ritual of Penitence. The pyramid at the end of the world. Atasan. He sent you to the land of women."

She nodded. "To here...the city of Grace."

"In the pyramid. It was you all along...and not Amina."

Nara stopped smiling and dropped her gaze to where the shaft of light played on filaments drifting in the air. She looked up at him again. "And who is this with you?"

"Crestal. As she said."

"I mean: Who *is* she, Flores?"

He glanced at Crestal as if debating whether complete honesty was the best policy in this instance. Reaching forth, he drew Crestal to his side. "My mate. And my love. Always."

Nara stopped smiling. From within, she forced the smile to return. "My own welcome to you, dear Crestal, and of course, to Flores, too. As special advisor to Lorenda over all the workers of Grace, I am at your service. Do not hesitate to call on me."

Lorenda interrupted. "Well, I am glad we all know each other. That makes your adjustment to Grace simpler, you men especially. This worker detachment will take you to the quarters that we always have prepared and waiting for visitors. We even have a meadow open to the sky for your reven-na to graze in complete security. Our leader will want to meet with you soon."

CHAPTER 18

With that, Lorenda walked away and soon turned a corner into an adjoining corridor. The three newcomers followed Nara and the worker-women up the broad avenue, marveling at its resplendent decorations framed by the seemingly never-ending portico of fluted pillars. Each pillar was at least twenty feet tall and cast the city of Grace in an aura of mystery and majesty. How could such a vast concourse inhabit a mountain? As they progressed, leading the two reven-na, their eyes fell on increasing numbers of women entering and departing via multiple connecting corridors, and they soon began to feel helpless, even lost, in their growing multitude—all women, all workers devoid of anything remotely feminine in Flores' eyes. All wasted no time and none loitered even a moment, intent on unobvious and unstated purposes.

After an hour of penetrating these masses, and traversing several huge sky-flung chambers, also glowing with vertical shafts and cleaned by aptly placed air shafts, the walls of which shone with marble and gold, they finally came to a set of small rooms aligned in a row.

Nara smiled and pointed. "Your new homes. Choose which you like. There are currently no women from the outside world living in Grace except for myself and you." Nara glanced at Crestal.

A broad opening lay at the end of the residential corridor. Flores glimpsed open sunlight and sward the color of redentine through the opening. "That is for your reven-na. Grace is famous for its hospitality." She grinned.

Flores omitted asking why they were the only guests if

the place were so hospitable.

"Thank you, Nara," Crestal said.

Nodding agreement, Tilsis removed the saddles from the beasts and led the beasts of burden to the pasture where he turned them loose to gambol happily.

Also nodding his appreciation, Flores waited for Nara to leave before turning his back and escorting Crestal within the nearest chamber—he noted with more than a bit of suspicion that two stolid worker-women took posts by the entrance. There could be no coming and going without their knowing.

Finding their new rooms more than adequate and beautiful with lapis lazuli and opal-marbled sides, Flores and Crestal settled into the first genuine beds they had seen since leaving Ven so many months before. Actual linen pillows containing bird feathers and five-limbed monkey fur beckoned to them, and before they knew what they were about, they collapsed in satisfied comfort.

The next day, appropriately late in Flores' opinion since he and Crestal could not have awakened any earlier even had they wished, Nara arrived at their rooms. Behind her was her usual escort of almost a dozen beefy-looking and militant in expression worker-women.

"Morning, my little friends," she gaily called, unable to suppress her tinkling laugh. "How did you like your web...I mean, your bed?" She laughed at her mistake.

Her mood was contagious, and Crestal replied, "Our quarters could not be better, Nara. I don't suppose a little refreshment might be available somewhere?"

"Only the best. But it will take some walking to get there." She breathed deeply. "The hour is already late, kids. I suggest we cover the distance at once. We don't want to be late for our meeting."

"Meeting?" Flores asked.

"Oh yes. Our meeting with Mother cannot be missed. Her schedule is busy...always busy." She pointed up the corridor toward the main avenue. "Mother insists on meeting every gila rescued from the outer world. Mother's love is endless."

The three newcomers fell in line and found that their guards—long experience led Flores to think of all 'escorts' in such terms—surrounded them and hurried them forward. Rejoining the main avenue, they were once more swamped by the enormous numbers of worker-women, and Flores once again noticed that no masculine face was to be seen. As no soldiers, no weapons, no recalcitrant slaves, no eunuchs, and no pretty women—only Nara.

She glanced with half a smile at Flores as if she were reading his mind. Then she looked ahead and let the half-smile become full, her youthful lustrous lips broadcasting beauty, as it were, in a desert of unbeauteous thorns, matched by the beauty of her bared legs and throat.

Flores found that, try as he might, he could not restrain his eyes from glancing at her form on occasion. Tilsis too, himself also no eunuch.

Suddenly the crowd parted. Their escort subtly but firmly pushed the three to one side, and the throng of women made a gap down the center of the main pillared avenue for a new throng—as out of place in the city of Grace as any Flores could imagine, he already becoming used to the idea of a city consisting entirely of females.

A hundred or so boys no more than three months of age, so of course fully functional as small eager warriors as all males on Maalstrom become by that age, were marching in unison, arms locked, faces vibrant and upraised, some already having tattooed themselves from obscure resources inside Grace and a few even sporting sharp shivs.

Flores peered at them with alarm. In less than a year they would be fully grown and if not acclimated to a warrior clan where older warriors could temper and discipline their warlike natures, they could become a threat to Grace itself.

"Nara," Flores said, "What clans will these join? Where

is Grace's army that will contain and train these boys before they become too old to control?" He stood looking at Nara in sincere puzzlement.

"Clans and armies? We have none."

"None," Flores exclaimed.

"None at all. Mother has taught us that there is no need for soldiers in Grace. They are only a disruption and a danger to us."

"What will you do with them, then?" Flores and Tilsis stared in equal confusion. "Preparing for battle is what men do, what they wish to do."

"We know that, Flores. We know that well here in Grace, just as I knew that when I was raised in the Temple of Ven, serving the goddess Vensa, when I observed the constant violence of the men in Her outer city. Violence is all that men are good for. It is indeed all they want. Therefore..." she glanced at the endless column of marching three-month-old boys with some clutching knives in their hands, "they are being expelled. Mother has decreed that all boys upon reaching this age must leave Grace forever, to find whatever home they can find in the outside world. They are being escorted to the outer gate where they will set out on their own and leave Grace in peace. It is what we wish. It is what they wish. They do not want to live in a city of only women."

Flores exchanged another confused look with Tilsis. Well, that was one solution.

The columns of boys finally passed, and the last disappeared in the direction of the city gate before the immense crowd of women returned, relief visible on their faces, and the three resumed their trek deeper into the womb of Grace.

The shafts of light grew taller, and the light they admitted grew paler, and the air that was channeled through the city less refreshing. For the first time, they saw groups of muscled women hauling material in deep-draft wagons, no motive power but their own, swathes of dirt on their cassocks, their destination some distant opening for dumping the results of their constant labor.

"We are always growing, always extending the corridors of Grace to other areas." She glanced at them. "You would be surprised, I think, if you knew how far." Nara paused. "Even I, who have been granted such privileges in what was once a foreign city, do not know exactly how far. I am not privileged to that extent."

For some reason, Flores felt a bit relieved to know that Nara's power in Grace was not infinite. She, too, after all, was a guest like them.

They arrived at a small courtyard and entered. Of light, there was almost none, and the three stumbled until Nara lit a portable oil-lamp. As the flame rose, it cast its pallid glare over a bizarre congeries of misshapen stems the size of stunted trees.

Flores squinted through the darkness to see. Nara brought the flame closer till his eyes took in the essence of what grew there.

"Mushrooms," he blurted.

"Of course," Nara said, "this is the sole food for our entire city." She peered on the grey stems in satisfaction. "This is the source of our strength, the energy that feeds our industrious multitudes as they labor within the earth, spreading the glory of Grace under the land. We have no need for other nourishment. We women of Grace do not defile our purity with the flesh of slaughtered animals. Our males' desire to consume flesh is another reason why we exile them into the wilderness. No true Mok wishes to eat meat. All you see here are vegetarians, preservers of Mother Maalstrom's gentle bounty."

"I-I don't know what to say," commented Flores, Crestal close by his side.

"No need to say anything," Nara continued. "Help yourself. Take what you wish from our holy plants and eat it raw. This substance requires no cooking, no expenditure of fuel. You will find it refreshes you instantly."

While Flores watched, their escort of worker-women waded into the midst of the stems and in short order left half the plants devoid of branches and consumed a number of round fruit hanging from the rest. Without having even to climb or fly to reach high branches, Flores noted, since these fungus plants were short and squat like hedgerows of bushes.

Memories rushed upon him of the fungus trees on the Isle of Vensor that fed flocks of malkops after they glided in on their leather wings from their world-wide wanderings. Such similarity could not be mere coincidence. But how they might be related, he could not imagine, except by the simple formula: the will of Vensor.

Crestal gorged herself—Flores less so—Tilsis hardly at all. The Turlicum found himself thinking of roast slabs of dismembered sikes such as he had observed grazing around the plain-girdled lake outside the city, a longing he thought best not to express.

He wondered more at Nara's comments about the extent of Grace's tunnels. Just how far did Grace's tunnels go? They seemed so vast already as they walked among the crowds of workers that it seemed impossible that anyone could personally experience them all.

They came to a central hub where several wide avenues intersected and at the center stood a cupola well-lit by an especially large shaft that traveled to a distant aperture set in the craggy mountains above.

"We must descend from here," Nara said, "if we are to keep our appointment." For a minute Nara stood as if waiting for something. Just when Flores thought she might be deliberately missing their appointment, Lorenda suddenly appeared out of the crowd with a new escort of taller, more muscled worker-women.

"Good morning," laughed Nara.

"Follow me down these steps," Lorenda replied without

a smile, peering carefully at the three newcomers.

At the prospect of plunging downward into darkness, Flores' tension returned, but as Flores' companions made no objection, he too reluctantly followed.

Down they climbed, down a circular stairwell, interrupted at frequent intervals by wide platforms lit now by infrequent long-lasting paraffin-lamps. However did the workers manage to remove such quantities of earth up such twisted steps? he wondered. Maybe there were other stairwells, larger and dirtier, even circular ramp-wells for wagons.

At the third such wide platform they were hit by a wash of steam. As the steam dissipated and he was able to see again, a scene hit his eyes such as he had not imagined. Strewn over the vast platform that stretched into dark oblivion were thousands of tan-colored eggs, over them hovering hundreds more worker-women, except here, far underground, they were not women but girls.

Still, no one comparable to Nara in beauty, or to the gorgeous, winged women he had witnessed during the Flight, these girls were merely younger versions of the laboring sexless workers of the city, lacking any of the signs of womanhood that a man's gaze naturally seeks. The girls stroked the eggs and fed them solutions of watery milk mixed with bits of mushroom, and a constant stream of girls carried the largest eggs past them to climb the steps to the upper regions, a few eggs separated by unobvious criteria.

Down they went again, farther into the depths of the planet. The next platform was as wide as the one above, but here the vast concourse of eggs were smaller, whiter, and the girls who tended them, younger. But still as sexless as those in the chambers above. As above, these girls exited in a constant stream, carrying the larger white eggs, headed to the chamber they had just seen overhead, while still more girls carried the smaller eggs into the chamber via another entrance.

To still lower levels they climbed down.

At what Flores deemed must be somewhere near the bottom of creation where the god of the underworld burned in anticipation of accepting those whom Vensor had rejected—those whom the malkops had failed to retrieve in war, and who therefore had been left to rot in the earth, their souls eternal prey to Atasan. Flores' soul recoiled by instinct at having penetrated so far into the realm of the Adversary of Men.

Strange sounds echoed from a huge chamber as they walked past, sounds that reminded Flores of the squirming of great slugs as they strove to fulfill some obscure task. Who was he kidding? Flores asked himself. He had seen enough in the Temple of Ven not to finally understand the motive forces behind Maalstrom. Inside that chamber could only be a cohort of enormous quasi-insect queens like Vensa Herself in Ven, but these queens not residing in a vat of water labeled a 'Sacred Spring' but laid upon soft dirt to live out their secluded lives giving birth like automatons, these queens of Grace incomparably larger than Vensa. In confirmation, he watched streams of girls entering and leaving, those entering bringing a huge supply of shredded mushrooms, those exiting carrying forth the small eggs for depositing upstairs, while more dozens of fully grown workers stared at the visitors with hostile suspicion even while laboring.

On they strode, hurried past the vulnerable birth chamber by their dour guards. A new vista opened before them: a vast cavern that stretched into pitch darkness that no light had ever pierced, the floor broken by disjointed gaps. As he glanced down, he realized they were as vertical as wells, no handholds visible on the sides, but falling down to the most remote depths of Maalstrom, if the planet indeed had any terminus to its depth. His guides strode past as if unconcerned, the sheerest depths apparently inspiring no fear in them, their eyes, half-blind on the surface, seeing better than any in this dim, barely lit interior.

At last, they paused before a simple wood-built double-door guarded by yet another squad of frowning worker-women, these the largest and most muscled Flores had seen, their clawed hands showing nails curved like scimitars.

Lorenda addressed the women guards. "Tell Mother we have come."

Nara immediately added, her voice trembling, indicating that not even she was entirely confident in the face of Lorenda and the perpetually present guards. "Yes, we have come for our appointment with Mother. She's expecting us."

For a time, they waited standing in the narrow corridor lit only dimly by two paraffin lamps flanking the double-doors. Once more, Flores felt dissatisfaction rise within, though whether it was due to the impatience of his nature—no longer willing to tolerate the slowness or apathy of others as he did when he was younger—or his eternal suspicion of the true motives of others, as his experiences had inexorably led him to.

The doors opened.

Flores felt his experiences meet with another surprise. Somehow, he had expected a slug-like queen like the ones he had just sensed in the prior chamber, or at least an overweight gila soon destined to join the land-bound queens, or even a winged girl set to fly in the next Flight, but before him stood a simple woman. And not a woman like the supervisor Lorenda, or another dour worker capable only of taking instructions, but an aged crone who had seen more Maalstrom years than even Flores could contemplate. Indeed, the lines of her face and her bountiful still blondish hair and the curves of her torso impelled into Flores' mind a sense of distant beauty to match that of a youthful malkop but long eroded though still redolent with hints of what she once had been.

"We are here, Mother," Lorenda said.

Nara was quick to make herself known also. "On time, as you requested!"

It became instantly clear to Flores that he had met the engine that ran Grace, which was not to be found in the perpetually squirming egg-makers of the previous chamber. This was Grace's true queen—a simple aged crone.

"Don't stand on ceremony, children, come in...come in. Have you had your morning refreshments?" Her voice creaked with such age that Flores could not help but think that some marvel had preserved her body in selective fashion, her voice alone betraying her true age.

"Yes, Mother." Nara answered before Lorenda could speak. "Thank you again for your kind thoughts."

"Kindness it is. But also the requirements of life. I always pay proper attention to the requirements of life and of our bountiful city of Nature's Grace."

Once inside Mother's chambers, Flores noticed that one side of the large room seemed devoted to studies of some sort, much as his own L-shaped chamber back in his estate of Turlicum in Ven where Flores and his ancestors had accumulated various stores of knowledge, including puzzling references to stars and orbits which he himself did not understand but which were accompanied by many scrolls of palimpsest and authored by Ven's more learned scribes.

Here, in Mother's chamber were similar items. Not just a large library of scrolls of palimpsest but a chalkboard scribbled with incomprehensible notations and tables covered by vats of fluids like an alchemist might keep, with a collection of rare glass containers. A strange acrid smell came from that side of the room, but not of ozone, which thought, at least, comforted Flores.

Mother was not alone with her usual coterie of stern women guards, but several other persons were also present, quite unexpected to be found within. The newcomers clapped their eyes on three other women who appeared behind Mother—for the first time Flores saw up-close candidates for Grace's Flight. Enthusiasm and joy flowed from their speech, from their smooth youthful faces. Not nude as they would be on the day of Flight, these girls were modestly clothed—but through a gap in their clothing on their upper spines bulged solid muscle to power large iridescent wings, though no wings were here present, apparently having been recently excised. Now land-bound, how could their Flight occur?

Also, for the first time, Flores and his friends caught sight of what he could only describe as drones. Sitting at the other end of the chamber sat three young men—also sporting solid muscles on their upper spines—also lacking any wings. They were dressed less completely than the winged girls and reclined in what Flores could only think of as studied indolence, their eyes rarely leaving the vivacious girls fluttering always near, contributing nothing but accepting drink and food offered by the dour workers. They said no more than did the mute Tilsis, leading Flores to think that perhaps they too were incapable of speech, though perhaps were merely incapable of directing their focus on anything but their assigned paramours, their shorts bulging greater than Flores would have supposed to see in normal Vensor males. Drones, indeed, he thought. Such males as these could never defend a city with sword and buckler but seemed made for something else.

A squeak came through an open door from a back chamber. Without waiting for an invitation, Flores slipped past the escorts in Mother's room and peeked—he glimpsed a large cage with iron bars and straw on the floor, inside the cage a pair of five-armed spider monkeys clinging to tree limbs set crosswise. Their eyes locked on Flores' stare and they spun on their tree limbs with happy excitement, squeaking louder. His gaze wandered farther, and he spied a cage with bats, then several more cages containing other animals, some familiar and others unfamiliar, and even farther back he glimpsed something huge and lumbering in a cage barred with thick irsrem that no amount of strength could break.

Glowering worker-women gently but firmly pushed Flores out of the doorway and shut it so he could no longer see what was happening in the other room.

Mother seemed not to notice but turned her attention on each of the newcomers. "Nara, I hear that one of your group is from the far city of Ven."

Nara stepped forward. "Yes, Mother." She glanced at Flores. "This man is Flores of the Turlicum Clan. I knew him well when we both lived in that city."

Nodding, Mother said, "As I knew *her* well. When Vensa lived among us."

Flores puzzled at this. The former Queen of Ven, Vensa, had once lived elsewhere at some time in Her long life? She had lived with Mother in Grace? How long ago must that have been?

"And Tilsis, another warrior from the city of Ven, an expert in war and fighting."

Without smiling, Mother slowly nodded at both Tilsis and Flores as if contemplating the potential consequences of allowing violent males inside Grace's walls.

"And of course the young woman I spoke of, the one who brought the men here, Crestal, who was a participant in one of our sacred Flights."

Flores turned to stare at Crestal. Of course, he had known this and he could not explain why a statement of this simple fact had struck him like a revelation. For the first time he found himself peering at her upper spine where the remnants of muscle that had once motored two enormous wings were still present, though atrophied until almost gone. He forced his eyes away.

Had Flores sensed something else, something in Nara's tone of voice, when she spoke of Crestal, when she mentioned that Crestal had brought the two male heretics into Grace? Could Nara's former passion for Flores and her vengeful nature be now so far removed from her that Flores and Crestal should now trust her? What choice did he have, submerged in this underground city, where Nara's word counted for more than a thousand of his excuses?

Mother brightened. "A survivor. What joy that brings to me, to see that one of our ambassadors to the outer world has returned to bring news of the success of my efforts."

Flores wondered what that phrase could have meant. Why should Mother ascribe Crestal's success to Mother's efforts and not to the efforts of the rest of Grace? But perhaps some things are not for a mere mortal to comprehend, even a mortal as fortunate and inquisitive as Flores. He noted that Nara looked a bit crestfallen as if she had hoped for a different response from Mother.

"What news do you bring, Crestal? If I heard your name from Nara rightly, since my hearing is not what it used to be."

Crestal nodded submissively. "My name is Crestal, yes." She looked up. Submission with her was always a façade. "The last Flight was glorious, Mother. I watched my sisters flood the sky with their numbers, heading for their destined ends. Flores helped by making their path safer."

Mother listened and smiled and nodded with happiness. "Good. Good. For that is how we claim the future, how Grace expands its endless numbers over the face of this desolate planet, how we will finally make Maalstrom our own."

"Yes, Mother. It is good." Crestal lowered her face again.

Nara ceased smiling.

Flores thought: how much more does Nara know of Mother's purposes? Any more at all? What, anyway, is a 'planet'? And why would Mother want to make Maalstrom her own?

Mother seemed to weaken. She slouched and two strong workers took hold of her arms and propped her up. "That is all for today, my children. I tire and must rest." She turned to Lorenda and the other workers. "Take these bright young things to their quarters. Leave their assigned male companions here. I must have my way with them before I can know what will come next." Mother glanced once at Nara—Flores noted that Mother's mind was instantly focused again. "Do not forget your own appointment, Nara. That is due soon. You know why."

Nara lowered her own face in submission—no trace of recalcitrance was possible in Mother's own quarters with Her squads at hand.

Flores glanced at Tilsis—each looked lost, no explanation of anything that had transpired in Mother's room coming to the minds of the two soldiers.

Mother gestured and Lorenda and her acolytes gently but firmly pushed the newcomers from Mother's chambers, and after another long walk past the various reproduction rooms, up the series of stairwells, and through corridors crowded with endless throngs of dull workers, they arrived at last at their previous quarters.

A delivery of mushrooms arrived and Crestal fell to devouring them with relish. Flores and Tilsis considerably less so, with some reluctance in fact, the two men already starting to feel famished by the plain vegetarian diet.

CHAPTER 19

N ara said, "That is all for now. You are dismissed."
The group of dull-witted workers dropped their gaze and nodded in submission then turned and crawled out of the tunnel they had just dug, heading back to more traveled areas of Grace where they could clean their sharp claws of the recent rock and dirt, and relax with a selection of fungus fruit until they might be needed again.

Nara watched as they made their single-minded way back to the main parts of the city. Once they were gone and she was quite alone, she walked for a time behind them as if planning similar activities—then halted.

Her eyes flitting in the almost dark for possible stray workers who might look and tell, she gradually fell back to where the newest tunnel addition to Grace lay. She had even had the foresight to dig a second tunnel close to the first, but in a different direction, containing some of the detritus pulled from the first tunnel. For what she had planned, it would not do for the results of her commandeering of the dullest of dull workers to be known.

Sucking a breath—not that it was inordinately easy for a surface dweller to breathe normally in every stretch of tunnel—she slid quietly inside the crude corridor and followed its length to the end.

Here she paused. Listened. Pursed lips. Frowned and furrowed her forehead. From somewhere a sound seemed to penetrate the *terminus ad quem*. Satisfied, she extracted from her tunic a steely span, and with infinite care, soundlessly carved a smaller sac-de-cul of the cul-de-sac. An hour passed. Still struggling to breathe, she set her face with determination and continued to scrape until she was rewarded—just before she felt she must collapse from the tension—by a very small hole.

Light penetrated through the hole, accompanied by an increase in volume of what sounded on the far side. Gradually expanding the hole to the size of her eye, she peeked through.

On the far side was a wide chamber filled with cages of animals, some of which she recognized, with apprehension; others were unfamiliar to her, which from their appearance inspired heart-stopping fear.

She glimpsed the five-armed monkeys—fortunately for her, swinging in their cage at the far end of the chamber. She saw isia—and wondered at the extent of the madness that alone could explain the presence of the poisonous centipedes. She watched a vicious ros itself eyeing another cage inhabited by a timorous youthful reven eager to flee the ros. Down the line she saw a sike, a vok, several bats, even a captured malkop, and Nara wondered at the daring and sacrilege of such an act, the abduction of one of divine Atasan's own children.

At the nearest end and close to the hole she had punched in the wall, was the largest cage of all, the cage with irsrem bars to house what its captors regarded as one of the strongest animals on Maalstrom: a large shaggy humanoid with two powerful legs, two immense arms, and a beetled brow with an expression of even greater dullness than the worker-women of Grace. The creature toyed with a thick bar of iron that it bent and unbent in play and occasionally touched the rotting carcass of a lizard draped over its sloped forehead as if displaying its prowess or rank to onlookers. A small sharp blade protruded from its side, which the creature seemed not to notice, or the thin blood trickling from the wound.

"A dragabond," Nara said to herself. "Whyever would Mother want to tinker with one of those, which I had thought were no more than fearful legends?"

Her eye moved past the cage with the dragabond to a smooth white table with six carved rorewood legs of immense age, but—like Mother—were prepared to endure longer. On the table sat several containers of clear tear-glass, irsrem, purified to eliminate its natural obscurant iridescence.

The first container was a cube enclosing a small cloud of minuscule insects hovering and buzzing over a layer of muddy water to keep them alive. Nara peered at this but no understanding for why these should be present came to her mind.

The second container was more to her liking. An oblong affair, it showcased what she sought with all her tunneling: a glass receptacle holding a sphere of natural irsrem that housed a nest of leroo-sa, the common hornet of Maalstrom. Suspended over the nest, an open pipe led straight through the ceiling all the way to the distant sky, fresh air constantly passing down the pipe and through tiny openings in the sides of the receptacle by hidden crosscurrents so that the hornets would be always refreshed and have access to the outer world.

Other containers were strewn about the table and in the corners of the chamber, but none held Nara's interest but the nest of hornets. Carefully, she cut a square opening in the wall and climbed through.

"Let Mother's annual sting be performed now. When I am done here today, I will control my own destiny, not the other way around. Then let Mother try to continue enforcing her rules. Flores has arrived. It is time to put into operation my next move."

With that, Nara approached the hornet nest. Opening the front panel—which had no lock—she emulated what she had seen Mother do several times. Holding her breath, she ignored the hornets that buzzed in surprise and placed her hands on either side of the nest. Instead of rising up in anger, the insects ceased moving, and she focused her mind on the nest as if charging a rapier with energy. A slight smell of ozone drifted as the nest's iridescence changed to violet, then blue, then green, and finally orange as the temperature within heightened.

She maintained the high temperature for as long as she felt necessary to affect the change she wished to the animals within, then, concerned with the passage of time and the growing possibility of discovery, she released the nest. The color of the sphere reversed its sequence and changed from orange, to green, to blue, to violet, and finally back to the natural glittering iridescence of wasp-produced irsrem.

She approached the cage containing several bats. Unlocking the simple mechanism, she slid one hand into the cage and soon snatched one of the small animals. Returning to the hornet nest, she opened the box containing the hornet nest and tossed the bat inside. The wasps, now fully recovered from the coma she had induced, attacked the bat. In less than a minute, every hornet in the nest had stung the bat and it collapsed dead.

Using a utensil, Nara removed the bat and shut the cage again. Hurrying to her hole, she replaced the square section, sealed it carefully from the other side leaving only the small eyehole, and fled out of the tunnel where she threw the bat's corpse into a pile of refuse and covered it deeply enough that it would never be found.

Returning by a circuitous route to her surface quarters, Nara cleaned herself, then made a quick appearance in various places where she would be certain to be seen, including at the door where Flores, Tilsis, and Crestal were residing and she loudly inquired as to their health and domestic needs.

Satisfied that she had been seen by large numbers of people, Nara made her way quickly back to the little cul-de-sac via unfrequented routes and sped up the tunnel to the end where, once again, she spied what she could spy through her little spy hole.

Just in time. As she surmised, Mother and her helpers returned to Mother's quarters and entered the chamber of captive life forms received from various trade sources or seized via expeditions into the wilds. Nara had seen much in Grace that had induced her to resort to deception—not that deception wasn't embedded so deeply in her, as the former master of intrigue in her former home of Vensa's Temple, that it only needed a spark to reawaken in Grace.

"Help me further, my daughters," wheezed the aged crone's voice. "Like so. Hold me up by my arms, thin as my wretched limbs are."

"Yes, Mother," came the replies, at least four or six, bright and vivacious, from girls who measured their lives in months, to their 'Mother', who measured her life in centuries.

"Well, what do you think? How about you, Alpha-10327?"

"Think, Mother? About what, Mother?"

"Why, about our current situation. Not that much really changes within Grace from one generation to the next. But, of course, your limited lifespan would know nothing about that. But I know...I know!"

Alpha-10327 answered, "Our current situation? Whatever do you mean, beloved Mother?"

"And what say you, Alpha-10244? What is your opinion on the politics that ever moves beneath the surface of our home Grace?"

Silence answered Mother.

"And there is my problem in a single word, or more precisely in no word whatever. No one in this whole infinite pile of dirt with its mindless egg-makers and dull administrators and vacuous workers that do nothing all day but move garbage from one place to another, no one in this entire vast enterprise can answer me the simplest question. None understands how this city came to be, why we are here, how this place is run, or what our future holds."

"How is that, Mother?" came several voices in response. "Why, you made our city, Mother. You are why we are here, you run this place, and you command our future."

Mother cleared her aged throat until the sound turned into a groan. "Yes. Yes, and yes. But then again—no! Do you little virgins destined never to know a man have any idea what fate awaits us all once these sere bones give up their last?"

"Bones, dear Mother?"

"Yes, bones. Do you infants actually believe that an old woman like myself will live forever?"

"But of course, dear Mother. Of course you will live forever." The answers came tumbling bright and vigorous.

"Not so, my dears, not so. Even I, who oversaw the first cups of soil removed from beneath my feet by my own daughters when they could still stand, even walk, before they begat their first eggs, the grandmothers of your grandmothers back before the beginning of time, even I will not live forever, but one day, and who knows when that day will come, I myself will lay myself down before the empty stars with my eyes clasped on one out of all the firmament, and I will die, wishing beyond wishes that I could return to the single one from whence I came and not have to sink into the dirt of this misbegotten planet, this Maalstrom."

"Do not speak of such, Mother," they echoed in reply.

Nara sucked her lips in reaction to the anguish she heard from the youths.

"Still, on we must go, my children. We must keep breathing just a little longer. We must try once more to reverse the damage."

The silence of the vivacious girls exchanging worried glances was more eloquent to Nara than further words.

"The business at hand—and hear this well—and although you yourselves haven't the intelligence to understand what I am about to say, I will soon communicate my decisions to Lorenda and the other managers."

"As you say, Mother."

"The two men who have entered Grace are a danger beyond calculation. Mere mortals with lifespans no greater than your own, my dears, they nevertheless bring the potential of tearing our city to pieces. Because they are strong and forthright and intelligent beyond what you yourselves know—which is why I insisted on meeting them. And above all because they are fertile males and will in time arouse the interest of fertile females within Grace. This I cannot have! This I swear to stop. Grace produces fertile females and its own fertile drones whose only function in life is to fertilize their appointed females and then die. That is how Grace survives. That is how Grace prospers, infinite pile of meaningless dirt though it is. Not by the visitation of wandering cutthroats!"

"If you say so, Mother."

"Therefore, I will order the two men killed. They cannot live in Grace. They therefore have no future."

"As you say, Mother. And the others?"

Nara breathed shallowly. Who else could 'the others' be but her and Crestal?

"Crestal is one of us. She too poses a danger in that she was once sent out on a Flight. But she has now returned. We have no need of further queens in Grace, and if she remains, even though I will require her to take the sting of the hornet regularly, she will one day resist. Therefore, after the two males are destroyed, Crestal must either be mated with a drone and enclosed in one of our egg-producing caverns, or she must be exiled beyond our walls to fend for herself as she was supposed to do with her Flight. Meantime, however, she brings interesting news of what is happening in the outside world. So, she may remain in Grace for now."

"And the last?"

Nara caught her breath.

"Nara of the city of Ven, she who came from Vensa

Herself, Vensa my old acquaintance, one of those who accompanied me from the single star in the sky, Nara who lived with Vensa in the forbidden Temple of Ven before Vensa was mercilessly killed by soldiers sent by her own wayward daughter, Nesta of the Temple of Nesta in the city of Neset..."

Her ear to the thin partition, Nara strained to hear Mother's final pronouncement on her fate.

"Nara has no potential for Grace. She will never tolerate being confined in a cavern to make eggs. She is not of our DNA but bears only the DNA of her mother, Vensa, and that of the hornet. That merciless hornet that so upturned our little colony when first my Mok-sa landed on Maalstrom. She lives and breathes wasp! She is never to be trusted. She cannot mate with any of our drones. But she brings to our city something besides risk. She brings news, and not merely of Ven and our environs as Crestal brings, but news of greater prospects, news even of the glass pyramid on the far side of the world where Atasan resides. This news is of the greatest value to me. Besides, of all my companions here in Grace, only Nara has the intelligence to provide me with the occasional conversation that I can find in no other person. Even I, your everlasting Mother, need an open ear at times, and a mouth that speaks of things besides digging and fungus crops. Moreover, she is the best administrator I have. She is worth more in organizing Grace than a hundred of my loathsome, empty-headed supervisors like Lorenda."

"As you say, Mother."

"Therefore, my pronouncement for Nara is that she remain among us—dangerous though she is—and that she continue receiving the sting of the hornet here in this room so that she may never become pregnant. Should she miss her annual sting even once, then she must die. For Nara as a pregnant hornet queen inside our city of diggers would doom us all, even me."

More silence as the girls exchanged their worried

glances.

"Now to business, my beloved offspring. Have our soldiers bring in the two drones from the antechamber. It is time to implement my latest experiment. Perhaps this time we will finally find a way to reverse the terrible curse that befell our sacred Mok-sa when my gentle people first landed on this primitive planet so very long ago. Before we ourselves, despite our innocence and pacifism, brought chaos and war to all we touched."

"Yes, Mother."

A few moments passed and the two male drones whom Nara had seen earlier when in Mother's quarters appeared to Nara's vision through her little eyehole camouflaged by the shade cast by the large cage imprisoning the dragabond.

Behind the males were several muscled worker-women, though it soon became clear that there would be no resistance—the promise of sating their genetic urge to at last mate with their appointed princesses was enough to guarantee cooperation in any project that Mother may have planned.

By the light of a dozen flaring oil-lamps, Nara's one searching eye witnessed Mother cross the room, and with the further aid of her bevy of eager girls—themselves not destined to mate with anyone—Mother opened a mere slit in the top of the square container of muddy water that buzzed with tiny insects. Sliding a slender item like stiff cloth through the slit, Mother paused but a moment, then slowly—and more carefully than if she were handling a piece of the suns—she extracted the item. Mother raised it to a lamp and examined it in detail.

"Yes, my little dears. My evil little gnats who have unleashed more terror than anyone can contemplate. You are stuck fast for me, your mistress, to do with as I please."

Mother turned to one of the drones. "Come here."

He instantly obeyed.

"Sit and bare your arm."

He sat in the wicker-work chair and extended his arm toward Mother. Leaning down, she gently pressed the side of the item with the gnats onto the drone's naked arm.

"There. That's it. Now you have but to wait for these little beetles to do their work. We, however, do not need to wait. Their industrious innovative is already penetrating your body, already changing your very nature, making you vulnerable to the next stage in your transformation."

The drone continued to sit, his face puzzled but calm. Far be it for a drone born in Grace to question whatever fate Mother had in store for him.

An assistant cranked up the largest oil-lamp and Mother carefully burned the stiff cloth until nothing remained of the stuck gnats.

Across the room, the girls helped Mother approach the cage with the five-armed monkeys. She produced a long thin metal tube and as the girls made sudden pleasant coos and ahs to distract the animals, Mother gently scraped the skin of one monkey with the tube.

They returned to the experiment table where Mother directed a firm stare at the drone. "Now open your mouth, my child. I promise you this will not hurt. It well may eventually open vistas before you that you cannot now imagine...however, I will undertake to analyze the changes as they occur. If we fail, then we fail, and you will be released to a new and amazing life in the wild. But if we succeed! If we succeed, then all that you see here in Grace, all that has happened across this alien world can finally be cured, be reversed, and peace and plenty will come to the last of the Mok-sa."

"As you say, Mother," the girls said.

The drone, being mute, merely smiled and nodded. He opened his mouth and Mother expelled the thin scrape of flesh she had taken from the monkey into his gullet, and he swallowed it without expression.

"Done. That's done," Mother proclaimed. "Now the

next." With the aid of her coterie of pulchritudinous exemplars of flesh, the ancient crone stepped to the cage with the dragabond. The creature stared at her through its glittering irsrem bars with even more dullness and incomprehension as did the drones, and the girls gave vent to pleasant mooing and cooing while smiling at the animal, always standing well clear of its reach.

Stretching her tube through the bars, Mother took advantage of the dragabond's distraction—she pressed the tube forward to scrape some skin as she had done with the monkey—Mother's hand slipped and by accident the tube jerked forward and imbedded itself in the animal's side not far from the embedded blade that still bled red.

The girls halted in fear. Mother too paused for a moment, forgetting that she stood within reach of the creature, who must now be aroused with pain and anger. Watching from the cover of the cage's shadow, Nara also covered her mouth for what must happen to Mother as the dragabond, renowned for its immense strength, retaliated against its tormentors.

Nothing happened.

The creature seemed not to notice, as it had still not noticed the blade stuck in its side though it had been bleeding for hours from its earlier accident. It merely stood and stared at the girls, taking in their pleasant pleasurable expressions.

"Thum," the dragabond mumbled. It touched its face and the lizard draped on its forehead. "Thum neg."

Mother yanked the tube out and stepped away. Everyone breathed easy again.

"I had forgotten that these animals are too stupid to feel pain. It has yet even to be aware that it backed onto that carving knife this morning. We must figure a way later to safely pull it out."

Returning to the experiment table, Mother went through the same process as she had done with the first drone. She extracted another stiff cloth with gnats stuck to one side. The second drone stepped near and exposed his arm, and Mother affixed it for a few seconds, then withdrew it to be burned.

Finally, Mother drilled the drone with her stare. "Open your mouth, my child."

He opened his mouth and she deposited the live sample of the dragabond and immediately clamped his mouth shut until he swallowed it.

"On this planet, swallowing live flesh is both an act of monstrous consequence...and an act of profound creation. I of all people should know. If only those damned Chaldeans had foreseen that."

"You are dismissed, my child," she said to the second drone. "Tomorrow I will examine the results to see if Grace has any hope remaining."

The drone nodded and casually departed in company of several dour workers.

"Now, where is that Nara?" Mother asked, more to herself than the others. "I wish to know which constellations are visible where she journeyed and which are not."

The eye aperture went dark, and on the far side of the thin partition, Nara sped rapidly back to her quarters.

CHAPTER 20

Once done with the day's work, Mother lay down to rest. Long she rested and long her mind was quiet, its hopes and contradictions sinking layer by layer deep into a nether world of white frozen capsules and buried wheat and monsters in the sky. And then dirt. Endless leagues of dirt.

When her mind slowly reassembled and ascended layer by layer and she once more knew who she was and what she was about, she rose and called to her happy, attentive girls.

"Bring Lorenda. And bring my haulers. Today they must haul. Prepare them for a trip, for there are substances that I need to properly evaluate the results of my recent tests, and I no longer possess any in Grace."

"Yes, Mother."

Before many minutes had passed, the girls had summoned Lorenda and a collection of workers and they carried Mother in their ample arms out of her private chambers, past the caverns of heaving reproduction, up the stairwells, and into the main avenue where swarmed uncountable numbers of neutered former-women going about their eternal digging and repairing.

Down one special corridor they went, pausing on occasion to make certain Mother had all she needed, until finally they arrived at a round, delicately carved door on massive hinges, much like the one that offered access to the city itself, but this door not disguised.

Lorenda posted a score of the tallest and most muscled dour workers and they cranked open the door on its ancient hinges. Rarely had these hinges been called to use. But though they protested, they obeyed. The door opened on a long empty corridor lit by occasional tufts of light punched down from vertical shafts above, the corridor gradually narrowing to a point invisible in the distance. No decoration or color or anything denoting civilization softened the harsh glare of live rock chiseled with rough scoops and the desolate patches of sun that dazzled and shifted on the flat smooth floor.

The workers brought a four-wheeled low-heeled wagon. Lorenda directed it be placed in the corridor. Under her watch, much fungus and water was placed in the wagon, a spare wooden wheel, and even a store of scarce Klopan wheat. Another score of exceptionally muscled workers entered and took up the long tongue that drew the carriage.

Gently, Mother was put in the back amid blankets.

"Are you confident for this, Mother?"

"Yes, Lorenda. It was often I used to make this trip in the past when I was only a few centuries in age. Now I am old."

Lorenda made no comment but continued arranging Mother's necessities for the long journey.

"And this may be my last trip. But it must be done. My experiments have exhausted all of my stores, and I must replenish them or admit defeat and give up my efforts entirely."

"Yes, Mother."

"Now shut the gate behind me. You know what could result if by some chance unfriendly persons discover this back way into our city. Shut it. And guard it well. Do not open it again until you hear my familiar knock."

"I will remain here always, Mother, awaiting your return."

With those final words, the little caravan set out in virtually complete darkness and Lorenda slammed the huge gate closed with an echoic thud.

The day passed without event and the little caravan crept

forward, taking care not to jostle or inconvenience Mother, but moving forward, ever forward. The hours crawled by like reluctant death, the air grew stagnant with only the aged cargo having any difficulty catching breath, the grey skin of the denatured beasts that hauled the wagon, sweating into the firmament, the endless miles of straightness arrowing far into the earth as if nothing else mattered or existed. The worker-women took up a systemic grunt, first ten on one side, then ten on the other, the sheathed claws of their hands pushing the lateral cross limbs with constant effort, even the stony walls seeming to take up the chant. The effort ate up mile after mile, steadier than a ship's prow eats the endless waves. The day came and went and the periodic vertical shafts ceased providing the suns' light. As the night came on, as thick as that on the far side of the river Styx, the wagon, like Charon's boat, seemed to float in a black-enveloped ether, the darkness taking life on its own. And still the rhythmic chant continued, one side after the other, no other hint anywhere in this starless sky that life of any sort existed. Chant after chant; night after day; day after night. On the journey went, the tunnel always straight without bend or turn, following its directionless, expressionless arrow ever forward to the goal with the force of a primeval nature impossible to divert or tame. No pause for any reason, the devils in their dungeon needing no break, their bodies as inhuman as their minds. After what seemed eons, and after Mother herself had slept and awakened and pondered and again slept many times, the caravan came at last to a halt at a small oval. End of the line. Nothing further. Nowhere else to go.

But up.

A slender ladder of steel rose perpendicularly out of the oval space, up a circular tube that was itself lit by a fragile hint of sunlight. At Mother's direction, the haulers found an oil-lamp inside the wagon and Mother lit it, the latter act being beyond the capability of the strongest but least mentally acute of Grace's workers.

With care, they helped her out of the wain. Coming to the ladder, two haulers climbed easily up with one arm while lifting Mother with the other till they came to a simple circle that barred their further progress. Mother signaled to her two escorts to wait and listen. Nothing being heard from the upper side of the seal, Mother directed that the small wheel set in the hither side be quietly turned.

The hauler turned the wheel. Cautiously pressed it upward.

They lifted Mother higher so that her head extended above the lip. A half-light poured into the shaft.

Mother's eyes lit up. "Yes, my darlings. Treasure it is. In truth, of the best and noblest kind. You are to wait here until I return. I will have no need of you until then."

"Yes, Mother."

With that, the aged and decrepit Mother of Grace slowly climbed the remaining three feet of ladder and stood free in the wonderland of her dreams. One last time, she had arrived.

She stood on a concrete platform lit from all directions as in a panorama but as through diaphanous veils, the world surrounding her gentle and flowing, oblongs and trapezoids beneath her feet merging and chasing each other like clouds.

Peering through the shifting light, she ensured no one else was in eyesight and she walked cautiously around the edge of a gigantic metal bullet that loomed over her closer than a moon, negotiating each step since it would not do for her diggers to rescue her and thus be found in this place. Coming upon a wide entrance, she stepped carefully onto the wide, low metal platform, one end of which was stuck six degrees in the concreted floor.

A vast dark gulf yawned above the lowered platform. Mother climbed the several staggered steps and entered the darkness. Her eyes adjusted and she soon espied a lone figure busy deep within the bullet, focused on some poorly lit activity.

Mother nodded.

She approached, no longer cautious.

The figure turned. She beheld a man every bit as old as she, bushy eyebrows overhanging one blue eye and one yellow, both broadening like saucers as they caught sight of her.

"So, it is you, after all," the man said. "I sensed you were still alive. How are you, my dear? I can't count the years."

"No one can, Yezd. And who would want to count so many?"

"Only the few of us still remaining from that great day. What will this world be like once we have all finally passed?"

"You are suggesting 'After us, the deluge'?"

"'*Before* us, the deluge', you mean!"

Mother looked puzzled, though perhaps it was merely pensive. "I never expected to see you again, Yezd, especially not here in Source. You vanished from our Mok-sa so long ago that I can hardly remember those days."

"An age. An epoch."

"Why did you disappear? We had need of you. The Chaldeans assigned you to our expedition to make certain nothing happened to us. Then you vanished. And we were slaughtered."

"And who was it did the slaughtering, Vedega? It was you! I left because I was in fear for my life. You lost your head, Alpha-1, and you killed all the men in Klopus. What else should I have done but flee?"

"Not all. I left two men with their lives. And the six remaining engineers."

"It was unnecessary what you did. As unnecessary as what the men themselves had done."

"You are wrong, Yezd. My firmness saved the colony. The men, with those two fanatics Lamoc and Khurko in charge, were murdering our women, killing the very reason that our expedition came to this wretched planet."

"You yourself had left the colony, Vedega. You did not need to return."

"Return? Of course I had to return. When I heard how Lamoc and Khurko were killing our precious cargo I had to hurry back to put things right."

"Oh, you put things right, alright. You shot Lamoc and all twenty-eight of the men—"

"Twenty-six only...less those whom the lynch mob had already killed."

"You permitted a whole two to survive while executing all that remained of our male companions. You even threatened to kill the engineers who had struggled so hard to build Klopus for you." Yezd let his eyes wander. "Oh, what a leader you turned out to be."

"Do not scorn my efforts, Yezd. I don't have to listen to such from you and your rotten Chaldeans. 'The Chaldeans are never wrong'. Indeed!"

"In time I could have found the answer to what was tearing our colony apart, Vedega. I only needed time."

"Time? Time was working against us. Every day another of our women became pregnant with hornet DNA. Every day another city was founded somewhere filled with nasty little insect soldiers thirsting to destroy our defenseless town."

"But you attacked them first!"

"Of course. It is not my nature to let an enemy move first. When danger appears, I move first!"

"So, you recruited the remaining women, all stung to prevent pregnancy, and you marched all the way to the far settlement of Ven where our companion Vensa had found a gushing spring to give forth her hornet progeny. And you attacked it, you tried to kill Vensa herself, one of our own colonist companions."

Vedega sighed. "And I failed. Even though we had guns versus their tiny spears, I failed. There were just too many.

My female Mok-sa trudged back to Klopus where we tried to set up a defense against Vensa. But that too failed. She sent a horde of her bloodthirsty little savages and they took our town and burned it and killed many of us before I managed to rescue the few women still alive and our last two males and flee east."

"East? Across the flaming crags?"

"Yes, to a place where not even Vensa could ever find us."

"But you did take my advice before I left."

"Yes, Yezd. Your last words were: 'I am worried about the gnats, Vedega. Concrete in the swamp around Source, just to be sure.' So, I had the marsh under our starship concreted in, to remove the gnats before more damage was done. It was then we women were forced out, and we watched from a distance while Vensa's little savages burned what was left of Klopus and even ransacked the interior of Source."

"Concreting in Source was a good move." He let his eyes wander about the darkened interior of the vast starship. "There was almost no power left in our starship anyhow. And without the gnats, no further infections could occur from other forms of life."

"But Vensa's little savages never left. From afar I watched them rebuild Klopus into what it is today, a nest of vipers that forever eat the young of my own people."

"You are stricken by this result—"

"I am a woman, Yezd. Your commander, but still a woman. Unlike you men, I must rescue those in need. But those most in need, my own offspring, I cannot rescue but must live with the knowledge that Klopus, like this entire planet you call Maalstrom, will always eat my young."

"A tragic situation, Vedega. You have my condolences." He raised his eyebrows. "But surely you know that one of our ancient companions now runs Klopus. Engineer Number Four. It was he saved Source from destruction by those 'bloodthirsty little savages' as you call them. It is good that your anger calmed enough to let our engineers live."

Now she shrugged. "They too were men. I'll have no truck with men in my own city."

"Which brings me to ask... How?"

"How was it that I never became a hornet queen like so many of our colonist women?"

He nodded. "How, Vedega?"

"It was during the project when we were concreting in the starship, after we had executed all the men except the engineers, and we were preparing Klopus to defend it, still thinking we could survive in our little town. I was helping spread lime with the assistance of engineer Number Three. That's when it happened."

"Happened?"

"I had failed to properly protect my skin from the gnats. Unlike the other colonists, I omitted to wear both gloves, and a red patch showed on the back of a finger where I had become infected. Still not fully understanding the consequences, I allowed my mouth to fall open and an insect flew in."

"Into your open mouth, Vedega?"

"Yes, into my open mouth."

He furrowed his bushy brows. "And what insect was it?"

She frowned and looked down. She shifted her feet.

"What insect?" Yezd repeated.

"A winged termite. A fertilized female seeking a home."

He yawned widely. "So, I begin at last to understand."

"I myself was not affected due to the protection I had acquired from regular stings of the hornet I had brought back from my wanderings, you see, one of the hornet hives so I would never become a queen like the others. But as it turned out, my own children were contaminated with the termite DNA, and they themselves...meaning my daughters, of course, since naturally I expelled all of my male children to fend their way in the outer world—"

"Naturally," Yezd said without further comment.

"My daughters became large, became huge until they could no longer stand, and they erupted eggs like a river gives forth its tide, and the eggs became efficient workers who craved nothing more than to dig into the bowels of Maalstrom and be far from the light of its burning suns."

"Now we come close to the edge," Yezd said.

"The edge?"

"Why you are here. In Source. What you are doing to the life forms on this planet, even I had not contemplated."

"Doing? Why, the same as you, Yezd. I am trying to find the solution to our problem. I am trying to reverse the effect of the hornets, which infected our colleagues after the gnats broke their DNA. How to finally eliminate the hornet cities that even now are spreading across the face of this planet, as each hornet queen begets more hornet queens."

"But what exactly have you been up to in your new home, dear Vedega? The things I have seen...the things I have heard. All coming from the East where no hornet queen yet resides."

"Experiments, Yezd. Just like yours, but my own."

"Vedega. You are not a scientist. You are a commander with nothing more than a loud set of lungs. You cannot solve problems in planetary biology. Only Milo—"

"Milo is gone. He took the rover and fled, as you know. With his wives, I might add. Traitors all."

"And he vanished, I am sorry to say. I never found what happened with him, though a few cities his wives founded have fallen to Vensa and her own efficient offspring."

"But for myself and my own, I must keep trying."

"The rum-na, Vedega. I have seen peculiar specimens in the steppes, calling themselves Swift of Foot. Was that your doing? The result of your experiments?"

She straightened her back. "Someone must try to fix what happened to our colony. You have achieved nothing even in one thousand years."

It was Yezd's turn to lower his gaze. "You are correct. But still your way can only worsen the problem. You are wrecking everything."

"And what have you done! Besides fly around on the backs of malkops."

"I have been to the glass pyramid in the southern ocean which was erected by all the malkops of the world working together. The pyramid sits atop this planet's magnetic pole. I do not know whether the pyramid caused the pole to shift to the Eye, or whether the malkops built the pyramid on the magnetic pole for their own purposes. I suspect the former."

"Magnetism?"

"Yes, I believe the magnetism of the black pillar beneath the pyramid enables its sculptures to regenerate spontaneously, as if alive. Elaborate sculptures that were never touched by human hands. There are many mysteries there that I wish to understand. As I mentioned to Engineer Number Four—the Oracle of Klopus who was here but recently—I attempted to report our situation to the Chaldeans by penetrating the Eye and with my bracelets tuning its magnetism, but I could only receive, not report. Seven bracelets, as it turned out, were not sufficient."

"You heard from Earth? After a thousand years?" For the first time, Mother showed surprise.

"Nothing more than 'Why are you not confirming your situation, Yezd? You must submit your report to us Chaldeans at once." Yezd shrugged again. "I am a Chaldean. So, I must find some way to report. Source was useless."

"You make your report. I will find the solution to our problems here on Maalstrom, where we actually live." Sarcasm found its way out of Mother's mouth.

"You are not an Omega, Alpha-1. You are only an Alpha. You should leave biology to Omegas like me. Only I have the training and the knowledge. Only I am a Chaldean."

"Go fly to your pyramid in the clouds, Yezd. I have no

more need of you. Or your engineers."

"Our engineers. Except they have all died but one. Only the Oracle still lives."

"Then let him remain where he is. We don't need men in Grace."

"Should I tell him that?"

Mother looked suddenly cagey. "No need. I have my secret ways, both into Source, and exiting. Your 'Oracle' cannot keep me out."

"Which explains the ghostly reputation that Source has earned among the inhabitants of Klopus. The noises at night, the stray lights."

"Neither you nor your last engineer can stop me from my goal, Yezd. If I wish to take Klopus back for myself, I could do so overnight, and not you or your so-called Oracle could stop me. There is no power on Maalstrom that can resist my progeny. Not even Vensa herself...if she still lived."

"I fear you may be correct. No matter. Do you wish now to collect the materials you need? I will not interfere. I have my own plans to tend to. And no power on Maalstrom can resist a Chaldean."

Mother snorted. "Boast if you will. I will take what I need and go." She recovered her equilibrium and seemed to brighten. "We were quite the pair in the old days, weren't we, Yezd? Not a person ever questioned our dual authority. We had only to speak and everyone obeyed."

"That is true, Vedega. But maybe now we should get on with our respective plans. I have come to believe that Earth might profit from what we have learned on Maalstrom."

She shrugged. Turning, she reached into a spare white cabinet and extracted a device, and with a flick, a stab of light illuminated the darkness. Her form shuffled painfully away deep into the interior as she collected various items and placed them in a small container.

A half-hour later, she was done and Vedega exited the starship, stepping down with Yezd's careful assistance onto the lowered platform, then to the ground. Once on firm footing again, she lurched around the corner of the bullet and crawled painfully back down the hole from whence she came.

When no further noise came from that direction, Yezd reentered the starship where he produced his own illumination tube and penetrated into the deepmost recesses of Source where he arrived at a chamber that resembled a foundry. Here he donned a white suit intersticed with lead and placed a similar covering over his head. Once prepared in this way, he flicked several switches and a wide curled span slowly rose, giving forth its own resplendent light. Inside, he looked upon a short tube, no more than millimeters in thickness. With supreme focus and extreme care, he positioned a micron-sharp device over the tube, and with infinite slowness, brought it down.

A high-pitched grinding sounded. The starship seemed to shudder, giving forth winks and moans as if preparing to take to the sky. All went dead. Lifting the grinder, Yezd gazed by the light of his mobile device at five new iridescent bracelets. And of the glowing tube, nothing more remained. There would be no more bracelets coming from Source.

All was done. Six for him; six still missing. Before, seven had been insufficient to accomplish his tasks. By what means could he complete his final goal with only six?

As Yezd placed the five new bracelets on his wrists, for a total of six, he made his tired way back to the lowered platform. He clicked a device on the high wall that hid the Oracle's gate, signaling Engineer Number Four that he should return and let Yezd out.

He waited and leaned. He turned. Why should there be a glint within the yawning abyss that opened into the starship's interior, when the last of its power was finally, irrevocably, exhausted? Yezd shook his head. It could only be the delusions of a thousand-year-old man.

CHAPTER 21

Back in her private quarters, Mother peered intently at Lorenda over the smooth whiteness of the experiment table. "How are they? What is their behavior?" Her stare communicated more than mere curiosity, but betrayed tension, anxiety.

"The drones are doing well, Mother. That is, as well as the other drones before..."

The fire in Mother's eyes cooled. In moments, her usual cast of disappointment returned, and she motioned. "Bring in the first drone." She sat as her squad of bright young women, dour women workers, and Lorenda fetched the first young male who had been inoculated with the scrape of the five-armed monkey after his DNA had been laid bare by the gnats. Five days had passed, and Mother examined the drone's half-clothed body.

"Signs. I wish there not to be signs, but that this one shall be normal. For if he is normal, then we have a chance to reverse the hornet infestation that swarms over Maalstrom. And to reverse the...termite element that pollutes my very body."

"Mother?" several asked.

"It is nothing, my beloveds. Nothing for you to concern your dull minds about." She continued to search the boy's body, running her hands over his torso by the lights of several flaring lamps. She halted, caught her breath.

Quickly, she ran her hands again over the boy's flank, rubbing, searching. There...a bump, ever so small but hard and bony, as of something alien beginning to make itself known.

She stood and washed her hands in a basin as having handled a leper. "He is done. Take him to the ejection station along with his wingless paramour. I haven't the heart to deny my own offspring the opportunity to live their lives as they may wish, lives that not even I can predict, given what kinds of life they will give birth to. I suggest a forested environment for their matrimony. Happiness, after all, lies in obeying one's nature, for though you may drive it out the door with a pitchfork, it will forever climb back in the window."

"As you say, Mother." Lorenda pointed to the drone and a pair of muscled worker-women took hold of him. They assisted him in covering his body with a thick tunic, then escorted him out of Mother's chambers.

"Now for the other."

A minute more and Lorenda escorted the second young male in. The male whom Mother had inoculated with the sliver of live flesh from the dragabond. As the dull-witted dragabond watched incomprehendingly from his cell of tear-glass, Mother examined the body of the second male who was as mute as the first.

"More changes here. Quicker than with the first drone." Mother eyed rough edges of fur beginning to appear on musculature that was already firmer and more defined than before. The dragabond inside its cage seemed to sense that some kind of kinship had made its appearance and shook the irsrem bars of its cage while staring hard at the young male. Noticing the blade in its side for the first time, it yanked the blade out and threw it between the bars.

The others drew back in alarm, but the blade only clattered on the floor. The creature shook its cage again, rocking not just the cage, but the walls of the chamber.

"What is it doing?" Mother yelled. "Lorenda, quick, send the second drone to the ejection tunnel with its mate." She stared in fright at the huge creature as it rocked the cage more and more, threatening to flatten the walls, driving thin cracks into the floor.

Lorenda ushered the drone out the door as a crowd of worker-women surrounded Mother, facing the dragabond with their honed claws bared in case the animal should burst from its cell. What was the sacrifice of one—or one thousand—to save the life of their Mother?

* * *

Several levels above, Flores and Crestal and Tilsis moped inside their limited quarters, wondering what exactly they were to do with themselves. Lorenda had provided them plentiful buds of fungus. Nara had showed them around the central plaza once more and introduced them to various corridors that opened up to other hubs and other magniloquent chambers flanked by amethyst and opals, lapis lazuli and gold, with silver threads in the walls and secret harbors housing gemstones that neither had guessed existed, colors and textures defying all imagination to report. All unearthed by the dull worker-women of the earth in their excavations down and down without surcease.

Yet in the end, even the marvels of the underworld ceased to sparkle in their eyes and they found an indescribable longing to see the suns once more. Even their skins calling out to, once more, feel light and heat. Anything but more dusty, shadowy avenues leading to only more shadowy, dusty vistas.

Nara knocked on their private door.

Flores opened the wide portal.

Nara looked disheveled, eyes wide, a dozen workers collected behind her. "Can you come quickly, Flores? And Tilsis? There has been a disturbance in Mother's quarters. The place is wrecked. Mother Herself is in danger."

"But certainly, Nara. We, of course, will hurry to help Mother. What has happened?"

"A beast. One of the most dangerous that reside on

Maalstrom, one which had been captured and imprisoned in Mother's rooms—it has broken loose."

Crestal shivered.

"She asked for us?" Flores asked as Tilsis threw on his fighting harness.

"Yes. And we must hurry to assist her. There is no time to lose. If ought happens to Mother, who knows what may follow?" She cast a quick glance at the worker-women around her. "And what will happen to us marooned here underground without Mother to look after us?"

Flores and Tilsis swapped nervous glances. Hardly anything worse could be imagined. Flores strapped on his own thick tunic. "Our weapons? My Nebelroc?"

"They will be provided. But we must make haste."

"As you say, Nara. You know best here in this strange world of fungi and half-blind slaves."

"By the way, Crestal, Mother has directed that you be allowed access to the southeast corridor, an upper-level avenue that opens onto a rotunda overlooking the lake. There you can partake of sunlight and wind to your heart's content."

Crestal glanced at Flores as he and Tilsis finished preparing for whatever battle they had been summoned to join.

"Will Flores and Tilsis..?"

"Yes, when the present emergency is done. Then they too will join you there. Mother knows how confining it must seem to you three to spend so much time beneath the earth."

"Let us not delay," Flores pronounced.

Crestal said, "Flores, are you—"

He pushed past Crestal into the outer hallway. "There can be no justification, Crestal, for neglecting our duty to assist Mother in her hour of need. We will meet you on the platform when our duty is done." With that, Flores, with Tilsis at his side, rushed down the hall toward the central hub leading down to Mother's quarters.

Nara and her dozen worker-women marched stolidly at their rear.

Forward they hurried, past the central hub, down the great staircase, past caverns and chambers, down again, past the complex of heaving reproduction where half a hundred of the strongest guards, women with the largest claws, stood alert, generations of breeding requiring them never to leave their post while hundreds of smaller women hurried past with thousands of eggs for the upper chambers, and more hundreds of muscled workers hurried the other way to help quell the disturbance in Mother's quarters.

They came to a smaller corridor—the one Flores believed he recognized as leading, after a turn or two, to Mother's chambers. Once more he glimpsed rocky apertures in the floor, falling away to the inmost depths of the world, steep as water wells but with flames flickering, no handholds visible in the sides, a phalanx of such openings stretching away into utter darkness, and Flores was careful to stick close to the one hallway that led safely to Mother. The dozens of muscled workers were no longer in sight.

"Halt here," Nara called. A torch with tow suddenly flared in her hand and her worker escort covered their eyes as if blinded.

"Nara. Why have we stopped? Where are the weapons you promised? We must not delay in helping—"

She turned toward the two men as if to answer Flores. Suddenly she shouted to their escort, "Take them and tie their hands."

"I—"

Still half stumbling in the dark, the men began to struggle but found the immense strength and superior numbers of their escort had them solidly pinned. The workers produced thick ropes and in moments had both defenseless men bound.

"Nara! What do you mean by this?"

The merry tinkling laugh returned. "A change in plans,

Flores."

"But, Mother—"

"Oh, yes. Mother indeed has an emergency, in fact she is struggling for her life even as we stand. But that is nothing for you to be concerned about...or me. If she survives, then all is well. But if she dies...then what will follow will be the grandest of developments. For I, Nara, will succeed her."

"What! How?"

"Slow Flores. Do you still not comprehend what you have seen so often now? You still do not understand the difference between you and me on the one hand, and Crestal and these absurd mole people on the other?"

She breathed deep and stepped closer while the workers held him fast, seemingly comprehending even less of what Nara said than Flores understood, whether due to their being less bright or simply less interested.

"Once before I approached you, Flores. I explained how the world actually works. And you rejected me."

Flores struggled against his bonds, again failed. "And what has changed, Nara? Do you think you have better arguments today than then?"

"What is there to argue, Flores? Nothing. Look about you. You and I...we are exactly the same. We both come from hornets that have buzzed this world since time began, since this world began, only temporarily interrupted by some two-legged simpletons who fell from the sky, and by their foolishness, contributed their life-force to the inexhaustible life-force of my kind, my wasp life-force. To *our* kind, Flores! For just as I am a hornet queen, you are also the product of a hornet queen and must be the mate of a hornet queen. How can you not see that? You are a drone just like those simpletons in Mother's chambers. Your destiny is to fertilize...a queen like me. We are destined to marry, Flores, you and me together, and no other. There can be no one for us but each other."

"No, Nara. You speak of dreams. We have no future

together."

"Think, Flores! Together, you and me, ruling all Maalstrom. That is the future I offer you. I have only to become pregnant by you, and to confine myself in a sacred spring brought into Grace from the lake outside, then to give birth to thousands of progeny...*our* progeny, Flores. And these stupid creatures that know nothing but digging and obeying will cease caring for their own offspring but will devote themselves to caring for ours. And in a few short years, Grace will be ruled entirely by our children. And finally, no more moles, no more digging in the ground like vermin, no more Grace. It will crumble to ruin while our descendants will go to war on the surface, expanding our rule across Maalstrom, burning Klopus, challenging Ven, destroying every other hornet queen whose city we encounter."

She stepped closer. Slid her hand over Flores' chest. "But it all depends on you."

"Do not make me repeat what I said before, Nara."

"Flores, don't you remember all the promises you made to me in the high scaffolds of the malkops? Oh, how I loved you."

"You deceived me then. You let me speak while thinking you were someone else."

"I still love you, Flores. Won't you come to me like you attempted to do in the city of glass? When you swore you would return with an army to rescue me?"

Flores was silent for only a moment. "No."

The laugh vanished. She swore and stamped a foot. "You dolt. Are you still such a fool as when we were in the Temple of Ven?"

"There are still others for you."

"Three-month-old boys? Idiot drones with no voice? Besides, Mother forces me to take the sting of the leroo each year, so it matters not how many men cross the threshold of Grace."

"Then how could we..."

She nodded gleefully. "I have found a way, Flores. With you and me it is still possible! I found a way into Mother's chambers. I held the sacred insect hive in my own hands. I ran up its temperature to enhance their poison, then I had them sting a bat to death, making them harmless for the next few days. Then I made my way back out of the room. When Mother requires me to take the sting tomorrow, it will have no effect, and I will become pregnant without her knowing. That is, I could become pregnant, if only...if you...in the very short time we have to make this happen..."

"No."

Again she stamped her foot. "Think, Flores! We have even less time to grab a world than we had in Vensa's Temple. Perhaps only minutes!"

"No."

"You think you can refuse me? With the power I wield in Grace?" Nara strode to Tilsis who had stood quietly the entire time of their exchange. "Behold." Nara grabbed Tilsis by one arm, and with the assistance of the guards, she walked him to the lip of one of the bottomless pits. Before Flores could speak, she shoved Tilsis over. His mute body bounced once, twice, off the stony sides, and vanished forever into the bowels of Maalstrom, a minuscule scarlet flaring from the deep.

"Nara!" Flores gushed tears. "You cannot do this! Mother will hear of it."

"She will—yes. Mother herself has given orders that both of you be killed. Her order is now halfway done. But I still offer you a way out."

"You think to obtain my cooperation this way? By threats and murder?"

"How else, Flores? You give me no choice but threats and force. For I will not be put off or dissuaded from my goal. Not this time. Your future is with me—or with no one."

"There is still Crestal. She will intercede with Mother

for me."

"Crestal?" The tinkling laugh returned. "Your termite queen whose only future lies in piling dirt into mountains of refuse?"

He thought. "What have you done with Crestal, Nara?"

"Do not fear for Crestal, my almost husband. She lives. But she is already by the lake in the company of a male drone."

"One of the drones? They have princesses already assigned."

"And one princess is missing." She smiled. "I wonder what became of her?" The laugh repeated. "Mother has also given her order that one princess and one drone be released into the outer world to make their life separate and apart from Grace. Even now, the escort is transporting them to the far side of the valley where the drone will fertilize Crestal."

Nara stared at Flores. "Did you not know, Flores, that your paramour has not received the sting of a hornet in over a year? That she is now exceedingly fertile?"

Flores struggled.

"But not to worry, dear Flores. Her drone has been inoculated with the life essence of one of Maalstrom's many creatures."

"Creature? What creature?"

"Do you really wish to know, since you will never see your Crestal again..?"

* * *

The floor cracked wider.

"Watch for the bottom of its cage," Mother croaked. "The bottom is splitting!"

Inside the cage, the dragabond jerked the irsrem bars with such prodigious strength that the entire structure began to warp, although constructed of iron and steel. But whereas no mortal muscle could ever bend or shatter the thick rods of tear-glass that bordered the front and sides, the floor and ceiling of the cage and the partial wainscoting that housed the bars were mere metal and thus little more than a moment's delay to a frustrated dragabond.

It rocked the cage one way—the next—then it warped and twisted. A glass rod sprang from its sockets and collapsed with a thud.

"Stop the thing," yelled Mother, creeping backward, too terror-stricken to think of turning, too ancient to run. "Seize it, Lorenda."

Lorenda signaled to the clutch of worker-women guarding Mother to intervene. Emotionless, they stepped forward like automatons, nine-inch claws extended.

With terrific force, the cage exploded—rods flung outward—the floor ripped in two—the dragabond emitted a deep chamber-shaking hoot followed by an angry growl.

The first guard-woman attempted to grab one of its arms. The beast hoisted her and tore the woman in two. Undeterred by the splash of blood from the doomed guard, two more stepped in to subdue the animal—the dragabond ripped each apart in turn.

It paused to touch the dead lizard still suspended on its sloping, almost flat forehead. "Thum neg. Thum neg!" Again, it roared.

"More," Lorenda yelled, adding her stern voice to Mother's. "More before it runs loose in the city."

Three woman workers hurried in—in seconds their bodies were torn to shreds, the beast flinging their remains about like trophies, splattering the distant walls and the other cages with torrents of blood.

The beast was out.

It moved among the other cages.

A horde of muscled guard-women rushed past Mother as she gained the refuge of the entrance, where she only just managed to squeeze past the entering flood. They surrounded the beast—slashed and tore with their enormous claws till the animal's blood mingled with that of its attackers. In moments, they too were rent into pieces by the dragabond, which, true to its nature, seemed to feel no pain from its own injuries but continued to rip its enemies in pieces.

Blood poured across the floor of the chamber in a tide, making the newest influx of guard-women slip and fall. The beast slipped too but ripped several more as it fell.

It regained its feet and in frustration pulled the bars from the cages housing several other animals, releasing isia, vok, sike, five-limbed monkeys, and bats. Not intimidated by any other species, the dragabond tore up the cage containing the ros, and it promptly leaped on the vok, which had defied its predatory glare for months, adding to the confusion in the chamber.

The bats fluttered about, searching for a way out—finding the vertical shaft over the leroo-sa hornets, they entered the shaft and escaped—the hornet nest spilled and rolled across the bloody floor, expelling its angry habitants into the air, which now filled with the buzzing of confused insects.

But the river of mole workers, programmed for nothing more than digging and defending, continued to grow until the chamber was literally jammed with their number. Each animal was ripped to ribbons. Every cage was pulled to pieces and the pieces dragged out. Piles of dirt were brought in and thrown helter-skelter so they might regain their footing in the lake of spilled blood while fighting.

For every worker-woman who fell beneath the awesome strength of the dragabond, two more took its place, the living constantly removing the dead to make room for more automatons.

The outer chamber filled with workers. Outside that chamber, the hallway filled with more workers. The network of corridors that led to the outer hallway filled with dour and sedate, but focused, workers, intent on their one purpose of rescuing Mother and eliminating the foreign creature that threatened Grace.

At last, even the dragabond began to tire. The effort of slaughtering a hundred or so workers was finally beginning to tell on even its superhuman strength and endurance. Three more it ripped apart—but not before their claws ripped more flesh from its body, now scarlet with a thousand such cuts. Not even a dragabond, which feared nothing on Maalstrom but its own kind, could forever ignore the torrents of blood shedding from its body, or forever ignore the signals of pain that, at last, made their way to its feeble brain.

It rent two more workers—threw their severed limbs across the room—pointed one last time to its lizard as if to say "Why are you not acknowledging me as your neg, your leader? I am Thum. Do you not see this lizard, my badge of authority?"

The workers closed in.

A flurry of enormous claws rose and fell without pause, leaving jagged wounds on the beast, more claws slashed its face—still uncomprehending—until no more remained but naked bone, blind to the fates that had brought it to this end and were now ending its life.

Another few minutes and the workers sliced the unresponsive body of the dragabond into slabs of hirsute bloody flesh for others to carry out and away, entirely out of Grace.

Mother ventured back in. All the animals had been despatched. Nothing was left of the dragabond but shreds of veins and clumps of hair. Lorenda directed workers to clean the leroo hornet nests and place them back beneath the air shafts, and even the fragments of cages were soon removed along with the remains of the other animals, all deceased, even the malkop.

Approaching the scene of the disaster, she casually inspected the place where the dragabond's cage had been.

"Do not be concerned, Mother. All will be put back as it

was shortly. Though it will take a little time to obtain more animals for your investigations. A caravan from beyond the lake will be here soon."

"Yes, Lorenda. I know," Mother's aged voice croaked. "This is merely an inconvenience. What is the death of a mere hundred or so of Grace's populace compared to the uncountable hordes that inhabit it? They will be replaced within the hour. Were it not for the burning suns that keep us underground, our numbers would soon cover Maalstrom up to our knees. Such is the power of my city. That Yezd should think on that."

"Who, Mother?"

"No one, Lorenda. No one of the slightest importance to us."

Mother edged closer to the area where the dragabond's cage had been. "Where is my flesh-sampler. I will have use for it again, if we can only find it." She peered. "What is this?" Behind where the cage had been, a square section of wall was gone, having collapsed. "Lorenda, here is a corridor where no corridor should be." Her body-assistants helping her, she leaned over and carefully picked up the collapsed section. "And here is a hole just large enough for eye or ear."

"Yes, Mother? Whatever could that mean?"

Her companions helped Mother stand straight. "One thing only, Lorenda," Mother said, her voice coarse as ever. "Only one. Bring my guards...here...to me. At once. She takes me for a fool. But I wasn't born yester-century."

With the help of her two muscled assistants to carry her, who were recently arrived therefore not covered in dragabond blood, Mother entered the tunnel that should not be, leading to a corridor that should not exist. Her horde of dully obedient moles, their claws sheathed but ready to be deployed at a single word, followed close behind, with Lorenda leading...

* * *

"Creature? What creature," Flores called out to Nara.

"Do you really wish to know," Nara continued, "since you will never see your Crestal again?"

Flores' eyes stabbed wildly.

"A dragabond, Flores, The very animal you yourself saw not many days ago in Mother's chamber. And the animal that even now is causing such havoc in her quarters overhead that she has no time to tend to you, or me."

Flores ceased struggling and stared straight ahead, the workers holding him fast.

Nara continued. "Your Crestal is gone, Flores. She will soon found her own city. A very special city. In fact, there are already many such cities scattered east and southeast of Grace because Mother has been experimenting with dragabond life essence for many lifetimes—as you perceive a lifetime. A city that will be half-termite like Crestal, and half dragabond like Crestal's new drone husband. The dragabond's powerful essence will in time overcome all of their termite nature. I know. I have seen the results. Mother too. But the foolish old crone labors on, as if another century of failed experiments might make a difference except to further pollute the life forms of our world."

An ancient hoarse voice sounded unexpectedly behind Nara. "And you, you would speak of pollution? Could there be any greater pollution than your mind and body, Nara?"

Nara spun round.

There stood...Mother. In the midst of a phalanx of muscled workers of Grace, their claws already unsheathing in the midst of coldly flaring torches that barely kept the midnight recesses of the vast cavern at bay. More workers streamed in behind Mother, led by Lorenda, still more from the way Nara and Flores had come. Escape was no longer possible.

At a finger movement from Mother, Lorenda tossed the square section of wall to the dusty floor.

"Care to discuss this, Nara? Would you bring me the

latest news from the great outdoors?" Mother smiled a smile of sheer triumph, as if having just won a great prize. "How entertaining our conversation shall be. I am most interested in your explanation of how this corridor and this fragile piece of wall with its little spyhole came to be."

"Mother! Oh, how glad I am you've come." Sweat beaded on Nara's face, gleaming through the semi-darkness. "See what I have uncovered for you. Flores, sneaking down here below your offices, I smoked him out, made him confess! I found him and Tilsis constructing this secret way so they could take your life." Her eyes darted.

"Tilsis!" Flores finally shouted. "She bound my companion and threw him into the pits."

"As you yourself commanded, Mother. See how I have obeyed your command."

Her escorts helped Mother approach Flores' side. Her eyes passed over him. Then she moved to Nara and gazed closely upon her. "And how, dear Nara, would this mortal from the outer world have the slightest inkling of the tangled pathways of Grace? How, dear Nara, when you yourself have kept the newcomers under close watch in their private quarters? And how, dear Nara, when no one but you and my closest lieutenants could possibly know how to execute such a plan?"

Mother moved even closer. Her eyes came so close to Nara's eyes that they almost touched. "You have a ring around your eye, my dear. A stain that might result from peering through an eyehole. This man has no such stain."

Lorenda held up the square piece and placed the eyehole over her own eye, which moved and wobbled through the spyhole where all could see.

The crone turned to Lorenda. "She is a contamination in our city, as I said from the start. I dared to trust just to add to my store of facts. Well, I have added. Now it is time to purify Grace, to purify it of all that have entered."

"No," shouted Nara. "You foolish woman. I have only

to become pregnant and your old bones will fall and shatter. You think to end my days here in this dungeon? I have prepared other tunnels, other ways for this situation. There will be no more stings of the hornet for me, Mother. I fixed your nests yesterday. Their stings will no longer prevent pregnancy, in me, or anyone. I have finished you! If Flores won't have me, I will find someone in the outer world."

With that, Nara flung herself backward where she traipsed over a narrow bridge to a rocky island thrust up like a pylon amid a jagged sea of pitfalls, the pits leading down to black invisible depths.

Nara continued shouting. "You think I have not foreseen this? I have my way, Mother. You are too late, too old, too feeble. You cannot win against a young, energetic woman like myself." She gave the slender bridge a kick and it collapsed, leaving no access to her island. With a grin of triumph, Nara turned to flee across another bridge to where a farther tunnel beckoned.

The finger moved.

With a rush, Mother's horde of mole women ran forward. The foremost threw themselves to the ground— opened their mouths—thick liquid erupted from their maws to mix with the dirt and in seconds the collapsed bridge began to reappear, coming into existence foot by foot. More workers ejaculated thick liquid, and a second bridge began taking form on Nara's left—a third on Nara's right.

Anxiously, Nara tested her escape bridge. It shook. Parts crumbled. Too decrepit to hold her weight, it suddenly fractured and fell, leaving Nara marooned on her little darkened island, shaking in sudden disappointment.

The three bridges came closer, each moment drying to the consistency of stone, sufficiently to add another foot. Without warning, the entire inner face of the network of pits came alive with worker-women, the endless depths inspiring no fear in them. More bridges appeared. Others brought more torches, though the half-blind workers needed no light at all to perform their task.

Five minutes elapsed and a half-dozen bridges of solid dirt ten feet thick and encased in mole saliva hard as rock neared Nara and her little island of stone. A score of workers waited on the bridges with their unsheathed knives stretched out.

"You can't! You cannot do this to a queen of Ven. Not to me, destined to bring the wonders of hornet life essence to the entire world. I am stronger than you, than your creatures, than all of Grace."

Flores watched, helpless, bound, unable to tear his eyes from the horror unfolding moment by moment.

The bridges came nearer. At a signal from Lorenda the nearest workers launched themselves through the intervening gap, striving to land on Nara's little refuge. They missed and fell into the depths without a sound.

More jumped. They too fell.

"Ha! You see. The gods save me even now."

Another foot closer came the stony arches. Another foot closer to Nara marooned on her pylon.

More ran and leaped—all fell into nothingness—one reached the island, clung with its claws. Nara kicked it and it too fell.

The bridges came closer. A dozen more ran forward—most fell to their deaths but three managed to cling to Nara's narrow perch. Frantically, she kicked them all to their deaths.

Another foot—another dozen leaped—six reached the island. All six were kicked into the bottomless Stygian darkness.

Nara screamed—the scream of the insane.

Closer still came the bridges. A dozen ran forward, leaped—all landed on the pinnacle next to Nara. But they did not touch her. Instead, they scraped at the stone beneath her feet. Desperately, she threw several over—more took their place.

At last, the bridges came very near to Nara's pylon—a

horde of workers rushed forward and tore at the little island till nothing remained but a thin stalagmite.

Nara slipped—held to the last handhold. For a moment she glared hate and madness. Then a half-dozen workers smothered her with their bodies—down they went with Nara in tow—all vanished into the endless, red-laced depths, Nara's lone scream echoing till no more could be heard.

Mother peered over the edge. "Maybe she should have settled for a little sting now and then," she cackled. "Could have avoided a good bit of unpleasantness." She turned to Flores. "Now what about you?"

He turned his face up defiantly. "Put me in a room with a sword and I will show you what about me."

"Hah. Just as I suspected. The violent thought processes of a man. Well, you may kill a dozen or so of my daughters—even a hundred. What good will that do you? Dispatching a thousand would do you no good. Ten thousand. Think on that, my friend."

Flores looked less certain but his anger and indignation would not let him give in.

"But what would be the point?" Mother turned away and began to walk back to her chambers as if she had forgotten Flores.

"Mother, what shall she we do with him?" Lorenda asked.

The crone paused, turned. She shrugged. "Give him his belongings and turn him loose by the lake. With Nara and Crestal gone, he is no longer a threat to us, though the presence of any man in Grace has its dangers. Also, he is useless for labor. It seems mushrooms do not agree with him." Away she walked, helped along by her coterie of 'daughters'.

CHAPTER 22

The following day, Flores stood by the lakeside with the reins of Tha-two in hand, watching fish dart and glide through the still waters. For a long time, he stood and thought in the shade cast by the perpetual ash cloud above.

What should he do? What could he do? Duty had always been his guide. But his episode with Amina had taught him the expendability of 'duty'. Now he longed for Crestal. But what was she in the end? Was she the same as Amina? Merely one more gila driving toward her own intrinsic goal, an elaborate play in which he had no more than a bit part? Could I be simply another drone, as blind and as caught up in the web of destiny as the mindless over-sexed winged males of Grace whose one goal in life was to mate with a winged half-termite queen in flight, then tumble happily to earth to die? Could it really be true that my every action, my every thought, are no more than expressions of my own unconscious instinctual drives? Am I not a thinking, reasoning child of the rational god Vensor, as we men have always proclaimed? Or am I, in my own way, just another automaton like Mother's innumerable obedient workers? Can I even say that my thoughts are my own?

Yes! As I proved at the pinnacle of the Eye in the pyramid when I—even I, a mere ant struggling on the face of this wild world by the decree of an uncaring heaven—had Atasan Himself, the ruler of this world, beneath the point of my sword. I was then no automaton. I had climbed to the heights of heaven, and with Macius as my guide, I challenged God in His home, and I pulled his very beard.

With my sword and my soldiers, I made the Heavens my own, conquering by force of arms HeavenHell, Atasan's glass city in the clouds. And when I allowed Atasan to live, it was I who made that decision, not a termite devoid of thought. True, I have learned that I am half hornet and not termite. But I am also half something else—whatever it was that came to this planet so long ago, Mother being one, and Yezd likely another. If they can bend Nature and the Heavens to their will—so can I!

I will not be thwarted. I will myself to find Crestal, although I know that in the end she is not like me, that she is even less like me than was Amina. But with the aid of the woodcraft which I learned from Tilsis, I will track her and I will find her. And I will do whatever I can to ensure her happiness even if it does not always accord with mine. That is not the chivalry of a Lord of the Turlicum of Ven speaking. That is my will, my judgment. Not Vensor's. Not Nature's. And not Atasan's. Mine alone. It is possible for a mere mortal to challenge the gods...and win!

Flores stirred. Tha-two curled its long neck and stared inquisitively into his eyes, knowing that a new journey had begun.

Rechecking his axe, Nebelroc, and a pair of irsrem and iron rapiers, with panniers and a lyart-hide buckler shield, and well-made boots of sike hide, Flores inspected his store of dried fish—threw out the revolting mushrooms Lorenda had given him—and pledged to murder and dismember the first sike he might come across to satiate his hunger for protein. Double checking his vok bladder filled with water, he turned his attention to the second reven, the one Tilsis had ridden.

No need for two, Flores thought.

"Sorry for you, my old friend." Flores poured a brief libation on the ground to Tilsis, and after removing all the appurtenances of civilization from the reven, he shooed it away. "Return to your home. Your service is over. I think

Tilsis would approve." The animal broke free and in moments dashed into the lake where it swam merrily into the distance, snatching fish and chewing marsh redentine, to mix with its wild cousins who eyed the newcomer with curiosity.

Flores mounted Tha-two, and with a slight kick, guided his reven around the southern curve of the lake, and headed for the far ridges to the east, crowned by dark pine forests, his eyes locked to the ground in search of two sets of footprints: Crestal and the wingless drone.

Might he already be too late? Flores set his jaw. Crestal is sensible and has a marvelous instinct for self-preservation. She would not dally in the middle of nowhere, certainly not so uncomfortably close to Grace, just to obey a primitive instinct by mating with the drone whom Mother had contaminated. Assuming she could even tolerate his ignorant, mute company.

And what would Flores do if he found them? He did not wish to think about that. But he felt his face and neck flush. At the moment, it would not do for him to speculate when other matters were so pressing.

For instance, how long will it take to reach those dark forests on the far ridges? Where might he find fresh water once he will have left the lake behind? Will there be sercotrope or redentine for his reven?

At least he would not have to plan for winter since the twin suns had long split apart and had passed spring and were quickly approaching their maximum separation—the heat of high summer would soon arrive.

The day passed.

A second day.

After the third, the grey ash that had previously covered the sky evaporated, allowing the suns' full light to rain down in all its splendor. The lake shrank in the distance and he neared the first ridge, hirsute with black tree-growth. To his surprise the trees were not pine after all but deciduous, and more, thick mats of growth that allowed a traveler only the narrowest of paths, the growth often touching overhead, giving Flores the sense of penetrating a greenish-black tunnel. He recalled the dark evil of the tunnels in Grace and shook himself to rid his mind of the evil memory.

His progress slowed and he found he often had to search for detours through the wild, rough, and stubborn wood. However, he finally managed to come to a stretch where the undergrowth was less and the overgrowth checkered with gaps that let down sunbeams.

The Turlicum slowed.

He had the odd feeling that eyes were on him. Turning his head, he gazed about but saw nothing. Shrugging it off, he kicked Tha-two forward again, and they penetrated more of the woody avenue. Wet leaves gave off steam as the day's sunlight found its way to the forest floor.

A loud click resounded.

Halting to stare, Flores slid Nebelroc in its holster to make certain it would be freely available, and Tha-two curled its long neck to gaze about with as much curiosity as did Flores.

Cautiously, Flores urged Tha-two to take a step when a voice erupted from close by.

"What do you want?"

Flores jerked. In a flash, he yanked Nebelroc from its holster and brandished it. But the click did not repeat, only another question from whoever was watching him.

"By what right do you invade our home? Do you think to steal from us?"

Still unable to make out the author of the voice from the dense foliage surrounding him, Flores stared ahead and to his left and up a bit where the foliage was thickest. "Who is there? What do you want from me?"

"My question exactly, intruder. What do you want from me and mine? What brought you to the vast splendor of the Empire of Melon?"

"I don't wish to offend you, sir, if I have stumbled on

your domain by accident. I assure you I am only passing through. I have no interest in your wood, or in taking anything that does not belong to me."

A gale of laughter rang out. "Why everything in this wood does not belong to you, you great fool. The leaves on the trees, the dirt beneath your feet, the sunlight on your skin all belong to our great Empire of Melon and are not here for intruders to take as they will just because they stumbled here by accident."

"Leaves and sunlight? You claim even those?"

"Of course, foolish man. What empire does not? And ours is the greatest of all."

Flores was losing patience. "If you are so great, why are you afraid to show yourself?"

"We are not stupid, not like you. We do not stumble about offending people in their homes without even taking precautions against their just response."

With that, Flores had had enough. As no one had yet come forward, he withdrew his four-foot rapier. Slowly he extended it to the patch of heavily leaved limbs where the voice seemed located and, with care, pushed one limb aside. To his surprise, a human face—a man's face with a half-whitened beard—came into light. Its two eyes stared hard at him and a toothy smile broke free.

"So, you are human after all, like me."

"Ha!" The face exploded with laughter. "Like you? I should hope not. Heaven help me if I should ever be so afflicted as to look like you. Why don't you come down from that fish-eater you are riding, you great oaf, and try your strength against me. I promise I will hold two arms behind my back just to make things even."

"What?" Now Flores laughed. "Now I know you are not right in the head. I will chop off both your arms just to teach you some manners." With that, Flores began to slide down from Tha-two, keeping his eyes on the leaf-circled face while also scanning to the sides and behind for signs of ambush. But, no other clicks sounding, he slid to the ground and stepped closer to the face.

"Now come down, braggart. I am ready to give you a lesson that you can take back to your Empire of Whatever, and Melon sounds to me quite ridiculous."

The face stopped smiling but made no move.

Reaching out with his rapier, Flores brought it down, and with a single motion, cut the limb off at its root.

"Yaaa!" the face screamed.

"What?" Flores yelled.

Before him, far from a human squatting on a branch as he had believed, was a face surrounded by five flexible arms, each clinging to separate branches.

"A five-armed monkey," Flores exclaimed. "With a human face and a human mind? Have I gone insane?"

The creature recovered and stared harshly down upon Flores. "You were insane when you first entered our empire, fool! You think I am alone? Our vengeance will rain down on you like an avalanche."

Flores sliced two more branches.

"How can you do that? Don't you know what will happen?"

"Let it come. I am waiting."

Instead of advancing on Flores—which would have been rather difficult since the monkey had no feet—it retreated higher into the trees where it was joined by more faces. They let loose a chorus of abuse but, to Flores' relief, threw nothing.

To chase them away, Flores threw a few rocks, and when a couple connected, bringing howls of anger, they had had enough and drifted away.

"Empire of Melon. That can only mean there are ripe dunmelons in the vicinity." And Flores remounted his reven and resumed his quest—but in even a more somber mood than before. "Mother's laboratory had five-armed monkeys in a cage. Could it have been she that brought human traits to such mindless creatures of the forest? I wonder how long she has been tinkering with Vensor's Nature."

On he went and, by afternoon, had left the forest behind. Winding his way through a shallow valley, he came out at the confluence of a pair of streams surrounded by rock-bound hollows.

He dismounted and stretched his legs while Tha-two drank from the stream, and Flores sank further into his depression. The prospect of combat with the things in the wood had briefly lifted his mood, but their cowardice had condemned him to more inaction. It did nothing to relieve the pain that swam in the lake of his heart. The pain that drew him ever forward to Crestal.

A peculiar movement caught his sight. His first impulse was to step behind Tha-two so the reven might provide cover. Who knew whether he had stumbled into another ambush, this time by men with arrows?

Across the glade strutted into view a clutch of two-legged creatures—not men. Still not sure if he had found Mother's workers far from home, or a band of Klopan warriors with strange headdress, or a gang of little tattooed savages expelled by Mother's Grace, he peered carefully without moving.

Closer they came, apparently intent on drinking from the same stream as he. They approached casually, seeming unconcerned by the sight of his carapaced and saddled reven, as any hostile men should be.

He stared hard.

How could he have failed to recognize the creatures? The passage of a season should not have clouded his memory so completely. He decided to wait in order to lift his mood.

They came to the stream and drank, their bushy beaks shaking with each movement, their widely placed eyes focusing and refocusing as if constantly scanning for predators. Their enormous bird-like legs grasped the ground as firmly as a vise, and their short bird-like limbs flapped, only the hands on their arms indicating that these were not quite the same as the fickle rum-na of Maalstrom's open steppe.

These creatures even talked. A steady exchange of speech was audible as they bent and splashed and rose and peered, ever ready to flee at the first sign of ambush.

"Give it up, Long-leg, you lost to me yesterday and you will lose to me today."

"You would like to think so, Flapper. But I've had a good fill of meadow-tubes since then. You are finished, you are."

"You two will never settle who is fastest. I showed the entire Dust-in-the-air herd last week that, though you may be fastest, I am quickest to detect ros-na and there is no predator in all the plains and forests that can surprise us so long as I am with you."

The mention of predators spooked the band of two dozen Swifters, and they all stood straight and spun their whiskered bird-beaks in every direction. Sensing no threats, they returned to drinking.

Still hidden behind his reven, Flores peered and made ready to move. He relished the scene that would unfold when he leaped from his position and the Swifters should realize that someone had been eyeing them while they let their guard drop. How they would squeal and bolt like rabbits. Flores grinned, anticipating the deliciousness of settling scores with these beasts who gave cowardice a whole new meaning.

Tha-two stopped drinking and raised its head.

The Swifters did likewise.

With no warning, a shattering roar crashed across the glade—they froze, for a split second utterly unable to move. From behind a stone, a predatory ros of the jungle sprang upon them, and sooner than Flores could follow with his eyes, the ros had seized one of the Swifters in its prehensile talons and ripped its neck in half.

It let loose another roar and the rest of the bird-like

creatures bolted, disappearing from view even faster than the ros had leaped.

Whipping Nebelroc from its home, Flores stood straight, ready to dispatch yet another of the predatory creatures, having reacquainted himself with the vicious beasts in the arena of Klopus. Tha-two hopped away after the Swifters, leaving Flores with no cover. He dug in one heel and spun his rapier in one hand, Nebelroc in the other.

The ros did not leap. To Flores' amazement, the animal showed no interest in him whatever, in fact seeming not to know he existed, its attention focused entirely on its kill. Yet it did not eat as Flores expected. Instead of tearing the Swifter to pieces with its one large beak bare of skin, this ros merely stared. As Flores gazed in wonder, the creature tore a small portion of flesh using its prehensile paw and transferred it to a small open mouth.

Only then did it finally strike Flores that this ros had no bare beak. Its head was as human as the five-armed monkey he had just met. A human head on a monstrous four-legged predator. Eating daintily as would a cultured human, eating the Swifter quickest to detect danger.

Am I losing my mind? What has gone wrong with the world? Flores stood, too stunned to move.

The thing eating the dead bird was mumbling to itself as it ate, the common language of Vensor-sa emanating from its mouth between bites. It gave a single glance at Flores, mumbled, "Go away," then returned to its meal.

Flores backed off, still brandishing his weapons.

The ros did not follow.

Finally, he turned and hurried after Tha-two, whom he knew would soon forget the danger and calm itself by snatching a fish from upstream. In half an hour, he was back on his mount, thankfully before the animal could slide into the water and damage his items.

Only then did it occur to Flores that he had also seen a ros in one of Mother's cages. That could be no accident.

Whatever the crone was up to, he was having to deal with the results in real life. What else might he encounter? An isia centipede with a human face? A lumbering sike discussing philosophy with other ungulates? Mother had even kept bats. Will they next pursue him demanding tribute for trespassing?

He swore. Humanoid or not, I will deal with these monstrosities that dare to bother me with one word: Nebelroc. And heaven help me if She stooped so low as to try to make reven-na more human, the beloved totem animals of my clan. Some things cannot be tolerated.

Flores hurried on but found he no longer knew which way to go. East? Southeast? The track of Crestal and the drone, always sparse to begin with, he had entirely lost. All he knew at this point was he did not wish to return west to Grace.

He decided to follow the stream farther towards its source.

After several days—thankfully without encountering any more abominations of Mother's making—he threaded a path through another patch of trees and entered a small glade surrounded by a circle of dense boles.

Something caught his eye.

At first, Flores did what any warrior far from home would do. He froze, then backed up. From the cover of the forest edge, he gazed at the thing lying in the glade. A flap of wings materialized overhead and he realized that whatever the thing was, it was dead, as no malkop would approach it unless it had died. So, there could be no danger.

He spurred his reven forward and the malkop flew higher for safety. Flores came near and a rush of happiness came over him—he had found the drone! Descending, he inspected the corpse and soon decided that it had been murdered before it had had a chance to mate, as the pool of blood intermixed with a vast amount of semen attested. Assuming he understood anything at all about Mother's bizarre offspring.

But who had killed it? Crestal was no murderer. The drone was not simply throat-cut, but massacred, its body rent into pieces. Yet he recognized its turn of face and jaw. There was no mistaking its identity. It was the drone that had accompanied Crestal, and even its eyes had reverted to two inset ommatidia like he had seen among the eunuchs of Klopus.

For a moment, Flores felt elated. His greatest fear had gone.

The trees erupted and a line of huge lumbering figures surrounded him.

CHAPTER 23

B efore Flores could react, Tha-two reared up in a cabré. He tumbled to the sward, barely managing to pull out Nebelroc as he fell. With a prodigious hop, the reven launched up and backward, turning as it landed—only to fall directly into the arms of Flores' latest adversaries.

Of all the beasts wandering the wastes of Maalstrom, only one could send a chill down his spine—dragabonds—like the one he had seen in Mother's cage, and which all alone had almost brought the city of Grace to ruin. The creatures were taller than men, huger than a reven, more hairy than a vok, their stupid placid faces betraying the near total vacuity of their slow dull brains. They were not quick, but they understood the concept of an ambush, and to Flores' chagrin, they had successfully executed their one maneuver, catching the Turlicum in their trap.

They had no weapons—needed none. Each dragabond relied on the strength of a dozen mortals in undertaking their single method of death-dealing, tearing their victim limb from limb. They had no shields—needed no shields. Their bodies were so large and their brains so dull that, by the time they realized they had been stabbed, their victim was usually torn apart, and pain was a sensation they barely felt.

Tha-two had no chance of escape. Attempting to slip between two dragabonds, they snagged its neck and ripped off its head to the sound of a single high squeal—the reven's body landed on the ground with a thud.

The largest dragabond stood before Flores. Raising its head to the sky it loosed a chest-cavernous howl of triumph sufficient to shake limbs off trees and birds from the sky, a sound that hammered Flores' ears and must have been audible for miles. The five other beasts paused in their advance to admire their chief and his great fat finger stroked a half-dead snake draped on its forehead as its badge of authority. The bite of the snake evoked nothing from the dragabond; he barely noticed but continued to howl. Only the chief possessed a weapon—a gnarled wooden stick serving as a club.

The training of a Simet warrior knows no pause, however. Before the howl ceased its reverberations, Flores snatched his rapier from his reven's saddle, and in one smooth motion, used the reven's body to leap into the air before its executioner. Flores plunged the rapier rapidly in both of the dragabond's eyes. Falling back, he leveraged the reven's body again to leap higher—Nebelroc sliced through the thick neck of the second dragabond. Even Flores' massive muscles and heavy razor-sharp steel axe could only cut half-way through the animal's neck, but blood exploded like a geyser.

The animal pursed its lips—fell backward with a crash.

Here could be no swordplay with honor as he would employ with a human enemy. Or even the calculated slaughter he used against the dishonored slavers of Klopus, who deserved no pity. These animals must be extinguished as quickly as possible in whatever fashion might work.

They came on again. Flores pierced and stabbed and sliced with rapier and axe. He whipped his spare shiv out of a boot and drove it clean through an opponent's densely muscled arm—they felt nothing but kept coming.

The beast he had blinded growled and tried to close with him—it stumbled over Tha-two and landed on top of the drone's inert body where it rolled and tripped one of its comrades.

Three more came at him. Flores forced the chill in his spine back down to its depths and steeled himself for whatever fate may ensue. They strode around their blinded comrade, their feet thumping like hammers. Again, Flores resorted to using the still bleeding body of his reven as a launching pad and flung himself upward, seemingly directly into the maw of the nearest beast. He swung Nebelroc up at an angle—the beast's jaw sliced free and hung by a shred.

Let's see if you feel that one, friend, Flores thought with a snide.

The injured dragabond halted—felt for its jaw—wondered where it went. It let out a pathetic whimper and sat, done with the hunt.

Two more lurched after Flores, and the one that fell recovered. Backing Flores past the drone, past the reven, past the near beheaded dragabond that lay on its back relishing death, the three came on. The leader with the snake pointed an accusatory finger at their intended victim. Its eyes widened as if signaling: Why do you not die, weak creature? It opened its mouth and slowly blurted, "Kral want food. Kral want eat."

Anticipating a long struggle, Flores stilled and resorted to whatever strategy he could think of to confute the creatures. With his axe raised, he pointed to himself with the hand holding the rapier and yelled, "Food no here. Kral no eat."

Momentarily, Kral stopped, and confusion stole over his face. He cocked his head, recomputing. "Food here. Kral want eat." He lurched toward Flores again, Kral's companions joining.

Flores brandished his weapons. Having been maneuvered past the reven, he would have no more opportunities to leap up to fight his attackers evenly and given their near complete insensitivity to the knife and the rapier, he had little to look forward to except a quick quartering by the three remaining dragabonds.

From the trees, a loud buzzing rang—the dragabonds halted.

Kral's confusion was replaced by concern, his eyes

widening, his sloped forehead suddenly free of wrinkles, his matted black hair rising up.

They turned to look.

Behind them, the wood expelled without warning a dozen human-like figures wielding clubs and swords who ran swiftly at the dragabonds. Without another snort or hoot, the latter turned and staggered back into the wood as fast, or the least slowly, that their tree-trunk legs could carry them.

"Well. It seems these two sides have met," Flores mumbled. "And one side prefers not to repeat the meeting."

His 'rescuers' swarmed quickly around him, needle points of irsrem swords aimed at his midriff, clubs raised overhead in case he chose to resist. Sensitized to encountering humanoid faces in unlikely places, Flores was pleasantly surprised to see that these bipeds, at least, had visages to match their overall appearance, with pointed faces surmounted by sharply swiveling eyes, their bodies between the size of human Vensor-sa on the one hand and huge dragabonds on the other. There was something about them that reminded Flores of the impervious beasts he had just fought and who had just fled. Darkness clung to these newcomers: their swarthy faces, their blackly furred bodies, top-knots of tied vok-hair stiff on their skulls that flowed down their backs, black as ever, most of their skulls shaved clean, short blue-black beards clinging to their chins.

The one closest to Flores peered intently at him. He looked at the two mortally injured dragabonds and the one Flores had beheaded. It stared at him up and down, pausing briefly to inspect his rapier and his axe. His face widened expressively, exuding admiration.

"You," it said, still pointing at Flores with a poniard. "I watched you deal with the dragabonds. By Vensor's Mother, you deserve this medal more than I, Relec of Sturm." Reaching to his half-sloped forehead, 'Relec' plucked off a poorly made copper coil image of a snake and handed it to Flores. "Leave this stranger in peace," he called to his comrades. They lowered their weapons and several briefly smiled as tensions relaxed.

Still alert to deception, Flores lowered his own weapons only slowly. "You saw these creatures come after me? What is your relationship to them?" He still peered suspiciously, concerned there may be a more elaborate ambush in play.

"Hah!" Relec snorted. "We hate and despise dragabonds. They come grunting out of the wilderness to rob and steal what we have. Nothing satisfies them. And they are so stupid that what they can't eat, they ruin. They see no value in anything they cannot eat."

One of Relec's comrades pointed to the dead dragabond and the carcass of the drone.

"We draks have done well. I, Relec, claim these resources in the name of our Queen of Sturm." He turned to Flores. More 'draks' appeared in the wood and came flooding out, soon numbering over one hundred, dragging behind them by means of ropes ten huge A-frame wooden sleds.

"Everyone, give me your attention," Relec called as his drak clan gathered about him. "This son of Vensor, this child of Vensor's Mother has won honor in a fair fight against the worst marauders that curse our trade route. Alone and with only these weak arms he slaughtered the enemy and rendered them harmless. He is one of us! Accept his gift of resources with gratefulness!"

They nodded and some smiled, and Flores got the impression that smiling was not something they often did. He affected his own smile in response but wondered just what 'resources' his new hosts were expecting from him. If they thought to obtain Nebelroc, they had best look to their own throats.

Nothing of the sort followed. At Relec's gesture, swinging his broad irsrem rapier in a circle above his head where the iridescence flickered in the light of late afternoon, the entire clan fell to setting an enormous bonfire in the center of the glade, and as Flores watched in horror and disgust, they unceremoniously threw the corpses of the dragabond and the drone into the blazing flames. Even the severely injured dragabonds did not escape but were promptly speared with a dozen shafts and thrown onto the pile before they ceased breathing, and Flores barely had time to retrieve the saddle and other equipage from his dead reven before that too was barbecued.

All were soon eaten. Within the hour, little remained of the corpses but bones, the draks ravenously downing every trace of flesh. Flores himself—careful to position his hammered snake on his head so all could see—eyed his new companions to make certain he was not next on the menu of these primitive creatures. They were sated, however, and all settled in for the remainder of the day and the coming night, and Flores was relieved to see that none seemed interested in his weapons, and he was left alone to sleep with his head on the saddle and his weapons still clutched nervously in his hands.

What else could he do? He must sleep. And if they wanted to end his life and consume his remains as well, there would be little he could do to stop them, given their superior numbers. So, he slept and gave himself fifty-fifty that he would see the suns again.

To his surprise, Flores awoke alive and intact. Relec approached and offered him a last morsel of flesh from the night's feast. Flores politely but firmly declined. Who knew what it might actually be? For all he knew, these draks may have a caravan of human slaves nearby to provide them with dessert.

But no slaves appeared. And the dragabonds did not return to molest them. And it became clear that Flores had come across a sizable caravan loaded with items to be transported to some highly anticipated destination.

"No time for us to waste," Relec shouted as the entire camp awoke and prepared to depart. In the clear light of morning, Flores got a better look at the heavy sleds. They had no wheels but each was merely an A-frame of average-sized tree trunks with open beds. A single drak, smaller than the foot soldiers, sat atop each A-frame on a small mount at the crossing of the trunks. What caught Flores' attention the most was not the sleds but these drak drivers. Each closely resembled Relec and the other footmen but were smaller and sported something odd on their backs.

Wings. Short, opaque wings.

Flores shook his head as he ate from his supplies tucked in the saddle. There were two types of draks, apparently. Were they princesses engaged in some bizarre variation of Mother's winged girls? A minute's inspection and Flores concluded that drak reproduction must be as different from the inhabitants of Grace as the latter were from the Vensor-sa of Ven. No face of a fertile princess of Grace could match the ugliness of these creatures with their rat-like physiognomy. They could only be male drones of this most peculiar race, Flores thought. And though winged, incapable of flight. Even as Flores stared, several drones stood on their little mounts and unleashed a furious buzzing with their veined blackened wings. Relec signaled approval, and Flores realized that the buzzing was their warning to any enemies in the vicinity that the caravan was large and lethal and that it would be best to avoid it.

"Relec," Flores called, forcing a wide smile—for he still was unsure exactly how he stood with his rescuers, despite their gift of the copper snake. "I am grateful for your assistance yesterday, my good friend. Now, however, my own destination cannot wait. It is time for me to resume my journey south."

Relec frowned. "What are you saying. Did I hear disloyalty from the newest member of our clan?" As if a switch had been turned, a score of drak heads snapped in Flores' direction, their coarse top-knots swinging across their broad backs, bared teeth rendering their pointy faces into the ugliest of expressions, a few drawing rapiers half out of their scabbards.

"Uh," Flores began—

"Since you are our newest member, I will forget what I heard, Snake-handler. But you must not forget that draks have a sacred duty to their clan, and since you are now one of us, that includes you! Show some gratitude for our sacrifice in saving your life. Now help me get the men moving. We have far to go before we can trade our cargo for the things we need and cannot make for ourselves."

Flores let out his breath. A close one—perhaps. He would have to think again about how to resume his journey.

The draks stopped frowning and resumed preparing to travel, and one pointed to the saddle on the ground, then glared at Flores. He pointed again and motioned to Flores. Lift it!

"This? I'm to do what exactly with it?"

"Carry it, Snake-handler. It is yours. You do not expect us to carry it, do you? Are we your servants?"

Flores omitted replying that it seemed he had become their servant. With a grunt, he lifted the heavy leather saddle and draped it across his back. Do they really expect me to...

"Pull the sleds," yelled Relec. And the caravan leapt forward, to Flores' surprise the drones on their little mounts producing short whips and whipping the draks pulling their sleds.

Yes, they really did expect him to.

Off Flores lurched, wondering if the weight would strengthen him, or kill him. Only time would tell. And probably not very much time.

Staggering alongside a hundred serious-minded draks grunting rhythmically, Flores struggled to keep up and was too preoccupied at first to notice the direction taken by the caravan. As the column threaded valley after valley, he was constantly engaged in repositioning the saddle and it soon dawned on him that they were retracing his former steps and moving considerably faster than he had traveled, though he had been mounted. The draks, each larger than Flores by half a foot took great strides. The drivers yelled and whipped the draks pulling their sleds without letup, vibrating their wings on occasion to warn of the caravan's approach like loud horns.

They were moving west, not southeast as Flores wished to go. But each time he took a step out of the line of march, weapons began to leave their sheaths and faces glowered at him until he reshouldered the saddle and rejoined the troop.

Two days passed this way. Each evening Flores collapsed and slept on the saddle, then next morning, he shouldered it again and staggered through the day.

When the caravan next stopped for the night, Flores felt his exhaustion was more than he had ever experienced. How much farther could he manage? The draks settling down, he decided that he had reached the end—come what may, he must ditch the saddle even if this provoked a drag-out battle with his new 'comrades'. The moons sweeping their varicolored sheets over the land, he took up his burden once more and walked casually to the nearest two-log sled and peered inside the large wickerwork bed stretched between the logs. The bed was mostly filled with tight leather sacks containing some viscous material with a vok-hair net draped over to prevent chafing.

What could it be? His mind could make no sense of it, and he had something else to do anyway. Gently, he laid the saddle down in an empty corner in the bed of one of the sleds. Then he stepped away.

Several draks watched—and did nothing.

For some time, Flores stood casually, suppressing his fight-or-flight instinct, waiting to see what the draks would do. Nothing at all. They looked, then went back to their own business.

Was his problem solved that easily?

Relec popped up beside him. "Why didn't you do that

earlier, Snake-handler?"

For a second, Flores eyed the sled as if worried that he may have merely exchanged one form of servitude for another—pulling a sled with a whip on his back.

"Relax, pulling a sled is not for you. As one of my best warriors, I want you walking guard. Unlike my draggers, you have proven yourself in battle." Relec turned and walked away.

Flores lay down by the fire. If anyone had ever felt the fool before this, Flores felt he had them beat by a mile. Silently cursing himself for a dull-witted jackass, he sat by the roaring evening fire and morosely munched his spare dinner while rubbing the ache in his arms and shoulders.

CHAPTER 24

The next day, a morose Flores joined the warriors as they hurried to resume their rapid pace.

To where? If Flores had been recruited as an admired but conscripted mercenary, he would at least like to know where they were headed. He soon realized the troop was following the very stream he had followed in the opposite direction days earlier, and before the day was out, this was confirmed when they came across the remains of a Swifter, the very one the human-faced ros had killed and eaten in his presence. Thank Vensor, the freakish ros was long gone.

On they hurried, the massive sleds creaking, the draks moaning as they labored, their drivers buzzing their wings every so often to herald their coming and occasionally snapping whips, and the foot soldiers under Relec stamping forward, ever forward, their sharp faces turning to and fro to inspect wood and meadow as they passed.

Flores did his best to imitate them.

After a time, Flores approached Relec as they strode to make time. "Relec, my friend, I am curious. Where is our clan going?"

The drak leader glanced once at him without interest, focused on making time, his rough bared feet stomping with every step, none of the draks wearing any boots or sandals. "Same as always, Snake-handler. Where all caravans go. And if we don't get there first, we'll get little or nothing in reward for our efforts. All season our workers back home have collected the crop, for months we've worked and prepared. It is finally time for us to exchange the product of our efforts for irsrem and iron, wine and lyart hides. Above all, we want weapons. The dragabonds threaten us everywhere, not to mention all the other abominations that lurk in the wilds." The drak leader scanned the adjacent woods again.

"What are...these abominations?"

"Part of the creation of Vensor."

"Maalstrom has great beauty. Its wildernesses too."

"I don't mean what Lord Vensor created. I do not fault our Father Vensor who lives in the sky. I mean She who created our god Vensor: Vensor's Mother. She who for her own mysterious reasons chose to populate Vensor's world with the most repulsive abominations one can conceive of."

"She?" Flores asked—already knowing the answer.

"She of the city that resides in Hell below. She who commands a million slaves, She who created even us. Mother," Relec practically hissed.

"Mother," Flores blurted out.

"We must avoid her city. Nothing good comes from there. She makes Atasan look like the savior of the world."

The Turlicum kept his lips shut. What good would it do to confess his acquaintance with the old woman and her experiments?

"So that city is not our goal?"

"Of course not. She never trades with us, and hardly with anyone. Her only interest is spreading evil over the land."

Flores hurried, stepping over a large stone to keep up. "I am relieved to hear that, Relec, my friend. I too have heard...uh, rumors about Her. I agree it is best to avoid that place."

"That is why we will soon curve to the south. The track is long established; there is no need to lay a new path. All caravan tracks lead to the same place anyhow. They will be waiting and will welcome us."

"And that place is..."

Relec glanced at Flores. "Klopus."

Flores halted. "Klopus!"

"Where else? Who else will give us rapiers and swords for truckloads of junk like essence?"

"Essence?"

It was Relec's turn to halt. "Snake-handler, you do not seem to know much. Where do you come from? I know you are not drak. Or dragabond. Or one of Mother's ground-dwelling slaves." Relec looked at Flores with a hint of pity. "Are you too one of Her unfortunate creations, though not privileged to be drak?"

"No, Relec. I am not of Her. I come from far away, a distance of many months. I have my own people, my own city. From where I come, they never heard of Vensor's Mother."

The drak leader looked relieved. "Then you should thank Gethos for your luck. Because little good comes from Her. And I say that even though we draks are among Her creations."

It was Flores' turn to gaze with pity. Could these dull-witted scavenging draks that eat carcasses killed by others have the capacity for self-pity? Could one of Mother's abominations be...almost human? The product of a union between a termite drone and one of Mother's eager princesses?

Flores put the tender feelings aside. It was best not to allow his feelings to extend to those he may have to murder. But he had seen the dragabond in one of Mother's cages, and its traits seemed manifest among these draks, leading Flores to a horrid conclusion. Had She tinkered with dragabonds to produce the likes of Relec? He could almost bet.

Then another thought upset Flores: Could all that he viewed be the product of Crestal's mating with the drone, as Nara had said would happen? But no. The drone was dead and clearly without having consummated its union with Crestal. That meant she was alive—somewhere. And since they lived in cities, according to Relec, Mother's tinkering with dragabonds must have occurred years—even centuries—earlier.

A week elapsed, and to Flores' increasing apprehension, they circled around Grace and made straight for Klopus. How to handle this delicate situation? As before, Flores could not afford to be recognized in Klopus. If the Klopans did not try to seize him, the draks may have him for dinner for the crime of angering the Klopans and disrupting the draks' all-important trade.

In the distance, the city gate of Klopus with all its pornographic imagery peculiar to the Eunuch Guild, at last came into view. As Relec had said, more than one drak city had sent caravans, and at least three other caravans of draks stood ill-eased on the wide fields before the walls, each eyeing the others with barely hidden jealousy.

"Relec. Why so many caravans from the same city? Why don't your people unite into one large caravan for better safety?"

The drak leader stared at Flores like he was insane. "The same city? You, Snake-handler, truly are ignorant of all things drak. Next you will tell me you are not aware that drak cities lie scattered over the entire southeast all the way to the most distant regions where even the stars are different, where at the farthest Land's End one can even see the Eye of Vensor blinking across the sea."

The Turlicum was taken aback. Not only at realizing the extent of his ignorance of Maalstrom, where he thought nothing remained for him to discover, but that any land anywhere could stretch so far into the southern ocean that one could see Vensor's Holy Isle and its crystal pyramid. He had never guessed but had always relied on the word of Macius.

Relec continued. "And this is why we must hurry. We must get in the queue before any more caravans arrive or Klopus will have nothing left for us and we will have to return to our home in Sturm empty-handed but for a few worthless lyart hides. That would not go well for us."

Flores stood and stared, shielding his face with his palm in an attempt to disguise himself.

"And although we have hurried as fast as possible, our biggest rival has already come before us."

"Which caravan in the queue is that?"

"None that you see. These caravans are but small groups from small villages. I speak of the largest city in the far south and their huge caravan run by the warrior Tobel, who is so large that some mistake him for a dragabond. His caravan was so quick that we passed them coming back from Klopus just before you joined us, and as he passed we heard Tobel boasting of his most recent success."

"Oh?"

"Didn't you see the drone?"

"Yes, I saw the drone. What of it?"

"That was Tobel's work. He found the drone in the company of a princess from Mother, young and fertile. Such has great value among draks, whose women are always scarce. Tobel killed the drone and seized the princess. He considers her a great find and declared that when he returns to his city of Sloter he will marry Crestal in formal ceremony before his Queen. Crestal tried to resist but what princess fresh from one of Mother's Flights can fight off a drak? Especially one almost as large as a dragabond? And she had already lost her wings so she could not fly away. All this Tobel loudly boasted to us to taunt us as they passed."

Flores stood electrified. Crestal! He had found her! But he had gone in the wrong direction and was no longer free to follow her. He thought better than to mention that Crestal's Flight had been years earlier and that she had shed her wings at least a decade ago—for a warrior no longer in control of his own destiny, like himself, to share feelings for another was not the wisest move.

For the rest of the evening, as the draks settled in under

the open sky with all its swirling moonlit colors, the draks having no concept of tents just as they had no concept of wheels or even domesticated animals, Flores lay with his head on a stone, his mind in a storm on how to get free and pursue Tobel to the distant city of Sloter.

When morning broke and Relec's draks stirred so as not to lose their place in the queue, Flores had made a plan. It all depended on one thing that he felt was certain: the feebleness of his captors' minds.

Still taking care not to expose his face to the Klopan soldiers who were beginning to inspect the drak caravans, Flores approached Relec. "By the way, my good friend, I meant to ask you about the many fine meals you have eaten on our trip. I stupidly refrained since eating the dead is not my custom. But as I am now a member of your clan, perhaps I should try your diet."

Relec looked smug as if having received a compliment. "You have come to your senses, Snake-handler. You really don't know what you are missing. There is nothing like a bonfire of seared flesh to get the juices flowing."

"On the other hand, I have my own customary diet that you may want to try."

He perked. "What would that be? Draks love only flesh."

"I was thinking of reven-na. The kind of creature that I rode on when I was surprised by the dragabonds. You yourself ate of that very animal after the beasts killed it. Do you admit it was tasty?"

Thinking back, Relec agreed. "Ah indeed! The flavor was magnificent. I have never stumbled upon one of their carcasses before."

"I myself would prefer to stay with my own custom for a while longer before sharing yours. Before the next feast, might I make a simple request?"

"What in the world do you mean?"

"I mean when we get to the front of the queue and begin

trading our goods for what Klopus has to offer, that you request a reven from the Klopans. I am a good warrior but not used to so much walking. I would like to ride the reven until we arrive at our next bivouac. Then we can share in quartering and eating the animal. Of course, you will have to tell the Klopans that you want the reven for eating, since no drak rides a reven; and be certain to insist on a large healthy one, otherwise, they may doubt you."

Relec turned the idea over in his head. Finally, he nodded. "Snake-handler, you are not just a good fighter, but you have good ideas. I never thought of riding the evening meal before roasting it. That seems not a bad plan. Just don't ask me to ride the thing. Only barbarians have such crazy customs as to make pets out of their dinner."

"Maybe later we can discuss another idea I have of using round wheels under your sleds instead of dragging loads across the earth."

Relec shook his head. "You propose violating the ancient rules that Vensor has put in place to preserve the draks. My people will oppose that." He shrugged. "Anyway, I have seen such things here at Klopus. But I have yet to see a tree that grows in a circle. Who has time to waste looking for something that does not exist in my part of the world?"

Flores nodded. "Of course, my friend. I cannot argue with that."

"When we get to the front, I will make a special request for a fat reven for our special evening meal. And you can rest your feet for a day before enjoying this new tasty meal along with us. You have some good ideas, Snake-handler. But some, like your wheels, are cock-eyed and will never work."

With that, Relec returned to inspecting his caravan and eyeing the rival caravans with distrust, and Flores decided now was the best time to remove the saddle. Depositing it behind a tuft of grass, he waited in the midst of the drak soldiers since they were no longer needed. Finally having some time to observe without demands on his time and body,

Flores did his best to mingle among them and stay out of a direct line of sight from the city gate or its walls.

The first caravan in queue dragged their four sleds opposite the main gate. As it opened, a host of Klopan soldiers emerged loaded with weaponry and assembled in two parallel lines while scores of slaves trudged between. Approaching the sleds, the slaves shouldered the many leather bags and bladders and hauled them inside the city to the main plaza while the draks stood and watched. When this was accomplished, more soldiers emerged carrying loads of weapons tied with rawhide and placed the weapons in the sled beds, and many casks of red wine alongside some lyart hides. Clearly, thought Flores, the Klopans did not trust either their own slaves or the draks with rapiers and swords and pikes, and the slavers motioned the draks to depart before distributing the weapons.

Once the first caravan had left, the second moved up and the procedure was repeated.

Then the third.

Finally, it was the turn of Relec and his draks, and with Flores still remaining some distance away, the long-established exchange was done. Relec signaled his draggers to drag his latest load of irsrem weaponry along with wine casks away from the city, and the soldier draks fell into line.

Where was the reven? Flores began to wonder if he had been double-crossed, or perhaps simple incompetence or bureaucratic oversight had frustrated his plan. Now he faced the prospect of standing alone in the middle of this open plain with no draks to cover him and a well-worn saddle by his feet and the caravan already leaving for home.

The Klopan soldiers turned and reentered their city and the gate began to shut.

Should he call to Relec? Relec was preoccupied organizing and shouting at his draks. Should he make a run for it? He could never cross the distance to the shelter of the nearest ridge and greenery before a Klopan patrol on reven-na galloped to the kill.

At that moment, the gates halted and a single reven belted through. Unsaddled, no reins, no stirrups, as virgin as one fresh from Maalstrom's plenteous rivers and lakes, it cantered and hopped in confusion as if wondering just what it was supposed to do.

The gates closed.

There was but one thing Flores could do. Throwing caution to the wind, he strode calmly to the beast with reins in hand and was able to place them over the reven's head, then walk the animal to his saddle. In full view of whomever may be on the city walls watching—and there were sure to be some alert soldiers ever distrustful of draks—he saddled the reven, ensured Nebelroc and his rapier were properly sheathed, leaped on top of the obedient animal, and cantered away. Not to rejoin Relec and his company but angled ninety degrees in a direction that would take him far from the draks' customary route.

Already sufficiently removed from the city to be unable to hear anything that might elapse inside and moving quickly enough to outrun any mounted pursuit, and far enough from the draks to prevent their catching up to him on foot, Flores tossed the copper snake from his forehead and melded into the wilderness, leaving a host of surprised drak faces and Klopan soldiers staring after him open-mouthed, and a distant buzzing from annoyed drak drivers.

Best of the luck of Gethos to you, my erstwhile clan-member, Flores thought. But you won't be eating this reven—or me. The city of Sloter, half a world away, awaits.

CHAPTER 25

S o, they think to train their warriors better after that character 'Flores' embarrassed their city? Yezd thought as he eyed a column of Klopans dragging two wagons filled with corpses, headed for the Nether Fields north of the city, the place where they traditionally deposited their dead.

There are many more corpses than usual, he observed. He watched from the coping of a stone enclosure demarking the deposits of Klopus' rulers, which were marked by a few upraised and tastefully carven altars, from a larger area strewn with larger concrete slabs barely raised up, the area reserved for commoners. But all were for the same purpose: to enable Vensor's malkops to retrieve their corpses as was their due and fly them away to Heaven. No Vensor city ever buried their dead.

By the light of early morning, a dozen slaves supervised the lyarts that dragged the wagons to the commoners' section, where, without ceremony, they dumped the score of bodies willy-nilly on the concrete slabs. They then returned to Klopus without a backward glance.

No hurry, Yezd reflected. I pass like a breeze in summer, invisible to all but whom I choose to reveal myself to. He fingered the six irsrem bracelets on his wrists. He must not lose them this time. Meanwhile, my plan is plotted out and in motion.

After the slaves had long disappeared, he approached the corpses and tinkered with the two largest and heaviest bodies. Then he waited.

As he expected, although he stood in open daylight, he

knew that no malkop could see him and they descended in the usual air-beating cloud to snatch up the dead. Which they rapidly did, flying away with them to Heaven—except for the two.

The malkops had gone. Only the two corpses remained. Another bevy of sky-dwelling malkops, called selks by some, kept eyeing the two with interest, perhaps wondering why no other malkop had taken them.

One came fluttering within reach—a larger malkop suited to carrying a heavy corpse hundreds of miles. Skittish as always, it scanned constantly the area around the body to make certain it was not putting its own life in danger, then finally it slowly alighted, and its pretty pale face with the blond hair flowing atop and its small expressive mouth smiling imparted pleasure at having found something to justify its existence.

It lit.

In a flash too quick to measure, Yezd threw a rope over the creature's neck and willed himself to become visible. Not to struggle, my little one, he thought. When all is done you will be well and you will remember nothing.

Surprisingly, the malkop did not struggle but stood upright beside the corpse and stared into Yezd's eyes. The Omega swung his arm overhead and drilled the creature with a stare and spoke aloud, loud enough for any to hear. "Now you listen to me, little one. By the power of my irsrem bracelets, you are now my servant, and you will fly me away from this place. I command you to fly me south without complaint or resistance."

Keeping the rope about the malkop's neck, Yezd climbed onto the creature's back with head lowered to avoid its wings, and in another moment the pair were rising through the clouds, aiming for some destination far to the south.

The cold air rushed past, freezing Yezd's wispy beard, specks of frost appearing in the malkop's hair, an endless vista spreading in every direction, shining under the eternal rays of Maalstrom's twin suns.

A day passed. A night. They flew over mountains and plains and plunged over the southern sea. And still they flew, the malkop's powerful wing muscles beating rhythmically, its face frozen with tear-drenched fright as its eyes streamed icy tears down its cheeks.

At last, when even Yezd felt he could not maintain his vigil any longer and began to wonder if his plan must end in failure, the malkop suddenly dropped out of the sky like a stone and aimed unerringly at a particular spot. Worry gripped Yezd since he still saw nothing but ocean.

A coastline rose up. The malkop dove until it came to an orchard on a cliff that overhung the sea. Before Yezd could think or plan, the malkop alighted among the trees and stood silently, looking at Yezd as if to say 'What more do you want from me?'

He dismounted and removed the rope. "So this is where you creatures go when left to your own devices. No matter. Fly, my pet. I set you free. I will find a new malkop when I am ready to further my journey." Without a backward glance, the creature took to the air and soon vanished.

Yezd beat his chest and sides to warm himself. He had not foreseen freezing while aloft, and he reproached himself for overlooking the obvious. Then he stopped—eyes peered down at him from all about. Pairs of eyes—human eyes—or at least human-like eyes. For he indeed stood within a forest, but it was a forest of which he had never dreamed, composed of trees he had never imagined.

The closest specimen was tree-like from the calves down but singularly un-tree-like from the knees up. Fixed permanently to the soil in this way, the 'tree' stared at Yezd from a body as human-like as any that Yezd had seen, entirely nude, clearly male, and deeply-tanned by constant exposure from the suns while flanked by two free-moving, human-like arms. This specimen seemed extremely old as its skull had lost all its hair. Yet its eyes gazed upon him with intelligence.

"How odd," Yezd murmured. "What more does this planet have to offer our little stranded colony? I wonder if they speak." He stepped closer to the tallest and oldest-appearing man-tree and asked, "Do you speak? Do you have a brain suitable for conversing?"

Silence.

"It matters not," Yezd said. "For what I have planned, conversation will only get in the way, anyhow."

But the man-tree kept eerily staring. As did the other man-trees stretching away to the horizon, thousands upon thousands, some old, some young, all obviously male and each spaced about twenty feet distance from the next with occasional apertures interspersed in the ground like wells, and in the farthest distance a shining wall of the kind that shields a city.

He scanned the skies. With a minor effort of will, Yezd threw his blanket of invisibility over himself again and waited.

He will come.

No more than half an hour passed when the twin divagated suns above shone down upon another malkop that burst with no warning through the cloud cover and aimed unerringly at the very spot where Yezd had landed. Beating the air above the Chaldean, the malkop spread its wide wings and softly alighted.

Nothing could be seen but an exhausted malkop folding its wings.

Nothing watched but a glimmer of sunlight in the air.

Letting his invisibility drop, Yezd sprang from his cover and leaped while shouting "Hi-hi-hi!" and something new materialized—clinging to the back of the malkop was a dark man of amphibian features, unsmiling, his face registering nothing of the surprise that had come over him. The malkop jerked and the dark man plummeted to the ground where he landed with a dull thud.

Yezd was instantly upon him.

"Where are they, you thief? You think to frustrate me by stealing the most potent weapons in this backward world?" While the dark man lay flat, struggling to regain his focus, Yezd rubbed his hands over the dark man's wrists and found two bracelets—he snatched them both and immediately placed them on his own wrists. "Is that all? That cannot be all! I know you stole six of them where are the rest you vile creature?"

The dark man sat up, shaking his head.

Yezd scrambled about the ground beneath the icy stare of the ancient weather-worn silent man-tree. On all fours, he scrambled about desperately. "They must be here—they must! Four more of the baubles and the universe will lie at my feet." He shook a thin fist at the dark man. "Did you toss them away, you fool? What would you do with them anyway? Give them to some gila for a mere night's pleasure?"

His hand found one. "Yes! It is here! Now three more and like the succubus and incubus I'll be done with you and this whole benighted planet."

The dark man sat up. With no more bracelets on his body, he had no power to intervene but could only watch.

"And another. That makes four. Only two more bracelets are still missing." He glanced at the dark man. "Did you—no, you had no opportunity. The remaining two have rolled away. I will need more time to find them, but meanwhile...as for *you*, thief of all thieves, I will finally deal with you so you can never inconvenience me again. Now, with ten irsrem rings on my wrists, no power in this world can frustrate me. And that includes you above all, my flat-faced friend."

Yezd pointed to the dark man. "You will listen to me now as I speak to your inner soul with the power of the irsrem bracelets. Stand up, you. I wish to know something about you, the man who wrecked all my plans several years ago and has forced me to turn everything upside down in an effort to correct what you did when you pretended to be under my spell, but were not, and stole my devices from my desolate outpost in the western forest. Stole them by attaching them to the ankle of a malkop I kept for transport, then letting the malkop fly away."

The dark man stood. A vacant expression seemed to take hold.

"Now tell me, my friend. You are under the spell of my bracelets and must answer. Just who are you?"

The dark man's body exploded in a tempest of poetic movement, his arms rippling with emotion even while his face remained stiff. "Macius," he said.

"Macius? Is that all? Macius of what, of where?"

Again his body exploded, his legs shuffling as to music though there was none, his ever-expressive body communicating more than his voice. "Macius. And Surge. Surge of the Xotl Clan of the city of Vaw and the Golden Cyclops."

"That is all? You think to throw me off with such pitiful remarks?"

Macius' arms paralleled and jerked back and forth. "I do not think. I steal."

"Ah! For once, I hear truth. Now, where are the remaining two bracelets?"

Macius stared into the distance. "Perhaps on the ground. Perhaps beneath. Or over the cliff and in the sea. Wherever they happened to land when you surprised me and caused me to fall, making the items roll away, and seal the fate of the unwary."

Yezd drilled Macius with his stare until he finally let it drop. "No, you do not lie...for once. None can lie under the influence of the rings of glass. I will have to spend more time searching to find the last two. But not with so dangerous a foe as you skulking about. Somehow, I must deal with you first."

He walked to the brink of one of the wells and peered over the edge. "Yes. A deep water well, doubtless to water these peculiar specimens by whoever tends them, if anyone does. This will do." Yezd went back to Macius who continued to stand and stare as ordered. "Follow me, my thief of Vaw. I have just the place for you." With that, Yezd marched Macius to the edge of the well. "Leap in, Macius. Or Surge. Or whatever your name may be. Leap into this well, my 'pet', and remain there until you cease breathing."

Macius did not hesitate, but commanded by the bracelets, he leapt into the well. With a single high splash, he disappeared in its depths.

"That's done. With that thief out of the way, I can recover the last two baubles. Nobody is safe until I find them. After that, I may finally go to the Eye. My only regret is that after one thousand years I still have no solution to bring the Chaldeans to solve their problem."

Returning to where he landed—and still filled with a sense of eeriness knowing that every man-tree in the forest was staring at him—he began to pace about in a circular search pattern, attempting to hurry due to the suns plummeting over the horizon.

In fifteen minutes, he still had found nothing and the suns had fallen and darkness was making it impossible to search any further, so with a reluctant sigh Yezd decided to rest beneath the trees until morning came and he could begin his search once more, and his eyes gazed on growing flocks of malkops hovering over the man-tree orchard and flapping higher then lower in waves as if intent on some obscure activity.

He stretched and yawned—perked at a stray noise.

The darkening forest erupted with snout-nosed swarthy barefoot creatures, snarling as they clambered over Yezd, the flocks of malkops instantly taking to the air in panic. A dozen draks fell dead—a dozen Yezd flung into the air—another dozen stumbled about as if bewitched—but their numbers were so great and he was taken by such surprise that Yezd was unable to deal with the draks even with the power of the bracelets.

Before he knew it, he was stunned, tied up, blindfolded, and a gag tied about his mouth, and he was carried off to those distant city walls while in his ears harsh barbarian voices growled "No intruders may disturb our orchard. No one may interrupt our production of essence."

Within the hour, Yezd found himself thrown in a cage of stout iron bars, his bracelets and whatever else he had had about his person strewn carelessly about the floor and out the entrance where most of the rings remained visible but quite out of reach, the draks trampling them beneath their feet as they departed.

Consciousness returned.

Friendly fingers removed his blindfold and gag.

"Old man, do not be concerned," a woman's voice said. "The draks will feed us soon. Though I fear they are only fattening us up so they can eat us."

Yezd sat up and rubbed his old bones. "And who am I addressing?" He peered through a shadowy interior half-lit by several guttering torches.

The woman was young and beautiful, even in shadow. "Crestal from the city of Ven. Welcome to Sloter."

CHAPTER 26

T he following morning two large draks approached the jail.

"Are you certain that is the mate you desire? I can think of a dozen drak princesses who are ready to drop their wings for a strong successful drak like you, Tobel."

"I am indeed successful and none have ever brought back more irsrem and wine than I did from my last trip to Klopus."

"Is there a problem, Tobel? I know competition for our female draks is fierce, but there must be many who would be happy to accept your magnificent gifts."

In the midst of the stone city of Sloter, the two draks paused outside the crudely built, iron-barred jail cell that had been constructed primarily to contain prisoners of war and other live captives in preparation for eating, but now unexpectedly housing two figures of mystery.

Tobel flexed massive arm muscles in the face of Tramar until he got the fawning submission he desired. Tramar was unusually strong, but Tobel was in a class by himself. "None are stronger than me. Do you agree?"

Tramar shrank back. "Of course I agree."

"And none are larger than me. Do you agree?"

His colleague Tramar blinked. "Certainly, I agree. I have yet to see another drak in our city larger than you."

"That is why the Queen put me in charge of the last three trading expeditions to far Klopus. Only the strongest and most energetic could succeed in crossing so many miles in only one month. I have always succeeded in what I set out to do, and woe to any who think to stand in my way."

Tramar bit his tongue. "Except—"

"Except the obvious. Our Queen of Sloter."

"So what then—"

"So what...nothing! I have made my choice. I choose no drak princess. Only the female residing in our Queen's jail."

"Shall we visit her then?"

The two draks, bare irsrem swords hooked onto hide belts around their waists, approached the entrance to the jail complex that contained a multiple of iron-barred cells, two prisoners per cell. They housed what those suppliants who wished to please the Queen believed may whet her palate.

Four drak guards armed with irsrem rapiers blocked their entry. "By whose leave?"

"This is Tobel, master of caravans, you fools," Tramar blurted. "Do you not recognize him?"

They exchanged nervous glances. "But these are still the Queen's future larder. If Tobel wishes to select the Queen's next meal, he will need to bring someone of higher rank to gain access."

"Tramar supervises the city's collection of essence," Tobel replied with indignation. "Nothing is more important to our fair city than that. Is he, too, not important enough to satisfy your stupid rule? It was I who brought the female inside there to Sloter, so she belongs to me, Tobel, and not to the Queen or to anyone else."

"You'll not get past us with such flimsy excuses. You may have commanded the caravan, but the Queen owned it, and the captain of Her guard, Zetan, ordered it. Now unless you want to feel our blades..."

Squinting in anger, Tobel stepped forward and half slipped his rapier from his belt.

The guards tensed.

A subdued buzzing sounded from some distance away among the ugly brick houses with wooden roofs that replicated throughout the city. From somewhere shouts broke out.

"A melee," commented one of the guards. He looked at one of his companions. "You know what that means."

"Free dinner," his companion answered.

With that, all four guards promptly abandoned their post and raced to partake, leaving Tobel and Tramar standing alone by the entrance. There being nothing left to block them, not even a door, they strolled casually inside as if they owned the place.

The front cell displayed the captive of choice. Tobel pointed at Crestal. "What did I tell you, Tramar? Is this female not the very image of beauty? Who would choose an angry fur-covered evil-eyed drak female with unwashed top-knot over this sun-kissed colorful angel from heaven? Look at her hair, the very colors of the gods." The caravan leader breathed deep in passion as his eyes ran over her semi-nude form, her body covered only by the simple tunic she had worn in Grace, now torn and disheveled and overly revealing.

Crestal dropped her gaze in embarrassment and turned away.

"Beauty? All I see is someone's future meal."

"Beware, Tramar. If you think she will fill your belly, then you will next fill mine."

"My error, Tobel. I instruct my tongue, but my tongue disobeys." Tramar eyed the exit where buzzing still drifted with the wind. His stomach growled. "Somewhere, someone is eating."

Tobel ignored him. "And what about this one?" He pointed to Yezd. "His ancient body won't fill a snake's pocket. The Queen will never wish to eat this gnarled stump. Why is he here?"

Tramar reared back. "Haven't you heard? This creature weaves evil magic with every glance. He killed half a hundred draks when my guards caught him making mischief in the orchard. It was all my orchard-guardians could do just to put him in this cell where he can't harm anyone else."

Tobel stepped backward while peering at Yezd askance. "Clearly, he is an infiltrator from those pathetic 'Vensors' as they call themselves, those weak creatures who are always hiding out in the port of Verlaw and trying to steal the secret of our orchard." Tobel shifted his gaze to a half dozen more occupants behind iron bars. "Like those we captured in our last raid." Tobel pointed at other prisoners. "Dinner for the Queen." He looked back at Tramar. "Half a hundred, you say?"

"At least. It was quite the feast when we ate their remains."

Now Tobel's stomach growled. He looked at Tramar. "Is it too late, you think?"

"Let us gather our factions and see what we can scavenge from the melee. I do not wish to go hungry again tonight."

With that, the two hurried out the entrance, their unshod feet accidentally kicking several shiny rings into a dark corner as Yezd watched and pretended indifference.

* * *

"Young lady. What sort of place have we landed in? And how long have you been here in this cell?" Yezd's one yellow and one blue eye flashed as curiosity took hold of the aged Omega. "And did I understand their comments correctly...that those two intend to devour some of their own kind?"

Crestal sighed and nodded. "I've been here for over a month, maybe two months of our quick Maalstrom days. Tobel found me in the far north and killed the drone who was assigned to me for reproduction."

Yezd twisted his white eyebrows. "Assigned you say? A drone you say? And why did you choose such a life?"

She stared at the ground, the inside of their jail cell showing the same unkempt stamped dirt floor as the hallway and the outer approaches. "When one comes from a place like mine, one soon learns that nothing that happens to one is by choice."

"And here you are, in the jail cell of a far city. This seems not the happiest outcome for a life so young. Of the city of Ven, you said? That is a long journey from here, as we are now deep in the southern hemisphere of this world."

"What is a hem-hemisphere?"

Yezd let one corner of his mouth smile. "Nothing important, little Crestal. Just as there is nothing important about you...or me. Just flotsam on the river of life. Temporary effusions in a flow of DNA. Who hopefully won't be eaten for a little while yet."

Crestal smiled at hearing a spark of optimism.

"Hey, old man," yelled a captive in another cell, just waking up. He cackled like one half-demented. "It's all just a flip of a coin, not that these two-legged animals would know what a coin is. Heads they eat me, tails I eat you." He burst into maniacal laughter.

A companion of his yawned and rubbed his eyes. "Sloterville it is, Cormor. Just a matter of time before they come for us all."

The half-demented one nodded too quickly. "What a place it is."

"How do you mean, sir?" Yezd asked.

"Mean? Haven't you figured it out? Why, in this nether side of hell, everyone eats each other. Like a great beast that is forever giving birth at one end while the other end consumes itself."

Yezd nodded. "The cosmic worm. The eternal return of the snake."

"No snake, old man," Cormor spat out. "Snakes don't last a day around here before encountering a barbecue. Haven't you noticed? These draks are never sated. They are never full. Nothing can ever fill their stomachs. As soon as they eat, renewed hunger seizes them, and if they are not put to work by whip and threats, they soon fall to killing and eating each other."

The landscape of conflicting orbs stared back. "A race of bipedal shrews, you are suggesting?"

Cormor stole a snide glance at his friend. "Just as I suspected, Sot. This old fart is crazier than me. He speaks of things that would make the gods mad."

A noise clicked by the entrance. The four guards had returned—except one was missing. Or, more to the point, only part of him had returned. The other three entered the jail and one tossed a half-roasted leg into the nearest cell.

"Don't say we never thought of you," the drak grinned, his prognathic face as projected as that of any wolfman under a harvest moon. He turned to his companions as they resumed their guard duty at the entrance. "A shame to waste such prime flesh on tomorrow's lunch."

"Lunch?" Yezd asked, looking at Crestal in surprise.

"No," she answered. "It's been weeks since anyone was taken from here."

The next morning, they came for Sot and dragged him screaming out of the jail—for lunch. The occupants of another dozen cells laughed and hooted to relieve their tension, knowing their turn also would come.

"I guess their Queen woke up hungry," Yezd suggested.

Crestal buried her face in her hands.

"Don't be disconsolate, young lady. There must be some reason why they have not come for you. For me, it is understandable. I am an old tasteless crow. But you, it must be because the large drak Tobel has you in his sights."

"That is worse," she wailed. "For weeks he has been coming here and feasting on me with his eyes."

"So, all that stands between dishonor by a drak and dinner by another, is this creature's infatuation with an escapee from the far Temple of Ven. Tell me, child, what was Vensa like in her final years?"

"Vensa?"

"Yes, Vensa. The former Queen of Ven before her daughter's soldiery burst into the Temple and slew her. Queen Nesta of Neset waited many-many years before finding an opening and murdering her own mother so her city of Neset could dominate her mother's city of Ven. But though Nesta succeeded, she still failed."

"I knew of Vensa but never knew her."

"Never knew her? But you said you are from Ven."

"From Ven. But not from Ven's Temple. I was the consort of a powerful noble of the city."

For a long moment, Yezd stared at Crestal.

"And which noble, my child?"

She breathed deeply. "Chief of the Serclaslers."

"Aah. Once again, I am beginning to see the greater picture: the famous Numsenmur."

Silently she nodded.

"Which means Soorkrul," Yezd added.

Crestal dropped her gaze again.

"Which means a sealed box all the way from Klopus."

She looked up in surprise. "How do you—"

"Which can only mean one more thing..."

"No! I do not wish it. I don't want to be one of Mother's possessions, living out my life in a mud cavern, reproducing endlessly with my mind turned off."

"I see. Of Ven...yet not of Ven. And of Grace...yet not of Grace."

"My life is complicated."

"You have given me much to think about, my child. Of underground dwellers, yet aspiring to be something different. Of hornet domestication yet not qualifying for hornet reproduction. Quite an interesting puzzle for an old Omega."

"Like I said, my life is complicated."

Yezd nodded, a new excitement spreading subtly. "I must think on this. More complications can lead to something simpler in the end. And to think that I was ready to make my move with nothing to show for a wasted millennium. Stark limbs in depths of blue! Eyes of amber beneath a radiant aureole! The cone of destiny! One begins by making the replica. The Constellation of Atasan casts its red rays over us even as we speak."

She shook her head at Yezd. "Just my luck. Cormor was right. I am stuck in here with a crazy man."

Cormor, now alone in his cell and contemplating how little time he must have left, yelled, "Crazy as Vensor's double. What did I say?" He grew serious. "Crazy as me. In the land of the self-eaters, only those who refuse to eat are sane."

Ignoring them, Yezd settled down to stare at a shadowy corner by the entrance while rubbing the side of his head with one finger. "I must find a way," he muttered to no one in particular.

CHAPTER 27

S everal weeks later, Tobel made ready for his weekly trip to the jail to glimpse the object of his passion when, in the street, a clutch of armed draks blocked his path. "Tobel of the caravans?"

He raised his chin. "Who else would I be? As if you don't know my face from all others in the city."

The draks exchanged hesitant glances. One pushed out his chest. "Tobel of the Queen's caravans, you have been summoned by the Queen to visit Her in the palace. At once and without delay." Several hands rested on the helves of irsrem swords.

The caravan chief pursed his lips. He glanced about. He was a patron with many loyal followers, but for once, he had ventured out with no backers. He exhaled. "But of course. You have only to ask and I shall hasten to obey my illustrious Queen."

"This way, then." They parted, and as Tobel passed through, the delegation assembled about him and escorted him to the palace.

Striding Sloter's main avenue, they passed block after block of stone houses composed of crudely formed bricks, some with neglected wooden roofs with gaps open to the weather. Hordes of small draks swarmed the little column, the word 'child' rather less descriptive than simply smaller versions of the adults, and more than a few clutched pieces of something edible in a hand or two, though it was not easy for any observer to identify what, or who, the pieces may have belonged to.

A much larger construction appeared at the end of the

avenue and Tobel encountered a second group of armed draks. They eyed Tobel and his escort.

"This is he?"

"Who else?" the escort smirked, their dignity offended at the suggestion that they do not know their job. "As if we don't know his face from all others in the city."

"Don't ruffle your fur, little drak. You think you are now a dragabond?"

"Keep talking like this and you'll soon hear buzzing close by." Two escorts loosened their rapiers at the prospect of another melee.

"Oh, calm yourself. The Queen is waiting. Take him in." The palace guards parted. One of the guards said to another, "Perhaps we should take his sword."

Too late. Tobel had passed through and was inside the palace, following a well-known approach through the dreary stone-ground walls under poorly dressed wooden lintels and ceiling joists until he came to the royal enclosure. This was a wide affair—not the throne-room itself, but the royal reception area where the captain of the guard screened all who would enter the last sanctuary.

"We have brought him, Zetan."

On an expansive poorly carved wooden chair on a low dais, surrounded by ten more palace guards, Zetan, the Queen's captain, squatted his enormous bulk. On either side of his chair were piled a variety of fresh flesh with which he indulged himself as if satiation were an ephemeral state always hovering just beyond his reach. He drilled Tobel with a sharp gaze. "So, you come at last. How many times has the Queen summoned you, Tobel? How many times have you ignored Her invitation?"

"None, Zetan. I have received no invitation before this."

"Well, now you know. You were summoned and you are here."

"And the day is bright and the sky is blue. So what?"

Zetan frowned. "And this is exactly why She has so

urgently requested your presence. This attitude of yours."

"My attitude is the same as yours, Zetan. What else can one expect from a proud drak?"

The captain's frown deepened. "Relax, Tobel. No one wishes to impugn your dignity. But She has only a simple question that She has asked me to put to you."

"Oh?"

"Yes." For a long moment, the room was silent as Zetan's ten guards flanking his large chair and the escort who brought him stood wordlessly, awaiting the question.

Tobel glanced skyward as if judging the passage of time, though the reception room was entirely roofed and no sky was visible. "Questions usually come with a question mark. And you are not the Queen, so make with it. I have things to do."

Zetan frowned. "So, here it is: Why do you keep telling everyone in the city that the prisoner Crestal belongs to you? Are you not aware that she belongs only to the Queen?"

Tobel sucked a breath as if preparing to launch into a shouting match. "To the Queen? The female Crestal belongs to no one but Tobel. It was I found her. It was I saved her from a mating with a putrid drone. It was I saved her from the wilds, entirely at my own risk. I have the right to make a prior claim on any item of value that I discover while driving the Queen's caravan through desert and swamp and forest, risking bandits and dragabonds, and all I claim in return is this one living soul, this creature with the colors of northern forests and ice-cold climes in her eyes. The Queen has no right to deny me this one Vensor, this one gila, whom I prefer over every drak female in Sloter." He put his hand on his rapier. "Is that answer enough for you?"

It was Zetan's turn to become heated. "I see more clearly now why the Queen's commands are having little effect in this matter. I do not wish to cause a scene here in the palace, or in Her prison. But listen to me and listen well. You are to give up your claim to this gila, for the Queen has selected her for her next feast. Her fate is sealed. And if you persist in this matter against the Queen's wishes, She shall strip you of your administration of trade caravans and you will go back to wrestling for your dinner in the city square." He put a fist on his side. "Is that plain enough for you?"

"Plain. Very plain."

"Now, you have new instructions. The Queen wills that you prepare a small trade of a few sleds. You are to take them to Verlaw and trade some of our store of essence for the prepared meats and that inedible stuff they call 'bread' that the Vensor-sa in Verlaw produce and which are suitable for our orchards, and obtain more wine for the palace."

Tobel bowed his head—the first sign of submission he had displayed since entering. "You know, of course, Zetan, that the men in Verlaw will never give us weapons. Thus, my hurried caravans to distant Klopus to obtain them. Have our drak citizens already lost or broken all I procured?"

"No, no, Tobel. Do not worry about that, though it is true the Queen's subjects have already broken many iron swords, and they have lost many irsrem rapiers. Curse their stupidity and negligence."

"For once we agree on something, Zetan."

"Go make ready. Scout out that perfidious city for tricks and traps. Then gather your sleds and proceed to make trade. That is all for today. You may leave."

Without ceremony, Tobel turned and stalked out of the reception hall, once again escorted, the chief burr of his passionate drak life still unresolved.

* * *

Sometime later, Tramar and Tobel stood on a hill, staring at the city walls of the port city of Verlaw by the rapidly fading light of late afternoon.

"What did I tell you, Tramar? See how much more smoke is coming from within the city walls of Verlaw.

Something is up, I tell you."

"Not my problem, Tobel. My business is keeping our orchard productive. Your business is whatever is happening on the other side of those walls. Zetan said to take them a few sleds of essence and come back with bread and wine."

"That's easy for you to suggest. No one resists your activities. But when I bring essence to Verlaw, they always complain how many of their people we draks have eaten." Sincere confusion seized Tobel's rat-like face. "Who can understand the strange ways of aliens? You don't see us draks complaining about how many draks we have eaten. Why, we have never eaten anyone still alive. So, what's their problem? I think they just like to complain."

"Strange people with strange customs, Tobel. Who can understand?" Tramar shrugged. "How can I explain to those Vensor-sa that by eating our own dead, we keep Heaven's malkops from neglecting their duties in Maalstrom's widespread groves. Otherwise, they would have no time for anything but flying around with dead draks in their clutches. What kind of world would that be?"

"A pointless exercise, indeed, my friend. I never saw any Eye of Vensor anyway, and I think those devious people in Verlaw made up the whole thing just to vex us draks. I never understood it."

"Well, enough complaining. My sleds are ready to take to Verlaw, so finish collecting what you need of essence to fill the sleds. The people of Verlaw won't give us the weapons we need, but they are happy to trade wine and a little bread and the prepared meats to supplement our orchards. That's what makes the essence of our orchards the very best."

"By order of the Queen?"

"Of course, by order of the Queen. How else does anything get done in Sloter?"

"By order of the Queen. And Zetan, captain of Her guard."

"What happens inside Verlaw is his problem. Not ours. Let's return and get to business and leave the rest to him."

They returned to Sloter.

The night came swiftly, and as Tumsenet plummeted overhead, the god cast entrancing shades of green over the city's scattered groves, illuminating surprising clandestine movements that began slowly but grew as the evening progressed. Occasional moonrays of flame threw shivers of light over a host of masculine faces as they stared upward as if athirst for visitations from unscheduled visitants. Invisible clouds plunged the orchards into impenetrable darkness. Then the clouds parted and exposed the most unexpected dance of nature one might imagine in this most unimaginable world. A high-pitched trilling rose from the man-trees, and in response, flocks of malkops hovered over the groves to listen. Individual selks flew lower to engage with single trees, then rose only to descend a second, and third time to different man-trees. The trilling rose to a crescendo from every tree as each malkop neared and the entire orchard came alive with vertical movement as the selks obeyed some unobvious impulse.

No one watched but draks, under Tramar, who was careful not to interfere with the economic basis for not only the city of Sloter, but for every drak city across the planet to the equator and beyond. The man-trees trilled and sang, their faces upturned with smiles of ecstasy, arms outstretched to embrace, their masculine members erect as for love. As each malkop descended, it would approach a man-tree, clasp it in its arms and lift its breechclout to slide onto the man-tree's member, a mutual embrace lasting but moments before the malkop returned to the air to visit another tree, and then others, dallying in the groves for temporary carnal pleasures before resuming their flight to whatever farther destination awaited, and collecting its own tribute of ejaculate in globes for the selks' own mysterious further purposes.

From the direction of Sloter, a stray noise disturbed the

eternal dance and a ripple crossed the orchard as the flocks took to the air only soon to descend again and resume their eternal orgy, the man-trees trilling and singing with ever greater abandon as more and more selks visited until the groves were thick with winged selks, their bare breasts flickering with moonlight, their blond manes compassing red-lipped faces, green and pale throwing ever-shifting loops over the ghostly scene, interspersed with fiery red from the stars of Atasan.

A sprinkle of lights moved through the groves. Each light was held by a drak dressed in simple tunic with sack over one shoulder and broad conical sunhat so as not to frighten the participants with their warlike visage. As each drak came near a man-tree, it withdrew from the sack bread and meat, and the tree accepted the food clumsily but with relish, quickly to return to its passionate trilling while the drak paused, and using a dull strigil, scraped the clear ejaculate that had accumulated around each man-tree's oaken ankles and placed it within a bag tied around the drak's waist. As the sack emptied of food and his bag filled with essence, each drak would return to Sloter until the entire orchard in a week's time was fed and harvested, selks and draks, and indirectly Klopus and every Vensor city, having obtained what they needed of the motive force of Maalstrom: essence from endless forests of Milos.

Thus, the night progressed.

Except not only draks were this night's witness. A man watched from the midst of green leafy trees on a near ridge and nodded all the while, for this was not the first time he had seen these groves, nor the first time he had observed the festive midnight dance of the malkops. When morning came, he was still watching as a large drak named Tobel filled two sleds with a portion of the week's take of essence and directed a score of draks to drag the sleds to the port of Verlaw to exchange the essence for wine and bread and meat consisting of some animal other than drak roadkill from the streets of the house of Sloter.

* * *

The port of Verlaw came into view and a hundred ships of the city of Vaw began to slow. Propelled by sails and ocean-going reven-na, the many ships, collected from a dozen ports by order of the new king Cetus of Vaw and his vizier Mens, prepared to settle upon Verlaw's one decrepit wharf like hungry bees on a single rusty flower. Summer was over and the suns were slowly merging in their ancient dance—as below, so above.

Too many ships for so small a port, they were forced to take turns disgorging their cargo—hard-faced soldiers with arms and armor, vitreous irsrem plates of varied colors denoting different regiments of trained warriors led by the Simet-sa of Vaw, the city's warrior elite. All day the ships landed. All day they disgorged until it became clear the town itself would not hold so many men comfortably.

The royal ship landed and the Cetus planted his stocky legs on the uncertain clapboards of the town's wharf, his eel-skin suit sheening with sunlight, his former uplifted yellow cape and cap now replaced by uplifted royal purple cape and cap.

"Take care, Cetus," said Mens, attempting to assist Fish, although a half dozen Vaw-sa warriors and sailors were closer.

"Do not lay your hand on me, Mens," Fish hissed. For a moment, Fish's fist raised and it appeared Mens was about to suffer the fate of Numtal, his former unfortunate aide, who went to his death with imprints of Fish's fists on his jaw. Growing chaos in the disgorgement process distracted Fish, and Mens breathed freely again.

After a time, Fish returned his attention to his vizier. "The wharf is clear, for the moment. What do we do next?"

He pointed. "The palace complex by their temple.

Redemer will doubtless be waiting for us there."

"Remind him that he asked for this."

"Indeed, he did. He asked for military assistance against the draks. We are here. We are ready."

Leading a hundred-armed men on foot—there being no room for reven-na on the tightly-packed ships—the Cetus and his vizier strode through the small town as the population—all males as befitting every Vensor city—arrived at the town's nerve center.

Redemer stood at the entrance with a score of well-armed soldiers of Verlaw, the best the beleaguered town could provide, but still poorly dressed compared to the many elite warriors of Vaw.

"Well met, Redemer. I have only one request for you: show us the largest table you have so we can plan our move."

"Yes, Cetus. Yes, Mens." With that, Redemer hurried to lead his well-armed 'saviors' into the palace where four more nobles awaited—the only elite the small town possessed. When they were all seated, Redemer spread out a large parchment with a map of Verlaw and the surrounding environs illustrated.

Mens studied it and soon looked up. "Good Redemer. How many of your people need rescuing?"

"A dozen were taken just last week. Doubtless all devoured by now by the draks. Can you believe they had the nerve to send a caravan of their filthy sleds demanding scarce bread and prepared meats for their secretive purposes, even while they were consuming our own people. Of course, we had to complete the trade." Redemer spat on the floor. "How I wish I could at long last take my revenge on them. They even took several more this morning!"

"That time has come, Redemer," Mens continued, "with the consent and leadership of our great Cetus."

Fish distorted his pink flabby face till the wrinkles of flesh welled up like fleshy subductions. "No more delays. I give the order."

Mens found the scribbles indicating the city of Sloter on the map and slammed his fist on it. "We want the secret of their essence. And we want the malkops destroyed; our own Vaw race produces no malkops. And we want every drak that we can find—dead! We will then invade Sloter and rescue whoever still breathes in the jail cells of our enemy. No further delays. We will move as soon as our army is deployed. When all is done and the city of Sloter is burned to the ground we can finally move to Stage Two of Vensed's plan."

Mens struck fist to chest, then saluted. "Hail Vensed! Aid us in our fight, in our struggle to cleanse the land of all infernal drak vermin."

"Hail! And done!"

CHAPTER 28

Yezd calculated yet again the distance between his jail cell and the nearest dust-riven lump in the dark corner by the jail's entrance. Rolling his long tunic and tightening it as well as he might, he stretched one arm through the vertical bars and arched it—he let the tunic flap.

Grunting, Yezd withdrew his arm. "Still too short." He turned to his companion of many weeks. "Dear child. I know how this may perturb you, but may I again request that you allow me to borrow your torn clothing. I understand your need for modesty..." Crestal and Yezd glanced at the other prisoners, now grown to at least a score with the draks' most recent foray against Verlaw, conducted after their peaceful trade had completed, and who leered at Crestal, few having seen a genuine gila in their lifetime, much less a nude one. "But I simply must add length to my tool. Otherwise, I shall never manage to reach yon devices."

"No, Yezd!"

"Hmmm," muttered Yezd. "Then there is only one other possibility. You there!" he called to another cell with its two inmates.

"Now what, madman of stone? What is your crazy scheme now?" They laughed.

"Sirs, I have been quiet until now due to the fact that I did not want to lose what is precious to me. But it seems that if I remain here much longer, I shall not survive a general barbecue by my captors."

"And your point being?"

"My point being that this little dusty item in the corner is not alone. There are several. I have need of them. They are all I possess in this miserable world and—"

"And?"

"They are of the greatest value to whomever happens to possess them."

"Value? Like what?"

Yezd ruffled his enormous white eyebrows in turn. "Like gold."

This brought a pause. "Like gold?"

"Gold. And silver mir. And more besides which I am fearful to state any louder out of concern that the others in this jail shall learn of it and somehow get it all for themselves."

The two men looked at each other. "Huh. They look like no more than dust-lumps ready to be swept out with the trash."

"You were not here when the draks first brought me. A great magician they called me, and they were not mistaken. Have you not seen how they avoid coming close in my presence? And how I have still not been eaten even though many others have? But I am desperate. I am sure my time is coming. So, all I request is one additional robe from either of you so I can extend my hook and finally seize the nearest gold bars. I promise to split my treasure with you when I recover it. Half for you, half for the drak who opens my cage. I ask for nothing for me but the chance to walk out of this jail."

The pair thought—whispered among themselves. They shrugged. "Oh, why not. We are only humoring a crazy old man. What's the loss but a robe?" With that decided, both disrobed and passed their tunics through bars into the cell with Crestal and Yezd. "Lucky stiff," one of the men said. "He gets to rub elbows with the most beautiful gila this side of Klopus while all we get is an entry on a drak menu. Cruel and unusual."

In minutes, Yezd had affixed the robes together into a single item with a hook at one end and prepared to start fishing when a commotion at the entrance interrupted...

* * *

"Stop, you," one of the guards outside the entrance called to someone not visible by those in the cells. "You are not allowed entrance by order of the Queen."

The three guards assigned to block unauthorized visitors found themselves thrust rudely aside, and the large drak Tobel burst into the jail, come again to see the object of his fascination, and this time accompanied by a dozen armed patrons more inclined to obey Tobel than Zetan, even if the latter did give orders in the name of the Queen.

Standing in the hall, Tobel let his eyes gaze once more over the disheveled fulsome body of Crestal, his rat-shaped visage sniveling as his eyes watered. "I do not know how you cast such a spell over me, Crestal of Klopus, when this old man here is supposed to be the wizard among us, while you are nothing but a stray lost gila." He put his fists on his hips. "How do you do it, witch? How have you alienated me from my natural female drak mates and made me love something strange and alien?"

"I have nothing to say, nothing to do with what you claim. This is all your doing, Tobel."

"There is gold involved!" shouted someone from across the cell-plex. "We heard them planning it. Is that enough to get us released?"

"Gold?" Tobel snarled. "What do draks care about gold? No one was born yet who can eat it. If that is all you have to offer, you may eat your fill of gold before I eat you."

They went silent.

Another commotion drifted in from outside. It grew louder and in a moment accumulated at the entrance with enough noise to threaten the outbreak of a melee.

One of the jail guards stuck his head inside the building. "We have summoned more guards, Tobel. They have already arrived. Zetan has sent a score of draks with rapiers and you have been summoned to the palace." The three guards snorted in triumph. "Now get out, Tobel! Before we drag your lover out and cook her in front of you."

Tobel glared. With a snap, he turned and strode out, signaling to his outnumbered loyalists to follow.

Off toward the palace they went, marching up the main avenue, Zetan's delegation harsh as ever, Tobel's faction taking their cue from their leader's explosive frustration. It soon became apparent that Tobel was far from alone this time, and the closer he came to the palace, the more of his followers joined in, until, as he approached the front gate, a veritable army of draks had assembled behind him—though it was far from plain whether they had accompanied Tobel out of loyalty or merely out of the sense that a general melee was about to ensue, which meant ringing the dinner bell.

Zetan's guard, who was formerly escorting Tobel with haughtiness, became less assured and soon seemed to be acting more as an honor guard for the most popular leader in Sloter. The gate guards gave way in an instant—careful to cast harsh glares at Tobel just in case Zetan himself may be watching them. Tobel swept his way into the Queen's antechamber, where, sure enough, the heavy-set Zetan, still striving to fill his bottomless stomach, sat on his expansive and unartfully carven chair. Upon Tobel's appearance, Zetan leaped up in alarm to see the number of hostile retainers behind his enemy.

"Is this how you honor the Queen, you oaf? By dragging your nest of vipers along with you when you are summoned to answer for your deeds?"

Tobel puffed himself up. "No one here dishonors our noble Queen, Zetan—only you by your constant interference when I attempt to perform my duties to Her."

"Duties? Like your constant visits to the witch of Sloter? The gila of an alien race who has bewitched you, as you yourself often say. Well, the Queen has made Her decision in this matter."

The caravan chief narrowed his eyes. "Will you pronounce what I suspect you wish to say?"

"Yes," Zetan shouted. At his outburst, his own soldiery in the Queen's anteroom assembled closely about their leader, matching a similar movement on the part of Tobel's backers. "Be it known to everyone in this room that the Queen has decided it is unhealthy for any citizen of Sloter to allow himself to fall under the spell of a foreign witch, and that the best approach at this time is for the witch to be removed from Sloter's jailhouse and brought here to the palace where the witch shall be executed and cooked and eaten at the Queen's next ceremonial meal in honor of our Drak god who resides on the highest peak of the Drak Mountains. May he sate His sacred appetite on this witch's blood."

Tobel exploded. "This is not acceptable, Zetan. I know it is not the Queen who wishes this, but you yourself. You want to taste this witch's blood just as much as I, but in a different way."

"In the drak way!"

"*Not* the drak way. Your way! I demand this be put to the Queen at once. I do not believe that She backs you in this. Our Queen would not wish to eat alien flesh."

"You think to challenge me in this, Tobel? You will not. You dare not. And you know why. Any who enter the throne room without my permission risks being struck dead by the power of Her gaze."

"I risk it, Zetan! It is you who dare not enter Her royal presence for fear of being struck down by Her infinite power."

By now both sides had approached face-to-face, a dozen draks armed with rapiers, protecting an enraged Zetan, and a score of armed draks surrounding Tobel. A single word from either side was ready to spark a general catastrophe.

At that moment, Tramar hurried into the antechamber

hauling a captive whose hands were bound in front with iron chain. "The Queen's chamber! My orchard guards have discovered another infiltrator like the old wizard. He killed many, so of course, we had to pause to eat a few as our hunger had become unbearable, but now I fulfill my duty to the Queen by bringing the criminal here. He was spying on the orchard." Tramar flicked his gaze over the others. "And something has happened in Verlaw town. They threw open their gate and a great army is rushing upon Sloter as I speak."

The chamber exploded in chaos. Without missing a beat, Tobel snapped out his rapier and threw himself on Zetan's protecting line of soldiery. Three fell quickly and the others retaliated, promptly slaughtering a half dozen of Tobel's draks. While a few from each side paused to wolf a bite from a corpse or two, the rest mixed in a general melee, and more soon crowded in the front gate, determined not to miss out on either the action or the rewards, and more than a few watching for 'accidental' shivs in their backs from starving 'comrades'.

For the moment, everyone forgot that an alien infiltrator stood in their midst. Flores of the Turlicum casually picked up a dropped irsrem sword, and prying it between links of his iron chain, snapped the links. With another smooth motion, he slid across the growing pool of blood and came up behind Zetan. One more swing and Zetan's head soared above the crowd.

Everyone halted.

Flores made for the throne room. To his surprise, Tobel shrieked, "Stop! You must not disturb the Queen's privacy!" The bravest drak in the kingdom of Sloter practically shook at the prospect of Flores approaching the Queen.

The Turlicum frowned, puzzled. Then, throwing caution aside, he burst into the Queen's chamber. Smaller than the antechamber, the Queen's chamber was composed of a simple bedroom with sparse woody furniture—the first furniture Flores had seen among draks—and a partition at the far end positioned by the wooden bed and a pair of dirty pillows.

As Flores came closer, the draks stopped fighting and collected behind him, apparently concerned at being struck dead by the power of Her stare and happy to let Flores take the blow.

But where was the Queen? Nothing stood in Her chamber but the bed and the partition, and as the bed was solidly fixed to the floor, there remained no place in all the room for the Queen to be but behind the partition.

Flores stepped to the partition—grabbed hold with one hand.

The draks froze as they watched, hands over mouths.

He flung it down. Behind the flimsy partition rested a simple chair—in the simple chair rested the Queen of Sloter. A corpse so dried and stiffened that She must have died centuries ago.

"Grab the impious intruder," Tobel yelled. "The Queen has appointed me captain of Her guard, and my first command is to take this infiltrator from Verlaw and serve him for dinner at the next ceremony."

A growing racket outside drowned out Tobel's words. The draks rushed out of the Queen's chamber, out of the antechamber, and out of the palace.

Flores followed unmolested and forgotten. The city was in flames.

"They are shooting at the malkops with arrows," Tramar shouted. "They are coming in our city gate."

Indeed, cohorts of Vaw and Verlaw soldiers in brightly colored irsrem armor were pouring through the streets of Sloter, creating a slaughter of their own. Draks fell by the hundred, even the female draks with their atrophied wings making them incapable of flight joined the battle and fell beneath the Vensors' blades, their soldiers sparing neither age nor sex. A mere extermination of a race of shrewish rats.

For a while, Flores stumbled about, searching for the jail

that housed Crestal. He had heard that much before Tramar had thrust him into the antechamber. But where to find it? Who could possibly know except for the draks? Suddenly he caught sight of a familiar figure. Tobel had separated himself from the fighting and seemed to be making his way unannounced to a side street. If anyone knew, it would be Tobel.

Flores followed. Sure enough, Tobel had abandoned the defense of his city to fulfill his private passion. He soon led Flores directly to the jail complex. As before, the guards had left, their duty to defend the city at least not having fled them.

Tobel dove in.

To Flores' surprise, however, Tobel reemerged almost instantly and with no one in tow. Tobel let out a howl of frustration, then ran off to join the struggle.

After Tobel left, Flores plunged into the jailhouse.

Most of the cells were empty. In the back area, Vaw warriors were snapping free the bars on the remaining prisoners.

"Fellows," Flores called to the Vaw warriors. "What happened to the gila whom the draks kept prisoner here?"

They called back, "You mean the old man and his slave?"

"Slave?" Flores exclaimed.

"Yes. He had already freed himself when we arrived. He gave the woman commands and she hurried to obey. They dressed themselves, then left. They refused our help."

"Did the old man say anything before he left?"

"Crazy as any, he was. He kept muttering something about gnats."

"Gnats!"

"Yep. As in insects. He said there was a small swamp nearby and he needed to visit the place before he went to the Eye of Vensor. May he rest in the Eye forever when he dies, which doubtless will happen soon given that he had no weapon of any sort yet was eager to wander the streets of Sloter."

It took Flores but a moment to plan. He took off out the entrance and raced down the main avenue of Sloter until he came to the open gate. Hiding for a minute behind a massive stone jamb while more columns of irsrem-weaponed warriors poured into Sloter to kill more draks, Flores saw his opportunity and slipped out of the city.

He raced to the orchard.

CHAPTER 29

Yezd dragged Crestal behind him effortlessly, surprisingly so given his advanced age, but unsurprisingly given the ten bracelets of power that he had retrieved from the jail entranceway. His power returned and his confidence high, he strode among the man-trees as evening fell once more over a Maalstrom Sloterhouse.

"Now do not complain, dear child. My need is great. My need is precise. I have planted my suggestions in your mind and your mind and mine have now become one. But you must please keep up with me for I am not entirely certain where the little marsh lies. I know it is southeast of the promontory in an isolated part of the vast grove of Sloter. And I must collect my required sample even though war and chaos rage around us. But have no fear. So long as you are with me, no harm will come to you."

A drak guardian of the trees sprang up before them. A beam of disapproval from Yezd sent the drak shrieking away as if some invisible demon were chasing him, then it tripped and fell dead. The pair resumed their trek. Farther along they came across a plethora of slain malkops, each with a Vaw arrow in its chest. Yezd shook his head and pressed on.

They came to a halt.

"It was here the accident happened. Two more," Yezd mumbled. "There are two more devices still at play somewhere close by. If not in yon nearest waterwell with the corpse of that thief." The Omega-trained Chaldean snuffled through the dirt and came up at the barked feet of what appeared to be the oldest man-tree in the entire vast forest.

"You won't find them there," sounded an unexpected voice.

Yezd froze. Slowly he stood erect and stared in frank amazement at the man-tree whose eyes drilled him with steady aim.

"Did you...can you speak?"

"Not only speak, but SingSong. Have you not opened your soul to the music of the trees? Is it possible that you could walk among the groves of heaven and not feel the root of the earth and the pull of the selks, who even now wish with all their heart to visit our sacred orchard?"

"It cannot be...not after all these years. Is it truly *you*, Milo?"

The man-tree lifted its sun-drenched face skyward as if searching ancient memory banks. "Yes, I did have that name at one time in my former life. Long long ago. Before I learned not to live for an uncertain future but to yearn and stir for the visitation of heaven's denizens, to embrace God's creatures with eternal love. My skin bare to their touch, abhorring the ancient confinement of clothes which had always stopped the touch of the Divine."

"By Vensor, Milo. Have you any idea how many years I have searched this planet for a sign of what happened to you? And here you stand."

"Here I love! Here I root and clasp and trill! Here I sing my SingSong as I have done for almost a thousand years since I left Klopus in a flying rover with my wives. They all left me, as they were wise to do. Khurko stole the rover—I managed to climb on at the last moment—the ailerons became stuck—we crossed the ocean and crash-landed on the little beach you see below us."

"The Chaldeans be praised," breathed Yezd. "That I should live so long to solve this mystery. How did. . .?

"A gnat it was. Only a little gnat. Followed by consuming the living fruit of this tree. That was all it took for the magnificent transformation to take place. Better by far than accidentally consuming hornets like what happened to our Mok-sa in Klopus."

"Yes, Milo. We figured out the causation of the infection after you left. Vedega returned and cemented in the swamp, but she consumed a termite by mistake."

If a man-tree could shrug, Milo shrugged. "I care not. Our enterprise was doomed from the start...unless you had some ulterior motive, some hidden instructions from your Chaldeans, as I always suspected."

"You were ever the clever one, Milo. After a thousand years, you still are. By the way, your striplings have spread far. They not only cover the country around here but have spread past the equator all the way almost to far Grace where Vedega lives underground with what is left of her Mok-sa."

"A termite, you said."

"For good or ill. That is her fate."

A hurrah rose from the city of Sloter.

"It seems the draks are rallying. I must take my leave, my old friend. It has done my heart good to hear your voice once more and to realize that something good has come from our colonization of this planet after all."

"You have a companion."

"Yes. And she is obedient, which is how she must remain. For that ulterior motive you mentioned, which is finally in my power to execute."

As the darkness settled, malkops hovered closer, seeking not just to snatch the bodies of their arrowed comrades, but to mingle with the man-trees, whose arms were outstretched to embrace, their male members erect and waiting, their faces shining with moonlight as their trilling rose to levels of ecstasy.

"We must collect our items, dear Crestal. Time is fleeting. I will have to be content with ten of the irsrem bracelets, as it is too late even to search for the remaining lost two. But ten is enough for the last stage of my Chaldeans' plan."

"Yezd."

He paused. "A last word, Milo?"

"You plan to visit the swamp? If you do, give my regards to Khurko."

"Khurko!"

"It is not only I who consumed the fruit of these orchard trees."

"I see..." With that, Yezd pulled Crestal after him, she emitting only a muffled yelp, and they made their way to the lost tract isolated by the draks by means of stones so that the gnats might not get loose and the strange inhabitants of the little lost grove not spread their striplings as the essence-productive forest of Milos had happily done.

Here they came upon a small grove of man-trees unlike any they had seen heretofore. These plant-men were robust, muscled, their raucous faces gleaming with clever evil, and Yezd was relieved to see that their feet were every bit as solidly implanted in the dirt as the Milo trees. While Yezd watched, a malkop flapped near, from curiosity. Instantly one of the trees snatched the selk and tore it apart with its hugely muscled arms. Devouring the flesh of the selk, it soon finished and wiped its mouth with the back of one hand, then tossed the half-eaten remains far into the bush behind it so as not to alert future prey.

"Poor Khurko," Yezd said. "Mad to the last. No wonder that even the draks won't allow his striplings to spread."

"Now, my dear. You must stand back. We cannot tarry more than a mere moment for this task as it is exceedingly dangerous." Yezd trekked alone a few yards behind Khurko to a marshy area. "Stay your distance, little creatures, the power of the irsrem protects me." Taking out a small flat container, he scooped up a portion, then sealed and pocketed it. From a tree he located a spherical ball, and snatching up another specimen, he placed it in another small container and pocketed it as well. He then made his way back to Crestal.

"Please open your mouth, dear child."

Unable to resist his will, Crestal obeyed. Producing a vial, Yezd poured some liquid into her throat.

"Just a little potion of mine from hornet DNA. Now we have no more time, child, to do the rest of what is required. The reef awaits. And no selk is going to offer us a ride in the midst of all this noise and fighting. We must search for a different way."

* * *

"I saw them. Both were there—right there!" Flores scurried across the orchard until he came to the spot where he had glimpsed Yezd and Crestal, close to the promontory overlooking the beach, in the midst of the oldest man-trees of the Sloter orchard.

"They were here. But which way did they go?" The Turlicum muttered to himself in a fit of pique. "All this time, all this distance, all my effort, and all I managed to obtain was a single glance. But I swear it was them!"

"Soul-as-well. Has it learned to sing? Has it learned to feel?"

Flores halted, stunned. For a long moment, he stared. Finally, a distant memory returned. "SingSong of the woods. You endure like stone and soil."

"I am Loving! I await the kiss of the Divine. Have no soul like lost wanderers like yourself. Need no soul." The man-tree let its eyes fall on Flores. "Split organ still hides its skin, splits mind from SingSong. I see pain, no place of belonging, hides behind clothing, cannot touch the Divine, knows not why it breathes, why it waits. It does not love but talks of loving, its voice dead, no SingSong possible from such."

"Yes, you spoke of this before. But I have no time to converse today. I search for a fugitive and the woman he stole from me."

A cloud drifted by casting moonglow over the orchard

and the man-tree lifted both arms and its male member to entice a pair of selks drifting overhead with the wind. They flew away and it returned its attention to Flores.

Flores asked, "I don't suppose you saw them...or perhaps any of your tree brethren saw..."

"Do not try to stop them, Soul-as-well. There is a better way."

The Turlicum returned the tree's stare with complete confusion. "Stop them? Of course I must stop them. But...what do you mean by 'a better way'?"

"You pursue a most ruthless man. You have no power to stop Yezd, but he has the power to end your life with a glance due to the many bracelets about his wrists. It was not long before now I witnessed another who interfered. The Omega Yezd threw him in that waterwell yonder. He must be long drowned by now. A man by the name of Macius."

"Macius! My friend and colleague." Flores hurried to the well the man-tree indicated. At the precipitous edge he peered down—bubbles were surfacing. The longer Flores peered, the more certain he became that an upturned face stared up into his own. "Good god Vensor! He still lives!" Rushing to find a long thick branch, he lowered it into the water and was shocked to see Macius pull himself up by his own efforts.

"How, Macius? What miracle is this?"

Macius sneezed and rubbed two orifices on the sides of his neck. "Perhaps I should have mentioned this to you about the peculiarities of my people of Vaw."

"What insane talk is this, Macius?"

"Do you not recall the name of my clan: the Xotl Clan?"

"I do."

"Do you not know the name of Fish's clan: the Xolotl Clan?"

"Indeed."

"We men of Vaw are descended from our Queen Morla who gained the abilities of Vaw's native axolotls. Which means we can grow gills if our life depends on it."

"The poisonous influence of Mother? This far away?"

"I don't know about any Mother, Flores. But I do know that the nature of us Vaw-sa is different from all other Vensors. We are not of hornets, but of axolotls. It is most difficult to drown a Vaw. We are even known to regrow limbs."

"Hornets. Axolotls. Termites. Man-trees. Dragabonds! This world of Maalstrom...a maelstrom of ever-changing life." Flores held his swirling head.

The voice called again. "You cannot stop Yezd. But you can still follow with the same protection he possesses."

Flores and Macius returned to the tree.

"I once had a name, you know. I was the chief ecology scientist of the Mok-sa colony that landed in Klopus in our ship called Source. I had seven wives, one pod out of twenty-eight total, prepared to settle this planet with the aid of seven engineers and their leader, Yezd. A one-way trip to colonize an empty planet. How wrong could anyone be?"

"Your name?"

"Milo Psi-2." The man-tree looked pensive. "Now how could I remember such an insignificant fact from one thousand years ago?"

"Milo, please pause your mind from wandering. You said we can follow Yezd and Crestal. How? I know the power of his bracelets. We dare not approach him."

Milo stretched out his arms toward Flores and Macius. "I have the remaining two. The two missing bracelets that Yezd sought so diligently but was unable to find. I picked them up months ago when Yezd was wrestling with Macius." Milo showed his gleaming wrists.

"Two irsrem bracelets!"

"You may take them."

Flores immediately denuded Milo of his bracelets. As he donned one, he caught Macius staring enviously at him.

"And why should I trust you again, Macius? You who

were so disloyal and greedy that you stole all I possessed back in Ven instead of delivering them to my safe as you had promised."

Macius repositioned his feet and bent his knees as if readying to leap. He shrugged and relaxed. "I am a thief, Flores. The greatest thief in the world. You knew that from almost the first minute we met. But I am no traitor or murderer." He stared again at the second bracelet in Flores' hand. "Besides, I happen to know where Yezd is going and how he will get there. I can lead you. But we must both be able to pass through the army of Vaw to accomplish your goal for they will attempt to halt us."

With a reluctant sigh, and the image of a beautiful gila still floating in his mind, Flores proceeded to hand over the second bracelet to Macius—he held it up suddenly out of reach. "Do not desert me again, Macius. I hold you to a pledge to carry through with me to the end."

Macius beat fist to chest. "I swear fealty to my Lord Turlicum, to the Eye and beyond."

Flores nodded—handed it over. Macius slid it on his own wrist.

Milo's voice suddenly rose.

"I looked from the planks to heaven,
At the man they called Youth,
We Mok-sa were immortal...one thousand years before now...
But we passed into the point of the comet.
Yezd began by making a replica
Of the Eye that sees all."

His listeners stared uncomprehending. "What do you mean by all that, old man?"

A long silence followed. Finally, Milo answered: "I no longer know how I felt. I no longer remember what prompted my utterance...

But what I know, I have known.
How can knowing cease knowing?

Matter is the lightest of all things,
Light also proceeds from the Eye,
The globe over my head
Its glassy, glaring surface
There are many fates in its reflections,
One sees them turning and moving
With heads now down, now up."

Milo ceased reciting and looked at Flores and Macius. "Yezd is taking Crestal to the Eye at the top of the pyramid to fulfill his final mission set by the Chaldeans before we Mok-sa set foot on this planet. With his bracelets there is nothing that can stop him, not even Atasan, the guardian of the Eye. But you can follow."

CHAPTER 30

Cetus spoke to the warrior chiefs of Vaw and to Redemer and his nobles. "Pile the bodies inside the city wall. I want no trace of this vile race to survive. Once everything is burned, knock down the walls so no drak ever sets foot in Sloter again."

"Yes, O Cetus. But do not lose sight of our greater goal. We have cleared the land of vermin, and claimed the orchards for ourselves, but Vensed has given us a sacred command. We have an army. They must be fed and kept busy. Atasan finds bad acts for the idle."

"We must move so soon?" Fish sat at a table in their tent, eyeing a spread of fishy splendor.

"Without delay, Cetus. I advise leaving a small detachment to finish destroying Sloter while the rest of the army moves to Land's End."

"And you are still certain that Vensed will prepare our way? You remember the disaster that befell our fleet a year ago. The selks upturned our whole fleet. What will keep them at bay when we invade their home this time?"

"We are twice as strong this time, Cetus. All the ports of the widespread sea have joined us. Our archers are more numerous than all the selks on Maalstrom. All the cities of Vaw-sa have gotten the word that more treasure lies beneath the glass pyramid of the heretic Vensor than anyone alive can imagine."

"And how can you be sure that they believe in this new religion of yours, Mens?"

Mens stared quietly out the window where flames still licked at Sloter. "Men always believe most deeply in whatever puts money in their pocket, Cetus. There is no faith without fortune. Poverty is always heresy."

Fish's admirable incisors ripped a great chunk of flesh from a large salmon. He raised one wrist. "Then let it be done."

Mens nodded. He turned to the assembled nobles. "Strand our boats. We will travel only by land after this. Round up all the wagons you can find and hook up the revenna that hauled our fleet so they will pull the wagons. Post our archers to ward off the selks. And above all, keep our soldiers' minds focused on the rewards that await them once they arrive at the pyramid."

"Humph," Fish grunted. "If only we had Macius once again to inspire the men. They were willing to follow that thief to the ends of the earth—as was I. I wonder what happened to our spastic dancer, the most famous thief of the entire ocean?"

By the end of the day, the army of Vaw—the crusade of Mens in the cause of the god Vensed—set out for Land's End, like a centipede of crowded thousands. No roads existed in this distant wilderness, exposed as it was to the depredations of roving hordes of draks, thankfully now mostly exterminated. An endless column of reven-na, pulled from their preferred ocean lanes and made to haul wagons on land where they bleated and hissed in complaint, led a vast concourse of soldiers equipped with pikes and swords and coral bucklers, the flanks covered by hundreds of archers to ward off the lethal emissaries of Atasan—his innumerable selks. Beauty from afar, red-clawed up close.

A week elapsed. Another. And still the vast concourse of ten thousand inched stolidly forward as the suns slowly merged, casting the southern hemisphere in comparative shade during the day, and falling under the harsh scarlet umbra of the devilish Constellation of Atasan by night. Brave as they were, the soldiers began to direct worried glances skyward as if perhaps lucre and wealth may not be sufficient after all to challenge an age-old belief, superstition though they knew it to be, fear outweighing both reward and poverty.

Indeed, they even began to level reproving stares at their leaders who rode ensconced in the foremost wagons, protected from the elements and sunburn, as if they suspected they had not been told the whole truth about their crusade. But through the carriage windows exposed by errant flaps, the faces of Mens and Fish and their coterie of haughty nobles shone confident and brash, no backsliding allowed among the commoners, and more than one deserter found himself dragged slowly to his death behind the final wagons bringing up the rear.

Mile after mile trudged by. A third week of travel paralleling a coast that seemed to increasingly narrow about the column, and then the sky's clouds billowed away and they perceived the first inclination of what their leaders hoped to challenge: from northeast and northwest, two uplifted columns aloft in the heavens conjoined at a point just ahead before merging and heading southwest. The columns consisted of uncountable numbers of selks. Engaged in their eternal tasks of carrying the corpses of humans and humanoids, and hauling globes of essence and purple lozenges of infant malkops about to be born, they hurried on their way to the distant pyramid where all knew they resided, matched by equal numbers passing the opposite way to retrieve more of the items the selks considered necessary to their way of life.

Some of the warriors tried to count as if to compare who might succeed in the coming contest. "We are ten thousand, that much we know," soldiers murmured. "We lost count of the number of selks at twenty thousand," replied others with recurring worry.

Yet they persevered until, after a trek of weeks, and the executions having grown to over a hundred, they arrived, at dusk, at the terminus they sought—Land's End, where the coasts came together to a point, focusing their minds and bodies on a sight so beautiful that no evil could possibly be attached. In the distance on the far horizon away in the swimming sea glimmered an iridescent flame, colors of the moons slipping one upon the other, and at the peak a shining beam like a lighthouse, though all knew that what they saw was but a minuscule portion of a mountain as high as any.

How much farther? How could any mortal walk on water as if it were a road?

Fish and Mens emerged from their protected carriages and beat their chests in fealty oaths. "The miracle begins here," announced Mens. "Remove all items that may reflect moonglow. Slaughter the reven-na and cover our swords and shields with the grease of their flesh."

"But how do we reach the pyramid?" asked scores of warriors. "We cannot swim half the ocean."

Fish silenced them with a glare. "Listen to my vizier. I have put my faith in him."

Absorbing their attention with a gentle pass of his arm, Mens said, "The way is open. You have only to step your foot in the water to see."

The vanguard stared, puzzled. They saw only water to the far horizon past Land's End and no more than a small disturbance far out in the sea.

"Behold the miracle." Mens stepped into the water and it came up to no more than his knees. Throwing caution aside, he strode farther and farther into the surf, and it became apparent that he stood upon a reef that supported his weight as far as he might wish to walk.

The men exchanged wondering stares. What other miracles might their pope and guru unlock for their pleasure and profit? Quickly they slaughtered the reven-na and moistened their blades to make them opaque, then, one by one, they shouldered their weapons and followed Mens out into the sea.

"Take care not to stray from the path," he yelled out.

"The road is straight as any and of the exact same height all the way to our goal, but no more than six feet in width. Do not stumble or slip. The sea on either side is as deep as any part of the Southern Ocean."

Having found their feet, the soldiers filed eagerly onto the sunken road, their souls again enthused with dreams of gold and silver mir and slaves and gilas and every fancy their minds could ignite.

"Make no noise, O believers, for the winged heretics are as aware of this approach as they are aware of the clashing rocks on the far side. We must arrive at the pyramid before dawn. They shall not attack us until the suns come up, but then, if we are not already inside the pyramid, we shall have to defend ourselves from the anger of the malkops."

Fish flopped his thick feet just behind Mens, the nobles immediately after, with the armed commoners following thickly behind, many wondering just how far their armor would sink them if they were to miss their footing.

The suns rushed to meet their bower to rest for the next day's efforts, a new day, a new creation waiting. The stars of Atasan threw their blood-red umbra over the column as it trudged with infinite care upon the reef, soon unable to see ought but dark water and sinuous forms collecting around their vulnerable limbs. Vensor's host of stars gathered, their smeared ecliptic betraying no hint of what universe they reflected.

Came midnight and still the column marched, the night unusual in the total absence of any moon for once, neither Nvediteg the storm-bringer, nor brown Talen inspirer of animals, not blue Gethos in all its fortune, not Nantifus the grey death, only a hint of greenish-tinged Tumsenet which lurked just below the horizon ready to burst forth when summoned by Vensor. Several times soldiers missed their mark and plunged silently over the edge to a mysterious fate; several times others vanished without a sound as if snatched by invisible predators. Still, they pressed on.

Swords of the Double Sun

Dawn at last showed its pink fingers curling in the distance when they turned back east to look, and the first sure sign of sunlight struck first the high peak of the edifice. No longer a mere lighthouse in the far distance, the suns burst forth to illumine a huge pyramid, world-spanning in size, larger than any structure they had seen or imagined in their feverish dreams. Smooth as marble, white as sheets, the sides were incapable of scaling until, as the eye was pulled up and up its sheer face, one's vision finally caught a glimpse of shining glass suspended in clouds, the very top a complex, sizable in itself, of layered terraces.

As the column viewed more and more of the pyramid, the men paused. Could they, mere mortals as they were, conceive of challenging such ancient, such time-defying rule?

Around the topmost terraced layers, a darker cloud seemed to hover and ripple.

"Forward," yelled Mens. "We are in time. We are still in darkness and have not yet been seen."

Directly ahead, the sunken road emerged suddenly from the deep and crept archly up past the beach that surrounded the pyramid and plunged into the structure's very heart where an open culvert gave wide access, perhaps to quickly drain the force of cyclones, but for what genuine purpose none could know, since none can truly know the mind of God.

Still concealed by darkness, the crusading army hurriedly abandoned the claustrophobic water and rushed up the slopes to gain the protection of the culvert before Vensor and Vensed burst forth in their fulsome glory to expose them to the rage of the pyramid's denizens. All depended on concealment. The rays of the suns crept down from the peak exposing more and more marble. Minute by minute the soldiers hurried out of the water and pushed their exhausted sinews to exert one more fire of aching nerves into cramping muscles. Lower and lower the sharp line of revealing light dropped like a summoning to an execution. Faster and faster the soldiers rushed into the culvert to abandon the sea as soon as possible and gain the safety of a lair, the ones first inside the pyramid already testing their blades in the feeble shade, preparing to storm the ramparts of Heaven in their search for gold and salvation.

At last, the remainder of the host crawled out of the deep and swept up the slope into the belly of the vast pyramid, just as the suns hammered the structure's eastern flank with the force of their rays, light bouncing up the slope to throw lurid shadows onto the faces of ten thousand men who found they were gathered beneath a side-arch governing a wide plateau of lakes and streams, even now the morning dew emitting a mist that rose into the marble-circumscribed sky.

Mens and Fish gently patted each other on their backs. "We have made it," hissed Mens. "Inside Heaven itself with hardly a casualty among our believers. There is no time to waste. We must organize expeditions into the bowels below—for that is where the treasure lies. The tombs and burials of millennia, waiting for the taking. Once we enter the pits, the selks will be unable to confront us as the paths below are too narrow for their wings. And when we have collected what we wish, we can exit this place by the same way we entered!"

"Bravo, Mens! All have heard of the fortune to be had in the burial pits of Vensor. It belongs to Vensed now, so let us make use of it."

Without warning, a clanging set off as of a brass pan, the harsh sound resounding across the plateau with a clamor.

"What?" Mens yelled in alarm. "What is that? What dolt is making that noise—he will alert the selks while we sit here helpless, unable yet to find the entrance to the pits."

"Find that idiot!" Fish called. "Shut him up immediately!"

Frantically, the entire host strutted about in a desperate search for the source of the noise—somewhere above, a buzzing commenced as of many wings on air.

From behind one edge of the open culvert, squatting upon a pylon of rock, a figure came into the dawn light as it streamed in. Not a soldier; not a malkop; but a simple figure of no consequence to the world or anyone.

"Hi-ho, I knew you would come! There was never any doubt in my mind as to what my treacherous subjects would do once they removed me from my throne. Steal! That is what they always wish to do. Especially my fat blubbery Fish, inspector of one of my minor wharves, who has now got it into his head that he is 'the Cetus', the king of Vaw, ruler of my kingdom."

Kot stood up and banged the pot with relish. "Come, selks! Come get them!" The echoes rocketed across the plateau and off the pitched ceiling perched a half-mile above. From many corners the sound of beating wings answered.

"And you, Mens! Disloyal to the last, as I always knew you would be. What a fitting pair you are. So, you thought to throw me to the dogs, send me through the streets beaten and abused by the mob, all so you two could fill your pockets with treasure? Well, I'll show you! Oh yes, I said I would take my revenge, and here it is! Ha-ha-ha!"

Throwing himself into banging his pot harder, Kot cackled and never looked up as a black cloud of angry selks swarmed from the interior of the pyramid and attacked the Vaw-sa. A thousand were snatched into the sky only to be dropped to their deaths. Hundreds more fell beneath a bloody avalanche of extended claws and open malkop mouths that spewed acid. A hundred selks collapsed pierced with arrows—thousands more took their place and soon covered what remained of the crusaders with a blanket of angry vengeance. Frantic, the soldiers panicked and bolted, searching for any place to hide, any nook that might preserve their life for a few more moments.

"Mens! What should I do?" Fish pealed.

"Oh, go to hell, Squawk," Mens answered. "Why do you

always leave everything on *my* doorstep?"

Seconds later, a selk snatched Mens in the air, rose half a hundred feet, then dashed him on a pile of rocks below.

Unable to face the ruin of everything, Fish tried to bolt out of the culvert and regain the relative safety of the sea— a flock of selks pelted him with stones, raised him in the air, then pulled him to pieces in a quartering impossible even for an axolotl to reverse.

A pair of selks approached Kot who still clanged his pot, dancing and hooting with joy. "Oh, so now you want me! Although I just saved your little glass kingdom, you ungrateful whirligigs."

Without a word, they snatched Kot into the air and slammed him down on the very pylon where he had stood, ending his life.

Hours passed.

As noon approached and it was clear that not one intruder remained alive, thousands more selks having entered the pyramid to purge it of the invaders, the winged guardians began to retrieve the corpses. Lifting them up in their strong arms, they flew them out of the culvert, around the pyramid, and into the apertures that gave access to the burial pits, where, by the end of the day, the pits had grown by precisely ten thousand, to nourish the next generation of selks.

When all was done and the day finally came to an end, two figures blinked into view.

"Come, dear child. The black tower awaits."

CHAPTER 31

Yezd pulled an unprotesting Crestal gently behind him, leaving the scene of the battle behind them. "Hold tight my hand, dear one. We are invisible to the selks, but the occupants of this strange city must not become aware of our presence. My talismans can protect us, but why tempt fate? The selks cannot speak, but what one learns, they all instantly know by some hidden process that is of no importance to our goal."

They crossed the length of the pitch-roofed plateau and entered the main chamber of the pyramid. Here a broad blanket of clouds obscured the higher structures, pouring dark rain upon the ground. Ignoring the downpour, they stepped around the rivulets that fell into larger streams, washing away leaves and stray branches from a scattered forest of needle-like boles of trees. They hurried past lakes of splashing fish; their feet kicked up clods of grass-gilt dirt.

The rain stopped and the upper reaches cleared of clouds and became visible. Far above, almost lost in chilly stratosphere, the bones of the enormous glass pyramid came together, arching to a point still lost in cloud. And at the center, as if an Atlas upholding the entire structure on its back, loomed a black tower, thick and rotund at its bottom and narrowing gradually with height until it formed its own needle as it met the inverted bowl.

"Hurry, my child. We must cross the fields of honey and we do not want to tarry among the owners."

Crestal's face for the first time reflected concern and fatigue. "May we rest, Yezd? I cannot keep going despite my sincere support for you."

Yezd paused. "Indeed, you are correct, child. My impatience imposes forgetfulness. It is not fair to ask so much of one who has not my years of experience and unusual predilections. We shall pause beside this lake and take our fill. There is little to fear. The talismans shall protect us from the malkops while we sleep."

For a moment he stood tall and threw his glance over the scene—an endless field of yellow althea flowers intervened between them and the black tower rising in the distance. "But my experience leads me to always be alert for the worst. There is always something that fate holds in balance for those with overweening hubris." He tapped his jaw in worry. Then he held out his hand and a fish leaped into it. "We may not strike a fire, my dear. That alone could alert the denizens of our presence. That will not do." Yezd tore the fish in half with his hands and he and Crestal consumed what they could and Yezd tossed the rest into the lake. Lying down, they slept as darkness enveloped them.

When they awoke, the suns had risen, throwing the entire vast terrarium into bright light. Before the pair stretched a broad isthmus passing between two lakes, strewn with yellow flowers into the distance until the eye came to the base of the pillar.

"We must not tarry, child. But to hurry would only arouse the ire of these fields. Measured progress, dear, measured progress." Yezd took Crestal's hand and led her into the maze of flowers, the yellow from their calyxes soon covering their thighs and calves. On they strode, yellow pollen rising in drifts about them, their bodies soon as yellow as the suns above.

Crestal slowed. "I am tired, Yezd. How much farther?"

"A while yet, child. We must not stop yet."

As in response, a locust-like swarm stirred from a far section of the field and rose into the air. The swarm turned in their direction. They soon took form as leroo-sa hornets, their yellow mandibles thirsting for ever more influxes of pollen.

"We must pause," Yezd said, the finality in his voice bringing Crestal to a sudden halt. "Do not move until I instruct you to."

Standing in the midst of the endless fields of altheas, the pair waited for their insect guardians to inspect them. They arrived by the hundred and swarmed about their legs, crawling up and down sniffing and licking. After ten minutes of this, their numbers lessened and they began to drift away.

"Now, child. Let us resume...slowly if you please."

"I feel suddenly sleepy. Why can't we stop here?"

"Not here, child. The sensation you feel comes from their probosces. It is a soporific. Which is why when they choose to sting, few can feel it."

They resumed walking and with Yezd hurrying Crestal forward and forward, the hours passed swiftly until they arrived, at last, at the bole of the black pillar—the structure of basaltic tachylite thrust from below like an eruption from the center of the planet, at this stage a thousand feet in radius. They searched for some way to mount it and climb to its upper regions.

Shortly, they found an on-ramp, a long low-slung ramp devoid of steps that seemed to circle the vast apparatus like a paved road, traveling up as their eyes climbed its dizzying height. The hornets had gone—taking most of the yellow pollen with them—and Yezd hurried Crestal up the ramp, following its counterclockwise route. Coming to the first flat stretch like the first stage of a sacred ziggurat, they paused. Yezd examined a tangle of black sculptures so thick that no basal surface could be discerned among them. Insects and tentacles, gilas and malkops, things from the deep and mysterious items from the sky proliferated across the face of the pillar as far as they could see.

"What is this, Yezd?" she asked, more just to speak than to hear an answer.

"What magnetism has wrought in a thousand years of

biological settlement of this strange abode. Should you snap an element, it would recreate itself overnight."

"Why, uncle?"

"It tells a story, my child. The story of my Mok-sa on Maalstrom, a story that lies resident in the DNA of every living thing on this planet. A story I hope to re-enact. Though it is too soon to attempt to explain such to a young girl like yourself. I beg you to place your faith in me and believe I have your best interests at heart. Have faith in a Chaldean universe."

At that moment, Yezd paused. His blue and yellow eyes fixed on some spot far below among the flowers where a stray glint seemed to flash where nothing glass or metallic should flash. His finger rubbed his chin. He gently pulled Crestal along. "No more time to rest, my child. We must hurry with greater speed after this."

"But I'm so tired, uncle. Why must we hurry so?"

"All of creation is not within my powers, child. God forever holds His final judgment close to His chest as befitting one that gambles with the universe. Not even I can predict what His cards may hold. May it be good, fortunate, propitious."

On they went. The flat platform ended in another upward ramp, and they climbed until Crestal could barely put one foot in front of another. A day passed. At last, Yezd permitted a short break. Night whelmed them, not even the varied colors of the moons able to penetrate the thick irsrem material that composed the sides of the world-encompassing pyramid.

Keeping one eye—the yellow one—unclosed, he watched the ramp they had passed while closing his blue eye for rest.

The next morning, he hurried Crestal up and forward again. Flocks of malkops passed by with their endless clicks echoing; none took interest in the camouflaged pair crawling slowly up the black tower.

Another day passed. Yezd produced a few shreds of dried lyart for them to chew—but spared no time for resting further. On they hurried.

Three days and they had circumnavigated the pillar several times and the yellow fields now stretched far below, no more than smears of yellow between blue lakes. The massive glass sides of the pyramid were coming closer, eager to join the pillar at the top.

They came to the final platform. They seemed upside down with their heads on the inside of a vast world-turning bowl. Above them, several wide tubes thrust through the bowl to the nether regions. As the pair watched, clouds of selks carrying globes of essence flowed from the air below and plunged into the tubes to vanish upward from sight, followed moments later by a reverse flow as more selks left empty-handed, billowing out of the tubes to spill breakneck at the dizzying height into unsupported air, only to beat their wings with pleasure at their mastery of gravity.

One tube was horizontal and dark, ignored by the hurtling flocks which preferred the vertical tubes. Into the shadowed tube, Yezd pulled Crestal.

They came out on a suspended platform uniting three immense corridors that surrounded the upthrusting black pillar. One corridor gave to the west where the suns could once more be seen directly with no glass to intervene, already plummeting toward their watery bower. The second gave toward the northeast. The third, the southeast. Beneath their feet were enormous holes and through these holes the selks poured in their infinite numbers.

At once, they ceased flying, and collecting into various parties according to their burdens, they walked to their various destinations, climbing more ramps to the higher echelons of the glass city in the clouds: lozenges, branches, moss-like globes of essence, though no more corpses as those were all destined for the burial pits below the base of the black tower. Stepping to one extremity, they saw a belt of selks far below entering the bottommost apertures bearing corpses, then flying out again after depositing what their fruit trees needed as nutrition, the malkops eating nothing else.

Crestal shrank back, giddy. "Do not fear, my child. They cannot see us. The bracelets are more effective than any passport into this realm. We have only to walk where we wish."

Walking to the edge, they gazed up the side of the glass city. Balconies, courts and apertures studded the side of the pyramid to rise to an apex above, to some level still invisible from their standpoint.

On they hurried. Chambers passed by, consisting of lattices of impossible height where selks rested in individual hex-sided chambers, the creatures having no need of ladders or stairs, but flapping to their homes, or flying out again to resume their duties after resting from their globe-trotting excursions.

Beside a wall, the pair paused. Selks had gathered to add a section of irsrem glass to the pyramid. Taking handfuls of essence in their mouths, the selks spewed it upon the desired location, where, mixed with their acidic solution, it glowed until hardening stronger than any other substance known.

Finding a cistern of water, the pair drank their fill. Then again they hurried on. Around the black pillar they continued to climb as ramps were found to further their way. The pillar now was no more than two hundred feet in diameter, and still they climbed—the temperature dropped as they penetrated ever higher stratosphere.

At last they came to the highest part of the dome, the apex of the pyramid atop the shining edifice of glass that crowned the entire world-spanning structure. A courtyard lay open to them, sufficient to house a thousand malkops, partially covered by a wide ceiling composed of an inverted hexscape overhead.

The courtyard was empty—but for a single inhabitant. Clinging to the underside of the hexscape with his multiform legs and thousand-faceted eyes, the ruler of the material world and its pyramid surveyed the pair in silence. Green scales burnished copper. Antennae alerted to the presence of Yezd and Crestal.

"Have no fear, child. Atasan is aware that we are here in His realm of Ra'Allah, or See-Face-of-God. But he knows we are only travelers, not invaders or looters. Walk with me without fear to the last stage of our journey."

They had come to the terminus of the pillar. Only a little more than one hundred feet in diameter, the pillar had become a hollow tube, the circumference of its low edge delicate with more black-magnetic carvings adorning the tachylite. Suspended above the tube was a sphere of irsrem a hundred feet across and faceted like the eyes of Atasan, the brazen globe circling slowly in time with the turning of the planet.

"We have come to the Eye. We are in the highest level of Heavenhell. Here it is best not to forget the poetic cycle of the Zeyd:

I flee to the Lord of Dawn from the Evil he created,
from the night when it falls,
from gilas who twist what should be straight,
from the One that Envies all.
I flee to the Lord of Man,
the King of Man, his God,
from the One who sneaks through portals,
who whispers evil in the hearts of men,
and the ways of selks and mortals.

From the beginning of time, the incubus and succubus have made their way via such portals. But it is time for this one to serve our need. Look into the sphere, child."

Crestal shrank back still. "I am afraid, uncle."

"There is nothing left to fear, dear Crestal. Merely a short energetic leap into the Eye, and it will do the rest. Come. I will hold you close."

Yezd glanced back toward where they had come. A glint

flashed. He looked back to the sphere. Together, they hurtled through the air over the narrow gap between the sphere and the circumscribing decorative edge of tachylite. Instead of plunging into the Abyss, or bouncing off the surface of the glass sphere, they passed cleanly through and found themselves inside, the glassy facets iridescent with light from all sides.

A tunnel of translucent hexagons beckoned. "Hold tightly, child. Now is not the time for us to become separated. The glass will attempt to deceive and trick us with every step. But we need do nothing more than walk firmly through."

Yezd took a step and the entire sphere flipped and skidded as one facet of the iridescent wall suddenly sped beneath their feet with an audible click, the entire sphere shifting without warning in response to his step. "Generations of contemplating the hives of the leroo-sa hornets enable one to negotiate this, the largest and most importunate hive of all. Here, insects rule. If we think like one, we shall penetrate the hive to its core."

He took more steps, with each step the sphere flipping so that the correct facet fell underneath their feet, the tunnel leading jaggedly deeper inside. "The way forward is to feel and invoke instinct, not to think rationally about what should or should not exist in this topsy-turvy world. Let it tug us to the end."

Soon they burst into a hollow chamber. "Atasan is absent, yet the walls are alive with His progeny. See how the hornets swarm the inside of their hive." Yezd pointed at a series of hexagonal panes clear of insects. "See how the hive offers portals to other times, other climes, other assemblages of physical properties, such as not even my Chaldeans understood."

"That one, uncle? Is that our goal?"

"Yes, child. The one leading to the empty cube. It is time for our final step." With a gentle push of his legs, Yezd floated Crestal into the air to the center of the hive—they floated to the panel with the image of the cube.

They passed through the portal. . .into another world.

A cube-shaped chamber encompassed them, dry ragged cloth drapes hanging off walls of bricks. Dust blew in an open doorway. The wall hangings displayed quotes from the Arabic Quran, the curved letters flapping in a dusty wind that penetrated the chamber.

Yezd and Crestal stepped through the open doorway and stood in the midst of a vast open courtyard bounded by many-storied structures. Looking back, they saw the chamber they had just exited was the interior of a cube forty feet tall whose exterior was also draped in cloth, black and gilt, also torn and neglected, as was all that met their eyes.

No person could be seen. Everywhere they looked was desolation, not a human left anywhere on Earth.

Yezd spoke, his age pressing on him. "You see, my child, how the Chaldeans are never wrong. We used this Ka'aba for millennia as a cover for our activities, and before Source left Earth, we knew what would be the final result of Earth's overpopulation...what you see before you now is the planet Earth, empty of people, as empty as Maalstrom was when our starship 'Source' first arrived on that deserted planet a thousand years ago."

Behind them, Flores and Macius emerged from the Ka'aba. Willing themselves visible, they flashed into view.

Yezd looked at them without surprise. "Take it in, gentlemen. My Chaldeans anticipated this. They are now all deceased, but my colleagues had hoped that we colonists on Maalstrom would one day find a solution to what they knew was coming...the eventual extinction of all human life on Earth. And we Mok-sa did indeed find a solution. Several in fact. Just not in the way my Chaldeans expected."

Yezd produced a container from beneath his robe. Raising it to the light, he showed several living fertilized leroo-sa hornet queens. From a second container, he showed several gnats.

"I have chosen Vensa over Vedega, the hornet over the termite. And now my mission is complete. The span of life granted to me by the Chaldeans is over, and I shall now die and join my dead colleagues. But you three...you know what must be done. I had hoped to deliver to my colleagues the knowledge of cold liquid carbon that the selks use in building their pyramid. But there is no need anymore, for Crestal has that secret within her. I commend her to you two. She must be stung with the gnats, then you must destroy the gnats at once. After her skin turns raw and red, she must consume the still-living body of a hornet queen. Thus, the cycle of the Vensor-sa shall begin on Earth as it did on Maalstrom, with Crestal as a new Vensa. She will then found a new world that will have no relation to the old."

With a deep sigh, Yezd lay down on the ground, and with a last easy breath, he died, contented and smiling.

Flores stood, confusion on his face. "Crestal, my love. Do you understand any of what Yezd said?"

Now free of Yezd's spell, she nodded. "I have seen all I need to see. Let's do what Yezd suggested. I am ready to form a Sacred Spring for my own progeny—with you as my husband, dear Flores. But we must first destroy the bracelets or they will eventually destroy us."

"With your help, Macius?" Flores inquired, looking to the thief.

His body exploded in movement. "All we need is a bonfire perfect for such vanities, Lord Flores. As for me, I wish not to return to Maalstrom. After finding the greatest treasure of all, nothing remains there for such as I. But I also do not wish to live on an Earth that has no people. You must do whatever it takes to repopulate this dead and empty world, Flores. And if sacrificing the bracelets is what is required, then so be it."

With that said, Flores sparked a fire in the Ka'aba that soon sent flames twisting into the sky. Retrieving Yezd's bracelets, and removing his own, and Macius handing his one bracelet to Flores, Flores tossed all into the fire where they popped and melted.

Then Flores carefully withdrew the gnats from Yezd's container and allowed them to penetrate Crestal's skin. Once the skin became red and raw, Crestal opened her mouth to receive the flesh of a living hornet queen.

She swallowed it. "Now come fertilize a queen, Flores my love."

Flores tossed the remaining gnats and hornets into the flames, where the pyre briefly flared.

"But what about my alien termite nature, Flores?" Crestal asked.

"Have faith in a Chaldean universe, Crestal. I am confident that Yezd somehow has provided."

The three walked out on the open concourse, once filled with thousands of pilgrims swarming counterclockwise, now the playground of leopards and snakes.

Somewhere up ahead, Sacred Springs flowed. They would find their own.

The dark man followed.

More from Glenn Lazar Roberts

Temple of the Double Sun
Two hundred colonists from Earth settle on a pristine planet orbiting two suns, but when women begin to vanish, paradise turns to murderous chaos, leaving Milo, a lowly ecologist, to solve the mystery before their new civilization is destroyed.

The Glow
Sam Trencher, to keep from bursting into flames, has to maintain balance, have the same coins in each pocket, and after six years away, he's going home to find his girl, but she's bequeathed to his worst enemy...and his temperature is rising.

Glenn Lazar Roberts is an international attorney and writer of sci-fi, horror, satire, and adventure fantasy novels. Glenn has taught college, professionally translated Arabic and Russian, and credits an eclectic group of famous writers for inspiring him to write, including Jack Vance, Robert E. Howard, Edgar Rice Burroughs, Mervyn Peake, H.P. Lovecraft, Ray Bradbury, Arthur C. Clarke, Isaac Asimov, and H.G. Wells, among many other Masters of the Art. "I love language. I am perpetually afloat on a sea of script." Roberts has edited the work of other aspiring writers and hosts a writing critique circle. When he's not writing he enjoys swimming. He lives in Houston with his wife and kids.